Betrayal

Other Books by Howard A. Losness

Escaped!
The Colombian
The Trick
Damaged Goods
Suicide Cliff
Cross Check
Once I was Lost
The Plot
Lost Woman

Short Stories

A Pocket Full of Pebbles

Young Adult Books

Little Eagle and the Sacred Waterfall
The Secret

Illustrated Children's Books

It's Fun to be Small
The Boy Who Lived Beneath the Sea
Zachary's Wild Balloon Ride
The Scarecrow and Farmer Rabbit
Humphrey Gets Lost
Sparrow's Vacation

BETRAYAL

Howard A. Losness

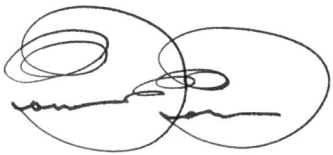

iUniverse, Inc.
New York Lincoln Shanghai

Betrayal

Copyright © 2006 by Howard A. Losness

All rights reserved. No part of this book may be used or reproduced by any means, graphic, electronic, or mechanical, including photocopying, recording, taping or by any information storage retrieval system without the written permission of the publisher except in the case of brief quotations embodied in critical articles and reviews.

iUniverse books may be ordered through booksellers or by contacting:

iUniverse
2021 Pine Lake Road, Suite 100
Lincoln, NE 68512
www.iuniverse.com
1-800-Authors (1-800-288-4677)

ISBN-13: 978-0-595-38206-4 (pbk)
ISBN-13: 978-0-595-82575-2 (ebk)
ISBN-10: 0-595-38206-1 (pbk)
ISBN-10: 0-595-82575-3 (ebk)

Printed in the United States of America

Chapter 1

There was a light fog hanging just above the ground and a light mist was falling when, at two o'clock in the afternoon, without forewarning, a driverless taxi sped past the Queen's Guard at Windsor Castle, crashing into the iron gate that was the entrance to the interior courtyard. What followed was an ear-shattering explosion that sent a deep crimson fireball and black smoke thirty feet into the air. The impact of the blast ripped the iron security gate off its hinges, instantly killing two of the honor guards and injuring bystanders, several of whom were on tour from America.

Within moments the grounds of the castle looked like an ant hill that had been hit by a sudden flood of water. Officials began screaming instructions as security men with ashen faces brandishing automatic weapons ran in every direction, seeking out any unfamiliar face, anyone out of place that might be carrying firearms. Finding none, they took up defensive positions around the entrance, preparing for a second wave of attack that could occur at any moment.

Outside of the grounds, the moment the blast occurred, visitors and tourists alike instinctively fell to the ground-covering their heads like turtles in a vain attempt to shield themselves from harm. Women and children screamed while men's eyes searched for impending harm at ground level.

A smaller, second explosion soon followed as one of the vehicle's gas tanks ignited sending another ball of fire and debris into the air and men to the ground.

* * * *

The dust had not yet settled in the courtyard when the telephone rang at Scotland Yard. "Scotland Yard. Sergeant Smyth speaking. State your business!"

"The Queen's as good as dead, mate," the raspy voice announced when the Sergeant answered. "Inform your precious Queen Mum that the little message at her gate today was just a minor diversion devised to get her attention. The next round will land on her pillow when she least expects it." The voice laughed sarcastically, taunting the Sergeant.

"Who is this?" the Sergeant demanded of the voice, the grit of his voice clearly angry, authoritative, challenging the caller. If the caller could have seen his face he would have been pleased to see the veins on the Sergeant's neck bulging and his clenched fist white from anger. The bomb had accomplished the intended duel responses: anger and frustration from the Yard coupled with a feeling of inadequacy that they had not been able to detect or divert the attack in the first place. And last but not least, there was fear from within the populace, the common folk who had to rely on the proper authority to protect man and country from terrorists.

"Why, none other than the Sons of Ireland, old sod," the voice replied, with an even tone that defied authority. "Who'd ya expect? Prince Charles?" He laughed again and rang off before the sergeant could respond, knowing that if he stayed on line much longer the call would be traced.

"Bloody cowards," the Sergeant said, as he looked at the Inspector, who was standing next to him with a receiver to his ear as well. "Why don't they come out and face us and fight like a man?" Sergeant Michael Smyth was a burly man, standing six foot four, with a bushy handlebar mustache and short-cropped brown hair. He had been the eldest of six children and had left home at the age of sixteen after his father had deserted them. His father had sought work and had been able to secure a position on a cargo ship bound for South Africa. Before leaving home, he wrote his wife a short note stating that he had taken half of the money that they had saved and hidden under their mattress. His final words were not to expect him to return, ever. There had been no sense of remorse in his words.

Realizing that his poor mum couldn't support herself and a family of six children, Michael Smyth lied about his age and joined the French Foreign Legion. Because he was large for his age, the Legion took him at his word that he was eighteen and accepted his application.

After serving three four-year tours, he opted to retire after being decorated twice for bravery and valor beyond the call of duty. He was the only member of his company that had survived a bloody battle that took place in Algiers in what was supposed to be a police action.

His company had been massacred and he had been hit by three bullets and had been left for dead When he came to, he bandaged his own wounds and hid in the underbrush for ten days, until his body became strong enough for travel. He survived on moisture gathered in the mornings from leaves and was forced to survive on a diet of ants, grubs and roots. He was a man who feared no one and detested those whose tactic was hit and run or who took shelter behind women and children.

"Better put in a call to Major Pennypacker," the Inspector said. "He'll want the details immediately so he can initiate countermeasures. We can't be having the bloody Irish thinkin' they can just drive their lolly onto the Queen's land, threaten her and be done with it. They've a lesson to learn, they do!"

His large fist hit the desk so hard that everything on the surface jumped. "And by gad, if I get my hands on the blackguards, it'll be their last breath! Ya can bet the farm on that!" He spoke with measured anger, looking the Sergeant in the eye. He was a solder's soldier. A man's man. Respected and feared at the same time.

"What you want done about guarding the castle, sir?"

"Get the Queen's best sharp shooters over there and make sure they're armed with automatic weapons. Twenty-four hour guard! All leaves are cancelled as of this moment. I want the guard changed every six hours, with a fifteen minute overlap. Put out an alert to all borders as well as on every road and path going out of town. I want every vehicle checked. Anything suspicious: detain them—no exceptions. Have security doubled at the airport, train stations and every port leading out of the country. I want every inch of water covered where an inflatable can be launched. Check everyone's passport twice. Anyone with even a hint of an Irish accent is to be detained so I can speak to them personally. Women and children included. Mess with me on my tour!" He snorted angrily, clinching his fist so his knuckles turned white. "I'll turn the country over, man by man, leaving no stone unturned until they're found!"

The Inspector had been with the British Royal Services Intelligence for twenty years before joining Scotland yard. He had lost the use of his left arm in a skirmish with the Irish three years prior to retirement and harbored neither lost love for the Irish, nor their kind.

"They've more than likely already covered their trail, Inspector," the Sergeant offered. "This was no amateur. It took an expert to load the explosives and maneuver the vehicle to the gate, then time the charges to go off at the precise moment of impact." Smyth had had plenty of experience with explosives when he had been with the Legion.

"I know," the Inspector said with resignation, "but maybe someone got sloppy. Now get on it!"

"Yes, sir!"

"Oh, and Sergeant?"

"Yes, sir?"

I want to know how they got hold of the taxi. Perhaps we've got an Irish sympathizer lingering on the transportation payroll."

The Sergeant nodded affirmation and hurried along his way. He'd been on the job too long to even think that they would find the culprit, but his role was not to question. As the Inspector had said, "…maybe someone got sloppy."

Right now, the taxi was the least of the Inspector's concerns. Guarding the Queen took all immediate priority. If indeed there was a British citizen responsible for making the taxi available to the Sons of Ireland, the Inspector knew he wouldn't be going anywhere. Security would find the driver assigned to the taxi and would sweat him. If there was something there, the Yard would get it out of him. They had their ways.

* * * *

Major Pennypacker had been informed of the attack on the castle within moments after it had happened. He knew the Sons of Ireland organization was simply trying to shake the British population in general and "The Yard", as he liked to call Scotland Yard, specifically. The terrorists knew they had no shot at getting the Queen by simply making a run at the gate with a bomb-laden taxi, of all things. It was more harassment than terrorism, like a mosquito buzzing around one's ear at night. You can hear him, but can't see him. Just the knowledge that the insect is there, flying around in the dark, waiting for you to go to sleep so he can fill his belly with your blood, is enough to make one weary.

They had succeeded in killing two palace guards, however. Pennypacker knew their goal was to shake up the population in general and to send a message to British Intelligence, wanting them to think that they could get to the Queen anytime they wanted. They were the mosquito in the dark: buzzing and waiting.

* * * *

In anticipation of the continued threat of an Irish attack, Major Pennypacker had been assigned to formulate and put into motion a counter plan several months prior to the current attack. Pennypacker was a thinking man's soldier. He played the game like a chess match, always placing himself in his adversaries' position, trying to think like his opponent, then preparing his offensive team for the attack, to be in position before the enemy had a chance to strike, waiting, ready to eliminate them.

The key is to lull them into complacency, thinking that they've got you on the run, he has said. Then, when their guard is relaxed, hit them where it will do the most good: at their leaders—inside the organization. Kill the brain and hands, and the feet become useless or, in the vernacular of chess, eliminate the power of the knights, rook and bishop, and all that's left are the pawns and royalty, who are helpless without their powerful fighting pieces.

His office was rather stark, considering his position in Her Majesty's service. Aside from a throw rug that he had brought back from India as a remembrance of a battle there, the highly polished hardwood floor was bare. A flint-lock, single-shot, long rifle had been mounted on the wall behind him. Next to the rifle hung a picture of Winston Churchill as a young soldier. Young Churchill was dressed in a British military uniform, holding a flint-lock, single-shot rifle in one hand and a pipe in the other.

Two leather chairs stood unoccupied in front of his wooden desk, uncluttered save a single pad and fountain pen which had been placed in the center. A rusty cannon ball occupied a position on one edge of his desk, cradled in a walnut dish especially designed for the object. Rumor had it that Major Pennypacker had carried the cannon ball all the way from a battlefield in North Africa as a remembrance of his career. Major Pennypacker sat behind his desk, leaning back, one foot propped up on the first drawer, the other firmly planted on the floor so he wouldn't fall back. He was smoking his pipe, which had been packed with his own blend, a mixture that was pleasant to the taste, but abhorrentto the nose. He was reading a portfolio that had been prepared for him on one Shawn Macafy. Macafy was the man, a Protestant Irishman, that MI had picked to infiltrate the organization called the Sons of Ireland, which had claimed responsibility for many terrorist activities against the British government and their people. He could add today's vain attempt against the Queen's castle to their list.

Pennypacker was well aware that history had dictated that Irish agents were to be used, but not trusted. More often than not, they had an agenda of their own. As a rule, their loyalty lay in the direction of their wallet. He who paid the most money, got the service—for the moment at least. So far, however, Major Pennypacker had found that the information received from British Intelligence about potential informers had proven to be accurate and fruitful.

Shawn Macafy had been born in Ireland of a Protestant family and, for most of his adult life, had generally tried to stay clear of political factions. His father, on the other hand, apparently an angry young man with a hot temper, had been actively involved in the Irish-British conflict ever since he had been old enough to be taught and understand the meaning of hatred. As a young lad, he had been capable of delivering a bomb hidden in a paper bag to a crowded bus or an official business establishment. In those days, no one had expected a tassel-topped, innocent-looking kid to be carrying death in his lunch sack. He had willingly worked for those who would use him to their end until, as a young man with a family, he had been killed in gunfire between the British and the Northern Irishmen. His son Shawn had then been but a lad of ten. No one seemed to know which side the bullet that had come from, not that it mattered. A bullet is a bullet, and dead is dead, irrespective of who shot it.

Ever since his father's death, Shawn had tried to avoid the politics of his country, although, at times, that task seemed a near impossibility. Being a pacifist was hard enough when politics was the main topic of every grown man in every pub of the land, let alone at the dinner table every night until the death of his father. Through the years he had learned to mask any political persuasions he might have felt, depending upon to whom he was talking.

Eventually, he came to the conclusion that those in charge of the Sons of Ireland, the Sons of Katy Elder, the Irish Republic Association and all the rest of the Northern Ireland political factions seemed to be perpetuating their own cause by constantly killing their "enemy" instead of trying to peaceably settle matters between the Irish and the British. They were not unlike a group of elderly military generals whose only purpose in life had heretofore been to direct and command men to fight battles. Any battle. Take away the lure of the battlefield and suddenly they're deprived of their single purpose for living. They become decorated military shells, capable of war stories at social functions. No more, and no less.

When it came to blowing up busses or cafes where women, children and innocent people were milling around—people who had nothing to do with the British-Northern Irish conflict—Shawn Macafy decided it was time to take a stand.

He had two children of his own: Mike, age twelve, and Aaron, age ten. He had no intention of raising them to be manipulated by some unfeeling, non-caring advocate of genocide, eventually seeing their lifeless bodies lying in the gutter, the result of some unknown gunman's conception of idealistic philosophy that had rationalized their slaughter to perpetuate "the cause".

He was a simple man who hadn't found much time for his sons, what with working in the factory from dusk to dawn, then hanging out with his friends at the pub after dinner, enjoying a pint or two and a friendly game of darts.

Of his two sons, Mike was his favorite, although he had named Aaron after the great American baseball player, Hank Aaron, hoping that one day he would match the talent and fafme of his namesake. When Shawn had been a child, his family had been too poor to even think of playing anything but street soccer or stickball. Any game they had played had been created within the minds of those who participated. Shawn Macafy vowed to do better for his sons. When it became apparent that it was Mike, and not Aaron, who was gifted with athletic abilities, he showered Mike with what little spare time he had.

As a result, Aaron, who had so little natural talent that he had trouble chewing gum and walking at the same time, was more or less shoved into the background, left to act the family clown for attention when people came over. The response was usually, "Grow up, Aaron. Act your age." He quickly learned that being chastised was better than getting no attention at all. In school, he was an average student who wore hand-me-down clothing. He had few friends. Those who would hang out with him were social misfits, much like himself.

They would entertain themselves by getting into mischief, such as ripping freshly washed shsirts from the clothesline of the likes of old Molly McGreggor, or rapping on the walls of the outhouse when Mrs. Malley was trying to catch a little solitude while thumbing through the latest "wish book". Once, they even tipped it over with her inside, just for spite. Unfortunately, Keil Thompson saw the act and told his mother, who told Aaron Macafy's mother, who told her husband, who soundly applied his belt on Aaron's bare bottom until he couldn't sit for a week.

Chapter 2

▼

Like every Irishman, Shawn Macafy wasn't in favor of British occupation. He was an Irishman at heart, irrespective of his heritage of being Protestant, a fact few men knew. But, now there were signs that the British appeared to be making a serious attempt to patch up the differences between the two countries. Constantly having their ear to the ground, looking for British sympathizers to aid their cause, or at the very least to be informed of terrorist activities in order to minimize bloodshed, the British underground eventually learned of Shawn Macafy's propensity towards peace. The decision was made to attempt to convert him.

It was outside O'Halloran's pub that a British agent first made contact. The barkeep had just announced last call when Shawn downed the last swallow of his pint. He wiped his face with his sleeve, patted the back of the man who was seated next to him, who had his head buried in his hands face down on the bar, then left. He had been walking for about fifteen minutes when he turned down the darkened street where his four-room house was located. A chill suddenly ran down his spine as he felt the presence of a man. He appeared from behind the shadows of a tree and fell in step just behind him.

Knowing that no acquaintance of his would be so dumb as to sneak up on a man in the dark of night without first making his presence known, Shawn Macafy instinctively turned on the man, swinging a sluggish roundhouse from his right. He clearly missed, clumsily falling to the ground as the man simply stepped aside, anticipating the move.

"Yer a mite too drunk to take me on, Shawn Macafy," the man said in perfect Irish, looking down at him with a smile.

"And who might you be, comin' up on a man in the middle of the night like this?" he demanded, lifting himself up on one elbow, squinting at the stranger through the darkness.

The man offered Macafy a hand, but he refused and got up under his own power.

"Tom," came the simple response.

"Tom? Tom who of where?"

"Just Tom will do for our purposes, Shawn Macafy."

"And just what might yer purpose be?" He straightened himself up, steadying himself against a broken fence, mimicking the stranger's language. "And how does it come that ya know my name?"

The man smiled, although he knew Macafy couldn't clearly see his face. Contact had been made and Macafy seemed receptive to conversation. Not a common event for a stranger in Northern Ireland. "We've been watching you. We think maybe we can be of some assistance," the man said. His voice betrayed his heritage.

"We? And just who might be 'we'?" He turned to square off against the stranger, wobbling slightly. "I'll tell ya who ya are. Yer a bloody Brit, that's who. And what might ya be wantin' with the likes of me?" He suddenly became offensive, looking around, for he knew that anyone caught consorting with the British in this neighborhood was askin' for a knife in the back with no explanation, thank you.

"And you, Shawn Macafy? What are you? A Protestant passing as Catholic in an Irish sector. A man without a cause."

Shawn Macafy was afraid of no man, but he didn't need the likes of a British stranger threatening him or telling him his business in his own neighborhood. The greatest threat one could have was to turn one's neighbors against each other. Neither he nor his family needed that sort of grief.

"What da ya want?" he demanded in a quiet, but firm voice, peering around through the darkness as if looking for unseen persons. He was sobering up very quickly.

"A word, Shawn Macafy. Just a word."

"You've had yer word, now off with ya before I ferget me manners."

"When I've had my word," the man insisted. "It won't take long, I assure you."

He knew he had three choices: listen, try to beat up on the man again or leave. He knew that he wasn't going to beat up on anyone in his present state, and simply leaving would assure him of the peace of mind he needed, so he chose the former. If he and his organization, whoever they were, had found him once, they could find him again. And, assuming no one was within hearing range, listening to what the man had to say wasn't going to cost him anything.

"Right. What is it then?"

"As I said, we've been watching you. We know that your Da was killed in a skirmish between your people and ours." He paused for a moment, letting the thought sink in. "And you've got two young'uns of yer own."

Macafy's mind flashed back to that day when they had brought his father home in a wagon, his body covered with some smelly fish-oil tarp. His eyes had been vacant as they had stared into space and his arms had waggled like some piece of limp spaghetti, moving without direction or purpose. He remembered his mother screaming terribly when she saw the body. She had shooed the children into the house, but not before they had seen their father's bloody body.

Shawn Macafy would never forget that sight, nor would he ever forgive those who had caused his father's death: the Irish dissidents and the British army. He blinked and was suddenly back to reality, facing the stranger. "And what business is that of yers?" he snapped, defensively.

That was the opening that the stranger had been waiting for. He relaxed the hand that held the Walther holstered inside his jacket. There would be no violence tonight. "It seems that every month someone's getting killed, either here in Northern Ireland or in my country," the man continued, ignoring his question. "Innocent women, men and children. Victims of senseless violence and anger." He paused to measure his words, letting the message sink in for a moment.

"One never knows when one walks down a street or gets on a bus if they'll live to return home in one piece. We know that you don't condone such behavior, Shawn Macafy, and neither do we." The tone of his voice softened with a message of firm resolve.

"It's been that way for years," Macafy snapped, visualizing the image of his father once more. "If you and your bastard cousins would simply get off our soil, the killin' would stop."

Common barroom logic.

"We both know better than that, Shawn Macafy. Neither you nor myself can unring a bell. History is dictating what goes on here every day. We can talk ourselves until we're blue in the face, then fight one another until we both drop dead from exhaustion, and in the end, nothing will have changed."

"I don't know if I agree with that logic," he said, sarcastically. "Still again, it would be nice to have a country at peace at least once in my lifetime. Not likely," he added, almost as an afterthought as he shoved his hands into his pockets.

Macafy shuffled his feet, unearthing a small stone. He picked it up and tossed it at a fence post, hesitating for a moment to hear the sound of a report, telling him that his aim was still on. "So, why talk about it?"

"Don't know if you heard or not, but last week there was an attempt on the Queen's castle. No one was hurt—not in the royal family, that is. A couple of the Queen's Guards were killed and some American tourists roughed up." He paused for a moment. "Now, you know that intelligence isn't going to let that sort of an incident go unpunished."

"What's that got to do with me? I wasn't there."

The man paused. "No, but you and your family are here. And when there's a retaliation, who can tell who'll be the next victims? Innocent or not," he added, knowing that Macafy knew he was right. "Anyone could be hit in the line of fire at any moment. Man, woman or child. Innocent or guilty. Gunfire and explosives aren't selective. You, of all people, should know that."

The message hit home. "Now see here," Macafy said, advancing on the man.

The stranger held up his hand. "That's not a threat, old sod. Just a thought to bear in mind next time you see a little one lyin' in the gutter with his little hand or arm blown off or his vacant eyes staring off into space, destined to never taste life again."

"Thanks to you bastards!"

"There's somethin' you don't know, Shawn Macafy."

"And I suppose you'll be tellin' me what that is?"

"I was about to." The man paused to light a cigarette.

For the first time, Macafy could see the image of his face through the flicker of the match as it played off his features. He had fine, small eyes and nose and lips that were a bit too sensitive for a man of his profession. Clean shaven. Not the type one would think would be in the strong arm business, he thought. Macafy shoved his hands in his pockets again as he smelled the man's cigarette. He wanted one in the worst way, but pride would keep him from asking. He swallowed dryly.

The man took a long draw, held it for a moment, then slowly let the smoke out. He tapped the end of the cigarette to dislodge the ash, licked his lips. Sensing Macafy's urge for a cigarette, he asked, "Smoke?"

He extending has hand with a pack of cigarettes, smiling slightly.

Macafy licked his dry lips. "Don't mind if I do."

The man gave him the pack with some matches. "Keep 'em. There's more where they came from." A bond had just been formed, fragile as it might be.

"Thanks, don't mind if I do. Don't get smokes much anymore." Macafy seemed to relax a bit as he lit a cigarette, then took a deep draw and held the flavor of the tobacco in his lungs for a long time. "Good smoke you Brits have," he said, as he exhaled slowly. "Got to give you that." He shoved the pack into his pocket and pulled the collar around his neck. "Now, what was it you were sayin'?"

"We have hard evidence that the majority of the bombs that are goin' off in your part of the world are set by Irish factions."

"Get out of here! Why would we want to kill our own? That's just British propaganda.

You have no proof!" He sounded insulted, but the truth of the matter was he had harbored such thoughts himself. What better way to fuel the flame of hatred than by blowing up a few innocent bystanders once in a while? Even if they are our own! Anything for the cause!

"But we have. Our intelligence far exceeds anything that you can imagine. Think about it. What better way to keep the conflict going, make the general population angry and full of hatred," he mouthed Macafy's exact thoughts, "than to have innocent, Irish people being killed?" He took a puff from his cigarette, letting Macafy think for a moment. He lowered his voice and looked around momentarily for effect. "If we aren't doing it, killing your people, what's to keep the spark of hatred alive?"

Shawn Macafy had no answer for him. "So, why are you tellin' me this?" The belligerence in his voice betrayed none of his own thoughts.

"As I said, we've been watchin' you. We know that you're not a British sympathizer, but by the same token we know that you don't like what's happening to your people, either." He paused for a moment to formulate his next words.

Shawn Macafy waited, looking around nervously. The longer he stood around talking to his stranger, the greater the risk of being seen. He took the last puff on his cigarette and ground it under his heel as he blew the smoke into the cold Irish air. He rubbed his hands together vigorously, then blew into them.

"There's someone we'd like you to talk to, that's all. Listen to what he's got to say, and if you decide that you don't want to help your people, then that will be the end of that. No obligations. No further contact will be made and no one will be the wiser."

"What's in it for me?"

Tom shrugged his shoulders. "Peace of mind. Love of country. Safety for your children. What else?"

"I got that now."

The man looked at Macafy, shrugged his shoulders and took a deep breath. "I guess they were wrong about you." He turned to leave. "Thanks for your time."

Macafy watched as he walked a few steps before calling after him. "What do you mean, they were wrong about me?"

"We thought you might have some interest in stoppin' the killin'. Guess we were wrong." He kept on walking.

"Hold on a minute." Macafy's voice was quiet as he looked around. "I guess it wouldn't hurt to listen," he said, waving the man to come back.

The man held his ground. "There's an address on the inside of that match cover. Be there at six o'clock tomorrow."

"Who will I meet?"

"Just be there. Leave the rest to us." He turned and disappeared into the cold night air.

Chapter 3

There was a slight drizzle in the air as Shawn Macafy made his way to the appointed place. A voice from behind a small vacant wooden building with a tin roof and broken windows called his name. He froze instantly, not knowing what to expect.

"Who's there?" he demanded.

"Over here," came the reply.

Macafy strained to see, but it was too dark and with the fog, everything was near invisible. *A good night for a killin'*, he thought.

"The meetin's been changed," the voice said, putting him at ease for the moment. "Over here."

Macafy cautiously stepped off the road, into the weed patch that led to the small abandoned structure. He wasn't drunk tonight, so his senses and reflexes were a lot keener than the last time he had met the stranger. Besides, he held a small revolver in his coat pocket, just in case. It was the only physical possession from his father that he owned. He had found it among his father's things after he had been killed that fateful day. He had never told anyone that he had it and had kept it hidden all these years.

The gun had been old when he had found it and had shown signs of rust on the inside of the barrel. At the time, he had done his best to clean it and had oiled the moving parts. The only bullets he had were the four that were in the cylinder. The barrel of the weapon was empty. Since ammunition was so hard to come by, he never fired it. For all he knew, it wouldn't even work. It might even blow up in his face. Even so, just having it in his possession gave him comfort.

The man behind the building wore a hat down over his eyes and a trench-coat with the collar turned up, so all Macafy could see was a portion of his face. He said nothing as he faced the stranger, not really knowing which side he represented. For all he knew, he could be an IRA agent or a member of the Sons of Ireland that had found out about him and was here to settle a score with an Irish traitor.

The meeting was brief. Macafy was given certain information that would assist him in infiltrating the Sons of Ireland, the group that currently seemed to be the most radical and dangerous to the British. Their actions were obviously affecting the welfare of the common Irish man as well, the man had pointed out.

Macafy listened intently as the man talked. He seemed to have knowledge of the group's operatives and knew where they liked to hang out. It occurred to him, as the man spoke, that if he had such awareness of the Sons of Ireland, why hadn't the British government moved in and eliminated them where they stood? Obviously, the answer was, they only had knowledge of some of the alleged members. From Macafy's point of view, the most important aspect of the man's information was that he knew their qualifications for admittance to the closed group.

Shawn Macafy had no intention of being a traitor to his heritage, nor was he going to be a turncoat to his country. It was imperative that he leave his contact with that understanding. His only objective was peace for Ireland and his people. Having had his own father killed and having seen several of his boyhood friends murdered, simply for religious or political beliefs, had been enough to convince him early on in life that someone had to do something to stop the senseless killing. If he was the appointed one, so be it!

"How will I be knowin' my contact?" Macafy asked. "I don't want anyone knowin' about this. Meetin' you is trouble enough," he said, looking around nervously.

"Here's a number that will ring through to the top if you need an emergency meeting." The man handed him a matchbook with the number imprinted under the matches. "It's my recommendation that you commit the number to memory, then destroy it."

"And who do I ask for?"

"The code name of your contact is Shilling."

"Shilling? Jesus, Mother and Joseph. Can't you people be more creative than that?"

"We wanted something that would be easy for you to remember."

"How about 'bullet', as in 'dead?'" he asked sarcastically. "It may appear to you Brits that we Irishmen are dumb as posts, but contrary to public opinion, we do have brains."

"No offense intended. Intelligence's motto is simplicity, unlike their American counterpart, who wants codes of colors, names and numbers just to wipe your ass."

"And my name?"

"Ducky."

"Oh, shit! Now you've gone and done it. I'll not be having a name like Ducky attached to me fer any man nor beast." He threw the match cover down on the ground and kicked it in anger.

"There's a method to every madness," the man said without emotion, picking up the match cover and handing it back to Macafy. "All correspondences are to be placed in a watertight container, then buried under the first pier to the north of the bay—the one with the number nineteen imprinted on it."

"What's that got to do with the name?"

"The code name Ducky was designated in case anyone should accidentally come across one of the messages. Reading it, they would think it was simply a lover's message."

Macafy nodded. "I guess that does make a certain amount of sense."

"Like I said, simplicity."

* * * *

It took a period of over a month until a set of circumstances materialized that would get the Sons of Ireland's attention. Macafy was to go to the designated pubs, throw down a few pints then vocally berate the British for killing his father, a fact that was well known amongst his cronies anyway. To be sure that he got their attention, the night would usually end up with a brawl, the result of some insult being hurled against one's heritage, jaw line or availability of one's sister. Afterwards, he would limp home, nursing his wounds, which were usually nowhere as bad as they appeared nor as he pretended. The scene had been set for the next act.

* * * *

The Sons of Ireland was a highly secretive organization. Only those within the group knew who they were. There was always the chance of a loose lip, however, usually the result of too many pints or the need to bolster one's ego. Once a man had been indoctrinated into the group, the only way out was by death: either accidental, by fighting the British or, in the case when one's loyalty was questioned, by execution.

One night when Macafy was at O'Halloran's pub downing his allotment of pints, a stranger slid up behind him and whispered in his ear. "Matey, I understand yer feelin's about the Brits. I'd feel the same way meself if'n me da was put down by the bastards."

Macafy took a sip from his pint without responding. This was the contact that he had been waiting for. Of that there was no doubt.

There was a pause, then, "There's a certain organization that might be interested in talkin' to ya'. Might ya be interested?"

Macafy instantly knew which organization he was talking about. He also knew better than to turn around to look at the man. If he wanted to make contact with the Sons of Ireland, he knew he had to play it cool. "'Pends on the organization," he responded without emotion, taking another sip from his pint, then wiping his mouth with the sleeve of his shirt.

The man didn't respond to Macafy's caustic remark. "Be at the corner by O'Flatery's clothing store at eight o'clock tonight. I needn't caution ya to be alone, do I, mate? Oh, and one more thing. Don't be carryin'." He patted Macafy's jacket pocket where he carried his pistol, letting him know that they had been watching him.

What else do they know? Macafy wondered as he drained his pint.

"That'd be a mistake, fer sure," the man said, hitting him lightly on the shoulder. "See ya, mate."

That evening at eight o'clock, Shawn Macafy was standing on the corner in front of O'Flatery's store when a gray van with no side windows and no license plates pulled up. "Shawn Macafy?" the driver asked.

"That'd be me."

The passenger stepped out of the van and strolled over to where Macafy was standing. Looking around, he said, "Would ya be so kind as to turn around?"

Although it sounded like a request, Macafy knew it was a command. Any resistance could result in a shiv between the ribs. As he turned to face the wall, two more men came out of the back of the van and quickly tied a handkerchief around his eyes while the first one patted him down, just to be sure he was clean. Then they steered him into the back of the van. "Watch yer head, mate," the driver said.

There were no seats and the drive to their destination was bumpy. It was apparent, from the number of times the driver turned sharp corners, that he was taking evasive action, just in case they were being followed. Normal procedure.

The occupants didn't speak and Macafy didn't ask questions. He knew the drill. They arrived at their destination, somewhere near the waterfront, Sean surmised, as he could smell the salt water and hear the waves lapping at the shore somewhere in the distance. Once the van stopped, he was led to what he assumed was an empty warehouse, as voices echoed when the men spoke.

For the first time, Macafy began to doubt that he had made the right decision—to infiltrate the Sons of Ireland. A quick flashback brought his father back to him, his vacant eyes staring into space with blood splattered all over his chest and onto his face. It wasn't that he was afraid of dying. That was the only way his lot was able to escape this wretched life. No. The last thing he wanted was to leave his sons without a father. Nothing was worth that sacrifice.

"I understand you've got an interest in the Sons of Ireland," a voice said once he was led to the spot in the room where he would be interrogated. The middle of the room, he deduced from the sound of voices around him.

"Could be, if their intentions are the same as mine," he said, with a belligerent tone.

A fist hit him solidly in the kidneys. Not enough to do damage, but enough to get his attention. "We'll be havin' no disrespect," the voice said coldly.

Macafy straightened up, giving no measure to the man who had hit him. With guarded tone, he responded, "None intended." He knew they respected toughness and honor. He intended to convey both to his audience.

"Now then, what makes you think that the likes of you can measure up to the cause?" a voice said, coldly.

"I can hold my own," Macafy said with a tone of arrogance. "Just turn me loose and give me your best man and I'll show you."

There were some challenging grunts from the group, but no one said anything. Although Macafy couldn't see, he knew that some of them knew him. "There'll be time enough for that," the spokesman said. "I hear your da got it from the Brits."

"You heard right. And I'd like nothing better than to return the favor." His voice had a bitter tone to it, which was not feigned.

"Well, maybe we can arrange that. But first, I hear by way of the grapevine that you've got friends on the British side of the street. We can't be havin' that, now can we, mate?"

"Me da always said, 'Have good friends, but know yer enemy.' I've spent considerable time cultivatin' a relationship with a certain element of the Brits, fer me own reasons. They got me da and, as I said, I intend on returnin' the favor. If that doesn't set well with you gents, just say the word and I'll be on me way. God be with you and no hard feelings."

There was a murmuring of whispers among the unseen group. Sean could tell that there were those who didn't like his arrogance, yet there were others who thought he would be an asset to the organization.

The meeting ended without a resolution as to Macafy's involvement. He was told that someone would be in touch with him later—when a decision had been made.

The drive back was much shorter, with less turns, but enough of an obvious attempt to confuse him about where he had been. They dropped him back in front of O'Flatery's. The van had driven off and turned the corner and disappeared by the time he had his blindfold off. He shoved it into his pocket with a smile. He would keep it as a souvenir. As he turned to go, he noticed a man across the street, leaning against a post, smoking, looking in his direction.

* * * *

It was a week before Macafy was contacted again. He had been on his way home from the pub when the same van pulled up alongside him. Without getting out, the driver instructed him to be outside O'Flatery's clothing store at nine PM sharp the following night.

Having issued his instructions, the van sped off, disappearing into the night, leaving Macafy alone with his thoughts. *I guess I passed muster,* he thought to himself as he made his way home. *I assume I'll be meetin' the top man soon.*

* * * *

Macafy was again blindfolded and loaded into the same windowless van. "Aren't you gents takin' this cat and mouse game a bit too seriously?" he said with a sneer.

"Shut your mouth, Irish. I don't like you none anyways. It wouldn't take but a wee bit of urgin' and I'd kick yer teeth out!"

It was obvious that there were hard feelings harbored towards him by some of the men. He also knew that no one would dare harm him unless he had been rejected by the group. Then he would be fair game. The disadvantage would be clear. He still didn't know any of the faces. Some of the voices, yes, but that wouldn't be enough to give him an edge if one or more of them decided to make sport of him.

"Touchy, ain't we? Yer old lady not givin' you any, laddie?"

A fist hit him hard in the ribs, and he heard one of the men wrestle with the one who had hit him, obviously restraining him. Macafy smiled to himself. He had made the right impression. "Maybe you won't be so handy with yer mitts when I've got me eyes uncovered and me hands free," he said.

The man grunted, but made no further comment.

Once they had arrived at their destination, he could tell that they must have traveled somewhere underground, even though his blindfold remained on. The room smelled musty and they descended several stairs before they arrived at their destination.

A strong pair of hands guided him to where he was seated on what felt like a barrel top. He appeared to be in the middle of a small room with voices coming from all sides. Everyone whispered except for the man who conducted the meeting. He was positioned directly in front of Macafy and came right to the point.

"In order to prove yourself worthy of being a member of the Sons of Ireland, Sean Macafy, there is a small task that will be necessary for you to perform." The voice had a tone of firm authority to it, used to giving orders and having them followed without question. Macafy could tell he was in control and needed no measure to prove it.

"And that might be?"

"In order to prove yourself loyal and willing to fight for the cause, you'll be instructed to kill a British official. We'll leave it up to you to pick your victim. You'll have one month to complete the task."

"Any requirements?"

"Only that you notify us when you're ready. We'll want to have a front row seat." The man was serious, but others in the room laughed. "When you've done that, the council will consider that you've proven your loyalty to the cause."

"How does killin' prove my loyalty? I'd kill the man who put me da down in a heartbeat."

"Maybe. But, the blood of a British official on your hands is our guarantee that you won't be becomin' a turncoat. If you fail in your task or choose not to perform, well, then, as they say, that will be the end of that." The man looked at his fellow Irish lads with a smile, sliding his index finger across his neck.

Without seeing the gesture, Macafy understood the phrase only too well. It needed no explanation. If he was to fail or backed down now, his body would be found in some back alley, his throat cut and his hands amputated as a sign of a traitor. Everyone knew the sign for failure in the Sons of Ireland. They further knew that, once a man had been killed in this way, all members of his family would be marked for death, as well. They left no survivors to retaliate, not even children.

Chapter 4

Ordinarily, Major Pennypacker would have assigned one of his staff to meet with the informant, but tension was riding high in the Royal Family and he had been instructed to handle the infiltration business personally. The Queen was nervous and made it clear that this was a task to be handled at the highest level. She wanted results—yesterday.

Pennypacker had arrived in their Northern Ireland safe house, an abandoned farmhouse in the country built on unforgiving land that was so hilly and laden with exposed rock that it could be considered virgin soil. The farmhouse itself had been built on the top of the small hill, giving its occupants a three-hundred-sixty-degree view of the surrounding area. That was its only saving grace.

"Major Pennypacker. Sean Macafy has arrived."

"Show him in."

Macafy was ushered into the study which Pennypacker used as an office. Major Pennypacker studied the man standing in front of him before speaking. Sean Macafy was a typical-looking, hard-working Irishman: not tall, five-foot-ten, stocky, with thick hands and neck. His face displayed the character of a man who had put his shoulder to the plow, so to speak. Signs of working as a laborer most of his life. He wore a pair of clean khaki pants and a blue work shirt. His shoes were workman's shoes—unpolished and worn, but clean. He had a full head of short, unruly brown hair and quick brown eyes that betrayed his intelligence.

"Welcome, Mr. Macafy," Major Pennypacker said, extending his hand. Sean Macafy's hands felt rough and powerful in contrast to the Major's, which were soft, thin and bony. "We've never spoken, but have communicated via messenger. It's a privilege to meet you in person."

Major Pennypacker was a tall, thin man with reddish-blond hair. He wore a herringbone jacket with leather patches on his elbows and carried a black riding whip which he continually hit against his leg as he paced the floor, talking.

He got right to the point. "As I'm sure you know, there's been an attack on the Queen's castle, Mr. Macafy." He looked at his guest to see if any expression betrayed his feelings. When he saw none, he continued. "The Sons of Ireland have claimed responsibility." He rubbed his hands for a moment, then his blue eyes hardened as they locked on Macafy's. "I needn't mention the consequences to your people if anything should happen to any member of the Royal Family, especially, the Queen."

Sean Macafy thought of his home, knowing full well that, in the event the British decided to wage an all-out war on his country, his people wouldn't stand a chance. The Sons of Ireland's and the IRA's success hinged on hit-and-run tactics and terrorist activities, although they didn't like using that term. "For the cause" was a more acceptable form of vernacular.

"I wouldn't like to see that happen," was Macafy's only response.

The Major studied him for a moment, as if wondering if he should proceed. Under the circumstances, he didn't see that he had much choice. Something needed to be done about the terrorist's attacks, and done now, short of military intervention.

"I understand you may be of some help regarding this organization, the Sons of Ireland." He stroked his chin, looking at Macafy. "A rough group of lads, I must say, although they're not Britain's primary concern at this moment, even considering the attack on Windsor Castle. Nonetheless, their act dictates that they need dealing with." He seemed to think for a moment as his eyes glazed over, probably thinking of other pressing military problems, then asked, "Tell me where you're at with the organization."

"There's been a hitch in my joinin' the group, Major," he said, wringing his hands in obvious despair. He didn't like being here, in the Major's farmhouse-hideaway, nor giving him information, for that matter. The Brits were the enemy. How did he know they wouldn't double-cross him and turn him over to some military faction when they were through with him? Or even end up putting a bullet in his head for that matter.

"How's that?"

"Well, you see, Major Pennypacker, before they agree to install me into the organization, I must prove myself."

The Major nodded and shrugged his shoulders. "That stands to reason. No organization worth its salt is going to let someone in without passing some sort of test."

"Aye! There's the rub."

"How's that?"

He looked at the Major. "They want me to kill a British official." A small smile uncontrollably crept across his face.

"Hmm. That could present a problem," Major Pennypacker said, rubbing his chin as he paced his office, unconsciously slapping his leg with the riding whip. "Tell you what, let me chew on this for a spell and I'll get back to you. Say, day after tomorrow?"

"Yes, sir."

"Oh, and Mr. Macafy. It won't do for us to meet here. Too many prying eyes. No use taking chances. I'll have someone meet you on the waterfront down by O'Malley's Bar and Grill. On the pier. Say, six o'clock?"

"I know the place."

"Right. Off with you then. And watch your backside."

"How will I know my contact?"

"Just be there. We'll take care of the rest."

Typical British, he thought as he left. *They always want to be so secretive and in charge. No wonder the Brits are always in trouble!*

*   *   *   *

It was near dusk when Sean Macafy strolled out onto the pier. There were a few fishermen here and there, leaning on the ledge with their poles lazily hanging over the edge. A hundred yards off shore, a light fog was rolling in. The eerie sound of a buoy bell sounded in the distance, keeping time with squawking sea gulls. The hollow sound of a foghorn sounded somewhere in the distance. At the end of the pier, a group of fishermen was tying up a small motorboat and putting their fishing gear on the platform under the pier.

Sean slowly walked down the pier, his hands in his pockets, as if he were just out for a casual walk, but his eyes saw everything and his ears heard all. He passed the first fisherman, an old man with a plaid coat and a cap pulled over his eyes. Next to him sat a tackle box and a bucket full of smelt for bait.

"Macafy," came his soft, horse voice as he walked past.

Without breaking stride, Macafy swung next to the man, leaned on the rail and looked out to the sea. To all outward appearances, he was simply a man out for a stroll, asking a fisherman how they're biting.

"You'll find a package at the end of the pier, sitting next to the first group of pilings. These are the explosives that you'll use to eliminate your mark. Do you know how to make a pipe bomb?"

"Child's play!" The tone of Macafy's voice conveyed the message that any Irishman worth his salt could make a simple pipe bomb, assuming he had the materials.

The fisherman nodded and proceeded to tell Macafy about the rest of the plan. When he had finished, he cast his bait back out into the cold waters.

Macafy slowly moved away from the rail, rubbing his hands together as if he were cold, then went to the other side of the pier. He stood there for a few minutes, looking down into the darkened waters, then retreated back towards the beach from where he'd come. When he came to the end of the pier, he took out a cigarette and lit it, taking care to look at every object, making sure he wasn't watched.

Under the pier, he spotted the bag, kicked some sand on it, then continued walking down the beach for a hundred yards, where he stopped. It was starting to get dark. The fog was at the end of the pier now, and those hearty souls that had been fishing were packing up, getting ready to leave. Macafy paused and faced the sea, looked around again, making sure no one had entered the scene, then turned around and wandered back, picking up a stone from time to time, tossing it into the sea.

By the time he was back under the pier, it was dark enough so no one could see him remove the plastic bag that contained its deadly contents. Moments later, he disappeared into the darkness.

Chapter 5

▼

Macafy had been instructed to stretch a tape horizontally across the middle of his living room window as an indication that he had picked his mark and to indicate that was ready to act. That night, after work, he was met by a man who identified himself only as "a son of Ireland", which obviously meant that he was the contact for the organization.

He was again blindfolded, driven to what felt to be the same meeting place as the previous underground musty meeting room. The drive took more than a half-hour due to the fact that the driver took several evasive turns, making sure his passenger couldn't decipher their destination and that they weren't being followed.

Once he had been led to the room, there was silence for a moment as he sat there blindfolded. "You indicated you were ready!" a voice said.

"That's correct."

"Well, Macafy, whom have you decided to hit?" the voice inquired.

"This coming Friday there will be a British diplomat riding in an official car. My information tells me he'll pass O'Halloran's Pub at four o'clock. That's when I'll strike and you'll get your kill."

"Where did you get your information?"

"That's my business."

"Don't get cute with us, Sean Macafy. You might not see the light of day." The voice was strict, but contained a tone of respect.

Sean took a deep breath. "I have my sources. I haven't been on the streets of Ireland for the past twenty-five years for nothing."

"What is the method of execution?"

"A pipe bomb," he said simply.

"Fair enough. That should give us high visibility."

There were some whispers then the spokesman said, "We'll be watching you, Sean Macafy, from a vantage point. Make it look good!"

"It'll be as good as it takes to make him dead," Macafy said coldly. He knew that any sign of hesitation would immediately be translated into mistrust.

* * * *

It was a normal day. The sun had broken out of the morning fog and calm and tranquility courted the street. It was business as usual as pedestrians walked the sidewalk with couples sitting out on the patio of the café sipping on a beverage of their choice. At three-thirty in the afternoon, O'Halloran's bar already had its usual bunch of early afternoon drinkers and regular pool players. A group of boys kicked a flat soccer ball down the street, stepping aside for an automobile whose driver honked at them. The boys offered a hand gesture to the driver and then continued on with their game. The Sons of Ireland were nowhere to be seen, assuming one knew for what to look.

Sean Macafy had loaded the explosives into a pipe bomb in his shed behind the house the previous night. Earlier that morning he was at the scene, where he placed it next to the curb, blending it in with the trash in the gutter, so it wasn't visible from the sidewalk. He had tied a dirty twine to one end of the bomb and had the other end in his hand as he sat at the bus stop bench next to the curb, reading a paper.

He held the paper parallel to the road so he could peer over it to see when the sedan was approaching. He was nervous, but to all outward appearances, appeared calm. He had never actually built a pipe bomb himself, but had been schooled in its construction, as had every Irish lad. He was anxious about its viability. *Worse case,* he thought as he held the paper, *no one will die today.*

He sat there all morning and into the afternoon, rising from time to time to stroll over to the small grocery store that was located next to the pub just to stretch his legs. At exactly four o'clock, a black sedan with dark-tinted windows appeared from the north. Macafy's hands suddenly began to perspire as he tightened the string so all the slack had been taken out of it. The moment of truth was about to be upon him. He set the paper down and concentrated fully on the oncoming vehicle. A woman with a shopping bag sat on the bench next to him, ignoring him. A man stood behind him, against the pub, leaning on a black umbrella. Across the street, two children were playing kick-ball.

The car approached Macafy's position. The lady on the bench stood up and looked down the street as if looking for the bus. The children kicked the ball into the street and it rolled toward the middle, curving back towards them as it reached the apex of the road.

The car was now twenty feet from Macafy. He jerked the pipe bomb up from the gutter, catching it in his hands. When the vehicle was ten feet from him, he tossed the pipe bomb under the front tires.

The pipe rattled under the car for a moment as the force of the tires kicked it under the chassis. What followed was a loud explosion. Crimson flames shot up from around the automobile, then a large screen of black smoke curled into the air. The whole front end of the sedan seemed to be on fire. The lady standing next to the bus stop screamed and dropped her package and ran. The man with the umbrella disappeared into the building and the children across the street simply stood and watched the fire as their ball rolled down the sidewalk. The people sitting at the curbside cafe screamed and they ran for shelter. The windows of the store and O'Halloran's pub shattered in the blast.

Sean Macafy stayed around for just an instant, curious to see what damage he had done to the automobile, knowing that it was rigged so, presumably, no one had actually been killed. Moments later, the air was filled with shrill sirens, as emergency vehicles suddenly appeared on the scene, taking charge of the sabotaged vehicle, their weapons drawn.

The mere sight of British officers brandishing weapons incited some Irish IRA wantabes, who began shooting. Suddenly, the air was filled with bullets, Irish shooting at the British and British defending themselves. Several innocent bystanders were shot in the exchange.

When it was all over, several civilians and two British soldiers lay dead. Among those killed was Sean Macafy. He had stayed to watch the action a moment too long.

Chapter 6

Sarah Macafy and her two boys sat outside Major Pennypacker's office, waiting for him to see them. With a sense of urgency, he had summoned them to his office via messenger. Without asking, she knew what the urgency was. She had lived with the violence in northern Ireland too long not to know. Her husband had been killed in an Irish-British confrontation involving a dissident organization and now her own and her children's lives were in danger.

She had one boy on each side of her as they sat on the hard wooden bench. Aaron lay with his head in his mother's lap, while Mike leaned his head on her shoulder. She nervously twisted Aaron's hair between her fingers, waiting to be called.

"I'm sorry to have had to make you wait," Major Pennypacker said, as she was finally ushered into his office, her two boys in tow. "Nasty business, that with the shooting," he said, sympathetically, taking care not to meet her eyes as he motioned for her to sit down.

"I don't want yer pity," she said bitterly. "'Tis because of the British that me husband's dead. Ifn' you Brits hadn't been so greedy as to wantin' to take our land and dominate our people, none of this would have happened," she said angrily.

"Well, lets not rehash history here today, Mrs. Macafy." He sighed. "I'm sorry for your loss," he said, meeting her eyes for the first time. The message he conveyed with the look was one of modest compassion tempered with dominant authority. He had a job to do, and a whining Irish widow wasn't about to change anything. "I only knew your husband a short while, but he seemed a right sort."

"My only concern now is for me children," she said with a firm upper lip. "I don' want them gettin' involved with the IRA, the Sons of Ireland, the Brits or none of that business."

"That's why I called you here today, Mrs. Macafy. For security reasons, as well as for your own safety I can't tell you what relationship we had with your husband, but I do feel a certain degree of responsibility for you and your children's welfare."

She was understandably angry with Pennypacker, the British and the Irish thugs who had been responsible for killing her husband, but all she could do now was play the only card she held: the pity-party, "Look what you've done to me" sympathy card.

"What ya goin' ta do 'bout it? I don' want me kids layin' in the streets, bleedin' to death 'cause them down at the pub decide to make us an example fer the rest of 'em, or when me boys are grown they've taken up the cause. Mind you, I'm as patriotic as the next lass, but this fightin' has got ta stop!" She had cried her eyes out and spent her emotions long ago. There were no more tears left. Only anger, fear and resentment.

"I couldn't agree more. I think the best thing for you and your boys is to relocate. Now if you…"

"Relocate? What's that mean? Relocate."

"To move you somewhere else, safe. Somewhere where you'll be out of harm's way. Away from the danger," he simplified the sentence, understanding that her degree of comprehension was limited.

"Can ya move us to America?" It was more of a request than a question.

"America!" His eyes widened. He had in mind moving them to a cottage adjoining the little farm they used as a safe-house in the country.

"I've always wanted ta take me boys ta America ta live. There, I know they'd be safe. There's no fightin' and killin' of the Irish there."

"Do you have relatives there?" From the security file he knew the answer to that question already, but was trying to drive a point home.

"No, sir. But I could get me a cleanin' job and raise me boys right. I'm a good worker, strong as a ox." She rolled up her sleeve and flexed her bicep.

Major Pennypacker smiled. "I'm sure you are, Mrs. Macafy. I just don't know. America." His eyes strayed to the upper corner of his office for a moment, as if visualizing the move in his mind's eye. "I'll have to give that some thought."

Then Sarah Macafy pulled out her ace, a move for which Pennypacker hadn't given this poor uneducated woman credit. "Ya had me man killed fer doin' fer yer organization." She set her mouth in a firm resolve. "The least ya could do is send us ta America, where we'd be safe. If ya can't do that, we ain't goin' nowhere." She suddenly stood up. "I can take care of meself and me boys, thank you," she said, jerking them to their feet.

She pretended to turn to go, pausing to make sure Pennypacker was paying attention. As she polished her rough, broken nails on her blouse, she said, "I know the IRA would pay well to know what I know about you Brits."

Pennypacker took a deep breath. The last thing he needed was for the clash between the English and the Irish to escalate. He also knew that she was right. He had used Sean Macafy to further his own cause. It was true, he wasn't directly responsible for her husband's death, but on the other hand, had he not sent him into harm's way by trying to infiltrate the Sons of Ireland, chances were he would be alive today.

He looked at the poor woman who stood there with one arm around each child, helpless as a sparrow with a broken wing. He knew, if they stayed in Ireland, it would only be a matter of time before something happened to one or both of her boys, if, for no other reason the organization did it for security measures.

He took a deep breath. "All right, Mrs. Macafy. You're right. I owe you at least that much." He made a note in Macafy's file and handed it to his aide. "The U.S. State Department owes me a favor." He smiled weakly. "I'll see what I can do about arranging passage for you and the boys to America. Either way, go home and get your affairs in order. I'll send a truck around this evening as soon as it gets dark, to collect you and the boys."

"We leavin' today?" Her eyes were wide with disbelief.

"No, but I have a hunch that you'll be safer if we collect you and the boys and keep you in a safe house until a decision's been made."

"Safe? Safe from who? We have no enemies."

The Major nodded. "That may be so, ma'am, but I prefer to come down on the side of caution. Be ready at dark. No furniture or household goods. Just bring personal belongings that you'll be taking to America, if I can arrange that. No more than one suitcase per person." No use telling her that there was a possibility that the Sons of Ireland had already found out that her husband had been working for the British and had arranged to have him killed. That being the case, he knew they'd be back for the rest of the family. Once an enemy of "the cause" had been uncovered, they would leave no survivors. They wanted no child to grow up to come back and hunt them down one by one once they came of age, or worse yet, to infiltrate the organization to their own end.

* * * *

At dusk an unmarked truck pulled up in front of Macafy's house. Within ten minutes, Sarah Macafy and her two children had their personal belongings loaded and were speeding down the road to the Major's safe house, where Macafy and Major Pennypacker had met previously.

* * * *

It was just before dawn when two figures ran from the old Macafy house on the corner. Everything was dark within and no one was stirring on the roads. Just as they had scrambled into the unmarked van and it had pulled away, there was a loud explosion. The house erupted into a ball of flames. The windows blew out and the roof was shattered into kindling, shooting twenty feet into the air. Nothing nor anyone in the house would survive the blast, nor the inferno that followed.

* * * *

Sarah Macafy had chosen the Seattle area to settle down in America. It had a similar climate to that of Ireland—hilly, wet and located by the sea. Major Pennypacker, through the cooperation of the American Consulate, had arranged for her to get a job as a cleaning woman in an office building, emptying wastebaskets, cleaning desks and washing floors. The pay was adequate by American standards, more than she had ever hoped to see in Ireland, but then, the cost of living in the States was much higher, too.

The first thing she did when she reached her destination was to change her name from Macafy to MacAffie. She wanted a different last name, just in case the IRA or the Sons of Ireland decided to come looking for her, to make an example of her. Yet she didn't want it to be so different that it would confuse her sons. Thus, she settled on a slightly different pronunciation and altered the spelling slightly. In her simple mind, she thought that that would be enough to throw anyone that might be looking for them off her trail.

* * * *

Sarah Macafy, now MacAffie, was aware of her shortcomings. To her credit, she didn't fool herself. She was unskilled and uneducated and she knew it. She wanted better for her sons. She knew that a proper education was mandatory for advancement in any society, especially here in America, where the culture was so diverse and affluent. There had been stories of immigrants who had come to America, poor and uneducated, who, through hard work and perseverance, had elevated themselves to great positions and wealth.

Nothing was spared to further her boys' education. When they wanted to advance themselves in one endeavor or another, be it socially or in sports, she did her best to accommodate them. She had made a vow to herself that she would make it up to them for losing their father. When her oldest child, Mike, wanted to play baseball, she dug into the cookie jar and bought him baseball shoes and a baseball mitt. When he needed a uniform for Little League, she went back to the cookie jar. Fortunately, Aaron required little special attention as he had no apparent skills and seemingly was too young to consider worrying about the future.

It was a rare occasion when she bought something for herself. Her life was unimportant. She lived through her children. She took them to the zoo, the cultural museum, to free plays in the park and down to the ocean at every opportunity, weather permitting, as it rained a lot in the state of Washington.

Chapter 7

▼

Major Pennypacker sat at his desk completing the ever-growing mountain of paperwork that the government wanted. It was six o'clock. "Will you be needing me any more Major?"

"No, Sergeant. I'll lock up when I leave," he said without looking up. "Lock the door behind you, if you don't mind. I'll be here for a few more hours. Bloody paperwork."

"Sorry sir."

Sergeant Smithers did as he was instructed, locking the door securely behind himself. There was a nasty fog rolling in. He hated driving on those narrow windy roads in the fog. *Never know when some bloke will come around the bend on yer side of the road,* he thought. He squinted his eyes, and looked at the grey sky and hiked his collar around his neck. *Thank God I've got side curtains on the Jeep to keep the cold out.*

The guard at the gate saluted the insignia on the Major's Jeep as Smithers drove out of the military compound. The fog was rolling in heavily now and visibility was no more than twenty feet, if that. Smithers strained to see the road, leaning against the steering wheel with his nose almost touching the glass.

Suddenly, his foot hit the brake as he forced the Jeep into a slide. He swerved to miss what appeared to be a female body lying alongside a black Mercedes 450 SEL. The wheels of the Jeep kicked up clumps of mud as it slid sideways. Suddenly, the vehicle vaulted over a partially buried rock, catapulting the jeep over and over again, until it finally came to a halt upside down in a ravine. The Sergeant, who had not been wearing a seat belt at the time, had been thrown from the vehicle on its first roll, and landed on the soft turf at the side of the road.

A man jumped out of the back seat of the black Mercedes and rushed towards the fallen man. The Sergeant opened his eyes just in time to see the blade of a knife coming down at him.

It was all over in a second. The blade had severed his spinal cord and slid under his skull, into his brain. Sergeant Smythers had felt nothing, even though his body had jumped as if it had been hit by a lightning bolt.

The man quickly went through his pockets as the woman, who had been lying on the roadside, brushed her coat, swore because she had gotten dirt on it. "Got 'em." He held the keys from the Sergeant's pocket for her to see.

*　　*　　*　　*

When the Jeep approached the entrance to the military compound it was near midnight. a light rain had begun falling and the Jeep's lights were on bright, reflecting on the dense fog. All the corporal at the gate house needed to see to wave him in was the insignia of a major on its bumper and the uniformed sergeant at the wheel.

There wasn't a soul on the streets, nor in the buildings, as they approached building D-ll-3, the security compound. The wooden sign outside the wooden building said Major Pennypacker—Chief of Security.

Looking around nervously, after fumbling with the keys for a moment the Sergeant let himself in. All the blinds were drawn before the lights went on in Major Pennypacker's office.

Ten minutes later, the Sergeant left the building without bothering to lock the door. He had what he had come for: a single file under his arm. The Jeep sped away.

Ten minutes later, the guard on duty tried the door knob as he had countless times before. Finding it unlocked, he entered the office of Major Pennypacker. It took only a minute to ascertain that all was not well. "Captain Sweetwater, this is Corporal Washington, sir. I'm standing in the middle of Major Pennypacker's office. You had better get down here immediately. It looks as if the Major's office has been compromised!"

It took only a few minutes for Captain Sweetwater to get to Major Pennypacker's office. "Call the main gate, corporal. Tell them it's a Code Red!"

* * * *

At the same time the Jeep with a major's insignia approached the gate house. The Corporal held out his hand and approached the driver. "Identification, please."

The Sergeant opened the plastic flap on the door and stuck out an automatic weapon with a silencer. It coughed twice and the Corporal fell to the ground, his vacant eyes staring up into the rain.

* * * *

"Major Pennypacker? Captain Sweetwater here. There's been an incident. I think you had better come down to the post right away, sir."

* * * *

Major Pennypacker walked around his office, picking up files that had obviously been discarded and had been thrown to the floor. Captain Sweetwater stood at attention next to the Corporal who had been on guard duty that night.

"I don't know what to say, sir. It must have been an outside job."

"Oh, it was an outside job, all right," he said, looking into his cabinet. "These boys knew what they were doing and they knew what they were looking for." He looked at the Captain. "Question is, did they find it?"

"We found this, sir." Sweetwater handed Pennypacker a note made up of pasted letters cut from newspapers. "Clever bunch of bastards," he said. "First they break into our security, they taunt us with this garbage." He read the message out loud. "*We missed the Queen, but your knight is down. His castle is gone. Next is the bishop, followed by her pawns. Check mate!*"

"We seem to have a chess player for a burglar," Sweetwater said.

"This is no burglar. This is a cold-blooded murderer, and we had better find who he's after, or there will be more blood shed! No one leaves until we find out what they were after."

It was 4:30 in the morning before all the files had been reassembled, correlated and matched with the master file and checked against the code in Pennypacker's computer.

Chapter 8

By the time Mike had graduated from high school, he had developed his athletic skills to the degree that he was awarded an athletic scholarship to the University of Washington to play baseball. It was in college that he found a new breed of friends. When he wasn't in class or playing sports, all of his time was spent with his cronies, listening to music, partying and drinking. His study habits were poor and his grades naturally followed suit. But, he was a jock! A star on the university's baseball team! He had heard from some of the football players that, if his grades slipped below par, the coaching staff would simply influence his teachers to issue him grades good enough to get by. For jocks, the teachers always made allowances, he was told. Even if it meant taking basket weaving or three physical education courses in order to elevate his grade-point average, they would find a way.

When he had been home—as a child—he had thought nothing of seeing his mother in old, worn dresses, her physical appearance in shambles, including her stringy hair and unmade-up, homely face. Once he started to visit his college friend's homes, whose mothers took pride not only in their homes but themselves, Mike suddenly became ashamed of his mother.

When he went away to college, he rarely came home for a visit, although he was only a few hours away by car. When school was out for the summer, he decided to find a job near the university. His drinking and late hours with fellow students, who were in college more for fun than an education took its toll on his grades. At the end of his freshman year his grades were so far below average that he didn't even bother going by the administration office to pick them up.

When Aaron had been young, he tried out for Little League, aspiring to be just like his older brother. Alas, he had no athletic abilities, at least none that were displayed on the baseball field. The rules of the game dictated that everyone had to play at least half of the game, however, thus the coach put him where he would be least likely to get in trouble—right field. In the unfortunate event anyone hit a ball in his direction, he would simply close his eyes and stick his mitt in the general direction of the ball, hoping that it would fall in. He was such a liability to his team that, in the end, the other kids shunned him or made fun of him to the degree that he finally was forced to quit. The coach, sensitive of the impact that rejection could have on a kid, offered him a way out. He offered him the job of being their bat boy!

When Aaron was a sophomore in high school he noticed that in the morning the sink contained a large quantity of his hair. He tried to compensate for the loss by combing the lower section of his hair over the rapidly expanding bald spot, but that just made him look rediculous. Losing his hair did nothing for his already diminishing self respect. He buried himself in his studies and, by the time he graduated, it was with honors.

* * * *

Mike's contribution to the varsity baseball team his freshman year had been significant. Not only had he been the only freshman to make varsity, but he led the team in both RBI's and home runs. His team had made the playoffs, but had been defeated in the college World Series during the second round eliminations.

The first week of his sophomore year, Mike received notification to report to the Dean's office. "Hey, Mike! We're going down to the bay sailing today!" Todd Elliot yelled as Mike was reading the notice found in his mailbox. "Why don't you join us?"

"Sorry. I can't. I've got an appointment with the Dean," he said, waving the letter in the air.

Todd waved at him. "He's just going to welcome you back to school and brown-nose you, telling you how great of a baseball player you are. Come on! Judy's going to be there," he urged him. "You know how great she looks in a bikini! If you don't grab her, Heilmeister will. You wouldn't want him to nose you out on your love-life!"

Mike shrugged shoulders and laughed as he folded the letter and jammed it into his back pocket. He jumped into the back seat of the red Chevrolet convertible. "Let's party!"

The next day he knocked on the Dean's door. "You wanted to see me, Dean Rosterman?"

"Yes, please. Have a seat, Mike. You just get in?"

"Ah, no. Actually, I got in late yesterday afternoon. Something came up. This is the first chance I've had to get in to see you." He smiled the winning smile that he had, knowing that it usually disarmed most adults.

"You had a great year, last year, playing baseball." The Dean shuffled a pile of papers from the center of his desk to the corner.

"Thank you. Yeah! We did have a great year, didn't we?" He swung one leg over the other, hiking up his pants to rub the hair on his leg. "I can hardly wait until the season starts. We're going to take it all this year!"

Dean Rosterman had a look of firm resolve on his face as he closed the file and looked Mike straight in the eye. "I'm afraid you won't be playing baseball this year, Mike."

"Wh-why? What happened?" The blood visibly drained from his face in shock. Suddenly, he smiled. "You're kidding. Aren't you?"

"I'm afraid not. Your grade point average was one-point-six, Mike. University policy is if you don't maintain at least a two point average per semester, an athlete isn't eligible for sports until they have a full semester of acceptable grades."

"But my scholarship…"

"That's been terminated, Mike. The terms of the scholarship are clear. If an athlete's GPA falls below a two-point, scholarship privileges are terminated."

Mike was stunned. "What can I do?" He was on the verge of tears. The scholarship was his only passport to college. Without it, he had no financial means of remaining in college.

Through the ten years of being Dean at the college, Rosterman had seen a herd of Mike MacAffies come and go through his office…jocks who thought the sun and moon set on their asses. Jocks who partied day and night, skipped classes and had their girlfriends do term papers for them.

Truth of the matter was, Dean Rosterman despised jocks. They were the envy of all the regular students. They walked around campus in tight jeans, flaunting their bodies like Roman soldiers in a slave market, taking their pick of the beautiful women. When Rosterman had been a college student, he had been what is affectionately called a nerd. He had hated jocks then, and was no more fond of them now.

"You can study hard, just like the rest of the students, and…" he said, looking him straight in the eye, challenging him to contradict him with, 'couldn't you fix my grades?" "With hard work and a little luck, maybe you can bring your grade point average up so you can play next year," he said with a slight smirk that betrayed his real feelings.

"But, I don't have any money! How will I live?"

"You should have thought of that before you decided to become a party animal!" He checked himself quickly. He rose and without offering his hand to Mike, and went to open the door for him. "Now, if you'll excuse me, I have a very busy schedule."

Mike felt too embarrassed to tell his friends or even his mother about his failure. He went directly from the Dean's office to the campus Coast Guard office without even bothering to go back to his room and pick up his stuff. He was not the first student to come through those doors in a desperate attempt to escape reality. After a fifteen-minute conversation with the Ensign, he signed up for three years' service. He would wait until Christmas to break the news to his mother, assuming he was still in the general area.

*   *   *   *

With Mike in college, Sarah now concentrated all her efforts on Aaron, who was by now eighteen years of age. She came to the realization that she had never given him much attention.

At this stage of his life, she wanted to be sure that he knew the value of a dollar. She was determined to instill in him the desire to advance in the world, to get ahead as she and her husband had never done. Money, she would preach, was the key to happiness and success. From wealth, everything else would flow.

When it came time for Aaron to choose a major in college, he decided to choose a career that would yield him the one thing that he craved even more than money, and that was attention. He considered politics, but when he realized how long it would take to work his way up the political ladder from city councilman to may to governor, then maybe senator or congressman, impatience steered him in another direction.

It wasn't until the minister stood in front of the high school graduating class that he realized the answer to all his dreams lay right in front of him. Where else could one be the center of attention and have complete command of his own destiny than being a pastor of his own church? The sky would be the limit!

Look at Billy Graham, Oral Roberts, even Jimmy Baker before his fall from grace. They had thousands of people looking to them for guidance. And the money they must make! Why, with the throngs of people attending each service, not to mention television and book sales, their income must be phenomenal! It was reported that Jimmy Baker's ministerer at the PTL brought in an excess of a million dollars a day!

He didn't hear a word of the graduation speeches. Instead he fantasized standing in front of thousands of people who would ssit in the confines of a magnificent church hanging on his every word. He decided right then and there that not only was he going to be his own master, but the master of his own flock. The potential for wealth and power was overwhelming!

That summer he applied to PLC, Pacific Lutheran College, in the state of Washington, declaring his major as theology. He had taken the first step of the rest of his life!

CHAPTER 9
▼

Boris Adamovich lived in the seaport town of Klaipeda. It was Lithuania's third-largest city and the main seaport of that small country which adjoined Russia on one side and the Baltic Sea on the other, and was under Russian rule. For years the main industry had been fishing and shipbuilding.

The weather wasn't so bad during the summer months, when one could actually walk down to the water and sink one's toes into the warm sand and enjoy the sunshine. The little fishing village was not known as a tourist town, but did enjoy the surplus of tourists who came from Palanga and ventured down to their quaint little village from time to time.

Palanga was Lithuania's main seaside resort, which was famous for its broad sandy beaches, elegant restaurants and carefree nightlife. Cool pine groves dotted tranquil sanatariums where the rich and famous would often come to rest and get away from the cares of political or public life.

Boris Adamovich had worked for the Lithuanian Shipping Company his entire life, as had his father, and his father before him. Now, his Sons—Yuri, Viktor and Nikolai—seemed destined to follow in their father's footsteps. The destiny of his only daughter, Nevenka, still lay undecided, although fate had a way of deciding such matters for Russian and Lithuanian women. Unless a family was well off—and they usually weren't—or they were especially athletically gifted—which was a rarity—the women were destined to marry young, get pregnant—not necessarily in that order—and become housebound for the duration of their youth, their bodies growing larger with each pregnancy, until they were permanently flour-sack size. They would then be destined to cook, clean and care for their families for the rest of their days.

In ship builder's terms Boris Adamovich was the equivalent of a common laborer, making just enough money for himself and his family to survive, assuming they baked their own bread, mended their clothes and had no higher aspirations than basic survival. It was a rare occasion when new clothing found its way into their household. Transportation was either by foot or, if one was fortunate in savings one's coins, a used bicycle might be purchased.

When Boris' wife got beyond the stage of being pregnant and their children were old enough to attend mandatory school, she, too, worked at the shipping company, picking up scrap metals that had been cut, sweeping floors or polishing the wooden hull of a ship that was in the final stages of completion.

In short, life for Boris Adamovich and his family was hard. It offered no way out of the caste system in which they found themselves. They accepted the fact that they were locked into Russia's eternal life-labor cycle. The only way out was death, which they fought on a daily basis. No one expected them to raise themselves above their present station in life without a miracle, and in Russia, miracles rarely happen.

In the winter, the air at Klaipeda was bitterly cold. In the evening, after work, Boris would put a large log on the fireplace and get a roaring fire going. Wood was not plentiful and, many a night he and his family had to huddle together in the same room of their small, three-room cottage to retain as much heat as possible. Their cottage had been in the Adamovich family for as long as anyone could remember. They had lived with Boris' parents until four years ago, when his mother had finally passed away at the age of eight-six, leaving the house to her eldest son, Boris. Tradition dictated that one day the house would pass to one of his children, who would work in the shipyards and raise his family. The chain would go on, unbroken.

Boris and his wife slept in their bedroom, while their sons Yuri, Viktor and Nikolai slept in the remaining bedroom along with Nevenka. Everyone shared the tiny bathroom that had indoor plumbing which had been added to their house a few years ago. The luxury of having indoor plumbing in Klaipeda was looked upon as a touch of aristocracy.

It was now summer, and Nevenka had just turned eighteen. Her long, flowing blond hair, coupled with her pale skin and blue eyes, made her a striking young woman as her body ripened into womanhood. Her ample breasts pushed at the soft cotton blouse that she wore, allowing the firm nipples to make a clear impression through the thin material. As a result of her maturity she got a lot of attention from the boys in her class, but really didn't pay much attention to them, as they all seemed to be so immature. Besides, she had no intentions of falling into the eternal trap of getting pregnant. For Nevenka, a career beyond working for the Lithuanian Shipping Company had become her goal—indeed, her self-appointed destiny ever since was had become old enough to be aware that there were other options in the world, albeit, mostly unattainable.

This particular day she had just arrived home from school and was sitting at the wooden plank kitchen table practicing book work when Yuri strolled in. She glanced up at her older brother and asked, "Have you been down to the shipyards to see about work yet?"

Yuri, the eldest, had just finished high school and was taking some time off before applying for work at the shipyard full time. He pulled a chair up next to his sister and ran his hands through his long, blond, unruly hair. "Nah. I think I'll take a short vacation. Maybe go to Palanga and see if I can't get a job in one of the resorts. Maybe I'll meet a rich woman." He laughed, grabbing his crotch.

He considered himself a ladies man. He was tall, strong and handsome—a man of the world for his young age. For his eighteenth birthday, he had saved up enough money to buy himself the gift that he had been looking for all year long: a weekend trip to Palanga. There, he had met the most beautiful woman he had ever known. When she had asked him if he was looking for a good time, he had said, "You bet!" It turned out that a good time with her meant paying for it in her little room upstairs over the bar where she worked.

At first he was crushed to discover that such a beautiful woman could be a prostitute, but the more he thought about it, the more he fantasized about having sex with her. As far as he was concerned, the money had been well spent. It had given him first-hand experience of a woman's anatomy while, at the same time, it had enabled him to turn his unbridled emotions loose. The bonus was that he had learned things about sex that he had never thought possible: positions, techniques and the pleasures that lie with an experienced woman.

"And maybe you'll get arrested for bothering them, too," Nevenka retorted harshly, looking at him with disgust.

Yuri laughed. He looked at his sister's blouse, admiring her breasts. He had noticed her slowly developing before his very eyes and, lately, had made it a point to peek through the crack in the bathroom door late at night to watch her bathing when she thought everyone was sleeping.

Even if Nevenka was his sister, he couldn't resist the desire to caress her ample breasts and run his fingers through the fine hair that grew between her legs. More than once he had lay in bed fantasizing about making love to her.

"Maybe you think that you're as fine as those bathing beauties in Palanga," he said, raking his fingers through her hair.

She made a face as she pushed his hand away without taking her eyes off her work. "I've seen some of those cows in bathing suits here in Klaipeda. I wouldn't want to be compared to them."

"Ah, yes. They don't have the equipment you do," he said, yielding to the temptation of running his hands over her breasts. He paused to pinch her nipple between his fingers, making it hard.

"What do you think you're doing?" she said, brushing his hand away. "Go play with yourself if you need relief. I've got studying to do."

"Studying? What for? You'll soon be through with school. Then you'll be just like the rest of them, looking for a husband to marry so you can get fat and pregnant and raise children." He laughed as he extended his hands over his stomach, mocking a pregnant woman.

"Not me!" she said, looking at her older brother harshly. "I'm not going to be like the rest of them. I'm going to make something of myself. Just you wait and see." The look on her face was one of determination.

"All you're going to do is make some man happy as he thrusts himself into you. Nine months later, you'll be as big as a cow and just as ugly," he laughed. "Here, let me show you what it's like."

He ran his hands under her skirt, slipping his fingers inside her underwear. He had just barely touched her when Nevenka hit him with her book so hard that it knocked him off his chair. "If you're so hard up, why don't you go down to the barn and play with yourself?"

Yuri smiled as he saw the fire in his sister's eyes. "What makes you think that I'd even consider such a thing with you around," he said, as he picked himself up off the floor, his eyes locked on her breasts.

"Because, I've seen you."

The smile on his face quickly changed to anger. "You lie!"

She smiled. "Late at night, when you think everyone is asleep, I've seen you, lying there in bed, jerking about like you were struck by electricity." She laughed, pointing her finger at him. "Moaning and groaning. Then when you're done, you wipe your hand on the bottom of the bed. How does it feel, playing with yourself? You're so ugly that your hand is the only lovemaking you can find."

Yuri was enraged and insulted as he looked at her. He jumped to his feet, knocking the chair across the room in anger. "I'll show you how it feels!"

Before she could stop him, he grabbed the top of her blouse with both his hands and ripped the soft material from her chest, exposing the breasts that heretofore he had only had the nerve to admire from a distance. He squeezed them his hands until they made an imprint on her milky-white skin.

"What do you think you're doing?" she said, flaying at him with her hands.

His strength was too much for her, and he pushed her back onto the table. He held her with one hand and grasped at her underpants with the other. In one strong motion, he tore the crotch off her panties, leaving what remained to dangle around her waist. With one hand he continued holding her on the table as they struggled, while he quickly fumbled to unbutton his pants with the other.

By this time Nevenka was exerting every ounce of strength she had against her brother, kicking, screaming and scratching.

Yuri was not to be denied as he forced his body against her. He had her pinned against the table as he guided himself into his sister, his hands holding her shoulders while his mouth sought out her breasts.

As he moved his head down to kiss her nipples, Nevenka let out a loud scream. At that moment the door to the house burst open. There, standing in the open doorway, holding his lunch pail in his hand, was their father, tired, sweaty and dirty from a day's work at the factory. His wife, equally tired from cleaning and polishing wood all day, stood wide-eyed behind him.

Boris Adamovich and his wife stood in suspended animation for what seemed an eternity as the realization of their eldest son raping their only daughter registered in their minds. The look on Nevenka's face was one of sheer panic—terror of what was happening to her.

Once Yuri saw his parents, the look on his face changed from one of complete dominance to total fear and subservience.

Within the confines of a moment, with a rage not to be denied, Boris Adamovich was upon his eldest son. He grabbed Yuri by the shoulder, throwing him across the room like a small animal. He was like a lion on a wounded zebra in a feeding frenzy, jerking him up off the floor and slamming him against the wall, then holding him two feet above the floor by his shirt, his eyes glazed with anger, slapping his son uncontrollably.

Suddenly, he released his grip. Standing over his son, he said, "You will leave this house and never return!" His voice contained measured rage. Gritting his teeth, his nose touching his Sons, he said, "I denounce you as my son! As of this moment, you are no longer a part of this family! Now go!" He pointed towards the door as his fury shot out of his eyes.

When he had let go, Yuri had slid helplessly to the floor, half-naked, unable to comprehend what had just taken place. He looked at his mother, who had diverted her eyes from both men and was standing there with her hands over her mouth, looking at her daughter. She knew that Boris had total authority. To go against him would only result in equally harsh treatment. Without further comment, Yuri inched by her at the door and, without looking back, disappeared.

Boris nodded to his wife with his head towards Nevenka, who sat huddled in the corner with her knees to her chin, clutching her torn blouse, sobbing uncontrollably.

CHAPTER 10

▼

The ferry rolled into the harbor of Seattle, from Canada full of tourists and sightseers. A small man wearing a dark olive-green plaid coat, dark green pants and a wool beret stood by himself, leaned on the railing, smoking a cigarette, staring out at the cities skyline, thinking how the rugged terrain reminded him of Ireland. To the untrained eye, he was obviously not a local man, but then, who was?

As the boat slowly drifted onto the loading dock, he waited until the majority of the foot traffic had departed before heading for the unloading zone. There, a line of yellow cabs waited.

He hailed one, gave the driver a piece of paper with an address on it, then sat back going over the plan in his mind.

The ride through town took twenty-two minutes. Although the driver had made several overtures of conversation with his passenger, they fell on deaf ears—either that, or the passenger wasn't in the mood for chit-chat. The driver did notice that his passenger, who in his wide range of experience was determined not to be a local, took no interest in the sites.

At his destination, 1400 Front Street, the address of a three story office building, he gave the taxi driver a twenty dollar bill, allowing four dollars and fifteen cents for a tip, and sent him on his way without a word.

The time was four-fifteen. Friday. Workers were beginning to depart the buildings in preparation for the upcoming weekend. The man stood across the street from 1400 Front Street, looking into a window that held camping and boating equipment. It was not the equipment in the window that he was looking at, however; it was the reflection of people departing the building across the street that he focused on.

By six o'clock most of the people seemed to have left the premises. A few moments later he noted an elderly woman dressed in a long, dark coat, wearing high-button shoes and a scarf around her neck, she entered the premises, carrying a bag which he presumed to be her lunch.

He waited an additional fifteen minutes before crushing his cigarette under the heel of his boot. No one had left the building for more than ten minutes now. At six-thirty he crossed the street, taking care to check to see that no one was around before entering the building through the double glass doors.

The lobby was empty. He stopped and listened for voices. There were none as he approached the elevator and punched the large red call button. The lit numbers above the elevator door indicated that the elevator was on the third floor. A few moments later a bell rang and the doors opened silently. The man stepped in, put on a pair of gloves, then pressed the three button on the elevator and waited.

As he stepped out of the elevator onto the carpeted hallway, he looked down the vacant hall at the glass doors. Only one door had a light shining through it. He walked to the door, listened for a moment, then turned the knob silently, peering in. He saw the figure of an elderly woman going slowly from desk to desk, picking up trash baskets, emptying them into a plastic bag. She didn't hear him as he walked behind her.

"Sarah Macafy?" he inquired in a soft voice.

Startled, she turned to face the man. "Yes. Do I know ya?"

"I was a friend of yer husband's, back in Ireland, before he got careless." He withdrew a cord from his pocket and wrapped one end around his gloved hand.

Sarah glanced around the room for something with which to defend herself, but she was too late. He wound the rope tightly around her neck and held it there until she slumped to the floor. The man then let loose of the rope and crossed himself. "Peace be with ya, Sarah Macafy."

Chapter 11

▼

Aaron MacAffie found a room above the College Side Inn. He knew that he needed to find a job so he applied at a small restaurant as a short order cook and was hired. Now, he had a cheap room and his food was free.

He had just finished putting on an aparon to start his shift when someone called out to him. "Aaron. There's a phone call for you. It's something about your mother. I think something's happened to her."

He ran into her house and picked up the receiver. As he listened, his shoulders sank. His mother had apparently been killed while working in an office building in Seattle. The police thought she might have interrupted a burglary, the voice said, although nothing seemed to be missing. They were sorry to have inform him of the tragedy.

Aaron took a Greyhound bus home for the funeral. Only he and his brother Mike were in attendance, along with the funeral director, the minister and some elderly woman playing the organ. After the service, the minister took Aaron aside and handed him an envelope.

"What's this?" He asked.

"Your mother was always concerned about your education, Aaron. She had a small insurance policy, enough to cover your books and tuition, in the event she passed away before you graduated. This is the policy."

Aaron looked at the minister as if he had difficulty comprehending what he had just said.

"She asked me to keep it for her," he responded before Aaron could ask the question. "I think she had a premonition or something." He nodded as he patted Aaron on the shoulder, then turned to leave. "It was your mother's fervent wish that you graduate and make something of yourself," he said over his shoulder. "Don't disappoint her."

*   *   *   *

Mike MacAffie was on leave from the Coast Guard hip, *Sea Hawk* which had docked in San Francisco. He and his bunk buddy, Holly Woodward from Palmdale, California, were touring the city. They had had few drinks on Fisherman's Wharf and were feeling no pain. Their goal was to pick up a couple girls and make a night of it. No one seemed to notice the little guy wearing a dark beret sitting at the bar, smoking a cigarette, watching them.

"I've had white, black and brown women, but I've yet to have some Oriental," Holly said, finishing his beer. Why don't we go down to Chinatown and get some of that horizontal stuff."

"I'm for it," Mike slurred with his eyes drooping. "You lead and I'll follow."

They took a cab down to Chinatown and started looking for bars. They walked into the first one they saw, called the Red Parrot Bar and Grill.

"This looks like it has some potential!"

The place was quiet, with soft Oriental string-instrument music playing. A couple of Chinese girls were sitting alone at the end of the bar, eyeing them as they walked in. "Pay dirt!" Mike said, nudging Hollywood.

"Can a couple of sea-going lads buy you girls a drink?" Mike asked.

Without hesitation, one of the girls said, "Sure. Pull up a stool, sailor."

After a couple of Singapore Slings later, the girls agreed to have a party with them, for a fee of a hundred dollars—apiece!

"I gotta take a leak before we go," Mike said, sliding off the bar seat. "Back in a minute."

He staggered to the bathroom and stood at the urinal with his eyes closed, his brain reeling slightly, visualizing the fun they were about to have with their women. There was a tap on his shoulder. "Yeah?" he responded, without opening his eyes, thinking it was his buddy. "We're goin' to get some pussy tonight!" He laughed.

"Might ya be Mike Macafy of Sean Macafy's kin?" the voice asked.

It was a voice Mike didn't recognize, but the accent was familiar. The man was a blur to him, standing behind him wearing a olive-colored coat with a dark cotton beret as he squinted his eyes. "Who wants to know?"

"The Sons of Ireland are inquirin'."

Mike spun around with a roundhouse, missing the man by a clean six inches. "Now why would ya be swingin' like that, me lad, if ya had no harm intended?"

"Any man who comes askin' about me Da, sayin' they're from the Old Country, is askin' fer trouble."

"Then ya be Sean's lad?"

"What of it?"

"Just askin'."

It happened so fast that, in his inebriated state, Mike MacAffie had no time to react. The little man brought a shiv of steel up under his rib cage, straight into his heart. It dropped him like a rock. He lay in the urinal with his eyes open, looking at the small man, but seeing nothing.

The man washed his hands, brushed his fingers through his coarse brown hair, then put his beret back on and left the restroom and the Red Parrot Bar and Grill.

His job was two-thirds completed.

* * * *

When Aaron MacAffie graduated from college with a degree in theology and a minor in business, the theology department found him a position in a Presbyterian church in the small town of Longview, Washington. Luther Magnason was the Pastor.

Aaron drove inmto town, found his way to the small church, parked his minivan on the gravel pad next to the church, put on his herringbone jacket with the patches on the elbows, combed what was left of his balding hair and walked into the parish office.

"So, you're my assistant," the Pastor said as Aaron was ushered into his study, a small room with pictures of members of his parish, plaques of commendation from the community, as well as his formal educational degrees, lining the walls. Two wooden chairs had been positioned in front of his small, simulated-walnut-top and stainless-steel desk.

The room totally lacked any character. Aaron looked around, disillusioned. He had hoped to be assigned to a more prosperous church—one with a greater availability of funds. More class.

If nothing else, the experience has humbling. It taught him that, while there might be some glamour in being called a minister, pastor of his own church, the leader of the flock, if there wasn't money in it, the whole purpose of his going into this field was defeated. Where was his image of Billy Graham, Oral Roberts? Even Jimmy Baker?

✳ ✳ ✳ ✳

Sunday church service had just concluded, and Pastor Magnason was standing at the door leading out of the church, greeting everyone as was his usual practice after services. He stood at one side of the door while Aaron MacAffie, his assistant and understudy, stood at the other. Those in a hurry came to his side of the line; otherwise, everyone stood in the Pastor's line to shake his hand.

Longview was not a large town, and Aaron had gotten to know most of the parishioners. When the short fellow with a reddish complexion and coarse brown hair, holding onto his beret, came to shake his hand, he greeted the man, saying, "I'm Aaron MacAffie. I don't believe I know your name."

"I be Matty McGown, lad. Glad to know yer acquaintance."

"You sound like an Irishman."

"That would be true."

"Well, I'm glad to make your acquaintance. I was born in Ireland myself. My father is still there. We had to bury him, bless his soul."

"Did ya now, indeed? And what was his name?"

"Sean Macafy. And a great sort of a man he was," Aaron said, slipping into an Irish brogue himself.

"Well, Aaron Macafy, it was sure and again nice meetin' ya. Ya be havin' a nice life, what's left of it."

Aaron furrowed his brow. *Strange thing to say*, he thought as he watched the small man walk away. When the congregation had finally left, Pastor Magnason and Aaron MacAffie retired to the Pastor's office, which was located next to the church. They had made it a practice to count and log in donations every Sunday directly after the service.

"I saw you talking to a new man after the service," the Pastor said as he dumped the money from the collection plates on his desk. "It sounded as if he might have been Irish."

"Yes. From Ireland, he said. Funny sort."

"Oh, how's that?"

"I dunno. Couldn't quite put my finger on it. Just seemed a little strange. You have many Irish in this town?"

"None that I know of." He opened the drawer of his desk and was rummaging around.

"Lose something, pastor?"

"It's that darn migraine," he said, rubbing his head. "I seem to be out of my prescription. I'm going to have to drive down to the corner store and be gittin' me a bottle of aspirin," he said in bad Irish brogue, kidding Aaron. "I'll be back in a flash. Don't be helpin' yerself to the funds now, ya hear?" He smiled, seemingly amused at his own joke.

"To be sure," Aaron said, playing along.

"Here. I'll be havin' a fiver from the collection fer the medicine," he said, continuing with the brogue as he picked up a five dollar bill from the collection. "Be back in a moment."

A moment later he was back in the office.

"That was quick. When you said a moment, you really meant it!"

"Can ya be belivin' it?" He said, still in the Irish brogue. "Me Bug has a flat. Could I be borrowin' yer wheels for a mite, mate?"

Aaron laughed and tossed him the keys to his van. "That's what ya git fer driving a yellow Volkswagen," he said. "Next time, drive American." He laughed.

A moment later there was a terrific explosion that shattered the windows of the office. Aaron ran out of the door, only to see his van engulfed in flames. *If Pastor Magnason was in the car, he's shaking hands with his maker*, Aaron thought.

Something made him think of the small Irishman at service today. A shiver ran down his spine and he ran inside to dial 911.

*   *   *   *

There was no funeral for the pastor, just a wake. After the service, Aaron decided that, with Pastor Magnason gone, there was certainly no reason to stick around. He tossed the keys to the Pastor's Volkswagen in the air, catching them in the palm of his hand. "I guess he won't be needin' this, either."

*   *   *   *

Aaron MacAffie was very surgical when it came to selecting the location of his future flock. He sought out a rich, free-thinking neighborhood. The current population was into reincarnation, out-of-body experiences, meditation, yoga, Scientology and New Age religion, he thought. They were breaking out of the traditional mold and reaching for something new. Something refreshing.

The majority of these free-thinkers were well-to-do folks who had time and money on their hands. This was the type of group Aaron MacAffie was seeking for his church.

Chapter 12

Nevenka's extra studies paid off when she applied for work in the office at the Lithuanian Shipping Company. After giving her an examination to test her comprehension and bookkeeping skills, they hired her to work in the office. The window of the owner's office looked out onto the general office area where all the women worked. The owner, Mr. Pavlinsky, positioned her right outside his office, where he could see her working next to the older, more portly women on his staff.

At first there was animosity, fed by envy of the other women, but Nevenka quickly overcame that with her disarming charm and smiles. She shouldered more than her share of the work each day, voluntarily stayed late after work each day to finish up after everyone else had left to go home. Her efforts did not go unnoticed by both staff and management alike.

Her work ethics were not accidental, rather by design, harbored for the desire to get ahead. It was an easy, logical step to appreciate the difference between working with a pencil and paper, pushing numbers around in a warm, clean office than working on the factory floor cleaning up after the workers or polishing wooden hulls, as her mother had done most of her adult life.

In the early hours each morning the family went to work together: her father, mother, Viktor and youngest brother Nikolai—or Niki, as he was nicknamed—and Nevenka. They parted company at the entrance to the building, her father, mother and brothers going into the mouth of the building to construct ships, while Nevenka went up the stairs into the offices. Each day, her mother would pause as her daughter climbed the stairs, admiring her, for she was the only woman in the history of her family who had raised herself above working as a common laborer or falling to the baby-factory category.

* * * *

Yuri, Nevenka's eldest brother who had raped her, spent many hours regretting what he had done, wondering what had gotten into him to lead him to commit such a heinous act. He knew that his father meant it when he had eradicated him from the family. He had no money. The only clothes he had were on his back and, in reality, he possessed no skills. His only real asset was his looks, which got him through many a hungry day and saved him many a night. He had honed his charm to the point that he could usually manipulate lonely women to take care of him. Eventually, even that became boring, as they were usually either older women, past their youth, in need of a young man's affection to bolster their ego, or were wealthy enough that they could toy with attractive young men such as Yuri.

He wandered about Russia until he met a friend in a park who had joined the Soviet Red Army. "The pay is not great, but I have a roof over my head and food in my belly every day. And wearing a uniform is great for getting women." He laughed. The following day Yuri joined the Red Army.

He never returned to visit his parents, but he sent letters to his mother from time to time. She always hid them from her husband, who still bore a grudge against his son for attacking Nevenka. One evening his name came up in a family discussion. Boris' fist tightened, then he banged on the table and left without comment. The message was clear. No one in the family ever spoke of him again.

One day Viktor found the bound bundle of letters from Yuri when he was rummaging around his mother's room looking for spare money for a date he had that night. He read how much his older brother enjoyed the army, despite the fact that the discipline was harsh. The rewards of being in the army seemed to far exceed being alone, out of work and without money.

When Viktor had finished mandatory schooling, he joined the Soviet Red Army to be with his brother.

* * * *

The air in Lithuania was filled with excitement as their government threatened to secede from the Soviet Union and become a free country. The Lithuanian Parliament proceeded to pass a sovereignty law, giving that body veto power over

Soviet laws, which had previously ruled over their country. The first amendment of the newly passed Lithuanian rule claimed that, from that moment on, all property within its territory should be Lithuanian, not Russian.

That night Lithuanians danced the night away around a bonfire. Prior to this such a celebration would had been banned by the Communists, who had stated that such a public gathering was an illegal and dangerous. The Catholic Church began to have regular Sunday morning services and schoolboys who had heretofore belonged to the Communist Young Pioneers organization joined the Boy Scouts. Communist names were stripped off main streets in Lithuanian towns and were replaced with the previously designated Lithuanian names.

* * * *

Vytautas Landsbergis was a fifty-eight-year-old man, born in Lithuania, who came from a family who had fought Russian domination years ago. It was through his intelligence and foresight that Lithuania strove for their independence. Gorbachev both feared and admired the man labelling him, *Gudri Lape,* the Clever Fox.

When news of the small state of Lithuania's declaration of independence from mother Russia spread, it was on everyone's lips. Soon, leaders from other countries were meeting in secret, talking and planning their secession from the Soviet Union, as well. Gorbachev's power was about to crumble around his own feet. Something had to be done.

He ordered an emergency meeting of his cabinet. "I will not allow this…this little bit of a country to withdraw from the Soviet Union," he said, slamming his fist on the table at the Great Hall in Moscow. "Who do they think they are, calling *us* foreigners?" He issued a long, stinging statement, accusing the Lithuanians of exploiting democracy and openness in order to incite their people to secede from the Soviet Union. "They have gone too far!" he warned, shaking his finger. The veins in his neck were bulging and his face was red with anger.

Landsbergis responded to the speech by stating that Lithuanians would fight for their independence. It was the big bear of the Soviet Union pitted against little Lithuania.

* * * *

The Red Army compound

The men had just completed an exhausting day of training in the field and had been dismissed. Private Yuri Adomovich lay on his bed, exhausted, his boots and sweat-drenched clothes still on, when the billet's doors shot open. Sergeant Pavlonovich stood in front of four armed soldiers, both feet firmly planted on the wooden plank floor.

"Private Yuri Adomovich of Lithuania!" the Sergeant barked, slapping a black swagger stick on his uniform.

As soon as the Sergeant had barged in the door, all activity and conversation in the billets ceased. Where there had been a dull din of chatter and movement the previous moment, one could now hear a pin drop. Each man froze as if in suspended animation. In the Red Army, superior officers have supreme control over their underlings, and everyone in the room was an underling. When their sergeants spoke, ice water ran through their veins and they responded without question or forethought.

All eyes had been focused on the men standing at the entrance of their billets. When Yuri's name was mentioned, all eyes focused on him. To be called by name and rank was expected, but when they had added the words "of Lithuania" to the command, everyone knew Yuri Adamovich was in for a hard time. Although the Red Army had made every attempt to keep word of Lithuania's secession from the troops ears, it was common knowledge that the little country could be their next destination if and when a dominating force was needed to return control to the Soviet Union. Yuri Adamovich was not prepared for that moment, but had concluded that he would deal with it in the event Soviet intervention was required. The one thing he knew beyond a doubt was that there was no way he would bear arms against his fellow countrymen, let alone his own family. The Soviet Red Army knew that, too.

"Sergeant!" Yuri Adomovich yelled as he jumped to his feet, standing at attention, eyes forward.

The Sergeant marched up to his bunk, the entourage of four armed soldiers following close behind. He reached out to Yuri's shoulder, where his Red Army patch had been sewn, and ripped it off with great vehemence.

Yuri's heart was pounding so hard it seemed to want to escape from his chest, yet he stood his ground firmly, looking straight ahead. He had been expecting trouble as a result of his being from Lithuania, but had rationalized that the Red Army would conclude that first and foremost he was a soldier, and therein lay his loyalty.

"Yuri Adomovich, you are hereby under arrest for treason! Take him to the stockade!" he commanded, pushing Yuri back forcefully so his head momentarily snapped back. None of the men in the barracks dared meet Yuri's eyes as they led him out of the building. To Yuri's credit, he stood tall and marched out proud, showing no fear.

✶ ✶ ✶ ✶

Viktor Adamovich, Yuri's younger brother, had been housed in another part of the compound, and had been getting ready for chow when his friend, who was the communications assistant, rushed in, out of breath. "Viktor! Your brother has been arrested!" His eyes were wild with excitement and fear.

"Arrested? How? Why?"

"Word from command is that they have labeled him a traitor because he lived in Lithuania!"

"Good God!"

"You've got to get out, Viktor! They'll be coming for you next. I've seen the order! Leave now. Go! Don't wait to take anything. Just go!" His eyes darted from Viktor to the door, as if expecting soldiers to crash in at any moment.

Viktor grabbed his money pouch and stuffed it into his pocket. He had saved some of his rubles. At least that would allow him to buy food.

"Hurry, Viktor!"

Viktor slapped his friend on the shoulder as he ran out the door. A moment later, he was back. "They're coming!"

"Hide!"

"Where?"

They both looked around in a panic. "In the shower! I'll pretend to be cleaning up. Hurry!"

The doors burst open. A red-faced man in uniform stormed in with four armed men behind him. Viktor Adamovich!" he yelled.

There was no one in the billets. "Check the toilets!"

One of the soldiers ran into the toilet area, where Viktor's friend, the communication assistant, was mopping down the floor. As the soldier ran in, Viktor's friend held up his hand. "Careful. The floor is wet. What do you want?"

"I'm looking for Viktor Adamovich!"

"There is no one here. Check the parade grounds. He's probably out there with the rest of his company."

The soldier ran back. "There's no one here! They're out on the parade field!"

The sound of boots exiting the empty billets echoed throughout the building as Viktor peered around the corner. "Thank you, my friend. I shall never forget you."

"Now, get out of here!"

Chapter 13

There were soldiers everywhere. *They're all looking for me,* Viktor thought as he slid from tree to bush to house, trying his best to remain invisible. An old woman was washing the family clothes, hanging them outside on the line, in the back yard. Viktor waited until she went into the house, then jumped the small picket fence that divided her house from the fields. There were men's clothing that looked like they would fit him. Hastily, he plucked a long-sleeved workman's shirt and a pair of brown pants from the line and ran behind the shed next door. The clothes were still wet and cold to the skin, but they would soon dry. He put them on over his army fatigues.

The plan was to try to make his way back to Lithuania without being caught. He had to warn his people of the atrocities that men like his brother were suffering…men who had offered up their lives in service for the greatness and good of the Soviet Union.

He was of average appearance and wearing workman's clothes, blended in with the common Russian man. At first he was sure that the soldiers would easily spot him. The soldiers in every army truck that passed by looked at him, but no one stopped. They were looking for a man in uniform!

When he finally got out of Moscow he kept to the side roads, jumping out of sight whenever a vehicle approached.

The following day, when he was on the outskirts of Moscow, he saw a young soldier standing by the side of the road smoking a cigarette, obviously waiting for a ride. Looking around to be sure that no one was watching, he casually walked up to the man. He had learned to speak fluent Russian in school and had not spoken his native tongue since joining the Red Army. In perfect Russian, he asked, "You look young for a soldier, about my age. Is it difficult to get into the army?"

Without hesitation, the young soldier responded, giving no indication that Viktor looked familiar. Victor decided to take a chance. "I have a friend from Lithuania that joined the army. I thought I would try to find him. Where to you suggest I go to find him?"

Viktor learned that there were rumors of several men from Lithuania who had joined the Red Army. When rumors of secession had spread, they had tried to escape after learning of what had happened to some of the soldiers from their country. Rumor had it that many had been captured and dragged back in chains. Some had been shot on the spot. There were reports that others had been beaten, raped, then had suffered a painful death.

Viktor thanked the solder and hurried on his way.

* * * *

"I understand we have a dissident amongst our troops," General Audalovid replied to his Captain. He pointed to a soldier standing guard at the entrance to the compound.

The Captain nodded towards Yuri. "That would be Yuri Adamovich," he responded. "He is from Lithuania," he said with his mouth turned down in disgust. "I have ordered him to be displayed on the parade grounds," he said, nodding towards the man who was chained to a post.

"A spy?" the General inquired, eyeing the soldier. "He has been in the Red Army for four years now. What has he done?"

"He is a Lithuanian," the Captain said with distaste. "He is suspected of spying for the enemy."

"The dog should be punished!"

The Captain nodded, with a slight smile creeping across his face. He loved dealing with dissidents.

"See what you can do to set an example for others to discourage such activity," the General said, nodding towards the soldier. "I do not want any of our men associating with traitors! Do I make myself clear?"

"Precisely," the Captain said, snapping a salute to his general. He knew precisely what his General expected to be done with the traitor.

* * * *

Vladimer Ryzhkov struck an imposing figure as he stood before the Lithuanian parliament, his long blond hair flowing over his shoulders like a lion's mane. His clear blue eyes and keen military mind betrayed his intelligence. He had but to speak and it was clear why he had been chosen as a military leader. Vladimer Ryzhkov wore the uniform of the new Lithuanian military order: gold braids around his right arm and a simple four-buttoned coat. A single star stood on his shoulder.

He had been a member of the KGB's elite intelligence force when he had learned of his country's move towards secession. He'd known that, should a movement materialize, his life wouldn't be worth a plugged ruble, despite the fact that he worked for the KGB. Without notice, he had packed up his belongings and had returned directly to Lithuania.

Without hesitation, Parliament appointed him in charge of national security, awarding him the immediate rank of General. "I have seen, first hand, the methods that Soviet KGB will utilize to maintain control over those forces that threaten Soviet power," he said. "As your General and Chief of Security, I tell you, on my mother's grave, that we will not bow to the Soviet Union, nor their strong-arm tactics!"

The members of Parliament and the officials who had gathered in Government Hall gave him thundering applause.

"I can tell you that Gorbachev is a very nervous man."

A number of hoots and yells came from the floor.

"Tomorrow, he is flying here, to Lithuania, to seek a settlement of the differences between our countries. Don't be fooled by the smile that he will wear. Like the birthmark he wears plainly upon his face, he wears two colors within his heart, as well: red for Russia, and black towards anyone who opposes him. He is here for two reasons: one, to initiate a settlement, but he's also on a spying mission to see how much he has shook us up with his empty threats."

More hoots and hollers from the floor were accompanied by shaking fists in the air.

"Shoot the bastard!"

"Send him to be tarred and feathered!"

Vladimer raised his hands and quieted the crowd. "Remember, while he is in Lithuania, he is our guest."

Hoots and boos followed.

Vladimer held his hands in the air. "Let's show him how dignified Lithuanians are. Don't lower yourselves to their level. Let's maintain our poise and dignity. That will go a lot further than animosity. We're better than they are! Don't you agree?"

Shouts and yells agreed with him.

"For security reasons, we are meeting in the small fishing village of Klaipeda. I want to show him how our people are going about their daily routine of working and are intent on making a living. An honest living!" He raised his fist into the air.

The crowd yelled its approval.

"Can you imagine how unnerved he must be to come here?" He smiled as he shot both fists into the air, his hair bouncing off his shoulders. His blue eyes danced in the lights of the great hall.

The crowd yelled again, feeling good that for the first time in their lives they were not afraid to voice their opinion.

"Did you know that this is the first time *any* republic leader has *ever* visited Lithuania! Does that tell you what they think of us?"

A yell rang out from the crowd. "Throw the Soviet soldiers from our land! Independence to Lithuania!"

Vladimer held up his hand. "Fear not. We shall prevail. Lithuania shall be independent!" He raised his hands, his palms facing the crowd. After they had yelled and clapped for several minutes, he said, "Take heart! The world is watching us. Gorbachev would not dare attack such a small country. Think how he would look to the rest of the world, attacking one of his own states? Slaughtering his own people!"

Again the crowd broke out into a chant, holding hands and dancing. "Independence, Independence, Independence!"

* * * *

Vladimer Ryzhkov, Chief of Security for the Lithuanian government, dressed in the General's uniform made by Lithuania's finest tailors, met Gorbachev and his entourage at the airport. Gorbachev's face was grave as he and Raisa, who was always at his side, along with his aides, exited the plane.

"Come," a solemn-faced Vladimer said, beckoning his guests with his hands. "I want to show you the Lithuanian people. These are the people for whom you have cared so little that you have never laid eyes on them. As you shall see, they are hard-working, simple people."

Gorbachev started to protest, but Raisa squeezed his arm, alerting him not to forget the reason for his visit. Begrudgingly, he held his tongue. The auto procession started, headed for the Lithuania Ship Building Company.

"Together, we must look for a solution," Gorbachev preached from the back seat of their limousine as they entered the compound of the Lithuanian Ship Building Company. "If somebody succeeds in splitting the great Soviet Union apart, they have bargained for more trouble than they could ever imagine! You remember that," he said, shaking his finger, looking harshly into Vladimer's eyes as if warning him. "You were once a member of the KGB, Vladimer Ryzhkov. You, of all people, should know better." There was no mistaking his meaning.

They made a quick tour of the manufacturing section of the ship building. Gorbachev nodded to the workers with a slight smile from time to time while Raisa pulled her colorful scarf over her forehead so as not to get any dirt on her hair…or to look into the people's eyes.

"The office is upstairs," Vladimer said, pointing his hand towards the stairs. "I would like you to meet the president of the company."

Reluctantly, Gorbachev ascended the stairs. He did not feel at home with these people, which was precisely the impression Vladimer wanted to convey to both to the Lithuanian people and to Gorbachev himself.

The entire office staff, including Nevenka Adomovich, immediately stood as Vladimer Ryzhkov, Gorbachev and Raisa and their security force entered the room. From the moment Nevenka saw Vladimer Ryzhkov, she couldn't take her eyes off him, even in the presence of the great Gorbachev. She had seen pictures of him in newspapers, and even on television, but never had she envisioned that she would actually see him in person…or, that he would be so magnificent. So beautiful.

When Vladimer's eyes met Nevenka's, normally she would have adverted her eyes, but she was so transfixed with the man that she was rendered immobile. Vladimer gave her a slight nod and smiled, then moved on. It wasn't until the woman standing beside Nevenka nudged her that she finally came back into focus and realized where she was.

"Are you all right?" the girl asked, holding onto Nevenka's arm. "You made quite a fool of yourself," she admonished her.

Nevenka shrugged her shoulders and smiled meekly. There had been no way to contain the feeling that had come over her when her eyes had met those of Vladimer Ryzhkov. It had been a once in a lifetime experience. One that she would never forget!

* * * *

Despite Gorbachev's efforts, Lithuania's Independence day came on March 11, 1990. All workers were given a holiday from work as Parliament unfurled its red, yellow and green Lithuanian flag. The people sang the old Lithuanian national anthem. Many of the elderly had tears in their eyes. Outside, crowds cheered as workmen systematically removed the Soviet hammer-and-sickle seal from every public building.

* * * *

Boris Adamovich was stunned when a personal gold-embossed engraved invitation to attend the independence ceremony came for him and his family. The celebration was to be held in the resort town of Palanga, fifteen miles north of Klaipeda, where they lived. The invitation stated that an official government car would arrive to pick them up at a specified time.

Her father was certain that someone must have made a mistake in inviting them to the ceremony. Why would anyone invite him? He was no one…nothing to anyone except his family. Only Nevenka had an inkling as to who had sent such an invitation, and she dared not think the why of it.

The limousine came as promised, and Boris Adamovich and his family, dressed in their finest clothing, were escorted to the ceremony. Although the back of the limousine was stocked with Russia's finest vodka and lead crystal glasses from which to drink it, Boris Adamovich would not allow himself to indulge, feeling that it would be a dishonor to whomever had sent the limousine, and might perhaps even taint the good fortune of he who smiled upon him. He sat quietly in the back seat, revelling in every moment of the ride to the celebration.

The ceremony was magnificent, with speeches, fireworks and food and drink for everyone. Nevenka was dressed in her finest white cotton dress. There was a soft summer breeze flowing through the evening air as music, song and vodka seemed to flow from everywhere. She stood alone, on the pier overlooking the Baltic Sea, with her eyes closed, enjoying the smells and sounds, when a deep, melodic, masculine voice behind her said, "I'm glad you could see your way to attend the celebration."

She turned to face Vladimer Ryzhkov. He was even more handsome and taller than she had remembered. Her blood pressure rose so fast it temporarily rendered her speechless. It was all she could do to simply stand there and look into his clear blue eyes. She had no idea if she said anything, or if her mouth was open, or if she even moved, for that matter. All time ceased to exist.

She finally summoned the strength to respond. "Yes. Isn't it great?"

"Forgive my lack of manners," he said, bowing slightly. "Allow me to introduce myself."

He took her hand and brushed his lips against her fingertips. "Vladimer Ryzhkov," he said with a deep voice that seemed to vibrate between her fingertips.

"Yes. I know," she said meekly, angry at herself for being unable to say anything intelligent.

"May we walk?" he offered, extending his hand towards the beach.

She was so stunned that words lost her.

Without waiting for a response, he took her arm and guided her towards the water. "I first saw you at the shipping factory in Klaipeda when we were giving Gorbachev and Raisa a tour. Do you remember seeing me?"

She looked shyly into his eyes. "How could I forget?" She wanted to say that he was the most beautiful man that she had ever laid eyes on. She wanted to inquire as to why he had taken the time to invite such an insignificant creature as herself to the ceremony, let alone send a limousine, which, up to now had been the highlight of her life, but instead, she said nothing.

He could have any woman he wanted. He was handsome, powerful and rich, no doubt. Although she knew she was pretty, Nevenka had no real conception of how beautiful she really was.

He stopped as they walked onto the beach, knelt down and gently removed her slippers. "I can't explain what it was that drew me to you," he said, "but I knew, the moment that our eyes met, destiny was taking command." He turned to face her. "Does that scare you?"

She blinked and smiled as she dared study the face of this magnificent creature standing before her. "A little."

He smiled too. "Good. Because it scares me, too."

They walked on the beach for what seemed an eternity, without speaking. Finally, Nevenka felt that she must ask a question that had been plaguing her for months. "What will happen to our little country?" she inquired, looking up into his face. It gave her a reason to look at him again without being guilty of staring. "I know that the Soviet Union will not let us withdraw from Russia without a fight. That concerns me."

"You are more intelligent and insightful than I had hoped," he said, smiling as he took her hand. They walked in silence for a moment before he answered. "I suspect there will be threats, maybe even reprisals from the Soviet Union, but that is the price of independence. We live in perilous times, Nevenka."

They continued walking before he spoke again. When he did, it was with measured words. Grave words. "It is not common knowledge, but my friends in the KGB tell me that many states under Soviet rule are talking about independence. In the months to come, I believe the Russian people will see their country come under a tremendous transformation. You are watching history in the making, Nevenka. This could very well be the end of the Soviet Union as we know it."

"That's scary."

"Yes, and exciting at the same time."

He stopped to face her. Taking both her hands in his, he said, "I must go to Moscow tomorrow, to meet with Gorbachev and his cabinet. I must try to convince them to leave Lithuania alone." He looked into her eyes and held her hands. "Forgive me for being so bold, but…" he hesitated for a moment, squeezing her hands gently. "Time is precious. Would you consent to…come with me?"

There was nothing more in the world that Nevenka wanted than to be with this exciting, bold young lion, but she hesitated, concerned about what her father would say. And what would she do in Moscow? She could only be in the way. She knew nothing of politics and could only diminish herself in this great man's eyes. And she had nothing to wear. What she had on was the best she had. She could not appear to be as poor as she really was.

"I'd love to," she said, "but, I can't. I'm sorry."

He nodded. "I understand," he replied softly. "May I see you when I return? We could meet, here in Palanga, and lounge on the beach, dine on the veranda of the hotel and watch the sunset together. Please, say you will meet me," he said with a smile that could not be refused. There was more than just an invitation spoken with his eyes, as well as his words.

"I'd like that."

"Good! It's settled then. Shall I call for you in Klaipeda?"

"No. I'll find my way back here to Palanga. It is only fifteen miles from home. I would prefer it."

He nodded. "I understand. Noon, Friday. Here, on the beach!"

"Yes. Noon, Friday." Her heart was beating so hard, she was afraid he would hear it over the soft lapping of the sea.

They walked back to the pier, hand in hand, not talking, just listening to the music in the air and feeling the magic in their souls that was being transmitted through their touch. He stopped at the pier, dusted the sand off her feet and replaced her shoes.

"I have one request," he said, facing her, looking deep into her eyes, holding onto her hands.

She was almost too scared to speak. "Yes?" she whispered.

"May I kiss you?"

Her whole body tingled. Never in her life had she even dared wish such a thing, and now, here it was, the most beautiful man on earth, *asking* for a kiss. "Yes," she said softly.

He held her face gently in his hands as his lips gently brushed against hers. She wished the moment would never end, that he would never stop. She would remember this time for the rest of her life.

Chapter 14

Yuri Adamovich stood strapped to a eight-foot post, his hands and legs bound by chains. His blouse had been ripped from his back. He winced, but gave no measure to his torturers as they laid the whip across his back time and time again until he sagged to his knees, bleeding, unconscious. He had done nothing wrong, but knew that no amount of pleading or denial of wrongdoing would do anything but fall on deaf ears. He was a proud man and would not beg for his life. Even as a child, when his father would whip him with his leather belt for discipline, he would not cry.

"Take the traitorous pig to the pit, where he is to stay until he revives," the captain said. "He is to be chained and is not to be given any food, nor water. When three days have passed, if he is still alive, return him to me. Then I will see if he wants to tell me who he is spying for." He slapped the whip against his leg. "Now! Bring me his brother! I have a special treat for him," he said, running his hand over a straight razor.

"He has not been found, sir," the soldier said, backing up just far enough to keep out of striking distance.

"Not found!" Fire fairly jumped from his nostrils as the Captain glared at the young soldier. "Either you find him, or you will take his place! Do you hear me, you whining pig?" he cracked the whip on the ground in front of the soldier, rasing a puff of dust.

* * * *

Vladimer had on his dress green uniform with red piping when he was ushered into the massive room. It contained a single rectangular table that measured no less than six feet wide and was thirty feet in length. High-backed red-velvet captain's chairs with padded seats and backs lined the perimeter of the table. The grey-veined marble walls were covered with oil paintings of past Russian heros who had served Russia, most of whom were military men or men who had been premiers. They had been painted in the Renaissance style of Rembrandt, with dark backgrounds, deep colors and somber faces. A black-veined marble bust of Vladimir Lenin stood in a corner of the room, a spotlight illuminating it from above. The shadows over his features gave him an ominous look. Three chandeliers, each measuring six feet in diameter, were suspended ten feet from a thirty-foot ceiling that was decorated with heavy gold wainscoting.

Vladimer had never been in such a room before, even when he had been in the KGB, and was humbled by the sheer greatness of its history. "Welcome," Gorbachev said, extending his hand as he walked into the room.

There were several men stationed around the table, all dressed in military uniforms decorated with colorful ribbons. Gorbachev made no attempt to introduce his staff, but Vladimer knew most of their faces from the time he had served in the KGB.

They made no overture towards greeting him, obviously showing their disdain for what they felt was a common traitor to Russia. Instead, they stood facing him with graven faces. "Please. Have a seat," Gorbachev said, waving his hand towards a vacant spot at the table.

Vladimer seated himself a few chairs from the last of the Russian military men, opposite Gorbachev. "It is an honor to meet with you," Vladimer said.

"Let me get right to the point," Gorbachev said, ignoring Vladimer's attempt to be congenial. There was no warmth to his voice. "It is of utmost importance that I impress upon you and your group of leaders that Lithuania's recent declaration of secession from the Soviet Union was a grave mistake." He paced behind his chair, not looking at Vladimer. It was an old KGB tactic, designed to intimidate the opponent. "We wish to convey the fact that, unless the secession is repealed within twenty-four hours, we will have no alternative but to take harsh measures."

The threat was not unexpected. Vladimer received it with a stoic face. It was important not to convey any hint of emotion to this governmental military panel.

Still standing, Gorbachev thumbed through a brown security folder that lay in front of him. "To start with, strict economic sanctions will be enforced. No food or fuel will be allowed to enter nor exit Lithuania. If such sanctions do not reverse your position, I will have no choice." More pacing, then he stopped to face Vladimer. "Much blood will be shed and there will be considerable loss of life. You will have *that* fact on your conscience, Vladimer Ryzhkov!"

When he had finished, General Vladimer Ryzhkov spoke. It was with a firm, but calm, voice of a man secure in his position, not easily intimidated by words. His deep voice rumbled through the great hall as he spoke. "I'm sorry you feel that way, your Excellency. But you see, the Lithuanian people feel there is nothing to be gained from continued dominance by the Soviet Union. You should know that the Lithuanian Parliament has been in contact with President Bush of the United States, asking for his intervention in the event military action is taken against our country. In addition…"

Gorbachev held up his hand. There was a condescending smile on his face. "President Bush is not stupid. He will not butt heads with a major power like the Soviet Union over a little country like Lithuania," he replied, cutting Vladimer off. "Don't be foolish! We are world powers. Lithuania is…" the mouth curled down as he measured his word carefully, "insignificant." He shrugged his shoulders as a sarcastic smile crossed his face. The look conveyed the disdain he felt for his guest and his little country.

Vladimer ignored the insult. "As I was about to say, our Parliament has been in contact with other world powers, as well, and has been assured that we will not be alone if a confrontation comes to pass. The eyes of the world will be on Lithuania."

Gorbachev ignored this attempt to intimidate him. "As we speak, Soviet tanks are rumbling through the streets of Vilnius and helicopters are dropping leaflets in Lithuanian towns to warn the citizens against the impending disaster."

He leaned forward on his knuckles. With a furrowed brow that was clearly intended to intimidate, his busy eyebrows furrowed as he growled, "You cannot prevail!"

Vladimer was not to be outdone. With a calm voice, he held his ground. "I must say, with all due respect for your position, your Excellency, it is common knowledge that unrest lies within many Soviet states. As you must know, I still have friends in the KGB." It was a lie that anyone in the KGB would put their job, let alone their life on the line to confide in a man who by now was considered a traitor, yet he dangled the carrot in front of his opponent anyway, taunting him.

"It is our opinion that, if you attack us, that action will only result in you relaxing your grip on adjoining states while you concentrate on Lithuania. The result will be that you will have a massive civil war on your hands, the likes of which Russia has never seen!" His voice was calm and his words measured.

The generals seated around the table moved uneasily, shooting glances at one another, but they held their tongues. It was true, what Vladimer had said. More than just rumors of widespread dissention had already reached their ears. That fact had been confirmed by members of the KGB, as well as by heads of states in those areas. There seemed to be a movement afoot that could result in many states seceding from the Soviet Union.

Gorbachev decided to play a trump card that he knew was weak, but counted on Vladimer Ryzhkov's allegiance to his heart to sway his thinking. "We are aware of the attention that you have been paying to one Nevenka Adamovich of Klaipeda." He lowered his head so just the top of his eyes met those of his guest. The lights from above darkened his brow, making him look like Lenin, which was intended. "It would bear noting that two of her brothers are presently serving in the Soviet Red Army. Their superiors do not look favorably upon sons of anti-patriots serving under them."

"Are you telling me that, because of my interest in an insignificant Lithuanian woman, you would harm her family?" He could not stop the flow of blood that ran to his face, betraying his anger. It was a cheap trick, and both he and Gorbachev knew it. And it had taken its toll.

Gorbachev simply shrugged his shoulders. "One never knows the fate of one's family in times of war. Many unfortunate things happen."

His meaning was clear. He fully intended to use Nevenka's brothers as pawns in this power struggle. Knowing that Vladimer Ryzhkov was a patriot of Lithuania, he was sure that Gorbachev was aware that Nevenka's brothers were disposable pawns. The woman was another matter.

Having been warned and insulted in the same breath, Vladimer bowed sharply and said, "I take it, then, this meeting has been concluded?"

Gorbachev nodded. "I trust you will deliver the appropriate message to your parliament."

Without comment, Vladimer bowed once more, then turned to leave. Before he had reached the ten-foot, heavy, wooden, sculptured doors, Gorbachev's voice said, "Beware that you are not reckless with your heart, Vladmier Ryzhkov. Much is at stake"

Again, the message was clear.

Chapter 15

As promised, Moscow had stopped all shipments of oil to Lithuania's only refinery at Mazeikiai and had cut off their supply of natural gas as well. Lithuanians took to riding bicycles, scrimping on what fuel they had left. When the Soviet leaders heard that the oil embargo had no apparent immediate effect on the little country, they resorted to cutting off all supplies of food, clothing and medicine.

In this same time frame, unrest had overtaken the citizens of the Soviet Union and the civil revolution was born. Immediately, the pinch was felt in both countries. Some enterprising Lithuanians were able to barter for supplies with sympathetic citizens from Moscow, Leningrad, Lvov and parts of Siberia where democratic groups had already won control over previously locally controlled Soviet governments.

What had begun as an isolated challenge from Lithuania had broadened so much that Gorbachev saw his union threatening to crumble before his very eyes. In an effort to make one last attempt to keep Lithuania in check, he sat down with his challenger to Soviet power, Boris Yeltsin, and leaders from the Baltic republics, as well as the leaders from eleven other republics.

The purpose was an attempt to pool their resources to maintain control, conveying a more compatible governmental body to the people, one in which the previous strangle hold was relaxed.

"We will not be divided," he shouted to the Soviet leaders at an emergency meeting as he slammed his fist on the large table. "If any more territories attempt splitting from the greater Soviet Union, there will be war! A terrible war!"

Vladimer had gotten word to Nevenka that he would be attending a meeting with Lithuanian leaders that was to take place in Palanga late Friday. Time would be precious, but he would try to find the time to spend a few hours with her if she could find a way to get to Palanga.

*   *   *   *

The day before the meeting Nevenka rode Niki's bike from Klaepida to Palanga under the cover of night. It took her two hours to go the fifteen miles, as she was forced to hide in the bushes each time a vehicle came down the road. Because fuel was almost unobtainable, it could be assumed that only those vehicles driving had access to fuel and therefore must contain members of the Red Army or someone from the Soviet Union. Since there had been widespread rumors of rape of Lithuanian women by the Soviet troops, she could take no chance of being caught.

As soon as she reached Palanga she rushed to the beach where she knew Vladimer would be waiting for her. She saw him standing there, facing the sea, like a giant statue, erected to protect all who came ashore. She raced up to him, jumping into his arms as he turned when he heard her footsteps in the sand.

He held Nevenka in his arms as she trembled. "Are you cold?" he asked, removing his coat and draping it around her shoulders.

She ignored his question and hung on tightly. "What is to become of us, Vladimer? The Red Army has been to our house several times looking for you! We have heard that they have killed my brothers, and now they threaten to arrest us, too. Just coming here was dangerous. There are rumors that Soviet soldiers have been raping our women."

"Shhh," he said, holding her head close to his chest. "They are just making noises like a wounded bull. They will do nothing." He knew better, but was trying to calm her. He had come to have deep feelings for Nevenka, and knew that the Red Army would not hesitate to try to capture him through her.

"They showed us pictures of my brother Yuri, chained to a post, beaten. His clothes had been torn from his body and a soldier stood over him holding a gun to his head." She sobbed. "They have killed him! I know it!"

He held her head close to his chest, stroking her hair. "Hush, little one. I'll think of something."

"My father was so shocked by Yuri's death that his heart couldn't take the strain. He collapsed when the news reached him. I fear that he will die, Vladimer. Then what will become of my mother?" She cried uncontrollably.

He cradled her head to his chest tightly, stroking her long hair. "You cannot go back home, Nevenka. They will capture you," he finally warned. "Gorbachev has warned me. You must stay with me. I will protect you. Together, we will find a way."

"I'm scared, Vladimer. I don't know what to do."

He held her hands and looked into her eyes. The tone of his voice was quiet, but deliberate. She knew that whatever he said, she must do without question. "I have a friend who has a house on the beach. You can stay there until my meetings are over. I'll return in the evening. We'll talk then. In the meantime, I'll send a messenger to your family, telling them you are all right, so they don't worry needlessly."

He took her to the edge of town, where there was a two-story house built on a rock cliff overlooking the ocean. It had a commanding view on both sides of the beach, as well as of the road. "You'll be safe here. Ondre is away on business, so you will have the house to yourself. No one will come to bother you." He kissed her gently on the lips, then held her tight.

She wanted to beg him to stay with her, but knew that he was an important man. The fate of Lithuania was far more important than her fear of being alone. She smiled. "Go. I will be all right."

Vladimer kissed her again and was gone. She watched as he walked away, his long hair swaying across his broad shoulders. *Only such a man could have the fate of our country on his shoulders*, she thought.

She walked in the sand with her bare feet, wadding in the water, tossing rocks into the sea and sitting on rocks, staring out into the vacant ocean, wondering what destiny held for her. She had found the man of her dreams. Was this just a moment in time, a flicker of light in the vast darkness of life, or dare she think that there was more to this relationship than just today? She closed her eyes and thought of her brother Yuri, and forgave him for what he had done to her.

* * * *

It was dark when Vladimer knocked lightly on the door before entering the house. Nevenka had lit a fire in the fireplace and was sitting on a large bear rug, warming herself. She didn't hear Vladimer come up behind her over the crackling of the fireplace and was startled when he put his hands on her shoulders.

She turned to smile up at him as he kissed the nape of her neck. "Did you have a successful day?" she inquired.

"I think everything is on track." He nestled down beside her, looking up into her eyes. "I must confess that I did have trouble concentrating on business, however, thinking of you here, all day, by yourself."

"I was all right."

"I know, but I wanted to be here with you."

She looked into his tired eyes and stroked his hair. "You're exhausted. Can I make you something?"

He laid her down on the bear rug, looking into her eyes. "I have everything I need right here."

They made love on the rug with the reflection from the fireplace dancing on the ceiling to the crackling of burning pitch. Then Vladimer fell into a deep sleep. He lay in Nevenka's arms dreaming of battles with Russians and saving the life of the woman he loved.

Nevenka had great difficulty sleeping, her mind vacillating between the unknown future and what would happen to Vladimer. This was the first time she had allowed anyone to make love to her since Yuri had raped her that fateful day at the house of her father. But she thought not of that, only of the intense love she had for the man she held in her arms. If her life were to end that day, she would die happy.

At daybreak Nevenka carefully got up so she wouldn't disturb Vladimer and went into the kitchen. She prepared breakfast for him: *biezpiens ar kartupeliem and krejumi*...cottage cheese with potatoes, sour cream and butter.

When she returned with the tray of food, Vladimer was just waking up. He smiled as he reached for her, allowing the rug to fall from him, exposing his naked body. Nevenka blushed as she said, "I brought some nourishment for you."

"You're all the nourishment I need."

She laughed as he pulled her down to him.

"Nourishment first," she said, beaming.

"You practical women." He smiled. "What would we do without you?"

Vladimer was famished and Nevenka loved watching him eat. When they had finished, they made love again, then fell asleep until noon. When they awoke, they made love again, then bathed and dressed. Vladimer took Nevenka by the hand and led her down to the beach, where they walked hand in hand in silence for a while.

"I've given this a lot of thought," he said, stopping to throw a pebble into the sea. "It's too dangerous for you to go home. You know that. They'll be watching your house. I'm sorry, but they think they can get to me through you. And they're right," he said stopping to look into her eyes. "I'd do anything to keep you from harm."

Nevenka smiled. "What should I do?"

"I want you to stay here for the next day or so. I've got contacts in Moscow that are sympathetic to our cause. I've got to find a way for you to get out of the reach of Gorbachev's men. Somewhere where you can be safe."

"What about my family? You saw what they did to Yuri. And God knows what happened to Viktor."

"Your family will be safe. Trust me. Their only interest is in capturing me. They figure if they can get their hands on me, they'll be able to squash the revolution. The fools!" He looked down into her eyes. "You are their only direct contact to me. They must not find you. You understand, don't you?"

She nodded. She was aware that the future of her country lay in Vladimer's hands. If he were to be taken prisoner, not only would she be crushed, but Lithuania would fall under Soviet dictatorship again "Yes. But I don't want you to leave me." Her voice was soft, pleading, not demanding.

He held her close to his chest. "You've got to be strong. I must leave now. I won't be long, I promise. It's for the best."

She nodded. "If you say so."

They hugged and walked back to the beach house. Vladimer left that day in the disguise of a peasant farm worker.

* * * *

Two days later Vladimer returned as promised. Nevenka lunged into his arms the moment he came into view. "I missed you so," she said, pressing her body to his. "Promise me you'll never leave me again."

"I've got good news," he said, trying to remain strong. "I've found a way out of Lithuania for you."

"For me? What about you? I'm not going anywhere without you, Vladimer. You, of all people, should know that." She could tell by his purposeful, distant demeanor that something serious was about to happen…something she wasn't going to like.

He held her at arm's length. The words came out with great difficulty, but they were the words of a man who would make the ultimate sacrifice for the woman he loved. "I've got this friend. She lives in Moscow." His words were labored. "Her name is Helena Makarov. She has organized a company to assist young women such as yourself to get out of the reach of Gorbachev and the Red Army."

"Out? Out to where?"

He studied her face. The words came hard. "America. She has made arrangements through diplomatic channels to…"

"America! Why would I want to go to America? I would never see you again. I won't go! I won't! I would rather die!"

"Listen to me," he said, taking firm hold of her shoulders. "You must do this thing for both of us. If they catch you, God only knows what will happen. And if you're not around, Gorbachev's men will not be able to get at me. I will be free to work underground and help our people. Lithuania needs me, Nevenka. We are at a critical crossroads here. You have to understand that. Please."

It was the most difficult thing he had ever said. Even if it was only partially true, he knew he had to get her out of the country if either one of them were to survive. He knew that the sacrifice meant that he might never see her again.

Nevenka didn't understand. Why couldn't she stay here with him, she wondered? It hurt deeply to think that Vladimer would send her away.

"You'll be safe." He put his arms around her, drawing her close to his chest. She felt a tear fall onto her head, and she understood. He was making the sacrifice for her sake.

"What do I have to do?" Her voice was barely audible. "My English is not good. We learned it in school, as you know, but I do not speak it well. What will I do? How will I get along in a strange land? I know no one. How will I get along without you, Vladimer?"

How could he tell her? The words stuck in his throat.

She looked up at her handsome prince. She loved looking into his manly face, which was framed by his long, flowing, blond hair. His crystal blue eyes were moist, but he had set his jaw firmly. He must not let her see his weakness.

"Vladimer?"

He took a deep breath. He had to tell her sometime. The sooner he cut the cord, the better it would be for both of them. "Listen to me, Nevenka. Helena has a service whereby she sends unwed women from Russia to America. I have arranged for you to be part of that group."

"A service? What kind of service?"

The sooner he said it, the sooner the deed would be done. He needed to be surgical about this matter. It was the same as if he were sending troops to take a fortified position, knowing most of them would meet a certain death. It had to be done. "She sends young, single women to American men who are looking for wives."

He saw the shock register on her face the instant he spoke the words. She pulled away from him abruptly, staring, unbelieving, into his eyes. A strange look came over her face, almost one of hatred "You are sending me away to America, halfway across the world, to marry a man I have never laid eyes on? This is not the nineteenth century, Vladimer. I will not be sold into slavery!" Her words were sharp, punctuated by anger and hurt. "If you do not want me, just say so. But don't sell me to some…some foreigner!"

"Please. You've got to understand."

"No! *You've* got to understand! I'm not going anywhere except back to Klaipeda, where my family loves me."

"You can not go back there and you know it," he said desperately.

"I'll explain to the soldiers that there is no longer anything between us," she spat, angrily. "Then they will leave me alone."

"Nevenka! Have you ever seen what they do to women they torture?" He shook his head in frustration. "You have seen pictures of what they did to your brother."

She looked at him with hurt eyes, her lips quivering, but said nothing.

"What they did to Yuri is nothing compared to the pain you would suffer if they captured you. Don't think for one moment you are dealing with a compassionate people. They think nothing of your life. They would torture you until they got what they wanted from you, then they would turn you over to field solders to do with you what they wanted. Do you know what that means?"

Her body quivered as her mind conjured up visions of filthy men groping her body, raping her, repeatedly.

"You know what Hitler did to the Jews? Well, you are the same as a Jew to the Soviet Union. You are not a Russian. You are a Lithuanian. We both know the difference," he said quietly.

"Then come with me," she pleaded, looking into his eyes, grabbing his hair with both hands, bringing his face down to hers. "We will both travel to America and start new lives. Please, Vladimer. If you love me, don't leave me!"

He lowered his eyes. He could not look at her. "I can't. You must understand my destiny is here, in Lithuania. I must free our people." He looked into her yes. "I can't concentrate on completing my duties if every hour of the day I'm worrying about you. I love you, Nevenka. More than anything in the world. I would give my life for you in an instant. You know that." He quickly wiped away a tear rolled down his cheek.

Nevenka slowly nodded her head. She understood. She just didn't like it. It has always been the destiny of great men to make sacrifices for their country. That is what makes great men great. "I understand," she finally said, barely audible, her lips trembling. "What is it you want me to do?"

"I have arranged for you to go to Moscow, to meet with Helena Makarov. You will travel by boat through the causeway to the Russian territory of Kaliningrad. No one will suspect you to travel that route. From there, you will be met by one of our people who will escort you to Moscow."

"Will I ever see you again?" She tried to be brave, but it was becoming increasingly difficult. This was a nightmare that had no ending.

He nodded. "I promise. As soon as the Soviet Union has accepted Lithuania's independence, I will come to America and find you. We will find a way to be together. You have my word."

"And if they capture you?"

He held her close to his chest. "Let's not think of such unpleasant things. Think only of the future."

Chapter 16

Nevenka made it to Moscow without incident and was delivered to the house of Helena Makarov, a plush, two-story brick residence located on the outskirts of town. She had a beautiful garden surrounded by six-foot-high brick walls which protected her from prying eyes and unwanted intruders.

There appeared to be a number of women living with her, all young, dark-haired and beautiful. Helena introduced Nevenka to each of them, then showed her to her room. "You will share this with two of the others, if you don't mind," she apologized. "We seem to have more guests than I had expected."

"Thank you for your kindness. I appreciate your taking an interest in me."

"Any friend of Vladimer Ryzhkov is a friend of mine." She smiled.

"Have you known Vladimer long?"

Helena's smile conveyed more than she intended. "We have been friends for a long time. When we were children, here in Moscow, our families were close, so we sort of grew up together."

"So you were close friends then."

"You might say that." She smiled that secretive smile again. Nevenka wasn't sure that she wanted to know more, so she didn't probe. Helena was older than Nevenka, closer to Vladimer's age. Even though she was probably in her early thirties, she was still a strikingly beautiful young woman. She had jet black hair and dark eyes that held much mystery. She carried herself with an air of great poise and confidence.

Nevenka could see that it would be easy for a man to be drawn to her. Her lips were full and sensuous. Although she wasn't wearing a low-cut dress, it was apparent that her figure was full and vivacious. She was the kind of person

Nevenka would like to have had as a friend. It was easy to see why she and Vladimer were so close. She only hoped he wasn't more than just a friend.

"Why don't you rest today? Tomorrow we'll begin processing you."

"Processing? Sounds like a packing plant." Even though she was nervous, she smiled.

"I guess, in a way, it is, although I never think of it in those terms. My role is to get as many refugees out of Russia as possible before the walls come crumbling down."

"Are things that bad?"

"I have friends in high places, and word from the grapevine is that the Soviet Union as we know it won't even be in existence soon."

"Why are all these other women leaving Russia?"

"Most of them are Jews."

"Jews?"

She nodded. "As you may know, Russian doesn't classify Jews as Russian citizens. Even though they have been born and raised in Russia, they're still considered outsiders. They're sort of a people without a country, you might say.

"For some reason that I have never been able to fathom, the Communists have always considered them less than second-class non-citizens, undesirables. If there is a civil breakdown in Russia, you'll find that people will look for anyone or anything as a scapegoat to blame their problems."

"And the Jews would be that scapegoat?"

She shook her head. "It's unbelievable, isn't it?"

"But, they're so beautiful," Nevenka said, looking at the woman sitting outside, chatting by the flower garden.

"I'm afraid beauty carries no weight beyond increasing one's longevity if they're handed over to the Red Army for fun and entertainment."

Nevenka grimaced. "I've been there. I wouldn't wish that on anyone."

"Then you understand the urgency of getting them out of the country."

"What happens tomorrow…when I'm processed?"

"Oh, it's no big deal. I have a hairdresser who comes in and does the girl's hair. Yours is so beautiful," she said, running her hand through Nevenka's long, blond hair. "I doubt anything will have to be done with it, beyond maybe a slight trim and a little backcombing to give it more body. Then we dress you up in attractive clothes and take your picture."

"Sounds fun."

"The fun part comes when we videotape each candidate."

"Videotape?"

"Umm. Americans like to see more than just a flat, two-dimensional picture. We take a videotape of each girl in the garden," she nodded towards the flowered area, "with the girl moving around a little, picking flowers, sitting and standing. Then we have them tell the camera something about themselves."

"Such as?"

"Where they lived, their likes and dislikes, something about their skills, their hobbies, and a little something about their background. We want to make you look as attractive as possible. The better you look, the better chance we have of getting an ideal position for each candidate."

"You make it sound as if it's a job."

She shrugged her shoulders and smiled. "In a way, it is. My job is to get you out of Russia safe and sound. What you do when you get to America is up to you. Bear in mind, if you decide not to get married to your sponsor, they could deport you back to Russia. Once they do that, I won't be able to help you. The authorities would process you through regular channels, and if you've got anything to hide, they'd find it. You can depend on that. And in your case, let's just say you don't want to get deported."

"I don't know if you're aware of it or not, but Vladimer and I are in love. I don't want to do this thing, go to America and marry someone I've never seen." Just the thought of it made her shiver. "He says that I must get out of Russia, because if they catch me, they'll use me as bait to get him."

"Yes, he told me. It's difficult being the love of such a strong and powerful man."

"Can't I stay here with you, and help you?"

Helena smiled. "You are the last bunch of girls that I am going to be able to help. As it is, the KGB has been watching my every move. It's only because Vladimer has friends there that I'm still in business, but that won't last long."

Nevenka was beginning to understand just how influential Vladimer was, both in Lithuania and here in the Soviet Union.

"When you go to America, I will be going with you. I will not be able to come back either. I'm this close from becoming a political prisoner myself," she said, holding two fingers an inch apart.

It was clear from the look on her face that the thought of leaving Moscow and her lovely house made her sad.

Chapter 17

The city of Los Altos is said to house more millionaires per capita than any other city in California, yet they don't flaunt their wealth like the rich of Beverly Hills, Palm Springs or Carmel-by-the-Sea. They don't drive Rolls Royces, nor display their wealth with heavily diamond-ringed fingers and gold chains. They do like extravagant houses, however. The average house ranges in value from a half-million dollars to several million, depending upon the location, acreage, square footage and views. Los Altos is located in the heartland of Silicon Valley, where millionaires play in the field of computer chips and high-end technology. This city, Aaron MacAffie decided, was to be his grazing ground.

He moved to town, rented a modest one-bedroom apartment to establish his residency and started his small church in the basement of one of his first parishioners. He called his church The Living Christ Church. As with all beginning establishments, it was a struggle getting started, but his small parish soon grew to overflowing capacity, leaving him with the enviable requirement of needing a larger facility.

To his flock he appeared to be a gregarious, single man with a halo of charisma around his now-shiny dome. Despite his ever-thinning hair, which was a constant source of irritation to him, wealthy women, mostly elderly and either widowed or divorced, who were entranced by his magnanimous personality, invited him into their homes for home-cooked meals.

Business-men in the community invited him to lunch at their country clubs and golf courses. For the first time in his life Aaron MacAffie was in seventh heaven! Every day he thanked God for his generosity.

A young, single, available man was like candy to single women…especially those who were widowed or divorced, neither of which appealed to him. The widowed were either too old or totally unappealing—usually both. And the divorced? Well, he wasn't going to be the main course for anyone's hand-me-downs or rejects. That, he thought, would not only be personally distasteful, but bad for business—church business.

One morning, while he was reading the newspaper over a cinnamon roll and cappuccino his eye caught an ad that included several smiling, attractive, young women. It read, *Beautiful Russian Women, "The Salt of the Earth". Call Lifetime Partners if you are interested.* There was a San Francisco telephone number to call for information. Without hesitation, he dialed the number.

"Lifetime Partners," answered a seductive woman's voice.

He hesitated for a moment. "Ah, yes. I, uh, saw your ad in this morning's paper and, well, I was wondering…"

"You were wondering what it was all about," she finished his sentence for him. Obviously she had had many such telephone calls.

"Yes."

"Are you presently unattached?"

"Yes, I am." *Preliminary questions,* he thought. *A necessary prelude. Can't be giving vital information to just every Tom, Dick and Harry.*

"Are you a citizen of the United States?"

A strange question, but he answered, "Yes," without thinking. Actually, he had been born in Ireland and hadn't officially applied for nor taken the citizenship examination, but that needn't become an obstacle.

"Are you gainfully employed?"

"I'm the pastor of The Living Christ Church here in Los Altos."

"Very good!" She sounded impressed. "May I have your name, please?"

"Only if you promise to give it back," he joked.

She didn't laugh. Either she didn't get it or had no sense of humor.

"And, your name?"

"Aaron MacAffie. Pastor Aaron MacAffie," he corrected himself. The title made him sound impressive, at least to MacAffie.

"Well, Mr., er, Pastor MacAffie, you'll appreciate the fact that we need to initiate a certain degree of precaution in these matters."

"Of course."

She launched into a well-rehearsed description of her service supplying available Russian women to qualified, available single men. The emphasis was on "qualified", as it was assumed that no married man would apply, though experience had demonstrated that the world was full of devious men. If a man could have more than one wife, what better way than having one from another country whom one could control and train as one saw fit?

"We take pictures and a video of available candidates for life partners, but we require a questionnaire be filled out before sending out additional information. You understand."

"Of course."

"We want to select the best possible match for our candidates. And for you," she hastened to add. "Do you have any questions at this point?"

"The pictures of those women in the paper...are those some of the women that are available? I mean, some of the available candidates?" he asked, holding the ad in his hand, selecting the one he like the best.

There was a hint of hesitation before she said, "Of course. Now, if I could get your address, I'll be happy to send you an application and we can get started."

The application came in the next day's mail. It consisted of two pages, with questions on each side, ranging from his name, age, address, occupation and marital history to political affiliations and hobbies. The upper right-hand corner contained a three-by-five-inch box which was designed to hold a photo of the applicant. There was an application fee of fifty dollars, which would be applied to the processing fee if and when the applicant successfully completed the application and was selected as a candidate for a Lifetime Partner. If, for any reason, the applicant was found to be an unsuitable candidate, the application fee would be forfeited. This would weed out the frivolous inquiries.

This could be an easy way for someone to pick up fifty bucks, he thought, but then the ad must have cost several hundred dollars, considering the size. Worse case, he'd blow fifty bucks. He'd spent that much on dinner.

MacAffie filled out the application and mailed it back that same day, along with a photo of himself in a suit and tie.

*　　*　　*　　*

Most men set a plan for themselves or goal for their life, be it a business goal or the toys they want to acquire once they become successful. Pastor Aaron MacAffie's plan was for his church to be the most successful church of its kind in America. The groundwork for achieving that plan lay in the wealth of its members. As new members enrolled, he meticulously retained information about each and every one of his flock; information such as where they lived, the type of job they had, their age, their likes and dislikes, strengths and weaknesses and, very importantly, their estimated net worth was logged in his computer.

As his parishioners thought he was simply compiling information for church records, they gladly supplied him with whatever information he asked. Everyone was categorized and analyzed according to their net worth. When he was through, he would have a list of Who's Who in Los Altos that would be the envy of the IRS.

* * * *

He had been in Los Altos for almost a year now, and was no closer to achieving his goal of building a new church than the day he had arrived. His vision of the church that he wanted to build was one that would be so distinctive, so unique, that people would drive miles just for the privilege of being in the structure. Everyone would know Pastor Aaron MacAffie's name. He had to be famous! That wasn't part of the plan, it *was* the plan.

CHAPTER 18

Aaron MacAffie sat at his desk holding a large packet postmarked from the Lifetime Partners Company in Moscow. His fingers shook a little as he tore open the large manila envelope. Among the contents that fell out was a videotape.

He slipped it into his VCR and flipped on the television. The tape began with scenes of various highlights of Russia and its culture. The camera panned museum walls bearing paintings depicting Russian heroes and great religious leaders, which surprised him, as he had thought religion had been discouraged in Russia over the centuries.

There were magnificent pictures taken from the Kremlin in Moscow, with its magnificent gold and silver domed structures reaching high into the sky like proud gods. That was followed by scenes from Russian workers toiling both in the fields and at factories, all seemingly happy at their work. The remainder of the tape focused on beautiful Russian women, some playing sports, others writing, painting and interacting with other women in what appeared to be a beautiful flower garden.

All in all, the video gave the appearance of healthy, self-satisfied Russian women. If this were the case, one might ask, why then would anyone want to leave such a happy environment to come to a strange land and marry someone she had never known? This thought never occurred to Aaron MacAffie as he pushed the pause button on the video so he could study each woman on the tape.

Having seen the video, he was satisfied that this was definitely something in which he could be interested. He turned his attention to the balance of the material that had been shipped to him in the packet. There were three separate pages, each containing pictures of women who had presumably been chosen and matched with his personality.

The first candidate was a woman with long dark hair and deep dark eyes. She had a very sensuous look about her. She stood five-foot-six, and was twenty-six years of age. She had been born and raised in Yalta, a resort on the Black Sea. She had worked as a hostess, greeting guests at the Tavrida Hotel, a facility that primarily catered to wealthy tourists visiting the resort. She was one of four children whose father had also worked at the hotel until his retirement. There was no mention of her mother, although it was assumed she took care of the household.

The second woman was from the city of Lvov. She had short dark hair and looked vivacious, with a charming smile. Her eyes portrayed a person who had a quick wit. She was shorter than the first, standing at five-foot two inches. The brochure said that she was an artist, working in a small factory that specialized in making pottery for sale in Moscow and Kiev. She was twenty-eight years of age and the youngest of three children. Her father was a bus driver and her mother a tour guide.

The third candidate for his consideration came from Lithuania. Unlike her counterparts, she had long blond hair that fell around her shoulders. She had soft blue eyes and a shy smile. She was five-foot six inches, was twenty-three years of age, and, like her father and three brothers, had worked in the shipyard, as an accountant. Her name was Nevenka Adamovich.

Aaron laid the pictures on his desk, side by side, studying each one intently as if buying an automobile. His eyes kept coming back to the blond. This was the candidate that interested him the most.

The accompanying letter stated that, if he so chose, MacAffie, hereafter to be called the "selector", could select one of the women, called the "candidate", from among those potential candidates that had been sent to him. When he had made his selection, he was to execute an agreement, which had been enclosed along with the rest of the material, called the Lifetime Partners Agreement. The agreement called for a one-time fee of ten thousand dollars, to be paid to an American escrow company in San Francisco which had been previously designated by the company. The fee was to be payment for transportation of the Lifetime Partner to the applicant's location, where the next process, getting acquainted, would take place. The agreement stated that in the event the match was found to be unsatisfactory within the first ten days from date both parties meet, that the funds, which were to be held in escrow, would be returned and there would be no further obligations to either party.

After the initial personal introduction, if the selector was satisfied with his acquisition and the candidate satisfied as well, they would let nature takes it's course. It would be assumed that eventually the two would be married. The arrangement of marriage and the costs related thereto were to be arranged and paid for by the applicant, of course.

As MacAffie studied the pictures he was excited by the prospect of marrying a Russian…especially one so beautiful, and a blond, no less. She had to be smart, he thought, being an accountant and all. He had always been attracted to the exotic.

The brochure said that the processing time was estimated to be six weeks from the date the contract had been executed and the funds received. Once he had made up his mind, Aaron MacAffie completed his part of the process without hesitation, including a cashier's check drawn from the church's coffers made out to Lifetime Partners Company.

* * * *

Helena called everyone into the living room one evening after they had finished dinner. She gave each woman an empty snifter glass, then poured each a portion of fine brandy. The look on her face was one of a mixed pleasure. "There have been reports of looting and hostilities in the square," she said, "and, although I regret having to say it, I no longer feel we are safe. The time has come for us to depart Moscow and the Soviet Union." She held a stack of documents in her hand. "I have arranged passports for each of you to depart by plane. We leave for America next week."

There was a murmur of excitement among the women. Everyone except Nevenka, and perhaps Helena was bubbling with excitement over the prospects of a new life. They giggled as they made wagers on who would land the wealthiest, most handsome husband, as everyone knew all Americans were wealthy.

"Does that mean that we've all been placed?" one of the girls asked.

"Everyone's got a home."

They yelled, danced and hugged one another. Nevenka faked a smile. She had hoped this day would never come. And now, here it was. She was going to a foreign country, halfway around the world, and chances were, she would never see her family or Vladimer again. She took solace in the fact that at least he was alive.

"You know, Helena. I don't really care if I go or stay, live or die," she said after they were alone later that evening, when Helena had come to her room.

"I'm sure Vladimer wouldn't be pleased to hear such talk," she said, sitting next to her on the edge of Nevenka's bed.

"I'll never see my parents again." She sobbed. "But, more than that, I'll never see Vladimer, either."

"I wouldn't accept the fact that you'll never see your family," she said. "Once you've established yourself in America, perhaps you can convince your new husband to sponsor them."

"Sponsor them?" She wiped a tear from her eye. "What does that mean, to sponsor them?"

"If someone in America wants someone from another country to come and live there, they must first have someone who will give them a job and a place to live, so the government will be assured that they won't end up on welfare."

"I don't understand welfare."

Helena laughed. "You will. Believe me, some day you'll understand the term all too well."

"So my new husband can sponsor, as you say, my family to come to America, too?"

Helena patted her hand and nodded.

A large smile came to her face and her eyes brightened. "Oh, do you think so? That would be wonderful!"

"And, as for Vladimer, If there's one thing I know about that man, he's persistent. If he's alive and well, you can be assured that he'll find a way to see you. Oh, I almost forgot. There's a message for you down in the parlor." She had a sly look that puzzled Nevenka. "Here, put a little lipstick on those lips," she said, smiling.

"Why?"

"Because the messenger is cute!" She laughed. "You never know," she winked, "you might get lucky."

Nevenka hit her friend on the shoulder goodnaturedly. "You Ruskies are all hot blooded." She smiled.

Nevenka walked down to the parlor, where the blinds had been drawn and it was dark. She saw the outline of a figure standing by the window, silhouetted by the blacklight. She hesitated for a moment, then lunged at the man. "Vladimer!" she squealed. "Where did you come from?"

"I come bearing good news," he said, sweeping her off her feet and swinging her around the room.

"You're the best news I could ask for!" She kissed him long and hard, then buried her face in his chest, holding on as if she would never see him again.

After a moment, she led him out to the veranda, where she could have a better look at him. She was shocked to see how haggard he looked. He had dark circles under his eyes and his hair looked as if he hadn't had a bath for weeks, and he hadn't, as one could tell from the body odor, but she didn't care. "Oh, Vladimer. How good it is to see you, alive and well."

"Alive, perhaps, but I don't know how well." He laughed. "But now that my eyes have beheld you, I feel great!" The love he felt for her was instantly evident in his eyes.

"You spoke of news. Tell me, is the conflict over?"

He shook his head. "I only wish it were. I fear the worst is yet to come. Citizens are looting and burning buildings. There is shooting in the streets and many citizens have pitted themselves against the Red Army. On top of that, one state is warring against the other."

"So there is no good news, then?"

Vladimer smiled. "When I heard that you were leaving soon, I knew that I had to see you."

"I'm so glad you did."

He held up his hand. "There's more. I went to Klaipeda to visit your family, to see if they were okay."

"Oh, Vladimer. I've been so worried about Papa. They're all right, then?"

"Yes. All four of them."

"Four?"

"Yes. That's the good news. Viktor escaped the Red Army and made his way out of Russia. He's back in Klaipeda, safe."

"He escaped?" She held her hand over her mouth, with her eyes wide in disbelief.

Vladimer nodded with a great smile.

"Oh, that's the best news ever. He's all right, then?"

"As good as gold. Once he crossed into Lithuanian territory, he found friends to help him get back home again. He was a little the worse for wear when he arrived, having eaten only what he could steal in the fields," he smiled, "but other than being a little thin…"

She hugged him. "Thank you," she whispered. "Thank you, thank you, thank you." Suddenly, she turned very quiet. "We leave for America tomorrow," she said softly, her fingers softly caressing his large, rugged hand.

"Yes, I know," he replied quietly.

"Vladimer! Can't I…"

He held his finger over her lips. "You already know the answer to that question. Above all, you must be saved. Should anything happen to me, you have to live for both of us."

"For all three of us, Vladimer."

He looked at her questioningly.

She returned the look with all the love that was within her soul. "You're going to be a father, Vladimer. We're going to have a child."

He fell to his knees and pressed his head to her stomach. "Oh, Nevenka. You have just given me the most precious gift any man could receive. A child. An heir! The greatest honor that could be bestowed upon me."

"You *must* live, Vladimer. I do not want a stranger raising our child. He is destined for greatness, like his father. That I know."

"He?"

She smiled. "You're not the only one who knows his destiny. I know that the life that grows within me is a male child, Vladimer. You must be there to teach him the way of the world. You must be there to be his mentor. I will not have a stranger, a foreigner, no less, raise our child. Especially an American."

Vladimer rose from his knees and held Nevenka's face in his hands. "By these words I promise that I will be with you always, both in spirit and soul."

* * * *

Dawn arrived too soon, and Vladimer left for the battle, while Nevenka, Helena and ten Jewish women prepared to leave for America. Although she could not bear to leave Vladimer, she now knew that her destiny was greater than both of them. She knew that no matter what happened, she and Vladimer Ryzhkov would be bound through all eternity with the child she carried.

CHAPTER 19

▼

Andrew Mullin had lived in Los Altos all his life, occupying the only remaining large parcel of residential land within the city limits, a ten-acre homestead, located just off the main street of town. His two-story, five-thousand-square-foot house included an in-laws quarters which was surrounded by a stand of fifty-year-old eucalyptus trees that reached more than one hundred feet into the air. The entire grounds was protected by wrought iron fencing, making entrance to the property accessible only through an electronic gate which could be activated from within the house.

Andrew Mullin was a jovial real estate developer in his late fifties, divorced and living alone. Although he stood no more than six feet tall, he weighed two hundred eighty pounds. His one joy in the world, aside from an occasional interlude with his children, who lived with his ex-wife, was making money, and he was good at it.

He was a workaholic who knew no other vice, aside from Margaret Jamesian, the little redhead that he fancied down at the title company. Every month or so he would causally arrange to meet her at Denny's in Monterey, where they would spend the weekend locked up in some motel room sewing wild oats. That was his only remedy for losing a quick ten pounds. It was also the only sex he would have for the next month or so.

No one could ever figure out why he bothered sneaking clear down to Monterey. There were motels in Palo Alto and San Jose, just fifteen minutes away. And, there was no one to hide from, unless it was from one of their exes, who could care less, anyway. Those in the know figured that slipping away to the coast probably just added to the excitement of the moment.

Andrew Mullin was a name dropper. Whenever he had conversations with new business associates, especially if he was trying to cut a new deal such as the development of his five-hundred-apartment-unit complex in Fresno or in building his hundred-unit hotel in Palo Alto, names flew like startled birds in an aviary.

Before negotiations were in progress, he would artfully set the stage with his potential investor, banker, purchaser or business partner, with such off-the-wall comments as, "King Hussein was in town on business last month. He stayed at my place while we tried to hammer out a coal deal with the Soviet Union that we've been working on for months," he would brag. His comments would have no relevance to their transaction, but he loved to impress people. "Once the deal is consummated with the Soviets," he'd continue, "we'll be the largest coal importers in the world. Could bring us millions."

When pressed for details, he would gloss over the triviality of the transaction with general comments pertaining to the distribution of coal to Third World nations, which you just knew would have to entail such a network of finely tuned, coordinated efforts that would be impossible to pull off with Mullin's one-man office.

Yet, once this story was told, he would press on about other major exploits of gigantic proportions too enormous for the common mind to fathom. When he was finished, it left one wondering why he was even bothering with such penny-ante deals such as the five-million-dollar hotel deal or two-point-five-million-dollar apartment complex development. And why pray tell, was he in need of investor's or financing?

Sometimes his schemes came together, at least that seemed to be the case for all outward appearances…like the land deal in Shasta County he claimed was going to be his retirement. "Developing a hundred-twenty acres, right near the lake, at the base of the mountain," he would brag, without any correlation to the current topic at hand. "Gonna time-share it! That's gonna to be my retirement. I'm gonna build a twenty-thousand-square-foot lodge and recreation room, have two pools, an RV park, mobile home park and residential lots surrounding the outlying area. It's gonna to be the hottest deal this side of Disneyland."

His eyes would glitter and his imagination would pick you up and carry you right along with him, whether or not you had initially wanted to go. The only thing was, he usually only had these transactions tied up with minimal option money. Between building his five hundred units in Fresno, working out his coal deal with King Hussein, finishing his hundred-unit hotel in Palo Alto—which was currently suffering from a lumber strike up north—and, at the same time, developing the several other smaller complexes that he had going from time to time, and coordinating his retirement community at lake Shasta, he rarely knew where his glasses were, let alone where his money was coming from, who his investors were or to whom he was obligated.

It was even rumored that once he had asked his secretary Myrna Lee for a ten-thousand-dollar loan, to make a couple of payments on the new house he had optioned in Carmel Valley. Yet, like cream in milk, he always seemed to float to the top.

Aaron MacAffie had noticed the gated grounds to the Mullin residence the first time he had hit town, but at the time hadn't given it much thought. Just another wealthy resident, he thought. As time marched on and he became more acquainted with the townsfolk, he noticed the name Andrew Mullin kept popping up in conversations. It was during one of those conversations that he finally tied the name to that large home surrounded by tall eucalyptus trees and the black wrought-iron fence just outside the center of town. Somehow, deep in his soul he knew that Andrew Mullin was going to be the key to his future.

At seven o'clock the following Monday morning he stationed himself outside Mullin's gate, across the street under a large elm tree, waiting for him to emerge. He didn't know what he was going to do when Mullin departed, but he waited anyway. *The Lord will show me the way,* he thought to himself, believing in his own fantasy. He spread a newspaper in front of him so no one would notice who he was.

At precisely eight o'clock, the wrought-iron gate swung open and Andrew Mullin pulled out in his white Jaguar Vandenplas. MacAffie waited for a moment, then pulled in behind him. The traffic was light so he stayed back a respectable distance, following him through town. There was no fear of losing sight of the Jaguar.

Mullin pulled into Murray's Donut Shop, parked his car and wandered in with a newspaper and what appeared to be a manilla folder under his arms. He ordered a cup of coffee and three chocolate donuts, then took a seat in one of the booths.

MacAffie parked his Volkswagen next to the white Jaguar and sauntered into the donut shop. He paced back and forth in front of the glass display case for a moment, glancing periodically at Andrew Mullin, who was already wolfing down his second donut.

"I'll have one of those cinnamon bear claws and a cup of hot chocolate," he told the elderly Chinese lady.

He took his food and sat in the next booth, facing Andrew Mullin. He let a few minutes pass, looking at Mullin, hoping that he could make eye contact, but Mullin seemed intent on reading his *Wall Street Journal*. Finally, MacAffie said, "Say, aren't you Andrew Mullin?"

Mullin looked up from his paper and stared blankly at the stranger. Then a smile appeared on his face. He was happy to be recognized, even by someone he didn't know. "Why, yes. Do I know you?"

That was MacAffie's invitation. Without hesitation, he picked up his bear claw and hot chocolate and sauntered over to Mullin's table. "Aaron MacAffie. Pastor Aaron MacAffie," he said, setting his loot down, then extending his hand. "I've heard a lot about you. I've been looking forward to meeting you. Thought I recognized you from the description."

Mullin laughed so his belly shook. "I guess I am sort of an enigma around town." He wiped his large hand on his shirt, then accepted Aaron MacAffie's hand.

"May I?" MacAffie said, motioning to the empty seat opposite his victim, then slid in without waiting for a response.

"Please," Mullin said, waving his hand to the spot where MacAffie was already sitting.

"I've heard so much about you I couldn't wait to meet you. Hope you don't mind. I'm not intruding, am I?"

Mullin laughed. "Not at all. Delighted to have a little company. No lectures," he said jokingly as he held up a finger.

"I'm off duty." MacAffie smiled back. "As I understand, you're a pretty successful developer. I admire people who can build something out of nothing. I've always wanted to be a builder myself."

Andrew Mullin was pleased that his reputation had preceded him. He loved the attention, and especially a stranger's admiration. "I've done a little building," he said, smiling. Modesty wasn't one of his long suits, just an introduction to the list of credits and name dropping that was about to follow.

"A *little* building? From what I've heard, you've built enough real estate to start your own country." He laughed. "Tell me. How do you do it? Stay so calm, I mean, in the face of all the tremendous pressures that must face one as prolific as yourself?"

Mullin was beaming now. MacAffie had skillfully led him straight into the carefully veiled trap that he had set for him. Now all he had to do was sit back, roll up his pants and endure the several feet of B.S. that was about to flow his way.

After twenty minutes, even MacAffie was getting bored with the King Hussein—Soviet Union coal mine stories. "That one of your current projects?" MacAffie asked, changing the subject, nodding towards the manilla file that Mullin had brought in with him.

Mullin smiled, pleased that MacAffie had expressed an interest. "Lake Shastina." He beamed. "I've got a hundred-twenty acres near Lake Shasta that I'm in the process of developing."

"Wow! How do you keep all those projects straight? I mean, you're developing a hotel, a five-hundred-unit-apartment complex, doing a coal deal with the Russians and now Lake Shasta! Boy, do I admire you. How do you get to all these places? I mean, you must spend all your time in the car. When do you have time to sleep?"

"I've got a little Cessna 172. When I need to get to one of my projects, I just crank her up and whip on up to the property. Much faster than a car." He beamed. "It's the only way to get around."

"You've got a pilot's license, to boot," MacAffie said, with exaggerated admiration. "Wow! Would you believe it if I told you that I've never been in a plane in my entire life?"

"Well, if you want, I'm flying to Shasta tomorrow. Come along if you like," he said, waving his arm.

"Do you mean it? Wow! That would be unbelievable!"

"Hey! Glad to have the company. It gets boring up there all by myself. Nothing but blue sky and clouds and the constant hum of the engine. It's enough to put one to sleep." He laughed.

MacAffie's eyes were sparkling with excitement. "I'd love to go. Where shall I meet you?" Things were progressing unbelievably well...much better than he had planned.

"Why don't you meet me at my place and I'll drive us to the San Carlos airport? That's where the plane is parked," he explained. "We'll take off from there"

MacAffie was beside himself. *What a stroke of good luck*, he thought. He'd met Andrew Mullin, was going to get to see his Los Altos estate and had been invited to fly up to see one of his projects all in one fell swoop.

"Do you know where I live?"

"Sorry," he lied as he shook his head.

Mullin gave him instructions, which MacAffie accepted as if he had never heard of the place.

"Seven o'clock too early for you? I like to get an early start so I can get back before dark. Hate flying at night," he said, wrinkling his nose.

"Seven is just fine. I'll be there. Anything special I should wear?"

"I'd wear something comfortable, loose clothing, and bring a jacket. It can get pretty cold up there."

Chapter 20

Aaron MacAffie pulled up to Mullin's gate at seven sharp. There was a freestanding speaker on the driver's side of the gated entrance, positioned window-high, with a button that rang a bell in the residence when someone wanted to get the occupant's attention.

"Aaron?" came the raspy, tinny sound of Mullin's voice over the small speaker. "That you?"

"Yeah. It's me, Mr. Mullin. Aaron MacAffie."

The ten foot-iron gate swung open and MacAffie drove onto the vast grounds that led up to the main house. The house was set back two hundred feet or more from the gate. The circular driveway that led up to the house was constructed of hand-laid red brick. Each side of the driveway had been planted with several varieties of colorful flowers with a background of two-foot-high well-manicured bushes. An expansive lawn had been planted behind the bushes on either side of the driveway that went from the front gate all the way to the house. The swimming pool was elevated and off to the right, situated under a grove of eucalyptus trees.

Andrew Mullin was sitting outside on a circular concrete picnic-type table, drinking a cup of coffee, waiting for him. He waved as Aaron drove up the driveway. He was wearing a red plaid Pendleton shirt and acid-washed blue jeans and hiking boots.

MacAffie parked his Volkswagen on the circular portion of the driveway in front of the house.

"Come on in for a moment," he said, taking Aaron by the shoulder and leading him towards the house. "I was just getting things ready. Care for a cup of coffee?"

Aaron hated coffee, but would have drunk peroxide just to get a chance to look around the house. "I'd love it. Thanks."

As he glanced around, he was surprised to see that the house was so ill kept. There were papers lying all over the large wooden kitchen table, as well as stacked on the Italian marble floor. Dishes were piled in the sink and dirty pots and pans sat on the stove which occupied a large island in the middle of the kitchen. Several large patches of some colored substance had boiled over on the stove, obviously a remnant of dinners past.

"Sorry for the mess. I do a lot of my homework right here in the house. I've got a cleaning lady who comes in twice a week, but she's been down with the flu the past week or so." He grinned as he looked around the kitchen. You know how it is when you're a bachelor."

"Being a single man myself, yes, I know." He smiled. "No family, then?" he probed as he selected a cup from the cupboard and examined it for cleanliness before pouring himself half a cup of coffee.

He was delighted that Mullin lived alone and was divorced. That could make things considerably easier down the line. Children could complicate his plan, but he'd have to cross that bridge when he came to it. He removed several newspapers that still had a rubber bands tied around them, dusting the seat momentarily with the back of his hand before sitting down.

"I've got two kids, a girl and a boy. They live down in Carmel with their mother. They're teenagers and have their own life. You know how it is with kids. All they want to do is hang out at the mall with kids their own age. They don't have much time for adults."

"So I've heard," he said as he picked up his cup, looked at it, then set it down without drinking any of its black contents. Apparently, he hadn't done dishes, either, as there was a small island of grease floating in the middle of the cup. He pushed it away when Mullin wasn't looking.

"You ever been married?"

"Nah. I'm too busy with the church," he lied. "No time for women." He thought about telling him about the Russian mail order-bride that he had contracted to bring over, but thought better of it. There was no way of knowing how Mullin might view such a wild venture and he didn't want to take the chance of endangering their friendship at this fragile date.

"Well, I'll just get my briefcase and we'll be on our way." As he turned his back, MacAffie poured the contents of his cup into a large bowl of stale rice, which soaked up the black substance, leaving no trace of the deed.

Mullin picked up MacAffie's cup. "More?" he asked.

"No. That was great. Thanks."

* * * *

Mullin drove to the San Carlos Airport, a ride taking no more than forty-five minutes. As he pulled off the freeway, there was a small green sign that read *San Carlos Airport*. MacAffie could see the control tower from the road which led to the small airport. Mullin passed an office building's parking lot and pulled onto the tarmac, where dozens of small airplanes were tied down. He stopped next to a single-engine, white-on-blue, four-passenger Cessna.

"Well, here she is." Mullin beamed. "Old Betsie has gotten me all over this grand land without so much as a flat tire," he said, patting the plane on its fuselage. It'll just take me a minute to check around the plane to be sure everything is ship-shape and we'll be on our way. Hop in if you like," he said, unlocking the passenger door. "You can stow your jacket on the back seat."

MacAffie had never been in a small plane before and was surprised to see so many instruments. He was also surprised to see a steering wheel on both sides of the airplane.

He watched Mullin as he meticulously walked around the aircraft, twisting the flaps, tugging at cables and kicking tires. "Well, that takes care of the formalities," he said, as he hopped in and locked the door after himself. "Buckle up there, Aaron. We don't plan on hittin' nothin', but it's good practice to be secure anyway, just in case." He laughed as he helped MacAffie buckle himself in.

Before he started the engine Mullin tested all the flaps, then took down a plastic card from overhead that contained a pre-printed checklist. He read each item aloud as he went through the checklist, tapping gauges with his forefinger, turning knobs and re-checking the flaps. When he was finished, he opened the plastic window and, yelled "Clear!" although there was no one within a hundred yards of the plane. He then closed the window and started the engine.

The engine chugged a few times and the rotor blade turned slowly, then the engine coughed and came to life, spitting out a puff of white smoke. The whirling noise was so loud that MacAffie couldn't hear himself think.

"Hang on, we're off!" Mullin yelled. He smiled to himself as he steered the plane onto the main runway.

The noise was too loud for conversation, so MacAffie simply sat back and watched, taking it all in like a kid with a new toy. Mullin taxied to the end of the runway, picked up the mike from the dash and talked to the tower, identifying himself, asking for clearance to take off.

Having been granted clearance to take off, he gave the plane full throttle, then released the brake and the plane rolled forward, picking up speed as it rattled down the runway. Aaron MacAffie hung on for dear life. He wished he had never agreed to go on the flight as the plane shook and rattled. *What have I gotten myself into*, he wondered as his fingers turned white from hanging on the side of his seat so tightly. Then, in a moment, the rattling stopped as the plane lifted off the ground. They were in the air, climbing rapidly. As the objects on the ground below became smaller by the moment, Mullin again talked to the tower. He replaced the mike and turned his attention to MacAffie, whose face displayed the discomfort that he obviously felt from his first flight in the small craft.

Once they had reached cruising altitude, the plane seemed to become quieter. The ground was far below now and flying suddenly lost its scariness. MacAffie relaxed and decided to take advantage of the time to pick Mullin's brain about his business, lifestyle and to get more details about the various projects he had on the boards.

* * * *

"There's Lake Shasta," Mullin said, banking the Cessna so MacAffie could look straight down, an exercise he could have well done without. "And there's the dam. See all the houseboats? Vacationers. If you ever need a place to unwind and relax, there's nothing like spending a week on a houseboat, fishing, swimming and just generally kickin' back. No telephones, no televisions and no salesmen. Nothin' to do but relax. You like to fish?"

"To tell you the truth, I've never been."

"Never been fishing? Well, we'll have to fix that. I've got a friend who has a thirty-footer moored at Silvercreek. Says I can use it anytime. Claims his houseboat is right next to Merle Haggard's boat. The country singer?" He looked at Aaron for confirmation.

He shrugged his shoulders. "I really don't keep up with country!" he yelled.

Mullin nodded, disappointed. One of his name-droppers hadn't worked. "Thing about bein' on a houseboat, all you gotta do is bring your own grub and drinks, of course. Everything else is supplied. What do you say? Interested?"

MacAffie shrugged his shoulders. "Sounds good to me." Actually, he thought he would hate fishing. He could think of nothing more disgusting that putting a hook through a piece of live bait squirming for its life, or removing the hook from a slimy fish who was obviously feeling the pain of it all.

"There's Mount Shasta straight ahead." He appeared to be heading right for the mountain with no apparent intention of turning. Mullin smiled as MacAffie's knuckles turned white as he gripped the sides of his seat. The Cessna was descending rapidly now and the engine noise made it nearly impossible to carry on a conversation. MacAffie gritted his teeth, closed his eyes and held on tight.

Mullin noticed his discomfort and smiled to himself. "You can't enjoy the sights with yer eyes closed," he said.

MacAffie opened his eyes and, with a sheepish grim, nodded.

Mullin enjoyed playing mind games with people from time to time. He glanced over at MacAffie, then purposely banked over the tree line a little too close.

There was no radio tower at Shasta, just an old wind sock indicating the strength and direction of the wind. Small crafts made what are called "visual landings" where they make a pass by the landing strip before landing. If no one appears to be in the process of taking off and no one else is in the same landing pattern, it's up to the pilot to use his best judgement.

The landing was a little bumpy, but MacAffie didn't care; he was delighted just to be back on good old Mother Earth. It was ten o'clock. The flight had taken a little under two hours.

"Well, we made it in one piece," Mullin said with a smile. There was an old station wagon that he had parked back in the corner of the tar-and-gravel parking lot. "It's not the Jag," he said with a smile, "but it's reliable. I figure no one's going to steal a heap like this." He laughed as he dusted off the windows with a rag that he kept on the front floor mat.

The driving time from the airport to the site was less than twenty minutes. Once Mullin had parked the car, MacAffie couldn't believe how beautiful it was. It was a woodsy setting nestled at the base of Mount Shasta, with giant redwoods, silver spruce and pine trees giving off that special smell that anyone who has ever spent much time in the wilderness loves.

MacAffie broke the silence of the forest with a sneeze.

Mullin laughed. "Catching a cold?"

"Nah. Just my sinuses acting up. Must be some ragweed or pollen in the air. I get plugged up every spring when things start blooming and there are pollen spores floating everywhere. It's miserable. If I don't take my allergy medication, I get so stuffed up I can't even breathe."

"I feel for you, buddy."

He blew his nose. "I'll be all right. I'm not going to let a little stuffy nose spoil this trip."

They walked the grounds and Mullin pointed out the location where he planned to build the clubhouse, the recreation room, and the RV park He even pointed out the area where the swimming pool was to be built. When they arrived at the place where the single-family lots were to be sold, he pointed out the area, then showed MacAffie a plot map that he held in his hand that outlined the subdivision.

MacAffie nodded as he pretended to understand. He then picked up a large pine cone, and bounced in his hand for a moment before tossing it at a grey squirrel that was playing upside-down on a tree trunk nearby. He took a deep breath and closed his eyes. "I like this place. You know what, Andrew, this is exactly what I need for a getaway spot. What a great place to visit."

"I knew you would like it."

"No. I'm serious. I want to own one of these lots. How much would it cost, Andy, for me to buy one? I don't want the best, just a nice little secluded spot where I can build a cottage where I can retreat when I need to clear my mind."

Mullin smiled. He was pleased that MacAffie liked his development. "Tell you what, if you're serious, I'll sell a lot to you at cost. Which one do you like?"

He took his time looking around before selecting a location that pleased him. "This one." MacAffie pointed to a corner lot overlooking the lake with a view of the mountain in the background.

"You've got good taste." Mullin smiled, patting his friend on the back. He made a circle around lot number 106 on his plot map and handed it to MacAffie. "There it is. It's yours."

MacAffie looked at him, puzzled, with his brow knitted. What do you mean, 'it's yours?'"

"Just what I said. It's yours. A gift to you and your church. I can write it off as part of a promotional campaign. That lot would retail for around fifty-thousand, so I'll simply make a fifty-thousand-dollar donation to your church in the form of the lot. It'll be a tax deduction to me and non-taxable to your church."

He laughed, and thumped MacAffie on his back with his big hand. "Come on, I'm hungry enough to eat the north end of a cow goin' south. Let's head back to town. There's this great little mom-and-pop restaurant that makes the best burgers in Shasta county. I'll buy."

"Wait a minute. Are you sure?" He couldn't believe that Andrew Mullin had just given him a lot worth fifty thousand dollars. "I can't tell you how much I appreciate this, but I can't accept a lot. That's too generous."

"Hey, what are friends for? Besides, that's just a drop in the bucket. I've got hundreds more where that came from."

*   *   *   *

After they had returned from lunch they prepared to fly back to the Bay Area. MacAffie watched carefully as Andrew Mullin checked the airplane over, pulling at the cables that moved the flaps, kicking the tires, looking under the bonnet, tugging at the various tubes and wires before closing the bonnet again.

"Everything all right? Looking for anything in particular?"

"No. I just like to check all the cables and stuff before I take off. Never know when something might jiggle loose on the old girl. Never do to have to make an emergency landing in this country." He smiled. "Too many trees. An unscheduled landing would be near-impossible."

"That's an unsettling thought."

Mullin laughed. "Don't worry. This old girls' got me more places than you could shake a stick at. Hop in. I'll let you fly 'er on the way home."

MacAffie was sure he was kidding. He wasn't. Once they were in the air, Mullin tapped one of the gages that had a little wing-like mechanism that moved up and down over a fixed horizontal line. "You see this line?" he asked, pointing to the moving horizontal line. "You just have to watch this gauge and keep the wings level with this fixed line. If you drop below the line, pull back on the stick a little. Conversely, if you go above the line, that means you're climbing, and you want to push it in a bit. If you turn like this," he said, turning the wheel, "the line tilts, which means you're turning. When you're several thousand feet in the air, with nothing but clean air and clouds around, you tend to lose your sense of what's level and what isn't. Just keep 'er straight and you'll be all right."

Nervously, MacAffie took the wheel while still looking at Mullin, obviously unsure of himself. Mullin simply laughed and took his hands off his wheel and said, "It's yours. See. It's not so bad. You're flying!"

MacAffie smiled. "I am, ain't I?"

Chapter 21

That afternoon, back at the office, Aaron MacAffie through about their trip to Shasta and the lot. He wanted to strike while the iron was hot and Mullin still remembered his promise to give him the lot. He went to the title company and got a blank Quit Claim Deed. He instructed his secretary, who was also a Notary Public for purposes of executing wills and legal documents for the church, to type up the deed on the Lake Shasta lot.

"Make the deed from Andrew Mullin to Aaron MacAffie in care of the Living Christ Church," he said, instructing her to leave that portion of the deed blank that called for a legal description. "I'll fill in the legal description of the lot once I get the information from Andrew," he explained.

Once the deed was typed, he smiled and took the typed document back to his office. Laying the document on his desk, he carefully cut the legal description from the preliminary report that Andrew Mullin had given to him. His hands trembled just a bit as he gently taped the lot description to that part of the deed that called for a legal description.

When he was finished, he held it at arm's length. He smiled to himself, satisfied with his handiwork. It looked all proper and legal. He only hoped Andrew wouldn't look it over too carefully, as he had instructed his secretary to make an obvious, but not uncommon typing error, on purpose.

∗ ∗ ∗ ∗

"Andy! Glad I caught you before you left," he said the next day, when he called Mullin's office. "Say, Andy, you remember that lot you said I could have up at Lake Shasta yesterday? Number 106? Well, hope you don't think I'm forward or anything, but I took the prerogative of having my secretary type up a Quit Claim Deed. I was wondering if I could buy you lunch and get your signature." He was careful not to ask him to meet him in his office, because he knew if Andrew caught the error that he had made, Mullin would simply have his secretary retype the deed, correcting the mistake, then everything would have been for naught.

MacAffie could tell by the tone of his voice that Mullin was slightly irritated, but he pressed on anyway. "It'll just take a moment of your time," he pleaded.

"All right, Aaron. How 'bout I meet you at Crockers Deli at one o'clock? That way we'll miss the crowd and will be assured of getting a table."

"See you there." MacAffie's hands trembled as he hung up the telephone. He carefully placed the document in a manila folder. Had he gone too far? He could be caught. Then what would people say? A man of the cloth! Cheating! He would be run out of town on a rough pole.

Had he been careful enough? These questions plagued him, but he was determined to proceed with his plan. He needed to do this thing.

He surprised himself at his devious boldness. The only thing that drove him forward was the thought that this was the only way he could get what he wanted most—a new church! And he was going to get it, at any cost.

MacAffie arrived at the deli a few minutes early. By this time, he had worked himself into a state of a panic. His mind was working overtime, thinking of all the ramifications that could result from his actions. So far, he hadn't committed himself, but once he had crossed that line, he knew there would be no turning back

Just then Andrew Mullin pulled up to the curb in his white Jaguar, parking next to a restricted yellow parking zone. He rolled his two-hundred-eighty pound frame out of the car and ambled in.

"Ah, you're here already, Aaron. Glad to see you." He extended his big hand as he caught his breath. "I hope you don't mind if I don't stay for lunch," he said as he sat down. "I've got a two o'clock in the city. I'm meeting Harlin Rockwell, the president of Northwestern Financial, to secure financing on my new Lemore project. Governor Pete Wilson approved my proposal to build a five-hundred-thousand square-foot security facility especially designed to house hardened criminals, but I need to acquire construction financing before I can commence building. I've already got the land tied up. Harlin assures me that, with the Governor's backing, I'll have no trouble obtaining a loan."

"I certainly admire your ambition. I don't know where you get your energy."

Mullin was too preoccupied with his appointment to be bothered with MacAffie's rhetoric. "If you don't mind, I'll just sign the deed and be on my way. You have it prepared already?"

"Right here," he said, carefully removing the single sheet of legal paper from his manilla envelope. "Had my secretary type it up. You'll note that I've attached the legal description of the lot to the body of the contract. I cut it out of the preliminary title report you gave me. That's all right, isn't it?"

"Well, the recorder prefers to have it typed," he said as he scanned the paper, "but they've been known to accept it this way. It'll be recorded in Shasta county anyway. Up there they're not quite as strict as they are here in Santa Clara county. It'd never pass muster here." He looked at the deed, and was about to sign it, when he said, "Oh, you've got the wrong county here," he said, pointing out the error by thumping his forefinger on the spot. "You typed in Santa Clara County instead of Shasta County."

MacAffie bit his lip. He had hoped Mullin wouldn't catch the mistake. He slapped his hand to his forehead in feigned frustration. "Darn! My secretary probably did that out of habit. All the recording she does for the church is in our county, you know." He smiled weakly. "I'll tell you what, once you've signed it, I'll just have her white out Shasta and type in the correct county when I get back to the office, if that's all right with you?"

Mullin wrinkled his nose and shrugged his shoulders. "It's going to have to be notarized anyway, so why don't you take it back to my office and have Myrna make the correction; then she can notarize the deed at the same time. Legally, I'm supposed to sign the document in her presence, but she knows my signature. Just tell her that I sent you over," he said, as he scribbled his name. He handed the paper back to MacAffie and smiled. "Got to run now. Sorry I can't stay for lunch."

Aaron MacAffie's hands were moist and his heart was pounding as he waved good-bye to his friend. He waited until Mullin had driven off, then breathed a sign of relief. He had skated through the first phase of his plan and was on to phase two—getting the document notarized.

※　　　※　　　※　　　※

He walked into Mullin's office, where his secretary, Myrna Lee, was chatting on the telephone. It sounded like a private call, as her voice perceptibly lowered when Aaron MacAffie walked in. "I'll call you back," she said into the phone's receiver, then turned her attention to MacAffie. "Can I help you, sir?

"Mr. Mullin…"

"Mr. Mullin is out of the office this afternoon," she interrupted. "Did you have an appointment?" she asked, thumbing through her appointment book.

MacAffie smiled his best condescending smile and said, "Yes, I know he isn't here. I just left him at the deli. He signed this Quit Claim Deed and sent me over to have it notarized." He handed the document to her, folded in half, hoping she wouldn't catch the discrepancy of the wrong county. "Said that you would know his signature and would notarize it without him being present."

Myrna had been trained to do as she was instructed by Andrew Mullin, without question.

Her boss was usually very fastidious about his work, so when Aaron MacAffie brought in the document with his signature, she simply took out her Notary Public book and recorded the transaction before stamping it in the designated spot, after which she signed and dated it.

"There you go. Will that do it?" she said, handing the document back to MacAffie.

Just as MacAffie was about to take it from her hand, she said, "Oh, I should make a copy for Andrew's file. He's very meticulous about copies," she said, slipping it out of his hand before he could protest. In a moment, the copy was made, and she handed the original back to MacAffie.

He nodded and said, "Thanks", then quickly departed, gritting his teeth.

Well, there was nothing he could do about it now. If the topic came up at a later date, he would simply have to plead ignorance and say that he had forgotten to have the county changed. After all, he wasn't going to record this instrument, anyway. At least, not in its present condition. At least, not right now.

Chapter 22

The plane from Moscow landed at Kennedy International Airport, where Helena Makarov and her Lifetime Partners anxiously deplaned. "Well ladies. Welcome to America," Helena said as they entered the main concourse.

"Wow! Will you look at all the people!" Nevenka exclaimed.

"And look how nice everyone is dressed. Boy! What a difference from Russia!" someone chimed in.

"What do we do now, Helena?" one of the women asked. "I'm anxious to meet my man!" She was all smiles, eager to start her next life. "Are they meeting us here?"

Helena laughed. "Don't be in such a hurry, Niki. You'll have a lifetime to be with your man. And no, they're not meeting us here. Come, let us get our luggage before someone steals it."

"They can have all the old clothes they want," Niki said with a twinkle in her eye. "I plan on having a whole new wardrobe."

"From New York!"

"Yeah!" several of the women chimed in. Now that they were here in America, they were getting into the swing of things.

They were giddy as they walked down the halls towards the luggage pick-up area. Some of the woman even felt brazen enough to make overtures to some of the men by smiling or winking at them or swaying their hips in an obvious fashion. The others just laughed.

"Careful, ladies. Some of these men may take your invitation seriously. Then what will you do?"

"Make love!"

They laughed

Once they had their bags, Helena led them outside, where a man wearing a dark blue suit and a matching cap was holding a sign with the name Helena Makarov written on it. "There's our ride," she said, pointing to the man.

"We're going to ride in *that*!" Nevenka said, astonished, looking at the large, white limousine. "I've never seen an automobile so large."

"May as well get used to a little luxury. Remember one thing," she said as they formed a circle around her. "Always set your standards high and never settle for second best. That's the motto of America. He who is diligent and works hard gets ahead. Here, there's no such thing as a caste system. The poorest, lowest man can raise to riches if he applies himself. It's done every day. You have a great advantage, coming from Russia," she said in Russian so no one would understand.

"Advantage?"

"How can coming from Russia be an advantage?"

"You may not understand this right away, but most people born in this country are lazy. They're used to having everything, so they expect everything."

"I don't understand."

"It's simple. If you've never had anything in life and the prospects of ever getting anything are simply beyond your reach, you tend to accept your station, although you may not like it. But..."

"But," Nevenka interrupted, "if you go to a country where you have the opportunity to get ahead, you'll work especially hard to achieve that goal, knowing that it's attainable."

Helena clapped her hands. "Precisely. That's why I said most American's are lazy. They don't know what it's like to do without, so they don't work hard to get what they already have."

"Well, I, for one, plan on doin' a lot of applying," Niki said, laughing. "Just show me the way!"

The girls giggled as they looked around.

The chauffeur put the women's luggage in the large trunk, then asked Helena where she wanted to go.

"Holiday Inn, please."

They put the sunroof down so they could look out of the top of the limousine. Some of the girls stood on the seat of the car with their heads sticking out of the top. They couldn't believe the skyscrapers, the number of automobiles, the people on the streets and, moreover, the stores displaying gorgeous clothes.

"Here we are, ladies!" Helena said when the limousine stopped in front of the hotel. When they entered the hotel lobby, their mouths dropped open at the magnificence of the interior. The ceiling went all the way to the top of the building. Plants grew out of each balcony. Several glass elevators slid up the side of the building, seemingly going up a hundred floors or more.

"Is this the presidential palace?"

"I've died and gone to Heaven."

Helena laughed and said, "No. This is just a hotel. Our hotel." This was her favorite part of her job, introducing Russian women to America for the first time. Their unbridled enthusiasm always amused her. And when they first walked into a department store or shopping mall, their disbelief in the availability of goods was truly astounding.

"Meet me in my room in half of an hour," she instructed everyone as they rode up the elevator. She gave each girl a key to their rooms. "Nevenka, you'll bunk with me," she said with a warm smile. "Room 2600."

* * * *

The women were all anxiously waiting in Nevenka's drawing room as Helena came out of her bedroom. The excitement was electric as they anxiously awaited the sealed packets that she had brought with her from Moscow. She hadn't wanted to distribute them until they had actually arrived in America, for fear that something might go wrong and everyone would be disappointed.

"Well, ladies. We made it to America. Today is your first day of freedom in a new country. Here are your marriage contracts," she said, as she passed out the folders to each woman, except Nevenka.

The women squealed as they opened the folders, seeing their prospective husbands for the first time. Helena had done well. There wasn't a disappointed woman in the group. True, each candidate wasn't Don Johnson or Brad Pitt, but there were no complaints.

"Now, I have scheduled periodic meetings for each of you to meet your Lifetime Partner here in the hotel tomorrow. I've rented a small conference room at the end of the hall. I know you'll be nervous. So am I!" She smiled. "Just remember, this is the first day of the rest of your life in Freedom USA. Enjoy it.

"You're in America now, so you might as well get used to speaking English. From this moment on, you are no longer a Russian. You're an American. Speak only English. You've all learned the language in school, so this is your chance to practice what you've learned. If you find that you have trouble communicating, don't be embarrassed. Remember, they asked for you; you didn't ask for them.

Believe me, they'll be patient and understanding; but, by the same token, so must you."

"Will you go with us? To the meeting, Helena?"

"Of course. That's part of my job. Besides," she said with a smile. "You're my babies now, and I have to be sure that you all go to good homes."

They were so nervous all they could do was giggle. Nevenka stood in the background, observing. She was happy for them, but there was no way that she was going to feel the giddiness that the rest of the women felt. Rather, she felt empty and sad. She thought of Vladimer and wondered what he was doing at this moment. She put her hand over her belly and wondered what sort of a child she would bring into the world…if he would ever see his father.

"Now, Zora, you're the first one up. Introductions start tomorrow morning at nine o'clock. Look your best. In the meantime, let's walk around this new country of yours and see what you think of it. Meet me back her in exactly twenty minutes, and we'll go touring."

When they had all left her room, Nevenka asked, "What about me, Helena? I didn't get a brochure."

"Your contact is on the West Coast, which is where I'm going. We'll go there together, day after tomorrow, after everyone has been placed." She held Nevenka's hands. "Are you all right? You're not nervous, are you?"

She nodded. "A little. I still don't know if I can do this thing. No, let me correct myself, I don't *want* to do this thing."

"I understand, but we've been over this a dozen times, Nevenka. You have no choice, unless you want to go back to Russia. It'll work out. You'll see. Give it time." Helena patted her on the shoulder.

Two days later they were on an airplane headed for San Francisco. "I'm so nervous," Nevenka said, wringing her hands as the aircraft banked over the bay, preparing to land at SFO. "Is that San Francisco?"

"None other than 'The City by the Bay.' It's a beautiful city, really. You're going to find great contrast between America and Lithuania, Nevenka. It's going to take a little adjustment, but you'll find that the weather is warmer and the abundance of things like food and clothing will astound you. For the most part, American people are warm and compassionate. In Russia you were taught that America was this big, horrible enemy to fear and hate. You will now have the opportunity, first hand, to judge for yourself."

She touched Helena's hand. "I appreciate everything you've done for me, believe me. It's not that. It's just that, well, I don't think I can go through with it. The marriage thing, I mean."

She looked out the window before responding. "I understand your feelings, Nevenka. You love Vladimer Ryzhkov. And nothing can take that away, but you've got to realize, he's worlds away. I hate to preach doom and gloom, but chances are, you'll never see him again. Who knows what fate has in store for Vladimer? He may even be…" She didn't finish the sentence. Patting Nevenka on the hand, she said, "You've got a new life here. It can be a great life. Try to make the most of it."

"And if I can't?"

Helena shrugged her shoulders. "I guess we'll cross that bridge when we come to it."

Suddenly it hit her. She was going to be alone, without Helena's guidance. What if she needed her? "Where will you be?" she asked anxiously.

Helena sensed the panic in her voice and squeezed her hand. She took a piece of paper from her handbag and wrote a phone number on it. "This is where I can be reached, day or night. I'm going to have an office right here in San Francisco. If you need me, just call."

Nevenka touched her hand. "You've been a good friend, Helena. I can see why Vladimer thought so highly of you."

"We'll both miss him, Nevenka. Here," she said, handing Nevenka a folder. "This is your new life."

Nevenka looked at Helena, then smiled slightly as she opened the file. "Is this my new husband?" she asked, looking at the photo provided by Aaron MacAffie.

"That's him."

She studied his face for a moment. His hair was receding, but he had a kind face. "He's certainly no Vladimer Ryzhkov."

Helena looked at her without comment, but her eyes conveyed the message. *Don't be picky. Be happy with what you've got.*

"He's a minister. I hope that doesn't create a problem for you. His church is called The Living Christ Church. He's located just down the Peninsula, in a small town called Los Altos. We probably flew over it when we came it."

"A minister." Nevenka studied the photo for a moment. "Helena. There's something that I need to tell you. Something that I probably should have told you before we left Russia."

Helena looked at her companion as the plane touched down. The look in Nevenka's eyes said it all. "You're carrying Vladimer's child."

A tear rolled down Nevenka's face.

"Oh, Nevenka. What are you going to do?"

"Do you mean am I going to get rid of it?"

Helena didn't answer, but simply looked into her eyes.

Nevenka knew what she was thinking. "It's Vladimer's child. I couldn't do anything to harm him or the child. It's the only bond left between us, Helena. This child is the only thing that will keep me alive. You've got to understand that."

"I understand. The question is, will Pastor MacAffie understand? Do you want me to go with you when you meet him?"

Nevenka shook her head. "Thanks, but this is something I need to do on my own. I only hope I won't be calling you this afternoon, asking you to come and get me." She managed a small smile as she wiped away her tears.

CHAPTER 23

"Pastor. There's a Miss..." she struggled with the name, "Adamovich? She's here to see you."

"What's it regarding?" MacAffie said, as he studied the layout of the parking lot for the new church he had planned on building sometime in the near future. "Does she have an appointment?"

"I don't see her on my appointment book. She does say that you were expecting her, though."

MacAffie made a face, then rolled up the plans of his new church, which were becoming pretty well worn by now. "Show her in."

A very attractive, well-built blond woman entered his office. She seemed shy. He had never seen her before, of that he was sure, otherwise he certainly would have remembered, although there was something familiar about her. She was simply dressed, but in good taste.

She wore little make-up and her shoulder-length blond hair glistened as it gently swayed from side to side as she entered his office.

She wore a timid, almost fearful look as she asked, "Are you Aaron MacAffie?" There was an accent that he couldn't pinpoint as she spoke.

MacAffie was temporarily stunned by her simple beauty. "I'm sorry, I didn't get your name," he said, unable to take his eyes off her. "Yes, I'm Pastor MacAffie. Come in, Please." He stood and motioned to the chair in front of his desk. "Please. Sit down."

Everything was suddenly rushing at her. Helena had offered to come with her. Now she wished she had accepted the invitation. "My name is Nevenka Adamovich." She smiled, extending her hand to MacAffie.

"Neven…" he stumbled with her name. "I'm sorry. Would you pronounce that again, slowly?" His smile was warm, almost apologetic for not understanding her the first time. "Forgive me, but I'm not familiar with the name."

Her light little laugh was charming and her smile radiant. "Nevenka. My friends in high school used to call me Neva." She smiled. "It's much easier to pronounce."

"Nevenka. I like that. What nationality is that? Russian?" He guessed from the inflection of her words. He had no sooner said the word than it dawned on him. "You're…you're Nevenka!" he stammered, pointing his finger at her with a bad effort at pronouncing her last name. "From Russia!"

She smiled shyly with her eyes downcast. She could feel her face getting red with embarrassment. Suddenly she felt like a garment that someone had ordered from a mail order catalog. "Yes. Lithuanian, actually. Lithuania was part of Russia, but then we seceded recently," she explained. "Now we're independent." She nodded nervously. "Yes, Nevenka Adamovich. That is me. Nevenka Adamovich from Lithuania."

Her spoken words were perfect, grammatically correct, each word enunciated as if separately wrapped in tissue, each containing its own meaning. He liked the way she spoke. And he *loved* the way she looked. She had already far exceeded his expectations.

MacAffie's face flushed as he extended his hand again, inviting her to sit down. "Where are you staying? When did you get in? Did you come alone?" One question stumbled rapidly over the other in nervous succession.

She simply sat looking at the man who had brought her halfway across the world, to marry her. She made no effort to impress him with either flattery or frivolity. She was too nervous to even answer his questions. He looked a little different from the picture he had sent. Shorter and a little stockier, she thought. Balder. There was no comparing him to Vladimer, as she quickly glanced at his hair. Then again, she recalled Helena's words, *Don't be too choosey.*

"I'm sorry," he finally said. "I'm just so excited that you're here. I never thought this day would come." He studied her face for a long moment, not allowing his eyes to venture beyond her neckline. His peripheral vision would have to take the rest of her in, for the moment, at least. "To be perfectly frank, I'm a little embarrassed. I've been anticipating this day for so long I didn't think it would ever happen."

His face started to become red with embarrassment. "I don't know where to go from here." For a man used to taking everything by the horns, he had never prepared for this day, thinking it was just a dream, a fantasy. But here it was.

Here she was. Sitting in the chair before him, as large as life and was beautiful as a spring day. He couldn't take his eyes off her.

Finally collecting his wits, he said, "Well, I guess the first thing to do is to get you settled. Do you have much luggage?'

"They allow us only one bag when we leave Russia. I have one bag." She looked around his office, taking it in for the first time. It was fairly stark. Not what she had expected. She had thought there would be religious memorabilia on his desk and on the walls. Instead, the only thing on his wall was his diploma, and his desk was cluttered with papers and some large rolled-up document the size of a poster.

"Will I be staying here? With you?" Her question was frank and direct, with the affirmative expected.

"I ah, well, we'll have to, ah, well for the time being..." He was stuck for words again and clearly beyond preparation. He felt like a child turned loose in a candy store with instructions to choose anything he wanted, but only one thing. What to do now? It was beyond comprehension that this woman was here to be his wife!

"I must confess to you that I'm a little nervous," she said softly.

"You're nervous!" He laughed. "I've never been so nervous in my entire life. I don't want to give you the wrong impression—I mean, I just don't go around ordering wives through the mail every day." His face was becoming quite red now, and he knew he was acting as if he had the IQ of a fence post. He gestured with his hands. "I'm sorry. I'm not usually this flustered."

"Flustered?"

"Tongue tied! Out of control. Scatterbrained." He laughed more out of nervousness and sheer delight than embarrassment.

She smiled. "Oh. I understand." She nodded. "Me, too."

"This has got to be a terribly frightening experience for you. First you get uprooted from your own country, then come to a strange land and, to top it off, meet with someone for the first time-me—who you're going to spend the rest of your life. Kinda of scary, huh?"

"More than kinda."

"I can imagine. I'm sorry I'm acting like such an idiot. Who knows what you must think of me?"

She smiled. "I think you are quite nice."

"I'll bet you're beat, traveling all the way from Russia. Did you leave today, or I guess maybe it was yesterday. I get confused with the time zones."

"Actually, we left three days ago. We spent two days in New York, then flew to San Francisco."

"We?"

She nodded. "Yes. Myself and Helena. She's a friend who works in San Francisco."

"Oh. It's good that you had someone to accompany you. Flying alone can probably be intimidating. Especially to a new country, language and all, you know?"

She nodded, although she didn't understand the word "intimidate".

"Tell you what," he said, rubbing his chin as if thinking. "I have a spare room in my living quarters over at the church. Why don't we get you settled in there, and you can rest up and freshen yourself. We can talk more later. Would you like that?"

She nodded. "That would be nice. I am a little tired, and it has been an overwhelming day."

"It's settled, then. I'll show you to your room, you can rest and this evening we can get to know one another a little. Would that be all right with you?"

She nodded with a sigh of relief. "Whatever you say, Mr. MacAffie."

"Please. My name is Aaron. Please call me Aaron."

"And you can call me Nevenka, or Neva, whichever is easiest for you."

Her smile was disarming and, oh, that body! To die for! He allowed his eyes to flow from her long blond hair to her strong shoulders, then quickly paused on the curvature of her chest before taking in the rest of her. He was falling in love with a woman he had never seen before. A woman that had come halfway around the world to be his wife. *His wife!* He couldn't wait.

It hadn't occurred to him what his congregation might think of his new acquisition. Well, that was the least of his worries now. At the moment, he had more on his mind.

* * * *

It had been a long trip and an even longer day. Now she was in a strange land with an unfamiliar man. She sat on her bed, exhausted, her mind fuzzy with confusion—Lithuania, her family, Vladimer and now this, a new man destined to be her husband...one she didn't know if she was even going to like, but had nonetheless agreed to marry.

It had been a trying day. She laid her head on the pillow, and cried softly. The next thing she knew it was dark outside. *I must have been sleeping for hours,* she thought as she sat upright. It was dark and she didn't know where she was. Suddenly, it all came back to her in a flash of pictures. The flight from New York, saying good-bye to Helena, the trip to Los Altos and, finally, meeting Aaron MacAffie. A shiver went down her spine and her skin began to tingle with fear.

Her eyes had just begun to search for a light switch when there was a soft knock at the door. "Nevenka?"

"Yes."

"It's Aaron. I've got dinner on the table. Could you use a bite to eat?"

"Yes. Just a moment, please." She opened the door a crack, shielding her eyes from the light.

MacAffie smiled at her. "Perhaps you would like to freshen up before dinner?"

She nodded. "That would be nice."

"Right next door is the bathroom. Take your time. When you're done, I'll be waiting in the dinning room. That just down the hall. Just follow your nose."

She smiled as she softly closed the door. She waited for a moment before going to the bathroom. The cold water felt invigorating as she washed her face. As she combed her hair she found herself staring at her face in the mirror. *Who are you, Nevenka Adamovich? Do I know you?* she thought as she studied her face. *What in God's name are you doing in this place?*

She made her way down the hall and found Aaron standing in the dinning room waiting for her. He had on a clean white shirt, black pants and a pair of slippers. "You look nice," she said, smiling.

"Thank you. So do you. Hope I didn't startle you."

She shook her head. "I must have been very tired. I've been sleeping too long."

"Nonsense. You've been through an ordeal that would exhaust anyone. How about it? Hungry?"

She smiled. "Starved."

"Good. How do you like your steak?"

"Steak? I don't know. I can't remember ever having had one. You decide."

"Well, I like mine a little pink in the middle, not too red and certainly not well-done. Is that all right with you?"

She nodded in agreement, smiling. She was grateful to be treated like a guest and not being pressured, as he might very well have done.

He held out his hand. "Come. I've put a Presto Log in the fireplace to take the chill out of the night air."

"Presto Log?"

He laughed lightly. "That's right. You probably haven't heard of such a thing. It's a log made from sawdust. They mold the sawdust together in the form of a log and add some chemicals to make the fire burn different colors. See?" He pointed to the fireplace, which was burning brightly with orange and blue flames.

He handed her a large snifter glass half-filled with a warm, dark-orange substance.

"Apricot brandy with a twist of lemon. Do you like brandy?"

"In Lithuania we mostly drink vodka." She sniffed the glass, then took a sip. "Umm, it is good," she said, cradling the glass in the palm of her hands as if warming them.

"Why don't you have a seat, and I'll put on a little music," he said, motioning for her to make herself comfortable on the couch in front of the fireplace. "How about Rimsky-Korsakov's Russian Easter Festival Overture?"

She shrugged her shoulders. "I don't think I've heard that one."

"Well, I'll put it on, and you can make yourself comfortable while I barbecue the steak. It shouldn't take but a few minutes."

She looked around the room after he had left. It was a comfortable room, with colorful Chinese throw rugs which had been placed over a hardwood floor. There were three couches surrounding the fireplace. A large glass table had been placed between them, bearing a metal sculpture of two dolphins jumping out of the water. A few inexpensive, but attractive, landscape paintings hung on the wall.

She snuggled on the couch next to the fireplace and slipped off her shoes, tucking her feet under herself, and closed her eyes. She was still tired, but a small wave of tranquility had started to overcome her. It felt good not to have to worry about the Red Army bursting through the door or having to worry about hiding. Her thoughts had just started to wander to Vladimer when MacAffie spoke.

"Dinner's served."

Aaron led her to the dining room where the overhead chandeliers had been turned down low. He pulled her chair out for her. The aroma of the food was overwhelming. On her plate was the largest steak she had ever seen, steaming hot, with a piece of butter melting on top. A baked potato and steamed asparagus were also on her plate, and there was a separate plate for the green salad that Aaron had prepared.

"This all looks too delicious to eat," she said, her mouth watering.

"Do you mind if we say grace first?"

She shook her head and bowed with her eyes closed.

"Lord, bless this food, and thank you for bringing Nevenka to me safe and sound. Bless her and help make her stay here in America everything that she wants it to be. Amen."

She reached over and touched his hand. "Thank you," she said, a tear trickling down her cheek. "That was the nicest thing anyone has ever said to me."

He looked at her and loved her even more. "So, what do you think of our country—America—now that you're here?"

"To be honest, I've only been here a little while, so, outside of walking the streets of New York for a few hours, I haven't had much time to digest anything. I can say I'm impressed with the large number of stores that carry such fine clothing, though." She smiled a little sheepishly.

MacAffie smiled. "I'm sure you'll acclimate yourself."

"Acclimate?"

"Get used to. You know, become acquainted with the stores."

"You'll have to forgive my poor English. I'm afraid all I know is what they taught in Russian schools. That is, when Lithuania was part of Russia."

"Oh. I didn't realize that Lithuania wasn't part of Russia. Hasn't it always been? I'm sorry to appear so ignorant. I know I've heard that Russia has been having its problems, but to be perfectly honest, I get so involved with my own little world here that I don't have time to keep up with world affairs."

Nevenka felt happy that he wasn't assuming a superior attitude. And the fact that she knew more about Russia's problems than he made her feel superior, in a way. "Lithuania first seceded from Russia, then other states followed," she explained. "Russia is having a very bad time of it right now."

"I'm sorry to hear that. Does that affect your family much?"

A sad look came over her face as she told him of the plight of her brothers in the Red Army. "I'm so sorry," he said, patting her hand. "It must not have been a good time for you to leave. Just when everything seemed to be coming apart."

"Yes," she said simply. "The timing was not so good. That is why I had to leave. But that is a story for another time." She threw back her shoulders and forced a smile. "But, here we are, and we must make the most of things."

"Here, in America, the only news we get about Russia is what is reported through the media—television and radio—and most of the time, that's blown way out of proportion. You must really feel badly about your brother. I know I would be devastated if that happened to mine," he lied. Actually, he and his brother had never been close and he hadn't heard from him since their mother had died.

"Yes," she said simply. Actually, she preferred not to discuss her family any further, for fear of bringing up old feelings, feelings that she had tried very hard to repress. She was grateful for his interest, however. That, in itself, made her feel good.

Chapter 24

Andrew Mullin was ushered into the office of Harlin Rockwell at Northwestern Financial Corporation in San Francisco. The company offices occupied two floors near the top of the Transamerica building and had a commanding view of the Golden Gate Bridge and the Bay. After standing by the window, admiring the beauty of the city for several minutes, he was ushered into Harlin Rockwell's office. He stopped in front of the door to admire the bronze plaque that read *Harlin Rockwell, President.* He blew his breath on the plaque and polished it with his coat sleeve. *I'll have to get me one of those,* he thought to himself. He envisioned the plaque: Andrew Mullin, President.

A man standing six feet-two, his jet-black hair combed straight back, with a matching pencil thin mustache walked out to meet him. He was dressed in a black pin-striped suit with a matching vest and a flaming-red tie. His black loafers had two little dangling leather straps.

Typical hot-shot hustler, Mullin thought to himself. The man had a big smile and wore too much cologne. He extended his hand with a two-carat zirconium on his pinkie. "Andrew! Nice to see you. You know Dora Hutchinson, don't you?"

Dora was Harlin Rockwell's personal assistant and on-site show-piece. She was an impressively statuesque woman, standing five-feet seven, with black hair, and she wore a short black skirt with a red sweater that fit snugly around her size thirty-eight D's. Everyone noticed Dora when she was around. Actually, it was somewhat distracting to have her in the same room when multi-million-dollar transactions were being discussed, but then, maybe that was the idea.

Mullin smiled as he took her hand. His eyes drifted down to her bulging chest, where her nipples stood erect through her sweater. He resisted the urge to reach out and give them a gentle, playful twist. "Nice to see you again, Dora."

Her eyes followed Mullin's as they fell to her breasts. She gave them a little boost outward, emphasizing her endowments, as if to taunt the big man. "Andrew," she replied in a simple greeting, as she blinked her fake eyelashes at him.

"I got a call from one of the aides in the Governor's office, inquiring about the status of your loan on the Lemore project," Harlin said, leading him into his office, motioning for him to sit in the chair opposite his desk. He opened the file that lay in the middle of his otherwise-uncluttered desk.

One not impressed with such fluff, Mullin inquired, "What did you tell them?"

"Simply that we had an appointment this morning to finalize the terms of your loan. He really wants to put this thing into high gear."

Mullin shrugged his shoulders, as if to say, "What do you expect?" He continued, "You have to remember that re-election time is just around the corner," he said, "and his thing is the law-and-order platform. Now that the state of California has executed David Bonin, the boy-killer, and Richard Allen Davis has been convicted for the kidnap and murder of Polly Klasss and has been sentenced to die, I think you're going to see the public demanding stricter law enforcement."

"You got that right!"

Mullin ignored his profound statement. "That means there's going to be greater demand for stricter crime control, which means he's going to need more detention space. It's one of the few state-sponsored construction projects that has complete public approval."

"Speaking of public approval, how's your Lake Shasta development coming along?" He wasn't really interested, but this was his form of small business talk, the preamble to negotiating the big stuff.

"Great! I just have to carve some time out of my otherwise-busy schedule to nudge the project along into the next phase. With the Hotel in Palo Alto nearing completion, the five hundred units in Fresno underway and now this project for the State of California on the boards, I've almost got more on my plate than I can handle."

"I take it that's not a complaint."

He motioned with his head. "I'd rather be busy than bored."

What he didn't tell Rockwell was that the lumber strike holding up completion of the hundred units in Palo Alto was killing him. The subs were demanding their next payment for payroll, but the bank wasn't making distributions, because the next phase hadn't been completed yet. A typical construction Catch Twenty-two.

To make matters worse, he had shelled out option money on some multiple-unit acreage, both in Visalia and Hanford, that he couldn't move forward on, because no bank was going to loan him additional money for land purchases when he had two unfinished projects and one on the boards. In short, Andrew Mullin was in a cash crunch and was teetering between financial ruin and developmental success, depending upon how the cards fell the next few months. He needed this project, more than he wanted Harlin to know.

He had fudged a little on his financial statement to keep Northwest Financial from digging too deeply into his current developments; otherwise, they might not have funded the prison project at all. He had been in the developmental game all his life. Financial ups and downs were just part of the process.

Harlin Rockwell withdrew a document from the folder. He handled it gingerly with two fingers, as if it were a letter bomb. He slid the contents across the desk to Andrew Mullin. "Here's the letter of commitment from Northwestern, Andrew. We're willing to give you a twelve-million-dollar construction loan, ten percent interest for two years. Two points."

"Two points! That's two hundred-forty thousand dollars! And I thought we agreed that you were only going to charge me eight-and-a-half percent." He laid the papers down. "What's going on here, Harlin?" This was the typical cat-and-mouse game that borrower and lender typically played when mega-dollars were at stake, especially when the State of California was footing the bill!

Harlin Rockwell shifted uneasily in his chair. Dora Hutchenson turned her chair towards Mullin, then slowly crossed her legs and arched her chest.

Mullin wasn't about to be distracted with such cheap tactics. He held his stare steady on Rockwell's face.

"The cost of funds have been going up, Andrew," he explained, lamely. "Besides, the State's paying for the project. Why be concerned?"

"Why be concerned? I have to make this baby work, that's why. If I have cost over-runs, you're not going to have to be the one to go to Governor Wilson and ask for more money. He's going to tell me that I made a contract with the State of California to build their correctional facility, and if I underbid it, that's my problem. I can't live with two points, nor ten percent interest, Harlin. It's as simple as that." Mullin shoved the letter back across the desk without even reading it.

"Maybe I can get the committee to add the points to the back-end of the loan," Rockwell offered lamely. "That way, you won't have to come up with any up-front money to fund the loan."

"Except architectural fees, permits, environmental studies and appraisal reports, all of which have to be in and paid for before you'll give me the loan." Mullin shook his head. "I'm sorry. Two points just won't cut it." He wanted this project, but he'd been around the construction block more than once, and if he had learned one thing, it was to have *all* your costs covered and included in your bid before committing yourself. "And don't forget, I have to make a profit, too," he added.

"Come on, Andrew, we both know you'll make between ten to twelve percent on this deal. That's one point-two to one-point-five-million bucks in your jeans." He looked at Andrew Mullin, as if to say, "Come on, who do you think you're fooling?"

"Have you ever seen a construction project come off as-bid?" Mullin retorted. "Take the hotel in Palo Alto and the five hundred units in Fresno." He knew he was on thin ice here, but it was necessary to make this man aware of the dangers of building a large complex like this too thinly capitalized. "With the lumber strike alone, I'm losing ten thousand dollars a day!" He breathed heavily, emphasizing the point. "How long do you think it would take for my profits to disappear at that rate, and that's not counting cost over-runs, labor disputes, plus God and nature stirring the soup from time to time. And you want to charge me two points and ten percent!" He shrugged his shoulders. "I'd rather pass on the deal, Harlin."

He knew that Rockwell had more on the line than just making the loan. He had the reputation of his company doing future business with the State of California.

Harlin was in a corner and couldn't afford to call Mullin's bluff. "All right. Tell you what I'll do. I'll slip you a half of a point on the back-end of the loan in the form of a consultation fee."

Andrew Mullin knew that was how the big boys justified their fees, by "slipping back some of the borrower's own money," as they liked to call it. In pure and simple words, it was payment under the table. The IRS wouldn't look too kindly at that part of the transaction if they ever got wind of it—and they never would. Mullin wouldn't report it as income, because it was his own money being refunded, and the lender wouldn't want to explain faking a high-front-end loan fee only to give a portion of it back to his borrower. Somehow the whole thing would get washed through the transaction, with labels such as promotional fees, advertising or travel expenses.

"And the ten percent?" He wasn't going to give up that easily. A percentage and a half over a year on the full-bore loan would equate to a hundred and eight thousand dollars, although he knew it would be less than that, because the lender only charged the borrower on the amount funded to date. It was common practice for financial institutions to hold back funding until certain stages of construction had been finished. That way the builder couldn't "go south" with the unused funds halfway through the project, as had happened with amazing frequency during the Sixties.

On the other hand, the more points and interest Rockwell could charge a borrower, the more money the company made, and the better he looked in his investors' eyes. It was a perpetual rolling ball, from borrower to lender to investor. Rockwell took a deep breath. "I'll see if I can get the Committee to cut back to nine-and-a-half," he suggested.

Mullin took a deep breath, more for effect than anything. "Make it nine and I'll do the deal."

Rockwell rolled his eyes. Dora uncrossed her legs and arched her back again, expanding her chest and glancing soulfully in Mullin's direction. Mullin paid no attention, even though her expanded chest was noted through his peripheral vision. His facial expression gave no indication that he was bluffing as he fixed his eyes on his adversary. He remained as stoic as a man about to be executed.

Rockwell made a gesture with his mouth. "I'll see what I can do," he said, finally. "You're a good customer, Andrew. I'll do my best for you." He rose to shake Andrew Mullin's hand.

Dora Hutchenson squirmed, then slid off her chair, adjusted her mini-skirt and realigned her breasts as they led Mullin into the outer office. "Be back in touch real soon," Rockwell said, giving Mullin a wink, as if that was supposed to mean something.

Dora Hutchenson blew him a kiss, then negotiated the distance between the door and Rockwell's office, her hips looking like a cat in a bag about to be thrown in the river. *Sure would like to be a fly on the wall in that office after hours,* Mullin thought as he smiled and closed the door after himself. *I'll bet a day's pay Harlin gets his hands full behind closed doors.*

Andrew Mullin was satisfied with the final negotiations. He knew that he had the clout of the Governor in his corner. His election might very well depend on getting the new correctional facility constructed. If Northwestern wouldn't make the loan, there were certainly other lenders that would love to get in the Governors jean's by getting his endorsement on their letterhead.

* * * *

There was a thank you package of fruit in a basket with a maroon and white ribbon on Andrew Mullin's desk when he returned from San Francisco. The note inside read, "I thoroughly enjoyed our time together. If you ever need company on one of your trips, give me a call. And my undying gratitude for your generous gift to the church." It was signed Pastor Aaron MacAffie.

"Myrna, get me Mr. MacAffie on the phone, will you?"

When Mullin called, MacAffie was sitting in his office with Nevenka talking about Lithuania's session from the Soviet Union. The topic seemed to fascinate him. "This is a personal call," he told her when his secretary advised him that Mullin was on the line. "Would you excuse me for a moment? This man needs private consultation," he lied. "I'll only be a moment, then maybe we can go out and grab a sandwich. I'll show you around town."

He didn't want Nevenka in the room when he talked to Mullin, because he thought the reason Mullin was calling was to inquire about the mistyped county on the Quit Claim Deed. Instead, he was pleasantly surprised when Mullin asked him if he would like to accompany him to the construction site in Fresno the following day.

"I'd be delighted." MacAffie wiped his damp hands on his pants. "Usual time and place?"

* * * *

Aaron took Nevenka to Mark's Tea Room for lunch, a quaint little bar and grill located on the main street of town. "I thought I would stop off at the market before we go back to the office, and pick up something for supper. You don't mind, do you?"

"I'd love to go with you. I've never been in an American market before. Will the lines be long?"

MacAffie laughed. "If what I've read about shopping in Russia is true, you're in for a surprise."

* * * *

The entrance to the store led directly into the vegetable section. From the moment they walked into the store, Nevenka couldn't believe her eyes. There were rows and rows of fresh fruits, vegetables and nuts. She just stood there, transfixed by all the food. And there were no lines! As a matter of fact, there couldn't have been more than a dozen people in the entire store!

She walked over to the produce section, expecting to be stopped at any moment. Aaron MacAffie watched with intent interest, not saying anything. She ran her fingers over the apples, feeling the firm, cool texture of their skin, then picked up a bunch of bananas and held them to her nose. She picked up a head of lettuce and squeezed it, then ran her fingers through the bin of walnuts.

She turned to MacAffie. "I just can't believe it! Is it always this way?" There was a look of disbelief painted on her face, as if this were all just a put-on for her benefit.

"What do you mean?"

"I mean, is there always this much food? Why aren't people buying it all up? Is anyone allowed to come in here, or just select people?"

MacAffie laughed. "No, this is a public store. Anyone who wants, can come in, even if they don't have a job or money. And yes, there's always this much food. I forget that food isn't plentiful in Russia."

"Or Lithuania."

"Same thing. Come on, I'll show you around the rest of the store."

Her mouth was open as they walked up one aisle and down the other. She picked up a package of pasta, then a can of soup, then spices, looking at them as if through the eyes of a child who had never seen toys before. "I just can't believe it." She gasped. "All this food. How many stores are there like this? Is this the only one?"

MacAffie laughed. "There are several in every town, sometimes one on each commercial street. There's big ones like this and small ones like the 7–11."

"7–11?"

"That's a chain of small stores that carry only limited things, like coffee, dairy products and a few staples, just in case you need only one item and don't want to stand in line just for a pack of cigarettes or a quart of milk."

She shook her head in disbelief. "America! I can't believe it! Why doesn't everyone live here?"

"I think many would like to, but we have immigration laws. One has to qualify before coming to America."

"Like I did?"

He smiled. "Yeah. Like you did. Come on, let's pick out some chicken for dinner."

*   *   *   *

The following morning, Aaron MacAffie pulled into Andrew Mullin's driveway. As soon as Mullin saw him, he came out the house with his briefcase to meet him before he had even turned off his motor. "Want me to drive?" Aaron offered.

Mullin smiled as he looked at MacAffie's Volkswagen, then shrugged his shoulders. "Why not? It's been a hundred years since I've been in one of these things. Do they still sound like a washing machine and ride like a tractor?"

"Worse."

At the airport, MacAffie paid special attention as Mullin checked the struts of the plane, the outside cables and the hose connections underneath the bonnet. "Ever find anything wrong?" he inquired, peering over his shoulder.

"No. But it's always good to check. All the cables have double lock nuts," he said, pointing out one of the wind flaps to MacAffie. "So it's near impossible for any of them to come loose. Nonetheless, it's always good practice to just walk around the plane and check, anyway. I did find an oil leak once," he said, lifting the bonnet for MacAffie to see the motor. "Got to maintain oil pressure and keep the hydraulic pressure up, or else the pistons in the hydraulic motor that moves the flaps can't move."

"I can imagine that could cause one to pause for concern."

Mullin laughed. "If you intend to land or turn, it could. He slammed down the bonnet, and hitched it up tight. "Ready?"

Chapter 25

▼

Aaron MacAffie was studying the artist's rendering of his proposed building structure the next evening when Nevenka entered his study. "What have you got there?" she inquired, looking over his shoulder.

"Oh! This is going to be my next church, our next church," he corrected himself as he moved so she could have a clear view of the rendering.

"Oh, this is pretty!" she exclaimed. "I've never seen a round building like this. Where are you going to build it?"

He tried to repress the sly smile that uncontrollably crept across his lips. "I've got my eye on a particular piece of property, but the opportune time to acquire it hasn't presented itself just yet."

She could tell by the glazed look in his eyes that he was totally enthralled with idea of building his project. She was impressed. She had never known anyone capable of owning such a building, let alone of designing and building one. "It looks like a lot of property," she said, looking over his shoulder. "Is it close by?" She noted the name of the street which was printed at the bottom of the rendering. She thought she remembered seeing a street with that name the previous day, when they had been out driving to the store.

"Closer than you think," he said, almost to himself.

"You said the time wasn't right. When will the time be right?" she inquired, naively.

He shrugged his shoulders. "There's ah…a couple technical things that need working through before the property will be available," he said, rolling up the plans. "I hope to have the building underway within the year. Now then, let's talk about us."

"Us?" A cold shiver ran down her spine. She knew quite well what he was driving at, but had hoped to postpone the discussion—preferably indefinitely.

"Yeah. I figure you've had a few days to get your feet on the ground. Maybe it's time we talked about the future. That is why you're here, isn't it?" He smiled as he extended his hand to her to sit down. So far, he had given her plenty of space, not rushing her, allowing time for her to feel comfortable with the situation. By the same token, there was a strain of insecurity flowing through his veins that told him he had better not wait too long. After all, she was a beautiful woman, one who could probably have anyone she wanted. He, on the other hand, was aware of the fact that he was a short, balding, moderately attractive man who would have to take what he could get. And he wanted Nevenka.

It was difficult having her in the same house, in the bedroom, right next door, yet not able to touch her. He desired her, in the worst way. He hadn't even kissed her yet!

She nodded with a lack of enthusiasm.

MacAffie noted her hesitation. "I just want you to know that I'm not pressuring you or anything like that, but, well, you know…" He shuffled his feet. "It's a little embarrassing to talk about."

She nodded with a shy little smile. "I understand. In Russia, many years ago, it was not uncommon for parents to decide who their daughters and sons were going to marry—with or without their consent. Sometimes a daughter married a man three or four times her age. That custom has long been—how do you say—done away with?"

"Abolished."

She nodded. "Yes. Abolished. I know how you must feel. Do not be embarrassed. I understand. I entered into the contract as well as you," she offered. "And I want you to know how much I appreciate the kindness you have shown me." She folded her hands in her lap and smiled. She had extended herself as far as she was going to. The next move would be Aaron's.

He simply smiled nervously and said, "Yes. Well, perhaps I can arrange to find some time alone to ourselves, away from this place, where we can get to know one another a little more."

"That would be nice." She greatly appreciated being treated like a lady. Before coming to America, her greatest fear had been of having being sent to a man who had no feelings outside of his own immediate gratification. She had seen enough of that in Russia.

* * * *

Aaron MacAffie didn't sleep much that night. His every thought was consumed by Nevenka...of having her. His loins ached for her. He lay there in bed alone, thinking how nice it would be to make love to her, to have her snuggle next to him, her nude body pressing against his while he caressed her velvet skin. The thought so dominated his mind that it took several hours for him to finally get to sleep.

The following morning at breakfast he suggested that they take the day off and drive down to Carmel. It was in the middle of the week, and there would be a minimal number of tourists on the streets and in the shops, he explained.

"This Carmel. It is a resort?" she asked, after he had described it to her.

"It sits right on the ocean," he explained. "Carmel is one of the crown jewels of California. You'll love it there." He smiled at her. "There's even a beach called Lover's Point," he said, touching her hand, hoping this would convey his intentions.

"Sounds delightful. What should I wear?"

He knew that, although it was summer, it could get cold there. He encouraged her to dress lightly, nonetheless. Worst case, she could cuddle next to him to keep warm.

Fortunately, for Nevenka, it was a warm, sunny day as they entered the gate of the Seventeen Mile Drive, where a uniformed man occupied the guardhouse.

"That will be ten dollars please."

"You have to pay to drive along the beach?" She looked at him in amazement as he took out his wallet and gave the man some money. "In Lithuania, the beach is free."

Aaron laughed. "It's free here, too. It's just that this is a very wealthy, private community and they want to control the amount of traffic that flows through here."

Nevenka's eyes were filled with amazement as Aaron pulled off the road to show her one cove after another, where they admired waves crashing against huge boulders, splashing aqua-colored mist high into the air, causing rainbows as the mist reached for the sky. "How beautiful!" she exclaimed. Her facial expressions were childlike...excited, yet simple.

"I told you you would enjoy it." He beamed. He pulled his Volkswagen onto a small patch of dirt just off the side of the road, where a grove of cypress trees was growing. "Come on, let's walk down the path. There's a private little beach that I discovered the last time I was here." He picked up a picnic basket from the back seat of his Volkswagen. "I brought a little something for us to enjoy."

The path wound past a lone cypress tree standing high on a pile of rocks, like a centurion guarding a city. Halfway down, the path all but disappeared, then suddenly opened up to a small, secluded beach with clear blue water lapping at crystal-white sand.

The moment Nevenka set foot on the beach, the sight took her breath away. "Take off your clothes, er, shoes." He grimaced at his Freudian slip. He kicked his tennis shoes off, then waded into the water. "Oh, that feels good!"

Before he could turn around, Nevenka was standing beside him. She bent down to scoop up a handful of sand, letting it fall between her fingers. She was wearing a pair of blue cotton shorts with a loose fitting blouse with a scooped neck.

"The water is much warmer here than at home. Cleaner, too," she said, putting a handful of water to her lips as she closed her eyes, savoring the feeling of the cool water.

Aaron couldn't help but notice that when she bent down the front of her blouse exposed her breasts, which caused an immediate reaction within his body.

"Come on, let's wade out a little," he said, encouraging her, hoping she wouldn't notice his erection.

She grabbed his hand as they waded out to their waists. Then, much to his surprise, Nevenka plunged head-on into the sea, taking a couple graceful strokes before standing up again, chest-deep. She laughed as she waded towards Aaron. The water made her blouse all but transparent and the cold sea made her nipples stand erect.

Aaron couldn't take his eyes off her. He knew right then and there that he had to have her, right here on the beach, no matter what the cost.

He tried to act nonchalant as he swam to her, making every effort to stay in front on her. He was unable to take his eyes off of her. They played in the water, splashing one another and laughing like children until they were exhausted. Then they waded back to the beach, hand in hand, still laughing.

"Here, I brought a blanket," he said, spreading a red-plaid Pendleton car blanket over the warm sand. "This sand is nearly impossible to get off when it sticks to you. Let me dry your hair," he said, kneeling behind her, gathering her long, blond hair in the towel, rubbing it briskly.

Just the act of touching her hair got him aroused again. He couldn't resist the temptation. He lifted her hair off her neck, then gently pressed his lips to the back of it. The touch of her skin felt so good!

Nevenka had never had any one pay quite as much attention to her in the same manner that Aaron did, and, although she had no feelings for him, she did allow herself to enjoy his touch. When he kissed her neck, her first reaction was to pull away, but discretion convinced her to remain calm.

Since Nevenka didn't seem to object to his advances, Aaron took that as a sign of approval. His next move was to softly caress her neck while still kissing her, then work his way over to her ear. From there, it was a short distance for his hand to slide down to her firm breast.

Nevenka closed her eyes and tried to imagine Vladimer touching her. Aaron laid her down on the blanket and began to kiss her softly, but passionately.

She resisted slightly at first, then let her starved sexual feelings have their way. This was the man she had come halfway around the world to marry, she rationalized. Be sensible. It was either this or the Red Army.

Within moments, Aaron had slipped his hand inside her pants and was caressing the soft down of her pubic hair. She moaned slightly as he felt inside her. She didn't resist as Aaron quickly unzipped her shorts, then slipped them off. He removed his own pants, then slid between her legs, slowly lowering himself onto her. She cried out slightly at first as he penetrated her. It had been some time since she had been with a man...Vladimer Ryzhkov, to be exact.

Her mind reeled giddily as he rhythmically made love to her, slowly at first, then with greater thrusts as passion and pure animal instinct took over. When it was over, he continued to lay on top of her, breathing heavily, suddenly at a loss as to what to say or do. This wasn't just a strange fling on the beach. This was the woman he had chosen to be his wife. "Are you okay?" he finally asked sheepishly, rolling over on one elbow.

She nodded.

"I'm...I don't know what to say. I don't know what got into me. I..."

She put her hand to his mouth.

He pressed her hand to his lips and a tear rolled down his cheeks. "I've never felt this way about a woman before," he confessed. "I know we've just recently met and, well, even so..." He held both her hands in his and got in front of her on his knees. "Would you marry me?"

She looked at him with a puzzled look. "I thought that was why you brought me here, to America?"

"It is. It was. I mean, I don't want you to think that you're obligated to marry me just because you're here. I mean, I want you to, you understand. It's just that..."

It was obvious that he was stumbling over his words. She had never had anyone make such a fuss over her, and she was flattered. Nevenka looked at the man beside her, on his knees in the sand, his dome glistening in the sun. This is not the man she intended to spend her life with, but she had come to convince herself that it was time she looked out for herself. The fact that she was carrying an unborn child inside her never left her thoughts for a moment's time. It was the welfare of this child that she must concern herself.

Vladimer was probably dead by now, and, even if he wasn't, she was certain that she had just been one of many insignificant conquests in his life. Helena was a living example of that truism, she was certain.

Life must go on. There was no life for her in Russia, which was where she would end up if she didn't marry this man. And in Russia, she knew her fate would be sealed by being thrown to the Red Army as a plaything. Helena had made that fact clear. As for her family, she would just have to hope for the best.

"What do you say?" Aaron persisted. "I don't want to rush you," he said holding her hand, "but if you could find it in your heart to be my wife, you'd never regret it."

She lowered her eyes. "Aaron. There is something I must tell you."

He sat down in the sand, looking into her sweet, innocent face. This was the most beautiful woman he'd ever seen. And she was here to be his wife! He was almost afraid to ask what it was she wanted to tell him.

"I am pregnant," she said, slowly and deliberately, not wanting to look into his eyes.

MacAffie fell back on the sand, supporting himself with his hands.

She closed her eyes, and a tear rolled down her cheek. "It was in Russia. The Red Army had killed my brother, and they were going to kill me, too. They took me and raped me. When they fell asleep, I escaped!" she lied. "This lady I told you about found me and took me in and gave me shelter." She kneaded her fingers in the sand. "I needed to escape. That is how I come to be in America." She looked into his eyes. "I am sorry to have deceived you. Can you forgive me?"

"Sorry? Why would you be sorry? It was you who were raped!" He reached for her, cradling her in his arms, caressing her wet hair. "You ought to be screaming mad!"

"I feel like I am, how do you say, damaged goods?"

"Don't even think like that. It could have happened to anyone. I admire your courage."

"You still want me?"

He held her at arm's length for a moment. "What kind of a man would I be if I condemned you for something that you had no control over?"

"Thank you," she said softly, then kissing his hand.

It was a moment before MacAffie spoke. When he did, his voice was one of concern, not condemnation. "Did you think about getting an abortion?"

"In Russia, there was no abortion. The Red Army had all doctors working on soldiers. There was no one to help."

Tears were flowing freely now. Nevenka knew there was no way he could verify or disprove her story. The truth as she told it was out and she was safe. The only question that remained: would he change his mind?

MacAffie held her at arm's length to study her face. It was so beautiful, and yet simple. He smiled to himself. She needed him almost as much as he needed her. Being pregnant forced her to be dependent upon him. He gently pulled her into his arms. "Don't worry. I'll take care of you. You're safe now."

He held her for several moments before asking, "How long ago?"

"Three months," came the simple reply.

"Well then, I guess we had better tie the knot soon, or tongues will wag."

She pulled away to look at him. "Tongues will wag?"

He laughed. "It's an American expression. It means people will talk."

"Oh. I see."

"So, I assume, you'll marry me?"

She smiled at him. "I would be honored," she said, taking his hand and pressing it to her breast.

CHAPTER 26

▼

They planned on leaving for Reno the following Sunday after church to get married. "I hear that the old MGM Grand Hotel is nice," he told Nevenka. "I think it's called a Hilton Hotel now. One of my staff said they have a beautiful chapel there. Are you excited?"

She smiled, but the smile masked her true feelings. All along, she had known that the reason she had come to America had been to get out of Russia to save her life. Ever since Vladimer had told her that she would be marrying an American, she had known. That didn't make it any easier. She would make the most out of it, though. After all, she had her baby to think of.

"Yes. It is exciting."

They pulled into the entrance of the Reno Hilton hotel at four-thirty in the afternoon. She had never seen such a grand entrance. They drove under the huge canopy which was the entrance to the hotel. A valet parked their car and a bellhop took their luggage. The moment they walked through the glass doors which were the entrance of the casino-hotel, the room buzzed with excitement. Bells and buzzers were sounding as gamblers hit jackpots on the electronic slot machines. A group of people standing around an oblong table was yelling as a young woman dressed in ski clothes threw dice down the table. There were mirrors and lights everywhere. It was the first time since her landing in New York that she had felt such a pang of excitement.

MacAffie registered with the hotel, and then they followed the bellhop up to their room. The room contained a large, round bed with a blue velvet covering. There was a small television in the bathroom, as well as in the main bedroom, and they could see the mountains towards Lake Tahoe.

When the bellhop had left, there was a moment of discomfort, as they were unsure what to do next. Finally, MacAffie said, "Tell you what, why don't you freshen up first? I'll take a walk around the casino and try my luck for a half-hour or so, then, when I come up, I'll change and we'll check out the chapel.

She was grateful for the time alone. She sat in the club chair next to the window, just staring out at the mountains, wondering what Vladimer was doing at this moment. Probably sleeping, she thought to herself as she smiled, visualizing his face. I wonder if he's sleeping alone? She shook her head and addressed the task ahead—preparing for her wedding.

✸   ✸   ✸   ✸

They walked down the large circular staircase that had mirrors on each wall, and on the ceiling, as well. A chandelier twelve feet in diameter hung from the ceiling, illuminating everything like a Hollywood movie set. "I feel like a princes descending the stairs of my castle," Nevenka gushed as she admired herself in the mirrored walls.

Aaron kissed her fingers. "You are a princess and this is your castle."

The wedding chapel was located at the end of a long corridor that was lined with boutiques selling everything from cut-glass figurines to old-time movie memorabilia. Nevenka enjoyed looking in the shops, seeing things that she hadn't even imagined existed.

The chapel was occupied by a couple who had just finished being married. They kissed one another, then rushed out the door, giggling. The bride had on a white wedding dress and carried a bouquet of white baby's breath and ferns. The groom wore striped pants, a black coat with tails and had a high hat with a matching cane, making him look as if he had come straight off a wedding cake.

Aaron and Nevenka looked at each other knowingly. He was dressed in his "preachers suit", a black suit with a white shirt and red tie. She wore her white cotton dress, the same one that she had worn when she had first met Vladimer Ryzhkov in Palanga. It was the only nice dress that she had. "I didn't even buy you flowers," Aaron said. His voice was guilt ridden.

"It's not important. Flowers will only wilt and die. It's the marriage union that's important."

MacAffie squeezed her hand. "I love you. Are you sure you don't mind—getting married here, I mean? I thought it best that we not get married in our church…the baby and all. You understand."

She nodded. "I understand. It's all right. It is for the best that we do it this way. This way, how do you say? Tongues won't wag."

They both laughed, and walked into the chapel. It was their turn.

The ceremony lasted all of ten minutes. The minister's wife played a small organ while the minister read the words from a sheet of paper that he had pasted inside of a Bible. Words that he knew by heart. Words that he had read a dozen times a day, every day since they had opened the business—and that was what it was, a business. "I now pronounce you man and wife. You may kiss the bride."

They signed the wedding certificate, and MacAffie paid the man a hundred dollars. It was done: They were now Mr. and Mrs. Aaron MacAffie. Somehow, the act seemed to be anti-climatic. The euphoric buzz that they had expected seemed to be missing. It was all so...sterilized and commercialized.

"Well, what would you like to do now?" he said, looking at his watch. It was only six-thirty. Too early to retire, too early for dinner and too late to go for a drive. "Would you like to roll a few bones?"

"Roll bones?"

He laughed. "Gamble. Would you like to gamble?"

She shook her head. "I don't know. I have never gambled before. How do you do it?"

"Have you ever played cards?"

"Yes. Sometimes, in Lithuania, we play this game called..."

"It's the same here. We call it Blackjack, or Twenty-One." He explained how to play the game by adding up numbers, allocating ten to the face cards and one or eleven to the Ace. "And then we have the slot machines. Maybe that would be more to your taste."

"The slot machines. Yes. I would like that, I think."

"All right. I'll play a little craps and you can do the machines. We'll see who makes the most money."

"Aaron?"

"Yes?"

"I don't have any money," she said apologetically.

"I'm sorry. I can give you fifty dollars. That's all I can spare. If you lose that, then I guess you're done for the day."

"That's a lot of money. Do you know how much fifty American dollars is in rubles?"

"Try not to think about in those terms. Here," he said, giving her two twenties and a ten-dollar bill. "There's a change girl. Just give her a twenty and ask for quarters. Then you can play any machine on this row. I'll be right over there," he motioned with his head. With that, he disappeared towards a group of screaming people who were gathered around a table where a man held a thin, curved stick and was scraping the chips off the table, saying, "Seven out! Don't come players and last on the come line wins."

Nevenka was putting in one quarter at a time, even though the machine allowed for up to three per pull of the handle. The first time, she hit three cherries. Ten coins spat out, and she was delighted. A moment later, three bells came up. Eighteen more coins came out. She squealed with delight as she scooped them out of the metal tray.

"You've got a lucky machine there," a husky male voice said from behind her.

She turned around and gasped at a tall handsome man with flowing blond hair stood behind her.

"I'm sorry. I didn't mean to frighten you."

"Oh, no. It's all right. For a moment there, I thought you were someone else. What is it you were saying?"

"The machine. It likes you. Stay with it and it will open up to you."

"Open up?"

He laughed. "It'll give you a jackpot."

She smiled, then gave him one more look before turning back to her machine. He was too good-looking to ignore, but she didn't feel comfortable talking to a stranger.

"You're not from here, are you?"

She glanced over her shoulder. He moved to the machine next to her and began putting in three quarters at a time. "No. I'm from Lithuania."

"Oh. A Russian. How long have you been in this country?" The tone of his voice was pleasant; not accusatory or unnecessarily probing, simply a gentle inquiry.

"Just a short time."

"And do you like it here?"

"Yes." She didn't want to encourage him to keep talking. Not because she didn't like him. Just the contrary. She was attracted to him. Maybe it was because he reminded her of Vladimer Ryzhkov.

"If you put three quarters in at a time, it will increase your winnings," he said as she hit a single cherry and the machine spit out three quarters. "You have a good machine there. May as well take advantage of its generosity as long as its in the mood to give." He smiled as he slipped in two of his own quarters after she had inserted just one again.

Three bells showed up on the face of the machine, and thirty-six quarters spit out. "See what I told you?"

She smiled and grabbed a handful of the quarters that had deposited themselves in the tray and handed them to the man.

"What's this for?"

"I would not have won them had you not put the two other quarters in the machine These are yours."

He laughed, and he gently cupped her fingers around the coins. "My pleasure. They're all yours."

She felt a sudden blush cross her face when his hand touched her. His hand felt like an electrical charge shot through her, turning on all her systems…the ones that had been lying dormant ever since she had left Russia. It embarrassed her, as she was sure it was obvious how she felt. She quickly diverted her eyes. "Thank you," she replied with a soft voice.

Time suddenly stood still as she continued putting coins into the machine. Suddenly, bells started ringing and coins were spitting themselves into the mental tray, clanging as they announced their arrival.

"You've hit the jackpot!" the man said, putting his arm around her shoulders, squeezing her.

Without thinking, Nevenka automatically tilted her head until her cheek touched his. Realizing what she had done, she pulled away and, for the first time, looked deep into the stranger's eyes. Their eyes locked, with messages being transmitted between them, ignoring the continued ringing of the machine's bell and the coins spilling out onto the floor.

"Looks like you hit the jackpot," the attendants voice said, breaking the trance that they were in. "Two-hundred-fifty dollars! The machine will pay you fifty dollars, and here is the two hundred," he said, handing her two crisp one-hundred-dollar bills.

"Is that you that's making all this noise?" MacAffie came walking up behind her, patting her on the back. He saw the bin full of coins and the two hundred dollar bills in her hands. "Congratulations! You're certainly doing better than me."

When the attendant had left and she had put the coins into a plastic pail provided by the casino, she looked around for the stranger. He was nowhere to be seen.

* * * *

After they had returned home that Tuesday night, MacAffie sat in his office thumbing through the mail while Nevenka unpacked and drew a bath.

"There's a letter from Lithuania," he said, handing it her. "It's probably from your mother."

She slit the envelope open and quickly read the short note, then let out a scream.

MacAffie came running into their bedroom. "What is it? What's happened?"

Tears were streaming from her eyes as she handed him the letter, although he couldn't read a word of it, because it was written in Lithuanian. "It's my father. He's dead."

"Oh, I'm so sorry," he said, cradling her in his arms, stroking her hair. "Is there anything I can do?"

She shook her head, unable to speak.

"How did he die?"

She sobbed, then took a deep breath. "My mother said he died of a broken heart."

MacAffie said nothing, but continued comforting her.

"I told you the Red Army killed my older brother. We are a very close family. When I left Russia, my father was so depressed I think he willed himself to die. He missed my older brother very much."

Chapter 27

Four months later

Aaron MacAffie rose from his desk, went to his file cabinet and removed the manilla folder which contained a single document, the Quit Claim Deed to the Shasta lot that Andrew Mullin had signed. He examined it for a moment, then carefully removed the lightly Scotch-taped legal description that he had added to the document prior to having Andrew Mullin sign it.

He went to his secretary's typewriter and carefully typed in the legal description of Andrew Mullin's ten-acre estate. He used the description that he had obtained from the preliminary title report that he had gotten from Sue Gillis at First American Title and Trust Company in San Jose five months previously, when he had obtained copies of blank Quit Claim Deeds.

When he had finished typing, he removed the document from the typewriter and held it at arm's length. It looked genuine. The same typewriter that had written the Grantor and Grantee and the date was now the same typewriter that had typed the legal description, and it had been signed by Andrew Mullin and notarized by his secretary five months previously.

He smiled to himself when he read the part that recited the county. "Santa Clara County," he said aloud.

It was perfect. The only flaw that gnawed at him was that copy that Myrna Lee had made when she had notarized the document. It had recited lot 106 of Mullin's Lake Shasta subdivision. Surely, he rationalized, she had filed it long ago, and, since he had never head from Andy, he was certain that it had been all but forgotten.

The next day, he drove down to the San Jose County building and walked into the Recorder's office at Seventy West Hedding Street. He filled out the necessary papers, listing information about the transaction for real estate tax purposes, paid the transfer fee in cash and handed the clerk the Quit Claim Deed. Once the clerk took his money and stamped the deed for recordation, there was no turning back.

Back at the parish, he had no sooner walked into the office, when Nevenka advised him that one of his parishioners had been involved in an automobile accident and had been transported to San Jose Hospital. Apparently, she was in a coma and wasn't expected to survive the afternoon. The family had requested that he come right over and minister to her.

Nevenka was now seven months along in her pregnancy with Vladimer's child, and although Aaron had urged her to stay home and take it easy, she insisted on working at the office. "I've got to do something to keep busy," she had said. "I go crazy, sitting home, watching American television game shows and soap operas about women who cheat on husbands."

The way she had of describing things always made him laugh. "If work is what makes you happy," he had said, patting her stomach, "then, by all means, work."

"Working at the office makes time go by quickly. Besides, I have much to learn."

"This is the part of the job that I don't like, Nevenka, running off to hospitals and funeral parlors. It's too damn depressing," he said as he threw Mullins file on his desk. "I'll return as soon as I can!" he yelled over his shoulder to his secretary. "If something comes up you can't handle, just take a message."

Nevenka watched as he rushed out to his little yellow Volkswagen. She smiled to herself with pride in her husband as the motor chirped and he drove out of the parking lot. She was about to close the door to his office when she noticed the file that he had flung onto his desk. Part of the contents had slipped out and lay face up. *I may as well file it,* she thought to herself as she picked it up.

Instinct or curiosity made her look at the document, then at the file that was labeled Shasta lot. Her eyes paused as they fell on Andrew Mullin's signature. She became even more confused when she read the legal description that designated the large measurements of a Los Alamos property—the same property she had previously seen on his church rendering. She shook her head and dropped the document into the large filing drawer of her husband's desk.

* * * *

Two months later, Nevenka had to stop working. It was nearing the last month of her pregnancy. It had not only become too difficult for her to perform the simplest of office duties, such as filing documents, but the Pastor was becoming nervous when anyone asked when she was due. It was just a short mathematical calculation to figure out that the child had either been conceived out of wedlock or that she was prematurely large. The last thing MacAffie wanted anyone to know was that the child wasn't his.

He had purchased a beeper to carry with him whenever he was out of her sight. If she had an emergency, her water broke or she started having cramps, she was to dial MacAffie's number on the beeper, followed by 911. This was their prearranged signal that it was time to go to the hospital. No matter where he was or what he was doing, he promised to be by her side within minutes.

That day came three weeks later, when he was in a staff meeting in his office. The beeper he had leased not only beeped, but vibrated. When it went off, it shook him up so much that he rushed out of the meeting without so much as telling anyone why he was leaving, although he assumed that they could figure that out for themselves. For those who weren't aware of the circumstances of his rapid departure, one might have suspected he had an imminent case of diarrhea.

* * * *

A healthy boy was born to Aaron and Nevenka MacAffie at El Camino Hospital in Mountain View. MacAffie paced outside in the waiting room, declining to be present during the birthing process. Once the baby was clean and the mother comfortable, the doctor came out and shook Aaron's hand. "Congratulations, Mr. MacAffie, you are the father of a healthy boy. All of the parts are there and he has a healthy attitude toward life." He laughed as he opened the door to the maternity ward.

In the room, Nevenka was cradling her child in her arms, smiling with satisfaction. "We have a boy, Husband."

Aaron MacAffie looked down at her robust, fair-skinned, blond-haired son as he yawned. He touched the baby's hand with his forefinger. Feeling the touch, the child instinctively took hold of it, squeezing tightly.

"Strong little tyke, isn't he? What shall we name him?"

"If you don't mind, I would like to name him after my grandfather, Vladimer Ryshkov."

He frowned slightly. That wasn't the sort of name that MacAffie had in mind. "Vladimer. Doesn't that sound too…Russian?"

"He is Russian," she said, looking at Aaron firmly. Her look suddenly softened. "In our country, it is customary to name the first-born son after our grandfathers. In Russia, Vladimer is a strong name. Very honorable."

"What's the second part?" He wrinkled his brow. "Riski?"

"Ryshkov."

"That's a first name?"

She smiled. "No. That was his grandmother's last name before they were married," she lied. "We honor both grandparents, the grandfather and the grandmother. It is our custom to so name them. That way they will not be forgotten."

MacAffie nodded. "I see. Well, I guess I can live with Vladimer. In America we don't use middle names that much, anyway. For all intents and purposes, it'll be Vladimer R. MacAffie." He smiled as he patted the little boy on the head.

She took his hand and smiled. "Thank you, Husband. Thank you for everything."

Six months later

"Pastor, there's a call for you on line one. It's Andrew Mullin."

"Andy! What a pleasant surprise! What's up?"

"I just wanted to remind you that we have a barbecue date at my place tonight."

"Wouldn't miss it for the world."

Andrew paused for a moment. "I have to fly up to Lake Shasta tomorrow," he said, offhandedly. "Meeting with the soils engineer. I thought you might care to join me."

MacAffie thought for a moment. He was interested in going, but he had pressing business at his desk that required his attention. "Gee, I'd love to Andy, but I've got meetings set up all day tomorrow that demand my attention. Thanks for the offer, though. Maybe next time."

"I'll let you fly," Mullin said, trying to entice him. MacAffie had come to love flying, and Mullin knew it. It was an underhanded trick, but what the heck. He wanted the company.

"What time you leaving?"

"The usual time. Seven A.M."

MacAffie paused for a moment, his mind suddenly racing ahead. The palms of his hands started to sweat and his heart pumped rapidly. "Sorry, Andy." He tried to control his voice. "I'll have to catch you on the next go-around. Thanks anyway."

"It was just a thought."

"Oh, speaking of dinner. I don't think Nevenka will be able to make it," MacAffie apologized. "Little Vladimer's got a touch of the flu or something."

"Well, then, I guess that makes it a guy's night." Mullin laughed. The inflection in his voice told MacAffie that he preferred it that way, anyway. He wasn't all that fond of children.

"I've got a stop to make in San Jose before I come over. I should be there around six."

"I'll have the baked potatoes waiting and the barbie hot. I thought we'd have a Caesar salad with our meal. That okay with you?"

"Perfect. I need to cut down on my caloric intake, anyway. A steak, baked potato and salad sounds perfect."

* * * *

"Nevenka. I've got an appointment with Andy Mullin this evening to discuss some business matters. I'll grab a bite with him, if you don't mind, so you'll have to make dinner for just yourself and Vladimer."

He seemed a little nervous as he went to his study to get his briefcase, but she attributed that to his busy schedule. "That's fine. Are you sure you don't want me to fix you something before you go?"

He shook his head. "I could be late, so don't wait up for me."

MacAffie's first stop before going to Mullin's place for dinner was the San Jose Airport. He parked his Volkswagen in the short-term parking lot, next to the terminal. He locked his car and walked to the Hertz car rental station.

A perky, young girl with a big smile inquired, "May I help you, sir?"

He was nervous as he looked around, making sure that no one saw or recognized him. It would never do to have one of his parishioners see him at the airport, then ask why he was at the car rental agency.

"I reserved a car. Aaron MacAffie."

She looked on the board behind her, where folders had been filed for car reservations. "Oh, yes. Here you are," she said, picking up the folder with the name MacAffie boldly printed in large black lettering. "You requested a compact car?" she asked, looking inside the folder.

"Yes."

"We're holding a Nissan for you. One moment, please." She typed his name in the computer. "Driver's license?"

He fumbled through his wallet, then handed it to her.

"This is your current address?"

"Yes!" he said sharply, then caught himself. *Don't make a scene*, he told himself. *Just get registered and get out of here!*

"Will you be needing insurance?"

"No, thanks. I don't plan on doing much driving."

The computer whizzed for a moment, then spit out a long, printed legal form. She handed him the rental agreement, with his name, address and license number already printed. "Just sign here and initial in the red circle where it indicates you decline insurance. You understand that you'll be responsible for any damage done to the vehicle?"

MacAffie nodded, and signed and initialled the agreement.

"Do you want to put this on your credit card?"

He was tempted to pay cash, but greed made him respond, "Yes. Here," he said, handing her his Visa card. By charging the rental car, he could be reimbursed from the church for the rental. If questioned by the bookkeeper, he'd simply say his car had been in the garage for repairs and he had to rent a car for the day. *Another reason to teach Nevenka to do the books,* he thought to himself.

"Your car is parked in slot forth-three. Just go out those double doors and to the right. There will be a man waiting to assist you."

"Is it black?" he inquired, handing her back the form "I specifically requested black."

"Yes, sir. Just as you requested. Will you be needing it long?"

"Just for the evening. I've got a late appointment in town. I should be back before midnight."

"Will you be needing a map of the city, Mr. MacAffie?"

He shook his head without further response and walked through the double doors.

Twenty minutes later, Aaron pulled into San Jose Blueprint's parking lot and headed for the Commercial Reproduction Department.

"Can I help you?" asked the young girl dressed in blue jeans and a baggy white sweatshirt with San Jose State imprinted on it.

"MacAffie. Pastor Aaron MacAffie," he said. "I've got some plans to pick up."

A moment later, the young girl returned with a long cylinder with a blue sheet wrapped around it with a rubber band. "Cash or charge?"

"Charge it. I've got an account here. The Living Christ church."

Moments later, he was on his way to Andrew Mullin's house for his steak dinner.

* * * *

Mullin had the barbecue red-hot when MacAffie arrived. Sitting on the side of the grill were two huge T-bone steaks. "You're just in time," he said as MacAffie stepped out of the Nissan. "The coals are hot and I'm famished."

"Me, too. This has been an exhilarating day." He smiled nervously.

"What's this?" Mullin asked, nodding towards the black car. "New wheels? Business must be picking up."

"No. The bug is in the hospital, getting a set of new tires and brakes. I just rented this for the day."

Mullin nodded. "I assume you got all your errands run?" he asked. The steaks sizzled as he slapped them on the hot grill.

"All done," he said with a sly smile.

"You seem especially pleased with yourself tonight," Mullin said, picking up on MacAffie's look. "You look like the cat who swallowed the canary. Anything you care to share?"

"It's a surprise. You'll know in time." He smiled as he popped the cork out of the tall bottle of wine that Mullin had sitting on the table.

* * * *

After dinner, Pastor Aaron MacAffie had one final errand to run before he returned home. It was well past ten o'clock when he left Andrew Mullin's house. He had been careful not to drink much wine, because the task that lay before him required that he maintain all his wits about him.

He drove the Nissan to the San Carlos airport, then backed the car up next to the six-foot galvanized-wire fence by one of the metal hangers, taking great care that no one had seen him. He sat in the car for several minutes, watching for any movement, listening to be sure that no one was around. When he was satisfied that he was alone, he removed a flashlight and two nine-sixteenth-inch wrenches wrapped inside a cloth that he'd had in his briefcase.

After taking one last look around, he made a mad dash out onto the tarmac, towards Andrew Mullin's Cessna 172. It was tied down in its usual spot. He stopped, crouched down by the tire, and watched and listened for a moment before quickly going around to the tail of the plane. There, he grabbed the right-hand tail flap and moved it with his hand, shining a small beam from the flashlight he held between his teeth. The light exposed the cable that was attached to the tail flaps.

On his knees, he quickly loosened, then removed, the outer lock-nut, then threw it as far as he could. He then loosened the other nut, so it was just held by a couple of threads. He tested the flap again to be sure it still worked, then ran back to the black Nissan.

His hands were sweating and his heart pounding so hard he had to put his hand over his chest in a vain attempt to slow it down. He was in a hurry, and couldn't remember where the ignition was on this car. He didn't want to turn on the interior lights, for fear someone might see him, so he fumbled around until he finally located the ignition, then started the car and jammed it in gear.

There was a loud crash! In his haste, he had become confused and had slipped the gear into reverse! He slammed the car into drive and sped from of the parking lot, leaving his lights off until he reached the street, just in case someone might have seen or heard him.

*   *   *   *

The small man dressed in dark-green checkered clothing and wearing a beret had followed Aaron MacAffie from his house to Andrew Mullins, then had parked outside his gate while they had dinner. *Enjoy your food, fool,* he thought as he watched them through high-powered night-vision binoculars. *Tonight you die!*

When MacAffie had gone into San Jose Blue Print, there had been no opportunity for the man in the beret to finish the job, and when he had rented a car at the airport, then drove on to San Carlos Airport, he had been too fascinated with what he saw to kill him, although that would have been the ideal spot to finish the job. When he had watched MacAffie sabotage the airplane through the night-vision binoculars, he hadn't been able to believe his eyes. He had waited until MacAffie had left, then he'd gone out onto the tarmac to see what he had done for himself.

Since Matty McGown had erroneously killed Pastor Magnason and the organization back home had later learned that Macafy had gotten away, he had been instructed that under no circumstances was anyone besides Macafy to perish by accident. The organization received a sizeable monthly donation from their American constituents. The one thing the Irish didn't need was adverse American publicity. It had taken all this time to track him down again, and the man had been advised that, if he messed up again, he needn't bother to come home.

* * * *

Traffic on the freeway was light that time of night. Nonetheless, MacAffie made sure he stayed within the speed limit. His heart nearly jumped out of his chest when he saw the red light flashing in his rear view mirror.

He didn't have a clue as to why he was being stopped. He knew he had been observing the proper speed limit. The only thing he could think was that someone had seen him at the San Carlos Airport and had reported him. Now what was he going to do?

A thousand thoughts raced through his mind as he watched the Highway Patrol officer approached the driver's side in the rear view mirror. "May I see your Driver's License and registration, please?" he demanded in a polite tone.

MacAffie tore out his wallet, and fumbled for his Driver's License as he searched the officer's face for the clue that would tell him how much trouble he was in. "This is a rental car," he said, handing the officer the registration from the glove compartment.

"Would you step to the rear of the car, please?"

This is it. I'm going to be arrested, he thought as he made his way to the back of the vehicle. For a brief moment he contemplated running, but knew that was futile.

"Your tail light is broken," the officer said, writing something in his book. "This is a fix-it ticket. Because you are driving the vehicle, it's against your diving record. You need to be sure that the car rental agency takes care of the broken tail light, otherwise your license may not be renewed when it becomes due."

MacAffie had to hold onto the car to prevent his knees from buckling. "Yes, sir. I'll take care of it. Thank you, sir."

The officer returned his license and registration and gave him the fix-it ticket. "Drive careful, ya hear?"

Once MacAffie got back to San Jose Airport, he pulled the black Nissan up in front of the car rental return space. He looked around for an attendant to return the keys and explain about the taillight, but no one was around that time of night. He scribbled a note on his contract, explaining the broken tail light, and dropped it, the fix-it ticket and the keys in the automatic check-in return, then briskly walked across the street to short-term parking, where he had parked his Volkswagen.

A few moments later he was back on the freeway, heading for home, still shaking from the experience.

✱ ✱ ✱ ✱

Matty McGown had parked his car at the airport, and used a public phone. This way, if the line to Ireland were tapped, no one would be able to trace the call. "You stab 'en, we slab 'em," came the answer when he dialed the international number. "Arthur's Funeral Home."

"Lemme talk to King Arthur."

"Who's callin'?"

"Matty McGown."

There was a long pause, and a curt voice answered. "I told you to never use this line! This had better be important!"

"I thought you might like to have a progress report on our man."

"What I want to hear is, 'Our man is dead!' I trust that is the case?"

"I just located him yesterday, and I haven't been able to make the hit. Did you know that he's a bloomin' minister?"

"A minister?"

"That's right. A man of the cloth. He's not Catholic, mind you. His church is called The Living Christ Church."

"Is it a scam?"

"I don't know. But listen to this." He proceeded to tell him what he had seen MacAffie do to Mullin's plane with his own eyes.

"That is a might peculiar and very interesting. Sounds like our friend is diggin' himself his own grave." There was a pause while he was thinking. "Maybe there's something there for the cause. This man may become more valuable alive than dead."

"What do you want me to do?"

"Keep an eye on him and don't, under any circumstances, let him identify you. Do I make myself clear?"

"Crystal clear, Arthur."

✱ ✱ ✱ ✱

Aaron MacAffie undressed in the bathroom, looked in on little Vladimer, then quietly slipped into bed, taking care not to awaken Nevenka. He was in no mood for idle chatter.

"How did your meeting go?" came her sleepy voice as he settled in.

"Oh, fine. Sorry to wake you, Nevenka."

She patted him on the shoulder. "I never go to sleep until you're in bed."

He didn't sleep much that night. His mind was busy with thoughts of the previous evening and what was about happen the following day. At five-thirty AM, the alarm went off. He jumped out of bed, and threw on a pair of tennis shoes, jeans and a sweatshirt.

"Where are you going in such a hurry?" Nevenka asked, shielding her eyes from the morning sun.

"Go back to sleep, Nevenka!" His voice was sharp. "I've got an early morning appointment. I'll see you at the office."

Ten minutes later he was on the freeway, heading back towards San Carlos. It was only a twenty-minute drive at that time of the morning, but he wanted to get there early. He didn't want to take a chance on having Andrew Mullin leave early and accidentally seeing him on the freeway. That would never do.

It was six-twenty when he pulled off the freeway and onto the side road that went around San Carlos Airport, feeding traffic to the various research and development buildings. He picked a spot by a clump of trees, where he could have a clear view of Andrew Mullin's blue-and-white Cessna 172, then parked his car.

He was calm now, but for some unknown reason, his hands were shaking as he held the eight-power, Minolta wide-angle binoculars to his eyes, searching the grounds for any movement. Here and there pilots drove onto the tarmac, parking their vehicles next to their planes, getting ready for their trips.

MacAffie looked at his watch. Six-forty-five. *Andrew Mullin should be pulling onto the tarmac at any moment,* he thought. The longer he waited, the more nervous he got. He already regretted what he had done the night before and was about to drive away when Mullin's white Jaguar came into view.

He pulled up next to his Cessna, got out of his Jaguar carrying his briefcase, set it on the wing of the plane, then went through his routine of checking out the exterior of the craft. MacAffie held his breath as he saw Mullin round the tail of the plane, give the flaps a quick pull, onto the front wing to complete his tour of the craft. Satisfied that everything was as it should be, he climbed in, went through the checklist, then started the engine. A moment later he was rolling down the runway.

MacAffie waited until the plane was in the air, climbing through the clouds, before he slowly drove away. Mullin's fate was now in the hands of the gods.

* * * *

Now that I'm awake, I may as well get up and get dressed, Nevenka thought.

Aaron's late night meeting with Mullin, and now this early get-away, had disturbed her. She went to his desk to see if he had left himself a memo regarding today's meeting. She was surprised to see his briefcase still sitting on the chair.

Nevenka snapped open the lock on his briefcase and withdrew his appointment book. There was nothing scheduled for early morning. She was curious about the bulky red cloth that was bound by a large rubber band. Carefully, she removed the rubber band and unwound the cloth. She stared at the flashlight and two wrenches that the cloth had concealed. Puzzled, she re-wrapped the items and returned them and the appointment book to the briefcase, then replaced it where she had found it.

* * * *

At nine o'clock, a young man wearing a red Stanford sweatshirt parked in the church parking lot and walked into the parish office. He carried a long cylinder under his arm. "Aaron MacAffie, please?"

Nevenka said that he was out at an early appointment. "Can I help you?"

"Mr. MacAffie left these plans in our car last night. I'm sure that he would want them back."

"Your car?"

"Yes. He rented an automobile from us, and forgot to take his belongings when he returned the vehicle. I work for City Delivery Service. I was given this to deliver."

Nevenka took the package, looking puzzled. "Thank you."

* * * *

That evening, before he went home, Aaron MacAffie withdrew the plans from the San Jose Blue Print cylinder and spread them out on his desk. He had been so preoccupied with the previous night's activities that it hadn't even registered that he had left them in the rented car.

His eyes sparkled as he looked at the artist's rendering of a domed structure with a cross prominently displayed on its peak. The laser-cut sign prominently displayed in front of the structure read, The Living Christ Church: Pastor Dr. Aaron MacAffie.

Chapter 28

Andrew Mullin had much on his mind as he drove to the San Carlos Airport. In a way, he was glad that his friend Aaron MacAffie wasn't accompanying him on this trip. It would give him time to think through the several financial problems that had been plaguing him relative to his various projects, especially the detention facility to be built for the state of California.

Construction on the correction facility was finally nearing completion. He would only make a hundred-eighty-thousand dollars on the deal. far short of his original projection. The points and increased interest rate that Northwest Financial had charged him had dug into his profits, but not as much as the steel union going on strike right in the middle of construction. That delay alone had cost him nearly two-hundred-thousand dollars in interest payments on his loan. In addition to that, they lost precious time which should have been spent completing the job. Instead, the workers were sitting around waiting for steel beams to be delivered from Pittsburgh Steel.

The hundred-fifty unit apartment building in Hanford was finally finished and he was expecting Northwest Financial to roll its four million, two-hundred-thousand dollar construction loan into permanent financing, as agreed. Two months prior to filing a notice of completion, however, Northwest had been gobbled up by a larger firm in New York. As a result of the take-over, the new administration had fired all of Northwest Financial's staff and advisors, installing their own team in their place.

When Andrew Mullin had received his letter from the new parent company, rescinding their commitment to issue permanent financing, he had been livid. The first thing he'd done was contact his attorney regarding his legal position.

"Why don't you come on over?" Mark Snyder had said. "Bring the letter and your file with you. Maybe there's a mouse hole the bastards forgot about."

Once Mark had read through the documents, he shook his head. "Do you want the good news or the bad news?" he asked cynically.

"What's the good news?"

"I think you may have a cause for action against these bastards."

Mullin's face lit up. "That's great. And the bad news?"

"You'll probably lose."

"Lose? I thought you said I had a case!"

"You do, but…"

"Well then, what's this 'you'll probably lose' bullshit?"

"I read about this company in the Wall Street Journal, Andy. They specialize in buying two types of paper: loans that are in serious default and loans where property values have fallen far below the loan balances, where the borrowers have substantial net worth. What they do is buy bad or delinquent notes from the banks for pennies on the dollar, then go after the borrower for deficiency judgements on the whole amount.

"In most cases, the borrower has signed the loan documents and personally guaranteed payment. He doesn't have a leg to stand on. When the New York boys send their legal staff after them, they crumble like yesterday's cookies and either make restitution on the full amount of the loan or bite the bullet and make arrangements for monthly payments until the outstanding principal balance, including legal fees, is retired. Either way, the lender makes an unconscionable return on their investment."

"But that doesn't apply to me," Mullin responded angrily. "I'm not in default!"

"You're not? You're the other category that they like to deal with. They know they've got you over the barrel. You've not only got your life's savings tied up in this deal, but your construction loan is due, and they know it, because they just bought the loan. If it's due, you're in default!"

Mullin looked like a cornered mouse

"Let's face it. They'd like nothing better than to take over your finished product for the amount of your unpaid principal balance. How much profit is there? They'd simply sell the building and make themselves a handsome profit."

"Can they do that?"

"Andy, they've got so much money, and their three floors of New York attorneys can throw so much paper at us, they'll bankrupt you in legal fees alone: depositions, show causes, request for documents, court appearances, answering complaints, ad nauseam. They've got you backed into a corner with nowhere to go, and they know it!"

"Bastards!" Mullin paced the floor for a few moments. "So what do we do?"

"As I see it, you have two choices: walk or deal."

"Great choices."

He shrugged his shoulders. "That's the trouble dealing with these mega-bucks banks. If they want to stick it to you, you have to bend over, grab your ankles and smile, like you're enjoying being screwed."

Mullin left Mark Snyder's office totally discouraged. Not one to take a beating sitting down, he decided to call the firm that had made him the loan: Northwest Financial. He asked to speak to Harlin Rockwell, but was told that he no longer worked for the company. "Well, give me whoever is in charge!" he barked.

A few moments later, a soft, feminine voice came on the line. "This is Miss Adleson. Can I help you?"

He knew immediately it was the old, pass-the-buck routine, but he launched into his tirade anyway. "This is Andrew Mullin," he said with very little control. "I'm in receipt of a letter of commitment from your company, giving me permanent financing on my apartment project in Hanford, and now I get…"

"One moment, please," came the obsequious voice, interrupting his tirade.

He swore as she put him on hold. He was getting hotter under the collar by the minute.

"Dunagan here," came a strong, in-control, male voice.

Mullin took a deep breath and started all over again. He was only halfway through his explanation when the man interrupted. "Do you have a loan number?"

Mullin recited the number.

"One moment, please."

He waited patiently for five minutes, until the voice returned. "Yes, Mr. Mullin. I have a copy of our correspondence in front of me. The letter Northwest Financial issued you at the origination of your construction loan has been rescinded and is no longer valid."

A redundant statement, Mullin thought. "How can you do that? Don't you know that you'll give me no alternative but to either sue you, or turn the apartment complex over to you? You know, as well as I, there's no permanent financing available in today's market. I relied on that loan!" The money market had dried up three months ago, and there were virtually no construction loans available, at any cost, for any period of time.

"I'm sorry, but you see, Northwest Financial has been absorbed by the Hong Kong Bank of New York Trust and Realty Investment Corporation." He was in control and knew it. His voice conveyed that fact to Mullin. "Northwest Financial is no longer an existing entity."

A foreign bank, no less. "So, what you're telling me is that you no longer intend to honor your commitment."

"The parent company is not honoring previous commitments made by Northwest Financial, sir" he said simply. The "sir" carried a condescending, insulting tone.

"So what am I supposed to do?"

"I can give you an extension on your loan for twelve months," he offered with a tone synonymous to giving a homeless person one's leftovers.

"And what would that cost me?"

"I could let you have it for a point."

Andrew Mullin took a deep breath to calm himself. "Let me see if I've got this right. You expect me to pay forty-two-thousand dollars to extend a loan that I have a written commitment to roll over into a permanent loan, without a fee?"

"Sixty months," the man responded simply, ignoring Mullin's sarcastic comments. "At ten percent per annum," he added.

"What! Five years! What the hell am I going to do with a five-year loan?"

No response came from the other end of the line.

"I'll get back to you!" Mullin had slammed the receiver down so hard that he cracked the telephone. That had been yesterday.

Andrew Mullin had all these things on his mind as he walked around his Cessna, going through his routine inspection, not even paying attention to what he was doing. After having completed his unconscious exterior inspection, he climbed into the cockpit and verbally ran through the checklist before opening the side window, sticking his head out and yelling, "Clear!"

Moments later, he was climbing to an altitude of three thousand feet, where he leveled off. It was a clear day and he was glad to be in the air. Flying was one of two forms of psychotherapy for Andrew Mullin. The other was construction.

Before long, he sighted Mount Shasta. The long fingers of Lake Shasta lay before him.

He saw the usual array of houseboats lazily making their way through the calm water. He slowly pushed in the yoke and started his descent.

As was his usual practice, he aimed for the mountain before banking right to prepare for his landing on the small landing strip. As he banked, the plane suddenly jerked violently, then veered to the left. He turned the wheel, but there was little response. Suddenly, everything was washed from his mind except the fluttering craft that held his life. Something had broken loose, he surmised as he tried to pull up. The plane wasn't responding.

He was too low, and was heading towards the tall pine trees when he realized he was going down. He automatically flipped on the radio and sent out the message: "Mayday! Mayday! This is Charley Alpha Mary niner-one-niner Cessna 152 on route to land at Shasta! Mayday! Control trouble…"

The plane hit the top of the first Douglas fir, flipping it over onto a smaller tree ten feet away. The wings snapped off as the fuselage threaded between two eighteen-inch tree trunks. The fuselage then plummeted straight towards the ground. The plane exploded on impact, blowing bits of the cockpit and everything therein over a hundred-foot area. The underbrush caught on fire, igniting the trees. Within moments, a small forest fire was raging out of control.

* * * *

Aaron MacAffie was sitting in his church office when he glanced at his watch. "Turn on the television, will you, Nevenka? Channel Five! I want to watch the six o'clock news."

He intently watched the television as Nevenka studied him. This was the first time since she had come to the office to work that she had seen him this intense, or that he had turned on the television, for that matter.

As he watched the news, he saw something that sent a cold chill down his spine. "There is a forest fire raging out of control in Shasta County," the newscaster was saying. The camera, apparently mounted on a helicopter, panned over burning trees, sending smoke into the atmosphere. "The fire was apparently caused by a downed airplane. Just before ten o'clock this morning, there was an emergency call indicating that a private plane had apparently been experiencing engine trouble. The call came from a pilot whose name is being withheld, pending notification of next of kin. It is unknown whether anyone survived the incident, but it is thought, from looking at the crash site, that it is doubtful that there were survivors. And, in the unlikely event there was a survivor, the fire would surely have gotten him.

"The exact cause of the accident is unknown at this time. Aviation officials indicate that they will be unable to get to the crash site until the fire is contained, which is estimated to be late tomorrow afternoon. This is Thomas Switchzer, from channel Five news."

Aaron MacAffie sat staring at the television set with his hands grasping the arms of his chair. Nevenka noticed that his knuckles were white from pressure. The newscast was still on, but, his mind had blanked out all connection to the outside world. He shuddered as his mind visualized the charred body of Andrew Mullin, still strapped inside the Cessna. He wondered what had gone through his mind those last moments before he had lost his life.

Had he suffered much? When had he known that he was going to die? There was a great burden of guilt hanging over MacAffie's shoulders that he hadn't anticipated. He had killed a man! Not directly—not with his own hands, of course, but nonetheless, he was responsible for the death of another human being—one that had trusted him. A friend! It didn't even occur to him what wrath God might inflict on the soul of one responsible for such a brutal act.

He sat there for a few more moments, his mind fully blank. He blinked only when Nevenka said, "Are you all right, Aaron? Your face looks pale."

He nodded slowly. "Yes. Yes, I'm okay." His voice seemed to have lost all of its vitality. "You can turn the television off now, thanks."

She studied his ashen face as she turned the set off. She sensed that something critical had happened, but could assign no significance to the forest fire. It did surprise her when he asked, "Would you excuse me for a moment, Nevenka? I would like to be alone, if you don't mind." There was a tear in his eye.

After she left, MacAffie sat in silence for several minutes, then slowly pulled the deed to Mullin's house out of the file. He held it in his hands as he examined the recorded document for a long moment. This deed was the only link between Andrew Mullin's death and himself, he thought as he looked at it. Although he had recorded it, it still wasn't too late to deed it back to Mullin, he thought. Maybe no one would be the wiser, but the vision of building his own church had so clouded and dominated his every thought for the past year, ever since he had met Andrew Mullin, nothing short of certain incarceration would alter his thinking. No, he had started out on this course of action. He was determined to see it through.

He replaced the deed in the manilla folder and, for the hundredth time, picked up the cylindrical tube that contained the floor-plans of his new church. His eyes glazed over as he looked at the plans. He had designed the interior to be built like a theater in the round, on a revolving stage, where he would be the center of attention at all times. The pulpit would be constructed of rich oak, constructed dead center, jutting twenty feet from floor level. The first four tiers, or layers, up from the congregation would be reserved for the choir and orchestra.

The next level would be for guest speakers and honored staff. Nevenka and his son would sit there, where they could admire him.

His parishioners had to be comfortable, so every seat in the temple was to be padded. The carpet would be deep crimson, of course. Aside from the simple cross at the top of the structure, the exterior of the building would give the illusion of a visiting space ship. He wanted it to be dynamic, outstanding, even outrageous.

He envisioned television cameras projecting his words to every television set on the West Coast. Eventually, people would come to know him the world over. Everyone would send donations, buy his books and seek his guidance.

He would be rich!

Pastor Aaron MacAffie would be king of the evangelists!

CHAPTER 29

▼

"In Russia, the whole family mourns the loss of a friend or loved one," Nevenka said, cradling little Vladimer as she noted her husband's apparent lack of sorrow over Andrew Mullin's death the following day after the name of the pilot who had crashed at Shasta had been released.

He shrugged his shoulders and made a face. "We weren't really that close," he rationalized. "When you're a pastor of a church, if you take the loss of every parishioner who passes away personally, you'll end up a basket case yourself. One has to learn to handle these matters objectively. They happen."

"But, he was your friend! You had dinner at his house. He took you on all those airplane rides. How could you not be close? Are all Americans so cold and distant that they keep their feelings to themselves?"

Since the loss of her brother, then subsequently her father, and Vladimer, of course, she had come to appreciate the value of friends and family. Should anything every happen to little Vladimer, she wouldn't want to live, she thought, cradling him to her breast, kissing him on the forehead.

✳ ✳ ✳ ✳

Pastor Aaron MacAffie presided over the funeral of Andrew Mullin. It was a beautiful morning. The dew was still glistening on the freshly cut grass. The sweet, pungent smell of flowers filtered through the air as the mourners gathered around the brushed-bronze casket which stood suspended above a fresh mound of dirt that, although it was covered with a green tarp, still had the hint of a musty odor.

Nevenka stood near her husband, holding little Vladimer in her arms, facing those in attendance. This would be her first funeral in America. She would be very interested to see how her husband conducted himself.

Local dignitaries and friends were present, along with Mullin's ex-wife Connie and their two children. Connie Mullin was an attractive blond woman who was well groomed and obviously took pride in her personal appearance. Her hair was cut short and she wore little makeup. She wore a black dress that was cut to just above the knees and a neckline that was slightly lower than what would normally be considered in good taste for a funeral. Around her neck she wore a heavy gold chain. A panda bear, China's symbol, dangled just above her pronounced cleavage. She seemed to be in remarkably good physical condition for her age, as demonstrated by her muscle tone and the color of her skin. He noticed several of the men in the galley eyeing her during the service, but they apparently had the good breeding not to approach her. Besides, she had her two children accompanying her and this, obviously, was not the time to play amorous games.

He also noted, with great pride, that Nevenka was the recipient of a lot of attention, as well. Many of those in attendance had never seen this beautiful, young, blond woman, and were shocked to learn that she was MacAffie's wife, and that they already had a child. Where had she come from, everyone wondered?

During the emotional eulogy, Pastor MacAffie spoke of Andrew Mullin's generosity to his family and friends, then launched into a short dissertation alluding to the generous legacy that he had left the church. He simply wanted to plant the seed against confrontations that he knew would follow…events that only he knew existed. He didn't press his luck by elaborating on the topic any further.

*   *   *   *

The will hadn't been read yet, but presumably, the children and his ex-wife were sure they would inherit his home, which, by now, was prime Los Alamos property. Then there were all his developments, the apartments, Lake Shasta and whatever other holdings he'd had that they weren't aware of. Little did they know that Andrew Mullin had ben up to his neck in debt when he had been killed and had been one step away from personal bankruptcy. People would later come to speculate that it was this despair over failing business matters that had driven Andrew Mullin to take his own life.

MacAffie had concerns of being investigated himself, because he was in possession of the deed to his home. He had thought the matter through several times, however, feeling comfortable with the logic he would eventually give those who would question him: that Mullin had deeded his house to Aaron MacAffie and the Living Christ Church for reasons only Mullin knew. Who could dispute the wish of a dead man?

But now, of course, everything was only speculation. Perhaps, knowing that he was deeply in debt, and having made the decision to end his life, Mullin had given the property to the church to protect it from creditors. Perhaps Mullin had wanted the church to have his house, knowing that MacAffie would made good use of it. One could even speculate that, having deeded it to the church, it had been his way of atoning for taking his own life. Whatever the reason, people would have to be satisfied that only Andrew Mullin knew the answer to these questions.

Pastor Aaron MacAffie felt relatively safe with this line of reasoning. Nonetheless, that didn't quell the butterflies that churned in his stomach. He was certain there was no way anyone could tie him to Andrew Mullin's death. No one had seen him at the airport messing with the Cessna, of that he was certain. And, everyone knew that he and Mullin had become fast friends.

He had carefully planned all of his moves, down to the minutest detail. Oh, sure, people would speculate, especially family members, that he had exercised some sort of power over Mullin's mind, but when they would think on it, they would know that no man could have power over Andrew Mullin's brain.

And what if someone asked why he had waited four months to record the deed? The answer was simple and irrefutable. Mullin had requested him to do so…or that he had waited because he didn't know any better.

Still, the copy that Myrna Lee had made of the original Quit Claim deed to the Shasta lot bothered him. If asked to produce it, he even had an explanation for its lack of existence. He lost it!

*   *   *   *

"Pastor. There's a phone call for you from a Mr. Adam Horwitz. He says he's an attorney representing the Mullin estate.

He had been expecting this call ever since the funeral. He just wasn't ready for it. He probably never would be, but knew it would be good to finally get it over with. "Pastor MacAffie," he answered with a calm, professional voice.

"Mr. MacAffie?"

"Yes, this is *Pastor* Aaron MacAffie." He put the emphasis on "pastor", wanting to set a professional tone for this conversation.

"This is Adam Horwitz, Pastor MacAffie. I'm an attorney representing Connie Mullin. This is in reference to the Andrew Mullin estate. We've been going through his documents, and it's come to our attention that there appears to be a conflict with one of his properties that seems to concern you." He waited to see if there was a response. Upon hearing none, he continued. "Could you come over to my office, say, tomorrow at nine o'clock, to discuss the matter?"

"Is this something that we can clear up on the phone?" He'd rather not get locked in an office with some shark from the legal profession if he could avoid it.

"No. I'm afraid this requires your personal attention."

"How long do you expect the matter to take? I've got a hectic schedule myself."

"I'm not sure. It all depends on how much light you can shed on a particular matter. Maybe an hour, give or take."

MacAffie paused. He knew there was no way he could avoid seeing the man. If he didn't go voluntarily, it could get ugly. He didn't want it to escalate into a court battle. The publicity alone would be devastating. He shrugged his shoulders. "I'll be there at nine sharp."

"Good. Oh, Mr. MacAffie?"

"Pastor."

"Excuse me, Pastor MacAffie," he corrected himself. "If you access to have legal counsel, I'd bring him along."

"Are you telling me that I need an attorney?"

"No, it's just that if you have counsel, you might want him to be present. There are some issues that…"

"I think I can answer most of your questions without concerning myself with legal consultation," he said, confidently.

"Very well. Hold on for a second. I'll give you back to my secretary, and she can give you instructions on how to get here. One moment!"

A form of power play, MacAffie thought. *No reason why he couldn't give me instructions himself. He wants to impress me with his importance.*

* * * *

MacAffie was led into a conference room that gave the impression of a human fishbowl. All the walls were glass, with the exception of an adjoining office wall. There was a large conference table in the middle of the room, with three leather captain's chairs on either side of the table and one at each end. "Mr. Horwitz will be with you in a moment," the secretary said, smiling. "Can I get you anything to drink?"

"Maybe a Pepsi, if you have one."

"But of course."

Before she returned, an elderly gentleman with a full head of grey hair and a bushy mustache entered the room, followed by the ex-Mrs. Mullin. They had caught Aaron MacAffie off guard with her presence, but it was not totally unexpected.

"I assume you know Mrs. Mullin?" Adam Horwitz asked.

"Yes," he said, standing to extend his hand. "We were introduced at the funeral. How are you?" he inquired.

She nodded, and stood her ground, not taking his hand, nor verbally acknowledging him.

"And I'm Adam Horwitz," the lawyer said, extending his hand.

"Your Pepsi," the secretary said, handing a glass full of the brown liquid and ice to Aaron MacAffie.

After everyone had been seated, Horwitz said, "I'll get right down to business, Mr. MacAffie." He opened a blue manilla file, laid it on his desk, then folded his hands. "As you may recall from my previous conversation, Mr. MacAffie, this concerns the Andrew Mullin estate." He paused to look at his client. "His residence, in particular."

His eyes studied MacAffie for a response. When none was forthcoming, he continued. "We seem to have a conflict relative to that property. On the one hand, we have Mr. Mullin's will, which, among other items, leaves his residence in Los Alamos to his two children. That will was dated May 28, 1985. Then," he flipped over some pages in the file, "let me fast forward to eighteen months ago, when he deeded the property to a Corporation located in Panama. We researched that corporation, and found that it was owned by another corporation located in the Cayman Islands. The sole asset of that corporation was Mr. Mullin's residence." He looked at Aaron MacAffie to be sure he was following. "Any questions to date?"

"Not that I can think of." He smiled. "This is all over my head. I assume there is some relevancy here?"

Horwitz ignored his inquiry. "Subsequent to Mr. Mullin's untimely demise, further research indicates that he was in deep financial difficulty and was probably about to go under. Do you see a picture forming here, Mr. MacAffie?" His voice was acidly caustic.

MacAffie starred at the file, not knowing what to say, so he said nothing.

"Then, we have this document." He handed a copy of a Quit Claim Deed to MacAffie. It was a copy of the deed that he had altered to change ownership from the lot in Shasta county to Mullin's residence. MacAffie felt the blood rushing to his head. He knew there was nothing to be done now except keep his cool, say as little as possible and ride the wave.

MacAffie handed the paper back to Horwitz without comment.

"We were hoping that you might help clear up a couple of areas that have us confused. First, could you describe the circumstances under which Andrew Mullin happened to give you a Quit Claim Deed to his house?"

MacAffie made every attempt to remain calm and maintain control over himself as his feet were about to be put to the fire. Despite this, his face became flushed, red all the way to the crown of his balding head. He shrugged his shoulders. "Well, I guess I met Andrew Mullin when I first came to town. I can't recall the exact circumstances under which we met, but, through a period of time extending through several meetings, it came to my attention that he seemed to be an individual reaching out for some stability in his life. You might say that we were drawn together like a moth to a flame."

"Who was the moth and who was the flame?" Horwitz said, making an attempt at sarcastic humor.

MacAffie ignored his comment, and instead looked at Mrs. Mullin, as if trying to make her understand that her ex-husband had needed his guidance badly. "As we got to know each other, we became close, almost inseparable friends. He would take me to his job sites, when he flew to Hanford, Fresno and, of course, Lake Shasta. Sometimes he would even let me fly his plane." He smiled, trying to add an air of lightness to his dissertation.

"Yes. And the house?" Horwitz asked, glancing at his watch, projecting that he was impatient.

Maybe he is late for a racquetball game down at the athletic club, MacAffie thought as he observed the obvious gesture.

"Could you describe the circumstances under which Mr. Mullin gave you a deed to his house?" Horwitz pressed.

"If you'll bear with me for a moment, I'm getting there."

Horwitz looked agitated, but said nothing. Mrs. Mullin grimaced. She wanted to know where this was going too.

"Well, apparently, according to Andrew, as you have already alluded, things weren't going well for him business-wise. He didn't exactly tell me what was on his mind," he added quickly, knowing that Horwitz would be following up with a question about his knowledge of Mullin's intimate business dealings. "But I could tell by his demeanor that he was under a lot of pressure and had a lot on his mind. Then, he began confiding in me. He told me things of a personal nature, things that bothered him a lot…about his family," he lied.

"Could you be more specific?" Horwitz pressed.

He looked at Mrs. Mullin, but addressed Horwitz's question. "I'm afraid not. Confidentiality, you understand."

"But, the man is dead!" Horwitz exclaimed, his apparent agitation increasing. "You can't break the confidence of a man who no longer exists!"

MacAffie smiled slightly. "All the more reason, Mr. Horwitz. A man's soul is nothing to trifle with. His body may be on Earth for only a moment, relatively speaking, but his soul lingers on forever. To violate the confidences he entrusted to me would, well, be unforgivable."

Horwitz snapped his pencil, for effect more than anything, thinking that he could intimidate MacAffie, but MacAffie knew that the umbrella of the pastoral cloth protected all confidentialities, and he planned on using it to its very last stitch.

"So, why don't you tell us about the Quit Claim Deed?" Horwitz pressed.

MacAffie took a long sip of his Pepsi, and swished it slowly in his mouth as if formulating his next thought. "During the time I had the privilege to know Andrew Mullin, he also came to know God."

Horwitz breathed deeply. He knew that MacAffie had him dancing on a string and there wasn't a damn thing he could do about it, except listen and hope that he erred.

"I can tell you this: Andrew Mullin felt that his asset would be best used by giving it to the Lord."

"So you had him deed the house to you? Is that it?" Horwitz snarled.

"Actually, no, that's not exactly how it happened." He looked at the ceiling, as if trying to recall the instance precisely. "This particular day, he called me to meet him at this deli that he liked to go to. Eric's?"

Horwitz nodded. He knew it well, a health-oriented deli that served sandwiches and homemade soup. He also knew that from a meeting with Mullin there, there would likely be no witnesses overhearing their conversation, if indeed there had ben a conversation.

"When he sat down, he handed me this piece of paper. The large lettering at the top read Quit Claim Deed. 'What's this?' I asked. 'The deed to my house,' he responded. When I quizzed him about it, he simply said that he wanted the church to have it when he passed away."

"That's it?" Horwitz exclaimed, almost coming out of his seat in disbelief.

"Actually, no. There was one condition."

"And that was?" Horwitz looked at his client with raised eyebrows.

"That whatever usage the church gave to the land, there was to be a memento acknowledging Andrew Mullin."

"A memento?" Horwitz couldn't believe his ears.

"Yes. You know. A plaque, sign or some declaration that showed that he had deeded the property to the church."

Horwitz looked at his client with obvious disbelief. "And he just gave you the deed to the property and told you this."

MacAffie nodded.

"And there was nothing in writing?"

"Andrew was a very trusting man…a true man of God."

"Did he make any specifications as to the preferred or exact usage of his property?"

MacAffie looked at him with a slight smile that bordered on being a smirk. "Odd you should ask. He specifically requested that the property be developed as some sort of facility for the church."

"Let me get this straight. You're saying that Andrew Mullin, heretofore a non-religious man, gave you a property worth well in excess of a million dollars and asked you to construct a church on it?" His voice was obviously disbelieving as he looked at his client with a dumbfounded look.

"That's the way I interpreted it." MacAffie smiled slightly as he licked his fingers and deliberately pressed the crease of his pants between his thumb and forefinger. "As a remembrance of his life here on Earth." MacAffie was happy with himself. He was performing well.

Mrs. Mullin suddenly shoved her chair back, knocking it to the floor. She stood and turned to face the window, tightly clutching her arms to her sides.

Horwitz jumped up and whispered something in her ear, then picked up her chair, positioning it back where it had been.

At this point, MacAffie knew he had them. Careful not to overplay his cards, he sat back and folded his arms. He was done.

Horwitz took a deep breath. He was losing ground, and he knew it. It was time he took another approach. He extracted a single sheet of paper from his file. "The date on the deed of transfer of his residence to you is October 21, 1994. The date of recordation is February 1, 1995! You held it for four months before recording it? Why, Mr. MacAffie?"

MacAffie looked at the ceiling, as if counting the holes in the acoustical tiles. "To be perfectly frank, I didn't know anything about recording deeds. I just thought that you held onto it."

Horwitz looked at Connie, making a slight smirk with his mouth. "And when did you learn to the contrary?"

"It was several months later when Andrew and I were flying to Lake Shasta. He asked me if I had recorded the deed to his property. I said, 'No. Was I supposed to?' I remember him laughing, and he said, yes, that I should have taken it down to the Recorder's Office in San Jose the day he had given the deed to me. He made me promise to do so the very next day."

Mrs. Mullin, who was still standing, looking out of the window, finally sat down.

Horwitz looked at her with eyes that said, this man is either lying through his teeth, or he's the dumbest person I've ever encountered. Instead he said, "Well, Mr. MacAffie, we'll have to do some further checking on this matter. As you may have surmised, Mrs. Mullin here is contesting the deed, and frankly, Mr. MacAffie, I knew Andrew Mullin all my life, and I never knew him to even go to church, let alone be religious. I must confess that you're adding insult to injury when you tell us that he deeded his most valuable asset to some religious foundation to be converted into a church!"

The word "church" had a nasty sound to it when he said it, and his closing comment angered MacAffie. He retaliated without thinking.

"You're telling me that you don't believe me?" He wanted to convey anger and insensibility to their accusation.

"That's about the long and the short of it," Horwitz said, coldly.

"Then, how do you suppose I came to be in possession of the deed?"

"I'm afraid I don't have the answer to that question, Mr. MacAffie. But I intend to find out!"

"*Pastor* MacAffie, if you don't mind. And I resent the implication." *When on the defense, go on the offense.* He rose abruptly and said, "Now, if you'll excuse me, I've got a church to run." Hearing no objection, he stormed out of the room, glad to be off the hot seat. Now he was confident that he had closed all the gaps. There was no way of proving that Andrew Mullin hadn't deeded his house to the church. Dead men don't talk.

"Well, where do we go from here?" Mrs. Mullin asked, her attorney when they were alone.

"Just between you, me and the fence post, I think that man's lying through his teeth."

"But, he's a minister."

"So he claims. We'll check on that, too. I've got a few loose ends that need looking into. Why don't we conclude for the day and I'll get back to you when I've uncovered something?"

He led her through the door, cradling her elbow in the palm of his hand. "Thanks for coming in, Connie. Sorry it couldn't have been more fruitful."

* * * *

Aaron MacAffie was whistling when he walked into his office at ten-fifteen. "Looks like you had a fruitful meeting," Nevenka said, seeing her husband in such a jovial mood.

"I kicked his butt!" he said before he even thought of what he was saying.

"I don't understand."

"They thought they were too smart for me, baby." He jammed his fist into the air. "They don't know who they're dealing with. No one beats Aaron MacAffie. No one!"

* * * *

Nevenka was getting acclimated to working in the office. She had been assigned the task of opening mail and sorting the important letters into one pile and putting advertisements, useless catalogs and requests for money into the round file, otherwise known as the waste basket. She had just finished opening the day's mail and held a bill for a Hertz car rental in her hand. In addition to the bill for the rental, the agency had enclosed a copy of the rental agreement signed by MacAffie that night, along with a maintenance and repair slip for a broken taillight assembly stapled to it. The amount owed was circled in red pencil with large letters saying "AMOUNT DUE!"

The cost of the taillight was two hundred fifty-nine dollars and the labor was another sixty. "There must be some mistake," she said aloud as she read and reread the rental agreement, noting the date and signature at the bottom.

She went into Aaron's office and thumbed through his appointment book. "Here's the date," she said, seeing *Mullin-dinner* penciled in. "I remember now," she said as she thumped the page with her forefinger. That was the night he'd gone to Andrew Mullin's place for a meeting. "Here's the notation I made in the margin." She furrowed her brow. Then she remembered the delivery of Aaron's plans the day after he had had his dinner with Mullin.

She examined the rental agreement one last time. "The car was rented at six-fifteen in the evening and returned at one-twenty the following morning!" She shook her head "That just doesn't make sense." Her mind flashed back on Aaron watching the televised newscast the following day, announcing that a plane had crashed in Shasta. She turned the page. MacAffie had written "Andrew Mullin killed in plane crash!!" on his calendar.

Chapter 30

▼

"Commander Terryman. Adam Horwitz is here to see you."

"Send him in."

"How are you, Pierce?' Horwitz inquired, strolling into his office, his hand extended. "Been playing any racquetball lately?"

"You ought to know that I'm too busy for such frivolity." He smiled widely. "Why, you looking for a game?"

"You can't hustle me, you bush-leaguer. I'm onto you. You lay low, making your opponent think you're out of shape and haven't played for months, then you get him on the court with his guard down and proceed to massacre him." He laughed, pointing his finger at him.

"I need all the advantages I can get. So, tell me, what brings you uptown?"

"Andrew Mullin. Or, more specifically, Connie Mullin."

"You still trying to get into her pants?" He laughed. "I thought you gave that up in high school."

"Just because Andy stole her from both of us, doesn't mean that I'm trying to take advantage of a grieving widow."

"Grieving, my ass. They've been divorced for five years...ever since she realized that Andy was married to his job and not her."

"Not to mention catching him in bed with that little redhead from the title company," Horwitz added.

"Details. The only thing Connie will grieve about is not getting his money. So, why are you really here? I'm a busy man, Adam, protecting society against blood suckers of the likes of you."

Horwitz took a chair across from Terryman's desk without being invited. "I suppose you heard that Andrew deeded his place to this Living Christ Church?"

Terryman nodded. "Sometimes you just can't figure people out, Adam."

"What do you mean?"

"I mean, who would have thought Andrew Mullin would have gotten religion? He didn't even have time for his wife and kids. His whole life was his job. Never seen a man so intent on making his mark in the world."

"That's the whole point. I just left that little jerk who calls himself a pastor. He's phony as a three-dollar bill, or I'm not Los Alamos's answer to Clarence Darrow."

"That's certainly debatable. As for Mullin, ever consider that maybe he killed himself on purpose? Maybe he did want to have a surviving monument erected to himself…sort of his way of living on in eternity, so to speak. He certainly had the ego for it."

Horwitz shook his head and made a face. "No way. You said it yourself: Andrew Mullin would never have given anything to the church, much less and especially his beloved house. He worked too hard to get what he had, and besides, I understand he was neck-deep in debt, facing financial ruin."

Terryman knew that Andrew Mullin always played things close to the vest. That's how he had lived his life. "You're implying there's skullduggery afoot?"

"A man doesn't go through the trouble to deed his house to a phony corporation in Panama which is owned by another corporation in the Cayman Islands, then, after all that pseudo-dodging, turn around and give the sole asset of the corporation to the likes of Aaron MacAffie. Especially, when he's got children to will it to."

"Let me get this straight." Terryman weaved his hands through the air, as if imitating an object moving. "You're implying that the good pastor *coerced* Mullin to give him his property, then killed him himself?" He shook his head. "That's a reach. Even for you, counselor."

"I'm saying there's treachery afoot, and I intend to get to the bottom of it. And I need your help."

"Aw." He pointed his finger at Horwitz. "There's the rub."

"I'm serious. Run a background check on this guy MacAffie. For openers, I have my doubts he's even an ordained minister. You would want to be discreet, of course. I wouldn't want him to find out that we're investigating him."

Terryman made a face, mocking Horwitz' words. "But of course not."

"Well, will you do it, or not?" He was showing visible signs of irritation. Terryman had gotten to him.

He got up from his chair and walked to the door, indicating that the meeting was over. "I'll make some gentle inquiries. If I uncover something, I'll get back to you." He slapped Horwitz on the shoulder. "Let me know if you get into her pants." He laughed as Horwitz looked at him in disgust.

*　　*　　*　　*

Myrna Lee was sitting at her desk filing her nails when the phone rang.

"Miss Lee? Adam Horwitz here. Could I have a few minutes? It concerns Andrew Mullin."

"Andrew? Why? What is it?"

"If I recall, you notarized all of his transactions: documents, deeds of trust, wills, that sort of thing. I wonder if you wouldn't mind looking back in your notary book for the year 1994. You notarized a document for Andrew that I'm researching—a Quit Claim Deed to an Aaron MacAffie. Do you remember that?"

She wrinkled her nose, a habit she had when she was thinking. "It sort of rings a bell. Do you have the month?"

"October twenty-first."

"You want to hold on for a moment?"

"Take your time."

"Ninety-four. October. Yes. Here it is. I notarized Andrew's signature on a deed to Mr. MacAffie."

"Do you recall the deed?"

There was a pause on the phone. "No. Not at the moment."

"Anything you can tell me about it? Anything at all?"

Another pause. "Just that it was a Quit Claim deed from Mullin to Aaron MacAffie. There's not much space in these little books for much more than bare-bones information," she apologized.

"Well, if you recall anything else, call me, will you?"

*　　*　　*　　*

"Mr. Horwitz. Pierce Terryman on line two."

"Adam? Pierce Terryman here. You were inquiring into Andrew Mullin's estate?"

"Yeah. Did you find something?" His voice had a tone of anxiety to it.

"Well, something came across my desk that may be of interest."

"I'm listening."

"I'm not saying there's any relevancy here, you understand."

"I understand. Tell me, goddammit."

Terryman smiled to himself. He loved pulling Horwitz's leg. He was always such an uptight asshole. "I'm in possession of a report from the FAA. Appears that Mullin's plane may have been tampered with. The report states that the right rear flap had the lock nut completely missing and the left wing flap had either worked its way off, or had been removed."

"So, what you're saying is that he *couldn't* guide his plane."

"According to the aviation expert that I talked to, there's no way he could have negotiated a controlled landing. And in that forest up there…"

Horwitz thought for a moment. "How could that happen? I thought that's why they called them lock-nuts. They were locked in place so they couldn't come loose."

Terryman shrugged his shoulders. "That's the principle."

"Do you think that someone might have removed them?"

"That's what the FAA wants to know. They're checking into Mullin's maintenance records, but you know what I think?"

"That there's something fishy afoot."

"As of today, I'm changing the status of Andrew Mullin's death from accidental death/suicide to homicide, pending the FAA's findings."

"That brings me back to our buddy, MacAffie. Anything new on him?"

"So far, he's clean. Born in northern Ireland. Apparently his father was killed in a gun battle with the British. After his death, his wife moved MacAffie and his older brother to the States. They changed their last name from Macafy to MacAffie for some reason.

"Sounds like there must have been some juice between this MacAffie fellow and the British. Maybe he was an undercover agent or something."

"Don't know. There's no mention of any connection with British intelligence. If there were, we'd never find out—not through regular channels, anyway."

"What else you got?"

"Well, this is the interesting part. Seems his mother was murdered a few years back while working as a cleaning woman in Seattle."

"Murdered!"

"Yeah. They never solved the crime. They put it down as a burglary gone bad."

"Like she interrupted a safe cracker, or something like that?"

"Something like that."

"Hmm."

"It gets better. His brother, who flunked out of college and joined the Navy, was also killed a few months later, in a Chinese bar in San Francisco. No motive. No suspects. Crime unsolved. Then…"

"There's more?"

"The minister where MacAffie was doing his internship in this little town in Washington was blown to smithereens in MacAffie's van."

"Sounds like he's one dangerous guy to have as a friend."

"He does seem to attract a certain element, doesn't he? So, let me summarize. His mother gets iced. The crime is unsolved. His brother gets iced. Unsolved. The minister gets iced in *MacAffie's* car."

"Unsolved?"

"Unsolved."

"So, either someone is trying to eliminate the MacAffie tribe, or there's an awful lot of coincidental murders in his wake."

"And you know how I feel about murders."

"So our minister is a true man of the cloth?"

"He graduated from a small religious college up north, with a degree in theology. He worked as an assistant, on-the-job-training in Longview, Washington, until the incident with his preacher-teacher, after which he came to our fair city."

"A black day for Los Alamos," he said, more to himself than Terryman. "So, what do we do now?"

"Well, so far, I have no reason to suspect him of anything other than being the unfortunate benefactor of a lot of unsolved deaths…"

"Or possibly being on someone's hit list."

"And there's no law against that."

"We can only hope whoever is trying to rub him out doesn't lose his eraser." Horwitz sneered.

"Very funny. Not in my town!"

Chapter 31

▼

Pastor Aaron MacAffie wasted no time getting the development of his new church underway. One of his parishioners, Orie Thompson, was a loan officer in charge of the New Wave Mortgage Company, a Japan-based, wealthy investment group looking for well-placed, secured, high-interest-rate loan opportunities.

Mullin's house had been free and clear, and the house alone had an appraised replacement value of one million two-hundred-thousand dollars. The excess land was valued at a dollar per square foot. All in all, the property appraised out at five million dollars, give or take a few thousand.

"My investor group would be willing to loan you the two-and-one-half million that you figure it would take to construct your new church facility, including all improvements," Thompson had said. "If you were to be the general contractor, as you propose, that could personally yield you something in the neighborhood of two hundred thousand dollars, assuming everything goes as planned."

He walked the grounds with Pastor MacAffie, putting his arm around his shoulders from time to time, as if confiding in him. "I noticed you built in an additional contingency fund of a hundred-thousand dollars in the deal," he said, tugging at MacAffie's shoulder, as if to say, "Good thinking." "I'd say, all things being equal, you should come out of this little development pretty well healed." He winked at MacAffie as if they had just hatched some diabolical secret known only to him.

MacAffie pulled away from the man's arm and stopped to look him directly in his eyes. "I noticed you have a twenty-five-thousand dollar fee for obtaining the loan." His voice contained a tone of displeasure, almost accusatory in nature.

"It's common practice to collect a point on loans of this size," Thompson said, defending himself. "If it were anyone else, I would have charged two points," he whined defensively.

"I would have thought, as a member of the church, you wouldn't have charged anything at all! It is, after all, God's work!"

His comment obviously incensed Thompson, but he didn't want to irritate his pastor and, even more so, didn't want to blow the deal. He had had a lean month and needed the money badly. "Don't forget, Pastor, I have a family to feed, too," he rationalized. His voice was almost pleading for leniency.

When MacAffie finally got through negotiating with Orie Thompson, he would end up paying a half of a point, and Thompson would be glad to get that. MacAffie, of course, would charge his church the full point and slip the other half to into his ever-growing pile of personal funds.

*   *   *   *

Forty-five days later, the loan was finalized and the building permits were issued. The Andrew Mullin estate started to take on a new look. As the construction crew moved in, the first to go was the stand of eucalyptus trees lining the driveway. The only trees allowed to remain were those standing in front of the old Mullin house, which would now become the pastor's home. The guest cottage would become the office, library and conference room.

An environmentalist group headed by one Larry Allen, a recent young graduate from San Jose State, petitioned the building department to allow the hundred-year-old eucalyptus trees to stand. When that failed, he tried to petition the local citizenry to allow the trees to remain, but that, too, was unsuccessful. As a last resort, he and his group tried to sabotage the earth-moving equipment. They even chained themselves to the trees, until the Pierce Terryman and his men showed up with bolt cutters and removed the locks and chains and threatened to arrest them for trespassing.

"I'm as much against developing this property as your are, Larz," he told the young, long-haired man, "but, the law is the law. They have a permit to remove the trees and there is nothing neither you nor I can do about it, so why don't you pack up your friends and go fishing?" He didn't particularly care for how Larry and his group looked, with their long hair and earrings, but Larry Allen was a son of one of guys he played tennis with every Saturday, so he went easy on him.

As a last resort, Allen and his pack of environmentalists picketed the site with placards nailed to one-by-two sticks, reading "Save the Trees." It was a slow day for news, so when the press showed up, Allen talked to them about the depletion of the ozone layer, destruction of the rain forest and the overuse of pesticides, enlightening the reporters and every citizen who came within earshot of the atrocities being committed upon Mother Earth, not the least of which was destroying the scrufty eucalyptus trees that supplied man with oxygen by osmosis.

While Allen was resting beneath one of the trees a man dressed in dark-olive-green clothing, wearing a beret eased next to him. "What they goin' ta build here, laddie?"

His accent gave him away, and Larry just smiled. He enjoyed talking to foreigners. They would usually listen to what he had to say with sympathy and understanding. "They want to destroy this group of trees to build a church. Can you imagine a man of God wanting to destroy such beautiful creatures?"

"This Macafy fella, is he the preacher?"

"Aaron MacAffie? Yeah, that's him. He's over there, talking to the contractor. Want to talk to him?"

"No. I was just curious. Thanks just the same."

"Hey, we're cuttin' out for the beach in a bit. Care to join us?"

"Thanks, but I think I'll stick around."

As soon as the first eucalyptus tree had hit the ground, Larz and his band of misfits retreated to Santa Cruz in Larry's blue Ford Aerostar, along with a keg of beer, a bag of pretzels, a football and a flea-bitten shaggy dog they had found wandering the streets.

*   *   *   *

As Nevenka thumbed through the mail, her eye caught the letter containing a Lithuanian stamp post-marked a week earlier. She was always nervous when she opened mail from home. She never knew if it meant good or bad news. The last letter she had received had informed her that her father was dead.

She cradled little Vladimer in her arms and tears welled in her eyes as she read the words of her mother, describing continued hardships in Lithuania. With the conflict raging out of control in the Soviet Union, it was becoming all the more difficult to get food. Fuel was apparently limited to what little driftwood they could find to burn. "You're lucky that you'll never suffer the hardships of Russia, little one," she wrote. "Even though you are in America, you are still a Russian. Don't ever forget it!"

She looked at the little blond child who was clearly developing the features of his father. Every time she looked at him, she thought of Vladimer Ryzhkov and her heart ached.

She felt guilty when she thought of the abundance of supplies in America, where no one wanted for food, clothing, nor fuel for their furnaces. *I've got to get your grandmother over here,* she thought to herself, stroking Vladimer's head. *Surely, Husband would have no objection to bringing them over and finding work for my brothers in his new church!*

*   *   *   *

"We received letter from Lithuania today," she told Aaron at dinner that night, showing him the envelope.

"Oh?" he said, without looking up as he shoved a forkful of meat and potatoes in his mouth. Then he washed it down with a large gulp of vine rose'.

She nodded, still holding the letter. "Things are not going well. They have very little to eat and they are cold." It was all she could do to maintain her composure as she brushed the blond locks back from Vladimer's head and kissed him.

"I wish you wouldn't do that!"

"Do what?" she asked.

"Keep fussing over that kid that way. You keep touching him like it's going to be his last day on Earth."

"In this day and age, you never know," she said, then kissing him again. "Maybe it will be."

MacAffie sighed. "Things will get better." His voice sounded compassionate. "You'll see."

"No, Husband. You do not know Russia. There is civil war in Russia. It is even on television six o'clock news," she said, pointing towards the television. "I am afraid for their lives!" She fought back the tears that were forming in her eyes again.

For the first time, he looked up from his food. "I'm sorry, Nevenka. I wish there were something I could do, but..."

"There is," she said, meeting his eyes. "Sponsor them to come to America!"

A cold shiver ran down MacAffie's back. This was not the first time she had brought up the topic of sponsoring her family, but it was the first time she had been this vehement about it.

"I'm right in the middle of pulling everything together on the new church, Nevenka. I don't have the time to get politically involved with bringing someone over from Russia and to do all the paper work required. Maybe after the church is built, okay?"

She looked at him with contempt, but held her tongue.

"Tell you what, I'll write them a check for five hundred dollars. Money talks, even in Russia."

"Lithuania," she corrected.

He shrugged his shoulders. "Whatever."

* * * *

The Living Christ Church got a ton of free publicity during the course of construction. The *San Jose Mercury and News* ran color pictures of the artist's rendering of the finished project on the front page of the religious section of the Sunday paper. The article included a picture of pastor Aaron MacAffie sporting a new look. He had himself fitted with a high-priced hairpiece. He looked more like a well-heeled businessman in his dark-blue, pin-striped, three-piece Eli Thomas business suit. His Pepsident smile should have given the readers a warning that there was a wolf hiding under that rug.

Dan McGowan of Channel Thirty-Six approached Pastor MacAffie for an interview, who showed his viewers pictures of the artists rendering of what the finished product would look like.

* * * *

The little man from Ireland grew a mustache and goatee, had his hair cut and bought himself some new clothing from Mervin's department store. With his new look, he blended in with the people who were always hanging around the construction site. They even got to know him as Joe from Scotland, as he couldn't get rid of his accent, although he tried.

* * * *

Six months later, the church was finished. With all the publicity, it was no wonder that the church was filled to capacity the first Sunday, which was, coincidentally, Easter Sunday. Twenty-five-hundred people filed in and filled the padded pews as the choir began singing, *The Old Rugged Cross*. Joe the Scotsman sat at the back of the church. It was Easter and, although he was Catholic, he rationalized that he should attend the Protestant church. Part of the job!

When everyone had been seated, the lights dimmed and the doors at the back of the church swung open to the sound of a cracking whip. What followed, no one who was present that day would ever forget. A young man, dressed in nothing but a loincloth, his long, straggly hair adorned by a crown of thorns, struggled down the center aisle under an old rugged cross constructed of twelve-inch-by-twelve-inch beams, ten feet long and five feet in width.

Sweat poured from his forehead. Obvious pain was painted on his bearded face. A gasp escaped from the crowd as a loud thud sounded. The man portraying Christ had fallen to his knees as he dropped one end of the cross. He held out his hand to one of the pews, where a man dressed in ragged clothes had been seated, carrying a tin of water. The man got up and offered the water to the Christ-portrayed.

The choir continued humming softly as the Roman soldier cracked his whip over the back of Christ again. Men and women in the church winced and tears welled up in their eyes as they shared his pain. Many could no longer look, closing their eyes or diverting them to the rock-colored panels on the sides of the church.

When Christ had reached the podium, he was strapped to the cross, where simulated nailing of his hands and feet took place as the hammer hit the wood. The timber was then raised and set into a receptacle on the revolving stage, facing the people. The agony and pain felt by the Christ actor and the congregation was clearly portrayed on their faces. It would be a safe statement to say that there wasn't a dry eye in the house.

Nevenka wore a new pink chiffon dress that her husband had purchased for her the previous week. She sat between the Pastor and the choir in a padded chair, holding young Vladimer in her lap. She looked radiant under the spotlights, although her face mirrored those of the congregation as Christ made his way down the aisle and was subjected to the punishment inflicted upon him.

Although she had not officially been presented to the congregation by her husband, many had met her by now, and, when the ceremony had been concluded, Nevenka and her son stood next to her husband at the door, greeting the congregation as they filed out of the church. As much attention was paid to her as to the Pastor.

Everyone wanted to shake Pastor MacAffie's hand or hug him for the tremendous experience they had witnessed on their first visit to his church. Those who had not previously had an opportunity to meet his wife were pleased to see this

Russian beauty up close and personal. No one had a clue that she had come from Russia with the express purpose of marrying their Pastor. And, everyone made a fuss over little Vladimer, but none spoke of the lack of similarities between father and son.

The Irishman slipped out of the church unnoticed.

※　　※　　※　　※

Matty McGown used his calling card to call Ireland from a pay telephone which was located in the Stanford Shopping Mall. "Lemme speak to King Arthur!" he demanded when a man answered at the other end.

"Matty! What did I tell you about calling here!"

"Relax. I'm in pay phone in one of these shopping malls. There's no way anyone can trace the call."

"What's up with our man of the cloth?"

"Today was openin' day fer his church. Ya oughta see the people come, mate. There must have been two t'ousand in attendance! And the money they put in the plate! I tell ya, there's a gold mine here."

"What about the man in the airplane that crashed? What's come of that?"

"So far's I can ascertain, nothin! I dunno how he done it, but after he did him in, somehow he got the bloke's land to build this glorious church on. Ya got ta see it, mate! It looks like a bloomin' space ship, it does."

"And nobody suspects a thing of our boy Macafy?"

He shook his head. "Not so's I can tell."

"You keep a keen ear to the ground there, Matty McGown. I want to know everything about this Aaron Macafy fella. Find out as much as you can. Somethin' tells me there's somethin' there for the cause. Keep a keen eye, mate."

※　　※　　※　　※

The Corporal sat next to his recording machine, shutting off the tape when the transmission had finished. "That appears to be about it for the moment, Major."

"It sounds like our friends are planning on using Macafy to further their own cause. We'll have to put a stop to that. Killin' his mother and brother are one thing…"

"Not to mention the preacher."

Major Pennypacker nodded. "That, too. I'm not going to get too upset if they get Macafy, but if those Irish bastards are able to tap into the funds at Macafy's church and they start bringing the in money to further the cause, there's where I draw the line."

"Don't you think we should warn Macafy, sir?"

"And how would we be doing' that, Corporal? You want to ring him up on the telly and say, 'By the way, Pastor, this is Major Pennypacker here, in good old London. I'm the one who got your da killed for helpin' us. Just want you to know that we know who strangled your mother, ran a shiv up your brother's heart and blew up the van that killed Pastor Magnason, which, by the by, was meant to kill you. Oh, and by the by, now the bloody man's there in town, wantin' to trade your life in exchange for a deal fer the cause. Don't want you givin' them any of yer blood money fer cause, now, ya hear?'" He turned to the man. "Is that what you had in mind, Corporal?"

The Corporal hated these cat-and-mouse conversations. Not only did he always lose, but they always ended up making him feel like a fool, to boot! "Well, no sir, I just thought maybe we should notify the authorities...to save his life, you know."

"Oh, I see. Call the US Constable and tell him that there are Irish terrorists in his country who are after an illegal that we snuck in under their noses, and would you please protect him and, while yer at it, send the Irishman back home, that is, if you can catch him. Oh, and by the by, our man is responsible for killin' several of your citizens. You will overlook that, won't you?' Is that what you had in mind?"

The Corporal didn't want to embarrass himself any further, so he said nothing, but simply looked at the Major.

Major Pennypacker patted him on the back. "You do the recordin', Corporal, and leave the thinkin' to me. I've got our British arse in deep enough as it is without hanging it out to dry, to boot. I do want to retire a Major, not a private."

"Yes, sir."

*   *   *   *

Matty McGowan's call to King Arthur had not only been monitored by Major Pennypacker, but had been routed from Ireland to Gempac, otherwise known as the Great Elite Military Power Control, a highly secret military group organized by and composed of high-ranking British military officers.

The room was very large and, aside from diffused lighting, was lit only by a large twenty-foot computer screen depicting the world's continents. Each continent contained various pin-point red blinking lights, more in some countries than others. There was a blinking light in northern Ireland, one in Bosnia, one in Kuwait, numerous lights in what was greater Russia, Palestine and every other hot spot on the globe currently experiencing violent political and civil unrest.

A completely separate and distinct screen of equal size occupied the opposite wall, showing a detailed map of Great Britain and all its constituents. Several lights blinked around northern Ireland, including an amber one with the typewritten inscription underneath it labeling "King Arthur."

"What do you think, sir?" The Captain said as he handed a printed letter of Matty McGown's conversation with King Arthur.

"I suspect that security will make a move if Ireland is successful in dominating Macafy. Until then, it's steady as she goes."

Chapter 32

Dawn and Eric Nesbit were in their mid-fifties and the proud parents of three grown, successful children. Laura, the eldest, had graduated from Stanford and was attending medical school at the University of Oregon. Mark and Matt, the twins, had decided that they, too, liked the Northwest and had applied for and were accepted by Lewis and Clark College in Portland, Oregon, where they could be close to their sister.

Eric's job at FiberOptics was Product Manager. He was responsible for marketing his company's product to the communication industry. Life was good for them. They had a healthy family and a beautiful home in an upper class neighborhood that Eric had built for them. One night after dinner, Dawn and Eric were sitting outside by the pool. "I feel so fulfilled," she said, "having you and this great house." She paused. "I was thinking, why don't we invite our minister over to bless the house, just as our lives have been blessed!"

Eric shrugged his shoulders. He wasn't as devout about his faith as Dawn, but had no problem with having their minister bless their house if that was what pleased her. Actually, he kind of liked the idea. They had belonged to the Living Christ Church almost since its inception and had become good friends with the minister, Pastor Aaron MacAffie. "Alright," he agreed. "Why don't you call him and invite him and his wife over for dinner after church Sunday?"

That Sunday, after service, Pastor Aaron MacAffie and Nevenka came over for dinner. He blessed both the dinner and the house at the same time.

"I was taken in by your sermon last week, Pastor," Dawn said. "You know, the more I think about it, the more sense it makes."

"You mean, rendering unto Caesar that which is Caesar's and rendering back to God that which is His?"

"Yes. How did you come up with a topic like that? I mean, what was your inspiration?"

"Well, if you consider the concept of ownership, in reality, God owns everything: your land, your country, the very Earth itself and indeed, the universe. We're all just here on a temporary basis, renting, so to speak."

"Like the poster I once saw." Eric laughed. "It was a cartoon drawing of the Earth, with people crowded everywhere, and this loud voice came down from the heavens, telling them that they've got three days to vacate, that he's leased out Earth."

Eric thought it was funny as he laughed at his own joke, but Dawn was into a more serious discussion and shot him a sharp glance.

Pastor MacAffie smiled without comment.

"Well, I thought it was funny," Eric said, almost to himself.

"I kinda liked it," Nevenka said, patting Eric's hand as she winked at him.

"Take the history of civilization, as we know it," the Pastor said. "Think back on any time in history, any date, any country, and you'll find that greed has been the undoing of not only every society, but the country, as a whole.

"Greed was the undoing of Napoleon. He tried to take over Russia," he said, looking at Nevenka, "and the weather defeated him, not the Russian army. Hitler tried to eradicate a whole race and take over the world in the process, and look what happened to him. Right here in our own country, before the settlers came from other lands, Indians lived here in harmony with the land."

"But even they fought with each other," Eric interjected.

"My point precisely. Even when there's plenty for everyone, greed overtakes common sense. History has dictated that everyone is greedy, from the leaders of our own country, down to the basic family structure.

"I once knew a couple who owned a very successful hotel. When they retired, they gave the hotel to their children, thinking that they were doing them a favor by giving it to them, hoping that they would continue on with the business. Know what they did?"

Eric and Dawn shrugged their shoulders.

"They fought about who was going to have control, who would make decisions and who would run the operation. They ended up selling the place, but not before they ran it into the ground. All their parent's hard work, gone down the drain."

"But isn't that what family is all about?" Eric asked. "Passing on what you've acquired during the course of your life to your children?"

"On the surface, that would seem to be the case. But, in reality, think what you're doing to your children by giving them everything."

"I don't get it," Eric said.

Pastor MacAffie smiled. He had them where he wanted them. "What's the greatest pleasure a young family can have?"

"A new house," Dawn said quickly, without thinking.

"Health and money, without the worry about bills," Eric added.

Pastor MacAffie smiled. "Self satisfaction."

Eric and Dawn looked at each other.

"Think about it! There's no greater satisfaction than working hard for something you want, whether it's a vacation, a car or a house, and achieving it. When you've worked hard for something, you really appreciate it. Don't you agree?"

Eric nodded. "That makes sense."

"Of course it does. Take this house, for example. You worked hard to get it, and now that you're got it, your really enjoying it."

"Well, it's something we've always wanted."

"That's right! And do you think if someone just came up and gave it to you that you would have anywhere near the appreciation for it that you do now? I mean, you've put years of hard-earned sweat and blood into getting this house."

He let his words sink in for a moment before continuing. "Take an automobile, for example. Lets say that you have two kids. One, you give him a new car, and the other, you make him get a job and work for it. Which kid is going to have the greatest pride and joy in his new car?"

"That's obvious," Eric said.

"Right! That's my point. God programmed us to appreciate that which we have worked for and to take for granted that which is given to us. Think how we deprive our children by giving them everything when we pass on. Oh, sure, we can and should pass on our personal heirlooms and stuff like that, but look what history has told us about when we give our children house and money."

He looked at his guests, who were waiting for his answer. "They sell the house and take the money and take trips, buy frivolous things like jewels and furs."

"And it's your contention that people should give their belongings to the church?" Eric asked.

"All things come from God. We know that. Right?" Without waiting for an answer to his rhetorical question, he continued. "It's our duty to return to him that which he has given us when we go to join him. I'm certain he'll reward such generosity."

"How?" Eric was not only pessimistic about his Pastor's philosophy, but suspicious as to his insight into God's mind. He never could figure out how ministers knew what God thought when they say, "God says…" or "God wants you to…" or, in Pastor MacAffie's case, when you give God something, "God will reward you!" *How does he know what God thinks, what he says or what he'll do?*

"God rewards good and punishes evil," was the Pastor's response to Eric's unspoken skepticism.

"Well, it's certainly something to think about," Dawn said, nodding to her husband.

"The time to do something is now," Pastor MacAffie said, "while you're young and vibrant. For the future, of course. Way in the future." He laughed, extending his hand, emphasizing the point.

"You mean like in a will?" Dawn asked.

"Yes. A Living Trust, it's called. We've done this with a number of our parishioners," he lied. "And we have staff on hand to deal with such matters, should you decide to go in that direction."

He had accomplished what he had intended: to plant the seed. Now it would be up to Dawn to germinate it, and he knew she would. Of course, he'd give her a little nudge along the way, just for insurance purposes.

After the Pastor and his wife had left, Eric said, "A little ballsy, don't you think?"

"You mean about the the trust? When you think about it, he has a good point."

"Deeding yor property to the church?"

"You have to remember that he's a man of God and after all, he's just looking out for his church," Dawn rationalized. She thought for a moment. "I think we should do it."

"What? Deed ouit stuff to the church?"

"After we're gone, of course. His comment about not spoiling the kids made a lot of sense to me. Don't you think?"

* * * *

At church the following Sunday Dawn saw a friend that she hadn't seen for a number of years. "Joanne! Is that you?" she remarked, holding her at arms length to admire her. "Why, you look simply ravishing! How do you keep yourself looking so young?" Joanne clearly looked five years younger than Dawn. She was trim, her face was radiant and she seemed to walk with an air of confidence that, frankly, Dawn had never noticed before.

"I've taken up running," she responded proudly. "I started two years ago, and simply love it! As soon as Sam goes to work, I put on my jogging clothes and take off." She sidled next to Dawn to whisper in her ear. "And you'll be amazed at the hunks I meet along the way." She giggled, elbowing Dawn in the ribs.

Dawn smiled, not at her seeing hunks, but jogging. "Maybe I should try something like that. Eric has his athletic club. It seems to do wonders for him."

"Watch him, honey!" She elbowed Dawn again. "They got more tight-assed, firmed bodied young chicks in those joints than you can shake a stick at. And they're all looking for a man!" She nodded for emphasis. "I've been there and seen 'em. Let me tell you, there's not a man alive whose eyes don't wander in those places. Those young things wear leotards so tight their tits bulge at the top and their suits are stuck up their ass like they got nothin' on at all. They're out there huntin', honey! Believe me! That's one of the reasons I took up jogging."

"You mean…"

"Competition. Ya gotta keep in the runnin', girl. Lag behind, and you can kiss your man good-bye. There's three tight-asses out there for every available man, just waiting for us to drop the ball." She winked as she walked away.

She does have a fetching figure for woman her age, Dawn thought.

The next day, Dawn was in SportsMart, trying on jogging suits. "I didn't realize they were so expensive," she commented to the saleswoman.

"If you want to look nice, you gotta' pay the price, honey." The small, trim saleslady smiled. "Most women who come in here to buy stuff never jogged a yard in their lives and frankly, don't intend to. They just want to look good." She laughed as she elbowed Dawn in the ribs. "The serious ones, they don't even wear jogging suits. Shorts and a skimpy top. That's it, and they're off to the races."

"I like this one," Dawn said, holding up a soft blue cotton top with dark-blue and crimson piping on the jacket and pants. Price: two-hundred-five dollars. "I'll take it."

* * * *

"Pastor. The Nesbits are here."

"Eric! Dawn! I'm so happy to see you. Come right in! You remember Nevenka, don't you?"

"Of course. Who could forget such a lovely lady?" Dawn said as she smiled at her. "And just who is this young man?" She knelt down to look little Vladimer in the face. "Such a handsome fellow." She looked at Nevenka, then MacAffie, looking for similarities. "He has your coloring," she said to Nevenka.

MacAffie forced a smile, but made no comment. He was getting tired of this "let's look for a comparison," routine, and finding none. He wasn't aware of it, but at that moment, the seed of dislike that had been lying dormant since before little Vladimer's birth had just taken root.

"Your file," Nevenka said, handing her husband a file with the label, "Eric and Dawn Nesbit—Living Trust".

"Looks like you're well prepared," Eric said, somewhat cynically. After many conversations about the topic, Dawn had worn him down. In the end he had relented and agreed to write the church into their will.

Dawn shot him a sharp look, then laughed nervously. "He's such a kidder."

"Well, we may as well get down to it, as they say in the movies. This is your copy of the trust, leaving your residence to the church in the event you both die..."

"Which I hope will be many years from now," Dawn said, nervously.

Eric made a face which everyone ignored.

"Many years." Pastor MacAffie agreed.

"Nevenka. Will you have Jo Ann come in, please? She's our notary," he explained. "Now then, if you'll just sign here, Dawn, and Eric, you can sign on the bottom line, and be sure to date it. When you're done, I'll witness your signature and Jo Ann will notarize it."

When all the signing was done, he gave Eric Nesbit his copy of the document. "Well, now, that didn't hurt, did it? I'm sure the Lord is smiling down on you. From this moment on, your life will be blessed."

"To be sure," Eric mumbled under his breath. "Come on, dear, I've got to get back to work."

CHAPTER 33

Dawn Nesbit started her jogging routine with a light run around the cul-de-sac, but soon discovered that she tired easily, so she slowed her pace to a brisk walk. At first she limited herself to just going around two blocks of her subdivision. The morning air was usually brisk. It felt good to fill her lungs with the cool, fresh morning air. When she arrived back home, her face was flushed and her skin tingled. She liked the looks of her complexion as she caught a glimpse of herself in the hall mirror. On top of that, she felt invigorated, alive.

Within a week she had worked up to a light jog around two blocks, and eventually she increased that to four blocks. Before long she was doing a mile. She couldn't believe the energy she had after finishing her run and taking a shower and putting on fresh clothes. She actually felt younger and more vibrant. And she looked better, too.

She varied her routes, first jogging behind her subdivision, then the next day, jogged towards the park where she had discovered a jogging trail posted with various exercise stations, such as stepping on a log ten times, designed to increase leg muscle tone; hopping over other logs for dexterity, stretching her legs and even chinning herself on horizontal bars for upper-body strength.

In time she began to familiarize herself with other joggers along the various routes she would take, making nodding acquaintances. It was on such a run that she met Tom Mathews, one of her neighbors from around the block.

At first it was just a nod and short greeting. "Hi, how's it going?" as they passed one another. Then, one time, they were jogging in the same direction, with Dawn about ten paces ahead of Mathews. He sped up and caught up with her.

"Mind if I jog along?" he asked.

The inquiry seemed innocent enough. *I mean, what can happen in the full light of day?* she thought. "Sure. Why not?"

"My name is Tom," he said, extending his hand as they jogged side by side.

"Dawn," she said simply, hesitating for a moment before reciprocating.

They jogged in silence for a few moments, then he asked, "I've seen you around. You live close by?"

She nodded. "Close. I don't like wandering too far from home." *No use giving out too much information. Never know what kind of guy this is.*

"I live in the Woolmont subdivision," he offered, nodding back to the direction from which they had come. "Been there every since it was new." They jogged for a few more moments before he probed. "And you?"

"Yeah. I live there, too, on Royal Court." Once she had said the name of her street, she bit her lip, wondering what had possessed her to even offer that much information. *Oh, well,* she rationalized, *how bad can it be, if he lives around the corner? I mean, we're neighbors! It's not like he's the Hillside Strangler!*

They jogged for a few more moments before they came to the end of the street and Dawn said, "It's been nice meeting you, Tom. This is where I turn back."

"See you again," he called over his shoulder, as she turned across the street to jog back towards home.

She didn't give it much thought when Tom Mathews came up behind her the following day as she came out of her cul-de-sac. "Hi again," he said, raising his hand. "Good timing." He beamed. "Mind if I jog along?"

She was sort of taken aback by his sudden appearance, but then thought nothing of it, until the following day, when it happened again. "We seem to get out about the same time." He laughed as he came up alongside of her.

She didn't really mind his jogging along with her. As a matter of fact, she sort of enjoyed the companionship of running with someone. It made the time pass quickly. They jogged and chatted about small matters: the weather, what their respective mates did and how long they had been running, what was good on TV…that sort of thing.

Their friendship quickly flourished to the point that Dawn looked forward to seeing him every day. She even found herself jogging in place a few times, waiting for him to come around the corner. She never mentioned her jogging partner to Eric and he never inquired if she had one, which made her feel more at ease, not that she had anything to hide.

That is, not until this one day in particular. It was overcast and the ground was damp from a light rain that had fallen the previous night. A light mist hung in the air. By this time, Dawn considered herself a veteran runner. A little mist wasn't going to keep her from her appointed rounds. A year ago, she wouldn't have even considered venturing out when it was damp. Might slip and fall or, worse yet, get her hair wet!

Tom Mathews was jogging in place as she came out of her cul-de-sac, waiting for her. "Nasty day," he commented as they fell in stride.

"Oh, I don't know. I kinda like the rain. Sort of invigorating, don't you think? Makes everything nice and clean. Smells nice, too," she said, as she took a deep breath with her eyes closed.

"Shall we jog through the park today, just in case the weather takes a turn for the worse?" He looked up at the grey sky. "That way, if it decides to get nasty, we can take refuge under the trees and you wouldn't get wet."

"That's considerate," she said, looking at him with a smile. As a rule, she wouldn't have jogged through the park, for fear of someone jumping out at her. There were lots of trees, with a little creek running through it, which was probably why the trees and underbrush were so prolific. Jogging with Tom alleviated her fear.

They had jogged towards the end of the park, and were ready to make a swing around the end of the batting cages where the little league kids played summer baseball, when suddenly there was a flash of lightening, followed by a loud clap of thunder. Moments later, they were in the middle of a cloudburst. Rain fell in sheets, as if someone had turned a hose on them.

"Yeow!" Dawn yelled as she raced back under the trees for shelter.

They stood under the large oak tree for protection, looking at each other and laughing. In the few brief moments that they had been exposed to the rain, they had both gotten so wet that they looked like drowned cats. Soon their laughter found them hugging each other, from the sheer exhaustion of laughing, if nothing else. In that moment, their eyes locked, and a second later their lips met with the moist love of Mother Nature dripping from their hair.

Within moments, they were kissing passionately and ripping each other's clothes off, oblivious to their surroundings or anyone who might have had the folly to venture out into the cloudburst. They made love right there under the shelter of the large oak tree, using their discarded jogging suits as bedding. It wasn't until they were both spent that a reality check set in, both realizing what they had done. It had seemed so natural, so right, that they had no immediate guilty feelings.

The rain let up as suddenly as it had started. It was only then that they became aware of their surroundings. "It's getting late," Dawn said, somewhat sheepishly, suddenly embarrassed by her nudity. She quickly covered herself with parts of her clothing, shooting glances ar Tom to see if he was watching while she pulled herself back together. When she finished dressing she brushed herself off. "We should get going."

They jogged home side by side without much comment, each lost in their own thoughts. The next few days Dawn stayed home and spend a lot of time staring at the hills out of their living room window, thinking. Was what she had done simply an thoughtless impulse provoked by a touch of temporary insanity, or had she secretly wanted this to happen? she asked herself. After all, she had been purposefully jogging with Tom Mathews for quite some time now. She certainly wasn't blameless. The guilt that she felt was overwhelming. She lay in the bed next to Eric wondering if he knew. She weas near hving a breakdown when she decided to do something about it.

The next day she phoned her minister. She had to talk to someone, someone she trusted. Nevenka answered the phone. "The Living Christ Church. Can I help you?"

Dawn didn't recognize Nevenka's voice. "Yes. This is Mrs. Nesbit. Dawn Nesbit. I need to see Pastor MacAffie as soon as possible. It's an emergency!"

Nevenka could tell by the tone of her voice that she was under a lot of stress. She looked at the Pastor's appointment book. It was full, but she knew she could move appointments around the following day. Old Mrs. Carter could certainly wait another day to bring the Pastor up to date on her never ending list of troubles. "I have an opening tomorrow at eleven. Would that be soon enough?"

"Yes. Thank you! Thank you very much!"

That evening Eric brought home the news that the factory was going to be down re-tooling some of the machinery and that everyone had been given the following week off.

"Tell you what!" he said. "Jacob said we could use his cabin. Why don't we take that trip to the Grand Canyon we've always talked about?"

Dawn saw that as the perfect opportunity to end her relationship with Tom, and to give him time to cool down at the same time. "That would be perfect. It couldn't come at a better time. What about the kids?"

"I thought maybe just the two of us would go," he said. "Sort of a second honeymoon. Do you mind?"

"Mind? I couldn't be more ecstatic!"

* * * *

"Pastor. Mrs. Nesbit is here for her eleven o'clock appointment," Nevenka said, as she gestured for Dawn to take a seat.

"Please, send her in."

Nevenka closed the door behind her, taking care to leave it ajar just enough so she could overhear what was being said.

"Now then, what can I do for you, Dawn? Nevenka said you sounded distressed. Everything all right at home?"

"I'm so embarrassed, pastor. I don't know what to do." She started crying.

MacAffie came around the desk and sat on the edge, facing her. "Now, now. It can't be all that bad, can it?" He handed her a box of tissue.

"It's the worst thing I've ever done. I'm so ashamed."

"Why don't you tell me all about it? I'm sure we can smooth things over." He put his arm around her shoulder and let her lay her head against his chest.

She dabbed at her eyes and blew her nose, then straightened up. She took a deep breath, looked at her Pastor, then said, "I've had an affair with one of our neighbors."

"How long has this been going on?"

She shook her head. "Just a short time." She blew her nose again. "It happened so fast.

I didn't even have time to think. One moment we were jogging together when a rain storm hit, and the next thing I knew we were..." She started to cry again.

"Does Eric know about..."

"No! And he can't know, either!" she said emphatically, looking up at him with eyes that displayed terror.

"And how about the other man? How does he feel about things?"

She dabbed her eyes and took a deep breath. She looked at her hands as she spoke. "I told him what we did was a mistake and I didn't want it to happen again."

"How did he respond to that?"

"He doesn't want to stop. He says he won't let me quit seeing him."

"What do you mean, he won't let you?"

"He threatened to tell Eric if I stopped seeing him." She cried again.

"All right. Listen. Can you talk Eric into taking you somewhere for a while? To get away? To give this thing time to cool down?"

She stopped crying and looked at him. "Did Eric call you?"

"No. Why?"

"Because we're leaving for the Grand Canyon day after tomorrow."

The wheels in MacAffie's head began spinning as he thought of the possibilities of solving several problems at once here.

He rose from his seat and patted her on the shoulder. "Tell you what. The two of you just go and have a great vacation. I'm convinced getting away will solve many problems. You and Eric have the most enjoyable vacation you've ever had."

"Are you sure?"

"Leave everything to me."

The next day, Eric and Dawn left for the Grand Canyon.

Chapter 34

It was eight o'clock in the evening, and the cold, foggy, February night was lit by crimson-orange flames exploding through the roof of the two-story house at the end of the cul-de-sac on Royal Court. The flames reached for the sky, licking the damp air with it's sharp tongue. The house was located in the elite, pricy subdivision above of the main town of Los Alamos, where the average price of a four-thousand-five-hundred square foot house appraised at over a million and change.

. From a distance, the colors of the flames danced on the evening fog like an unsettled spirit. People from the small cul-de-sac were huddled in groups, talking amongst themselves in hushed tones, as if witnessing an illegal hanging. Aside from the crackling of burning wood, and the angry roar of the fire giving it a life of its own, the air was silent. No one made any attempt to put out the fire, because it had already fully engulfed the designer house.

The air was suddenly pierced by the wail of fire engines, as the Fire Department, led by a yellow Jeep Cherokee, driven by Fire Chief Earnest Fitzgerald, rolled into the cul-de-sac. The house was located at the very end of the street, on the left-hand side. All the houses on the cul-de-sac contained three-car garages, so there were virtually no vehicles parked on the street itself. That would soon change, however, as first the emergency vehicles arrived, followed in short order by roaming television vans whose reporters, with their hand-held cameras, were already feeding live data to their mother stations. Next would come the curious, the ambulance chasers, and the inevitable opportunist looking for a way to take advantage of someone else's disaster.

The men from the fire trucks wasted no time unraveling their hoses, but the heat was so intense that they were unable to get within fifty feet of the blaze. The firemen had on their protective yellow heat-resistant fire-fighting gear, complete with oxygen tanks and clear masks to protect their face, and eyes from sparks. They showered the inferno with streams of water, but that was instantly converted into the hissing sounding of steam as it reached the flames.

Terry Poon and Paul Koslowski, owners of the homes on either side of burning house, had positioned themselves on their respective roofs, trying to wet down their houses with garden hoses in an effort to keep their houses cool enough so they wouldn't ignite from sparks of the inferno. Their pitiful efforts were as unless as an ant crawling up an elephant's leg with rape on its mind. Even though they were forty feet from the blazing house, the paint had already begun to blister and some of the exterior siding was already smoking.

According to the neighbors, there had been an explosion that had occurred simultaneously with the fire, which had presumably caused the fire. All of the windows of the houses on either side facing the burning house had been shattered from an explosion.

The form of a person could be seen in the second-story window of the house on the right, frantically pulling down flaming curtains in an attempt to curb any further damage to his home.

The Los Alamos Police Watch Commander, Pierce Terryman, drove up in his white Bronco shortly after the Fire Chief had arrived. He had heard about the fire on his scanner as he had left his office for the day. It was his habit to remain abreast of anything that occurred within his jurisdiction, even a fire.

"Any idea what happened here?" Terryman asked Fire Chief Earnest Fitzgerald as he eyed the roaring blaze.

"Just got here myself. By the looks of the damage to the houses on either side, my guess would be either a bomb or gas explosion."

Terryman nodded. "I doubt anyone could have survived the blast, let alone the fire," he said, almost matter-of-factly.

"Anyone know what happened here?" Fire Chief Fitzgerald asked, addressing the huddled onlookers.

At first there was silence, as if no one dared speak of the atrocity, lest a hex befall them.

"It was the explosion," a man said, stepping forward to speak for the group.

"Your name?"

"Davis. Jerry Davis. I live at…"

"1427", Fitzgerald interjected, looking at his computer-fed locate-log of the neighborhood. "And, the Nesbits live here." He nodded towards the inferno, still not yielding to the water.

"Eric and Dawn Nesbit," Davis affirmed.

"This explosion…do you happen to know if it occurred before or after the fire?"

"My wife and I were in the kitchen." He nodded towards his house, which was next to Paul Koslowski. "We had just finished putting the dishes away when this tremendous explosion took place. It nearly knocked us off our feet! The dishes rattled and…"

"Do you know anything about the Nesbits?" he interrupted. "If they were home, or could have been in the house?" he asked, squinting as he watched the firemen pour water on the flames. Time was precious, and if someone were trapped inside the house, he had to know—and he had to know now, if there were any chances of saving anyone, although he knew, from looking at the blaze, no live, breathing creature could have survived either the blast or the inferno raging within. He knew that sending one or more of his men into the fire would bring certain disaster. Yet, if there were the possibility of someone being in the house, alive, they'd go in. That was their job and they were prepared to do it if their leader so commanded.

"They're on vacation," a new voice offered from behind the group.

"And, you are?" he inquired, looking at the man. He recognized him from the religious television program that his wife periodically watched on Sundays.

"MacAffie. Pastor Aaron MacAffie," he announced with an air of dignity. Emerging from the crowd was a stocky man dressed in a sports jacket, slacks and a white mock-turtleneck sweater. He appeared to be very well groomed, with a hair piece that seemed a little out of place.

Watch Commander Pierce Terryman wanted to hear more about the explosion, so when Fire Chief Fitzgerald turned his attention to MacAffie, he quizzed Davis in greater detail. If there was an accidental explosion, that would be Fitzgerald's department. If there was a crime, such as a bomb resulting in a potential homicide, then he would head up the investigation.

MacAffie detected a puzzled look in Fitzgerald's face, realizing that the Fire Chief must be wondering what he was doing here as he pretended to quickly scan his computer-director for the name MacAffie, not finding it.

"I'm their Pastor," he added quickly, anticipating his next question. "I saw the whole sky light up from my church…The Living Christ Church." Everyone knew of his church. Mentioning it would lend credibility to his being there. "Knew there must be a tragedy and thought that I might be of some service."

"Do-gooders," Fitzgerald grunted under his breath. There's one in every crowd, every fire. Someone always shows up, pretending to want to help…and some are genuine in their intentions, but this is a job for trained experts. Amateurs simply muddle up the operating and get in the way, or worse yet, get hurt or killed.

"Do you know the whereabouts of the Nesbits?" he asked Pastor MacAffie. The tone of Fitzgerald's voice was quick and to the point. He didn't have time for idle chitchat, and his manner conveyed that message. If he could get confirmation that no one was in the structure, he would breathe easier.

"They're on vacation in the Grand Canyon. Been gone for over a week now. Eric had said he would be home tomorrow night, in time for Sunday's service. He's a deacon in my church, you know," as if everyone knew the church's business. "Boy, they're going to be in for a rude surprise when they see this," he said, holding his hand over his eyes to shield them from the glare. "Any idea how it happened?"

Fitzgerald grunted again. Idle chitchat. All he wanted was the facts. He ignored MacAffie's inquiry. "Know when they're expected back? What time?"

"Knowing Eric and Dawn and how they like to squeeze every minute out of a vacation, I would guess late afternoon tomorrow, early evening. About this time," the Pastor said, looking at his watch.

"Grand Canyon! In the wintertime?" Jerry Davis, who was apparently through talking to Commander Perryman, asked. "That's the worst time to go. Roads are closed and you can't enjoy the beauty of the place. I mean, we're talkin' snow, man. Haven't you been watchin' the telly? There's a wicked snowstorm brewing there right now. The forecast for the past week called for tons of the stuff. I'd hate to be there."

"That's why they went…to see God's country in its finest spender. No bottle throwin', trash spreadin', bumper-to-bumper tourists—just the Nesbits and God," the preacher said, badly mimicking a Southern drawl.

"Well, I can assure you they won't even see the ground, let alone cans and bottles!" Davis exclaimed. "They'll be lucky if they aren't snowed in for the duration. That's not for me, thank you."

Just the thought of all that snow made Davis shiver. He shrugged his shoulders and inched closer to the fire, extending his hands to get warm. The flames were subsiding now and there was a bite in the air. "Hope he's got fire insurance," he muttered aloud.

"You can be sure that he's adequately covered," the Pastor said, confidently. "I helped him put together his insurance package," he added quickly when he noticed Fitzgerald had shot him a quick glance.

When the fire had been fully extinguished, one of the firemen strung a band of bright-yellow plastic tape with the lettering, "Police Line—No Trespassing" around the perimeter of what was left of the Nesbit's house. The only things left standing which indicated that a house had even once stood where the pile of ashes now lay were two rock fireplaces reaching majestically towards the sky like two sentries, guarding the grounds. The pile of rubble lay fuming, emitting an occasional spit or hiss as the flaming monster sucked its last breath.

Tomorrow the investigative team would sift through the ashes, looking for clues to determine what had caused the blast. "Probably a leaky gas joint," Fitzgerald guessed, "ignited by the pilot light in the water heater. Wouldn't be the first time. We're just lucky that no one was home when it happened."

Fitzgerald was the last to leave. He noticed a lone figure standing on a lawn under the shadow of an olive tree. He pulled his Cherokee in next to the sidewalk, parallel to the figure. He was dressed in a leather jacket, blue jeans and a dark green beret and was leaning against the tree with his hands in his pockets.

"You live near here?" Fitzgerald inquired without emotion. Years of being on the job had taught him that the less a person feels threatened, the more at ease he will feel and the more information he'll yield.

"Nay," came the response. "Just passin' through when I saw the blaze in the sky. Never could resist a good fire."

The man had an obvious foreign accent, Fitzgerald thought—Irish or Scottish. No reason why he should be here, then again, considering the fire, no reason why not. "Mind if I get your name?" Fitzgerald asked, taking out his clipboard.

"McGown. Matty McGown."

"Do you live here, in Los Alamos, Mr. McGown?"

He shook his head as he looked around. Fitzgerald wondered if he was thinking of running.

"I'm just visitin'."

"Do you mind if I see your ID?"

It appeared somewhat unusual for someone to have stayed at the burn site for so long, after the fire had been extinguished and everyone had vacated...especially standing so far back from where the fire had been—unless were was some specific reason for his being there, of course.

The man dug into the back of his pants and pulled out an black wallet, wrinkled over years of use. "As I said, I'm just passin' through. The only ID I have is from Ireland." He pulled out an Irish identification card and handed it up to Fitzgerald.

He wrote down the man's name and identification number, then handed the card back to him.

Fitzgerald nodded as he studied McGown's face, looking for a reason to detain him.

Finding none, he said, "Well, the excitement is all over here, Mr. McGown." He nodded towards the smoldering embers. "I suggest you be on your way."

The man nodded. Fitzgerald watched as he slowly made his way up the street. He followed a few yards behind, until he saw him get into a rental car with an Avis tag on the rear windshield. He made a note of the license number as the car pulled away.

Chapter 35

▼

Fitzgerald's team was on the scene early the next morning, ready to start their investigation. They established an evidence table which would contain any item that they might find and wanted to preserve.

In addition to the people that lived on the street, a small group of curious passerbys had wandered into the cul-de-sac to watch. Matty McGown was present among those curious people, although he made a point to remain all but obscure, standing behind a tree or next to a van.

A uniformed officer who had been assigned to stand guard over the site kept everyone behind the yellow no-trespassing tape. It was normal operating procedure to preserve the scene of a fire in those cases where arson might have been the cause. Even if a faulty gas line had been ignited by a pilot light and was thought to have been the cause of fire, Fitzgerald's policy fell on the side of caution.

It wasn't long before one of the firemen rushed to his vehicle, pulling the mike from his car. He spoke quietly, so those edging toward him to listen couldn't hear when he said, "Chief, you better get down here right away. And maybe you should notify Commander Terryman, too. You'll both want to see this!"

Fitzgerald and Terryman arrived within moments of each other, Fitzgerald in his yellow Cherokee and Terryman in his unmarked white Bronco. As soon as Matty McGown spotted Fitzgerald he backed into the shadows, making sure Fitzgerald didn't see him.

"What's up, Scott? Must be important, to get you riled up enough to get us both down here at once." Fitzgerald's voice was all business sprinkled with a vein of concern as he looked towards the long, black plastic evidence container that lay on the table behind the yellow tape.

Fireman Scott made no response as he lifted the lid.

Fitzgerald and Terryman viewed the contents of the box, then gave each other a knowing glance. What lie in the box was the skull of a human being, seared clean by the fire. "There's more," Scott said. "There are two of them."

"The Nesbits," Terryman said, as he straightened his six-foot-four frame and stretched backwards, a habit that he had acquired over the years which, in body language, meant a resigned indication that they had their work cut out for them. "Any location of the source of the blast or where the fire started yet?" he asked, as he brushed his yellow shock of hair back with his big hands, knowing the answer without asking it.

"Too early to tell. I'll know more tomorrow."

"Soon as you get the balance of the remains collected," he said with a nod towards the pile of debris, "get everything down to forensics." He sneezed, and pulled a white handkerchief from his back pocket and blew his nose. "It doesn't look like there's much left to examine. Any evidence of foul play, assuming there was some, was been eradicated by the fire, but let the boys from the lab to their thing."

"Getting a cold there, big fella?" Fitzgerald asked, banging him on the back.

"Damned sinuses. Happens every time I get around soot and ashes." He blew his nose hard again.

"Careful. Might blow what few brain cells you got left." He laughed.

"Very funny."

"Never become a fireman," Fitzgerald ribbed him, with good humor.

"Never fear. That's why I'm a cop. No ashes."

By this time, reporters from the *San Jose Mercury News* and Channel 36 had arrived on the scene and were already busy taking pictures and interviewing neighbors on camera, following up on the fire of the night before.

"Chief Fitzgerald! Have you uncovered any evidence of foul play? I understand there was an explosion just before the fire," the reporter from the television station inquired in a demanding voice, looking at his notes and, at the same time, balancing his microphone. "I see that the Los Alamos Watch Commander, Pierce Terryman, is on the scene," he said, glancing towards Terryman and pointing the mike in his direction. History had told him talking to Pierce Terryman or any of his men would yield virtually no information. He doubted that Fitzgerald would tell him anything, either, but still, it was his job to ask. "Have you uncovered any bodies?"

Standard reporter questions. Fitzgerald had heard them a million times and had fielded them just as often. Procedure was to throw them just enough crumbs to so they'd have a story to report: the obvious facts, such as there was a fire and the house had burned down. That way they'd go away happy and not bug him about any facets of the investigation that he wasn't ready to disclose yet.

"Preliminary indication is that the blast was a result of a faulty gas line that was probably ignited by the pilot light in the water heater," Fitzgerald told the reporter. "If we uncover anything that alters that theory, that information will be made available as it's known." A statement without making a statement.

Having gleaned all they could from the Fire Chief, the reporters switched their interest to the Watch Commander. Might as well interview everyone. That way their boss wouldn't fault them for not asking. "Detective Terryman! Why are you here! Is foul play suspected?"

"We like to keep ourselves apprised of anything that might affect our citizens...coming down on the side of precaution, if you will." Another non-statement. "At this stage of our investigation, there is no indication of foul play, just an unfortunate fire that might have been averted with a little caution."

"I understand," he smiled as he quickly consulted his handwritten notes, "that Eric and Dawn Nesbit haven't been notified of the loss of their home yet. What, if anything, is being done to locate them?"

"My understanding is that they were scheduled to be on holiday to the Grand Canyon." A true fact, as far as it went.

"So they could be on their way home as we speak?"

"Could be. I can't verify that one way or another."

"What are they collecting over there? Those men putting things into the plastic containers?"

Commander Terryman looked over his shoulder. With a trained stoic look that betrayed none of the seriousness of the matter, he simply said, "Material to be examined to determine various factors relative to the fire."

Matty McGown, who had overheard the conversation between the reporters and Commander Terryman, made his departure from the scene before everyone else. He had heard enough to confirm what he already knew—that someone had died in the fire. The one thing he didn't want to was to have Fitzgerald find him there. After last night, he would have a hard time explaining his presence. King Arthur had made it clear that he wasn't to get involved with the law.

*   *   *   *

"What have you got for me, Scott?" Pierce Terryman asked as he entered the forensics lab the next day.

"There wasn't anything in the human remains you brought me that showed any indication of foul play. I can't even tell you if the victims died in the fire. For that matter, I can't even tell you how long they had been dead. The fire purged almost all of the evidence. I can say that the skeletal remains indicated no physical stress, such as broken bones, cracked skulls or bullet holes." He looked at Terryman, as if expecting him to question his results, yet knowing that there was nothing for him to question. "It'll be a few days before we can verify that the victims were the Nesbits," he said with a voice the hinted at routine procedure. "We're taking dental X-rays of the skulls as we speak. As soon as the film is developed, we'll try to locate their dentist, then shoot the negatives over for positive ID."

* * * *

Terryman met Chief Fitzgerald in the main hall, just before leaving. "Been to forensics?" Pierce asked.

"I just was on my way over there after my meeting with the mayor. Any news?"

Terryman shook his head. "A dead end so far...no pun intended. The fire destroyed any clue as to cause of death, assuming it was something other than the explosion and the fire. Chin says it'll be a few days before he can pull all the pieces together for a positive ID. How about you? Anything new from your end?"

"Well, all the tests aren't in yet." He paused for a moment before continuing. "But there seems to be an indication that the victims died in the kitchen, probably just after coming home. They probably parked their car in the garage and entered the house through the laundry room. My people examined the stove: gas." He looked at Terryman for emphasis, knowing that he would get his meaning before he finished the sentence.

"They found one of the burners turned on. Apparently, when the Nesbits left for their vacation, someone must not have turned the burner off. They were gone a long time, and the house simply filled with gas. My guess is that, when they turned on the lights, there might have been a spark in the switch or something that ignited the gas and—well, as Paul Harvey would say, 'you know the rest of the story.'"

"Except that if a gas burner *was* left on, presumably the stove's pilot light would have burned the gas," Terryman offered.

"Unless the pilot was faulty or somehow got extinguished."

"I don't know," Terryman said. "It's a little loose for my taste. The stove isn't that old and it's a little too coincidental for a burner to be left on and the pilot light to be extinguished all at the same time."

"That's why I'm tossing the ball to you. We'll keep sifting, but in the meantime, maybe you should start a background check on this guy, Nesbit. See if he's got any skeletons hiding in the closet. Maybe he had an enemy or owed someone money."

"Or, someone just wanted him dead!"

"There's a thought!"

"Someone wanted him dead."

"So, you have suspect, or are you going to just dangle the carrot there all day?"

"How about a secret lover?"

"One that wants them *both* dead! Come on."

"Hey! Anything's possible. Haven't you ever heard of the 'If I can't have you, neither can anyone else' theory?"

"You've been watching too much television."

Chapter 36

"Major Pennypacker! If you've got a few minutes, sir, perhaps you could stop over. I've had a recent communication from the Irish operative working in America."

"Matty Gown to King Arthur?"

"Yes, sir."

"Be right down."

It was a three-minute walk from Major Pennypacker's office on the main floor of the security building, where they had a room set up specifically to monitor calls from Matty McGown to the Sons of Ireland, ever since they had learned of the Northern Irish political terrorist faction trying to extend their establishment in America through Aaron MacAffie. It had been a growing concern of Pennypacker's that the British intelligence keep American governmental officials out of and unaware of the goings-on between their government and the Sons of Ireland. If the CIA ever found out that British military intelligence had installed a hot target like the Macafy's in their country, it would not only be a major embarrassment, but MI 5 would be the laughing-stock of the intelligence world. You just don't take your dirty laundry to a foreign soil, then lose it. They didn't even tell their overseas intelligence, MI 6, about the operation for fear of ridicule.

Pennypacker slapped his riding crop against his leg as he walked into the small, stark room, void of furnishings except for the recording and listening equipment that had been hooked into the line leading directly to King Arthur's connection. As of yet, no one on the British side knew who King Arthur was. The name was obviously intentionally bogus, designed to protect his identification.

It had been no problem for intelligence to trace the line to the location of the telephone, but that had proved useless as well. The telephone line led into a large warehouse, where over a hundred men worked and where countless patronized, bringing or taking merchandise in a daily manner. The telephone line was located somewhere within that warehouse...perhaps in an office, a corner or even in some storage crate or a secret room. They would never know without a search, and a search would blow their cover, so they were limited to knowing what they did about who was answering the line, which was next to nothing.

"Play the tape!"

The Corporal slipped the tape out of the recording machine and snapped it into another, totally separate, unattached recording device. They couldn't take the chance of replaying the tape in the original recording machine, because, in the unlikely event another incoming telephone transmission came over the wire, they would be forced to choose whether to record the new message over the old message, thus erasing it, or to let it go and not record it at all. Neither option was acceptable. The Corporal installed a new tape in the receiving machine, put on his earphones and played the tape for Major Pennypacker.

The transmission from America was clear, due to their advanced telephone technology, while the reception from northern Ireland was full of static.

"King Arthur. Matty McGown here."

"I know who you are," the voice snapped. "You don't have to say your name!"

Pennypacker smiled as he lit his pipe and sat back in the chair provided by the corporal.

"Remember my telling you that our man Macafy had set up the demise of his flying friend, one Andrew Mullin?"

"Yes, Matty, I remember."

Even with the bad connection, Pennypacker could tell that King Arthur wasn't patient with his man in America.

"Well, since that time he's added a couple of his flock to the list."

"What do you mean?"

"I watched him go into this vacant house one evening while the owners were on vacation."

"And?"

"Well, I don't exactly know what he did or how he did it, but..."

"How do you know he wasn't just watering the plants or feeding the dog?" King Arthur interrupted.

It was Matty McGown who was getting a little short now. The pitch of his voice elevated in frustration. "He parked his car down the street so no one would spot him. Then he walked up to the house, dressed all in black, looked around kinda sneaky-like, then slipped in through a side window. I watched him!" he said defensively, before the other voice had a chance to challenge him. "The lights never came on in the house the whole time he was in there. A few minutes later he ran down the street and drove away."

"That's it?"

"A few days later the people must'a come home, because their house blew up with them inside! This guys a loon, I tell ya."

There was a silence on the other end for a moment. "Maybe it's time we elevate our plan to the next step, Matty."

"What do ya want me ta do? Rough him up?"

There was another moment of silence. Pennypacker could hear a discussion in the background of King Arthur, but the line had so much static that he couldn't make out the words. "Tell you what. Watch him for a while longer, then report back to me. By that time, we'll have a plan."

"You're the boss."

"And, Matty?"

"Yeah."

"Don't get caught doin' nothin'. I'd hate to have to send Benny over there to take care of business, if you get my meanin'."

Matty got his "meanin", all right. Benny was the organization's enforcer. If you saw Benny comin' your way, it usually meant that you were destined for the meat locker.

The line went dead. "We've got to trace that line," Pennypacker said, nervously slapping his leg with the riding crop. "Who's our best telephone man?"

"That'd be Sean McTavish."

"Have him get over to the warehouse and find the location of that line. Things are heating up much too fast. I want to know who we're dealin' with! No confrontations. Just ID the source!"

* * * *

Sean McTavish was a small man, standing no more than five-foot-five. He was dark-complected, wore a bushy mustache and usually three-days-growth of heavy beard. There was nothing special about the man that would cause him to stand out as he walked into the Macintosh and Sons Warehouse.

"What can I do for ya, mate?" the man behind the desk asked.

"I've got some art works that I inherited from the family, and I have no room to keep them in the house, so quite naturally, I thought of storing them. I asked an art dealer who would be reputable, and they recommended you."

"Sure. We can store anything you want. As you can tell, we have over five-hundred-thousand square feet of warehouse here. We can store anything from a Sherman tank to your aunt Meg's jewelry." He laughed.

"The paintings are quite old, and the art gallery said that I should keep them where they won't be damaged. Is that a problem?"

"Nah. We label everything according to name and contents and can insure up to a million dollars per item."

"Would it be possible to look around a little? Just to satisfy myself, you understand. It's my wife. She's, how shall I say…"

He waved his hand. "Say no more, mate. I've got a mother-in-law that's the same way. Just walk around the center aisles and mind the jitneys. Wouldn't want you to get rolled over." He laughed. "And no openin' boxes, either." He smiled as he waved his hand.

"Won't be but a minute. I'll just leave when I've had a quick look, just so I can tell the missus. You understand."

The clerk waved his hand over his shoulder as he went on to the next customer.

Sean walked down the musty-smelling aisles. There were rows upon rows of merchandise piled ten to thirty feet tall in the building with a eight-foot aisle in between. Sean McTavish knew exactly where the telephone wires came into the warehouse, so it was no great feat to locate them against the back wall of the building. There was no activity in this area; still, he had to keep an ear open to any sound, just in case there were guards roaming around. To a certain degree, he could feign being lost if detected, but preferred not to be caught and questioned.

In the unfortunate event he were caught and searched, he would have a very difficult time explaining the sophisticated detection equipment on his person, hidden in the under garment that he wore just beneath his coat, let alone the small automatic weapon equipped with a silencer that he carried strapped to his ankle.

He located the telephone wire and traced it to a large wooden box, four feet square and five feet tall sitting on ground level against the back wall. "Now that's interestin'. The phone wires go into this box, here." Upon examination, the boxed proved to be secured by two hex screws, both at the top and at the bottom. In a matter of seconds Sean had the screws out. The side of the box swung open to his touch, as the other side was secured by hinges that had been mounted on the inside of the container, so as not to be seen from the outside.

Inside the box had been built a small desk-like apparatus with a stool for a seat. From the looks of the small stool, it had had a lot of use. The varnish was worn bare on the outer edges. On the crude desk, a telephone receiver had been taped into a receptacle. The other side of the receptacle was an identical receiver, only reversed.

"Now, isn't that cute. The calls comes in and is automatically forwarded on to another location. Hmm. Let's try something."

He took out his instrument and hooked it up to the receiver, then dialed the number and pushed a button, engaging the line. There was a ring, then, "Gempac!" came the simple response.

"Yes, I was wondering if I might talk to the man in charge of purchasing."

"Who ya callin', mate?"

He recited the number

"Where did you get this number?" came the demand.

"Some bloke gave it to me. "Could you tell me where you're located, so I might come over?"

"You got a wrong number!" the voice snapped.

The line went dead.

"Well, that's mighty interstin'."

Sean replaced the equipment as it had ben, secured the box as he had found it and left.

*   *   *   *

The Captain on duty at Gempac, the Greater Elite Military Power Control station in London, buzzed the General as soon as the telephone call came in.

"What is it, Captain?"

"I think our line has been compromised, General. There's no way anyone could have dialed this station direct unless they came through the Irish connection."

"Have it looked into immediately. Probably some fool stumbled upon the connection and was playing mind games. Nonetheless, one can't be too careful, now can we, Captain?"

"No, sir!"

Chapter 37

The Nesbit children—Laura, twenty-nine, the eldest daughter, and the twins, Mark and Matt, twenty-six—arrived at their parents family attorney's office together. They were ushered into a walnut-paneled office, where one wall had been lined with law books, while the other walls contained oil paintings depicting life in early-American horse-and-buggy days. The floor was hardwood planking, stained black walnut, on top of which a deep, plush maroon Chinese carpet had been placed in front of a black leather couch. The desk was an authentic French Eighteenth-century piece, adorned by a single brass lamp.

"I want to express how sorry I am for your loss," Andrea Houesman said, as he entered his office and shook the hands of the Nesbit children before taking his seat. He had been Eric Nesbit's friend, racquetball partner and lawyer for the past ten years.

When Eric and Dawn had come to his office, asking him to add a codicil to their will last year, he had been guardedly pessimistic, especially when he had been informed of the new terms of the will, but then, he had just been looking out for what he thought was the family's best interest.

He could see that the kids were uneasy being there, fidgeting, wanting to get the ordeal over with. Deep circles were still imbedded under Laura's eyes, the result of many hours of grief. The boys seemed to be holding their own.

"We're waiting for one additional party before we begin," Houesman said. His voice was almost apologetic, but the children dismissed it as an expression of his feelings towards their parents.

At that moment, his secretary rang through to his desk, announcing that the other member of the will-reading party had just arrived.

He instructed her to usher him in.

"Pastor MacAffie," Houesman said in an unenthusiastic voice, rising to shake his hand as he motioned for MacAffie to take a seat next to the Nesbit children. "I assume you know Laura, Mark and Matt Nesbit?"

"But of course," he said with a large smile. "I'm so sorry for your loss. Your parents were wonderful disciples of God and the church. We'll all miss them." His words and the tone of his voice didn't match expression on his face, which was anything but maudlin.

MacAffie took a chair beside Laura and, in sitting down, slid it back a foot, so as to be out of the line of her peripheral vision. He unbuttoned his coat, put one leg up on his knee and bushed his black polished boots with his hand while he waited for the will to be read, a portion of the contents of which, he already knew.

The Nesbit children looked at one another, wondering what MacAffie was doing at a meeting of the reading of their parent's will, but they had the good breeding not to inquire. They would find out soon enough.

"Well, now that we're all here, I may as well start," Houesman stated, in his most-lawyer-type voice. "This will was originally executed five years ago, then…" he paused, "last year a codicil was added."

He looked at the Nesbit children, as if attempting to convey an unspoken message, then went on the read the essentials of the will. "'To my three surviving children, Laura, Mark and Matt Nesbit, Eric Nobel Nesbit and Dawn Ann Nesbit hereby bequeath our entire investment portfolio, any cash in the bank and current invested stocks and bonds, which our attorney Andrea Houesman has in his possession, to be divided equally between the three surviving children. In the event one of the children predeceases us, the estate shall be divided equally between the surviving children. In the event there are no surviving family members at the reading of this will, our entire estate shall go the Living Christ Church, Pastor Aaron MacAffie presiding.'"

So that's why he's here, Laura thought to herself.

"Do you have any questions about the will at this point?" Houesman asked, looking specifically at the Nesbit children.

Matt raised his hand. "What about our house? I assume that's included, although you haven't specifically made mention of it."

"What house?" Laura said, looking at Matt as if he were a bug. "Just in case you forgot, it was burned to the ground, with our parents inside!" She started crying.

Pastor MacAffie started to put his hand on her shoulder, but then thought better of it.

"I know that, Laura," Matt said. But the house was insured. I was speaking figuratively when I said 'the house.' Obviously, I meant the insurance to rebuild the house."

"Well, who else would they give it to?" They had by this time been so absorbed in the reading of their parents last will and testament that they had but forgotten that Pastor MacAffie was still sitting in the background.

Houseman shifted nervously in his chair, taking care not to look the Nesbit children in the eyes, and said, "Well, let's finish reading the will." He held the paper at arms length then cleared his throat. "There is one remaining provision that will, I'm sure, clear up any questions you may have relative to the issue concerning the disposition of the house or what remains, i.e. the lot and the insurance to rebuild same."

He paused, adjusted his reading glasses, exhaled deeply, then began reading the last passage of Eric and Dawn Nesbit's will.

"This is the codicil that was added to the will last year. 'To Aaron MacAffie and the Living Christ Church, to further his wonderful work with the Lord and in gratitude for his giving us his guidance these past years, we hereby bequeath our home at 1414 Royal Court, Los Alamos Hills, California. The personal property contained within the house shall be divided between the surviving children as they see fit, to be agreed upon amongst themselves.'"

The three Nesbit children sat in stunned silence, disbelieving what they had just heard. It was Laura who that broke the silence. "Personal property? Big deal! What personal property?

Everything was burnt up in the fire!" She was crying openly now, her tears masking the anger and frustration she felt.

Matt put his arm around her shoulder as he looked to Houesman for guidance.

Houseman was obviously feeling uncomfortable as he looked up at his clients. He made a facial gesture that indicated there was nothing he could do, then he said, "That concludes the reading of the will." He deliberately closed the folder and sat with his hands folded on his desk.

There was silence for a moment. It was Laura who spoke first. She had stopped crying now. Her voice was tempered, but still had a bite that indicated her anger. "How could our parents have given our house to someone else? A church!" She shot a glance to Aaron MacAffie, who was busy examining his fingernails. "It's our house. We were raised there. It's not fair!" She broke down crying again.

Matt put his arm around his sister again, but she shook it off in anger.

"You said something earlier about their revising the will," Matt probed, looking sympathetically at his sister.

Houesman took a deep breath. "Yes. Your father had called to make the appointment. He said he wanted to discuss modifying the will. When your parents arrived, they handed me a typewritten page indicating the change they wanted to make." He took another deep breath. "It was obvious that he hadn't been happy with the change, but apparently it was something that he and your mother had discussed and had apparently agreed upon, even if he didn't like it—willing their house to the church."

"Did you know about this?" Matt turned to ask Aaron MacAffie. The tone of his voice contained a degree of accusatory self-indulgence.

MacAffie finished studying his fingernails and turned his attention to the grain in the paneling behind Matt's head, not wanting to meet his piercing eyes. "Your parents came to me and said they wanted to do something for the church." His voice had an even, guarded tone. He knew that he was on the defensive here, but had to try to smooth things over, then get out of the office.

The Nesbits had issued their last will and testament. He knew that short of a court order, nothing could undo that act. "Something that would make a major contribution to our ministry," he continued. "We're live on TV now, you know?" he beamed, looking momentarily at each child, as if seeking praise. "Two hours every week. I'm working on being on television daily. Our goal is to go national as soon as we have enough contributions. I'm sure that's what your parents had in mind when they made their contribution to the church. You can understand that, can't you?"

"For you to go on television?" Matt asked, unbelieving.

"That, and to further the word of God. That is the main objective here." His voice took on a tone of admonishment as he looked sternly at Matt for the first time.

Matt wanted to say, "And to further your ever expanding ego". Instead, he chose to remain mute, gritting his teeth, knowing that whatever he said would have no impact on his parent's decision to will their home to MacAffie and the church. He was well aware of MacAffie's evangelistic ambitions, that he had started his church in the basement of a parishioner's home, then had graduated to ever-larger facilities, each time through gifts and generous donations of either money or space.

The will had been read and there was little else to be done. Aaron MacAffie was the first to leave, offering his hand to each of the Nesbit Children, who, except Laura, received it with cool reservation. She simply turned her back.

As Aaron MacAffie walked out of the law offices, it was all he could do to keep from smiling. Outside the door, he clenched his fist in exuberance, as he could barely believe his good fortune. He had estimated that the insurance claim on the house would be in the approximate amount of seven-hundred-fifty-thousand dollars, plus he would have the lot to sell, which should bring an additional three-to-four-hundred-thousand. That would pay off a lot of pressing bills and allow for a handsome bonus to himself.

Chapter 38

▼

The nine o'clock service was filled to near capacity, as usual. This was the service that was to be recorded for television, to be shown on Channel 44 at eleven AM. This gave the producers time to edit out anything they didn't want to show the general public, such as church announcements, passing the collection plate or anything that wasn't showy enough to hold the watchers interest.

This was the time of day when Pastor Aaron MacAffie was fresh and at his best: early and "on". The camera panned the choir as they sang *Just A Closer Walk With Thee* which MacAffie had the conductor jazz up the tempo to sound like an old Negro spiritual. The choir was standing, fully encompassing the circular stage, three rows deep. They were dressed in their magnificent crimson robes with white sashes, rocking and clapping their hands, with each member smiling and looking up as if singing personally to the Lord. The audience responded by rocking back and forth in their seats, many clapping their hands to the choir's beat.

When the choir had finished, Aaron MacAffie rose from his seat next to his wife and their two-year-old son. He took deliberate steps to the oak pulpit, dressed in his opal-white robe with crimson sash. He looked ten years younger with his new hairpiece, which was neatly combed into his own hair.

The camera zoomed in for a close-up. His voice started out deep and quiet, filling the huge base speakers which had been generously placed throughout the circular church, suspended from its magnificent eighteen-inch glue-lam beams.

"You have all heard of Eric and Dawn Nesbit's untimely death." He paused with his head bowed for a moment, immortalizing the moment in everyone's minds. The camera panned the congregation, then fixed back on Pastor MacAffie. "God has called them to sit at his feet." His voice sounded soulful, his face maudlin. "They will suffer the effects of this world no more. They have paid the ultimate price by unwittingly giving their life to the fire demon."

Several "Amens" came from the audience. Many of the audience held their palms to the sky.

Center stage continued its slow, circular motion bringing Pastor Aaron MacAffie face to face with each and every person present in his magnificent temple. "Eric and Dawn Nesbit's deaths will not be forgotten, however."

"Amen!"

"The Lord foresaw their demise and led them to the church before their death, instructing them to will their worldly possessions to God before they met their Maker."

"Praise the Lord!"

Pastor MacAffie studied the rows of anxious faces as they slowly passed by his pulpit. "Aaron and Dawn were asked by God to donate their home to the house of the Lord. To you." he extended his arms. "To the Living Christ Church!"

"Amen! Praise the Lord!"

His voice was heavy with emotion now and his hands were shaking in the air as he turned to face the oncoming audience. The television cameras came in for a close-up shot, catching every facial inflection. MacAffie's lips trembled and he managed to manufacture a tear, which rolled down his cheek. The camera zoomed in even closer, tracking its slow path as it spilled onto his lips.

Several "Praise the Lords" rose from the congregation. The choir hummed their version of *The Old Rugged Cross* in the background as the camera panned first the choir, then the congregation. The congregation was getting into the emotional flow of his well chosen words. Pastor MacAffie would expertly play off their emotions as he delivered his message, a message specially designed to tug at the purse strings of those in his congregation who felt a need to be closer to God. He knew that there were those in attendance who thought that doing something special with their assets, like the Nesbits had done when they had willed their house to the church, was what they would like to do, too.

When Pastor Aaron MacAffie got through with them, he hoped to have such a surge of emotion riding through his flock that they would all rise to their feet, not unlike a Billy Graham crusade, and march forward, throwing their wallets at him.

"Ladies and gentlemen of the Living Christ Church, Eric and Dawn are sitting at the Lord's feet right now, being rewarded for their generous donation, for having the forethought of thinking of their church before themselves."

A multitude of "Amens" and "Praise the Lords" came from the congregation. The choir hummed a little louder as Pastor MacAffie's voice increased in volume and he rose to his tiptoes in an effort to seem overwhelming. Perspiration began to form on his forehead in the heat of the overhead lights. He expertly dabbed at his forehead with a white handkerchief without missing a beat. That would be cut from the film to be shown at the eleven o'clock televised service. His flock couldn't see their leader sweat. It wouldn't be dignified.

"When I learned of Eric and Dawn's untimely death, the Lord spoke to me and told me to immortalize their gift by inscribing their names on a stained glass window of this magnificent house!" His hands were widespread, encompassing the whole congregation. "Now, whenever you look upon that stained-glass window," he pointed towards a side panel where the names Eric and Dawn Nesbit had artistically been painted with liquid lead, "you will think of their generous donation to the church and envision their spirits sitting at the feet of our Lord."

Enthusiastic, "Amen! Praise the Lord."

The lights in the church dimmed and the glass panel lit up as one of the light crew, who had been positioned in the balcony above, pressed a button, activating exterior spot lights that had been previously placed outside the window, so when they were turned on, it looked as if the sun was shinning especially through that window and that window alone.

Every head turned to face the light. The congregation audibly gasped, which was followed by more "Praise the Lords" and then a spontaneous applause. The camera panned the stained-glass window and slowly zoomed in on the names, *Eric and Dawn Nesbit.*

"That's God's light, shinning through the souls of Eric and Dawn Nesbit." Pastor MacAffie's voice boomed over the speakers. The voices of the choir crescendoed. Now the congregation was on their feet, many with their hands raised to the air, praising God.

Aaron MacAffie had done well. He was leading his sheep as if he had a magic wand. Wherever he pointed, they would go. The congregation was rocking to his every word, anesthetized by the magical voices of the choir.

The time to strike was now. The time for which he had brought them to this point of heightened emotion. The point when they were the most vulnerable. The point when some of those in his congregation would now give him anything he wanted, just as he had done with Eric and Dawn Nesbit months before their untimely deaths.

Nevenka sat next to the choir, facing her husband as her mind flashed back on the night they had gone to the Nesbit's for dinner and the day that they had executed their will. She moved uneasily on her chair, clutching the hand of little Vladimer.

"God is speaking to someone in this house right now," Pastor MacAffie said, looking over his congregation, his hands outstretched. "I can hear his voice. I can feel his power." His fists were clenched now, pumping up and down like pistons. Then his voice suddenly became soft, like flowing honey, as he extended an opened hand to the audience. "I know you can feel it, too. He's asking you to be special…special like Dawn and Eric. He's inviting you to make a covenant with Him by giving Him your worldly treasures when you rise to meet Him in His glory. That which He gave you during your life, you can give to His church in death. Your name will live on forever," he said, pointing to Dawn and Eric Nesbit's names in the stained-glass window.

He stepped down from his pulpit and walked down to stand in front of the congregation. "If you can feel God's hand on your shoulder, brothers and sisters, rise and give Him praise!" He strolled deliberately in front of the parishioners, looking them in the eyes as he spoke. "Show Him that you love Him." He raised both hands over his head. "Stand up and reach for God. Praise the Lord. Give thanks to your Creator!"

The choir was humming as loudly as they could now, adding to the emotion of the moment. The television cameras panned the faces in the crowd. Emotions and tears were flowing like rivers. Pastor MacAffie's opal-white robe was changing colors like an eternal fire, illuminated by the alternating blue and red spots above.

Who could resist such words? Emotion flowed through the air on each note from the choir. If you were in the congregation, you *knew* God was talking to you that very moment, telling you that you were special. He was telling you to stand! Raise your hands and lock fingers with Him! Now! Now was the time! Give!

The choir started singing *Just A Closer Walk With Thee*. Tears were rolling down women's faces. Husbands were hugging their wives. An elderly couple stood up, their hands raised into the air. God had spoken to them. They agreed, they'd do it! They wanted that eternal light and their name on a stained-glass panel. They wanted eternal life! They wanted to give. They would give.

Soon, other parishioners were standing, raising their hands and giving praise to God and, before long, there were several hundred people standing. All the stained-glass panels were lit now and the electricity in the air was ecstatic! There wasn't a dry eye in the house. Aaron MacAffie had them rocking. He had them right where he wanted them. They were his. He looked out at the sea of raised hands, floating like so many helium balloons.

"God wants you! Those of you standing, those of you who have shown Him your loyalty and devotion, come down to the front right now! That's right, come down the aisles and stand right in front of me for a special prayer. God wants to see your face up close and personal. He wants to thank you! Come on." He waved. "Those of you in the back of the church, we'll wait for you."

The choir continued humming *Just a Closer Walk With Thee*. The camera panned over the throngs of faces as they filed down to the front, hand in hand, wiping tears that were streaming down their faces. They didn't know whether to laugh or cry, they were so happy to be touched by the Lord.

Nevenka held tight onto her Son's hands. The power that this man who she called her husband had over these people frightened her. What frightened her even more was the length that he would go to in order to manipulate them to get what he wanted.

"If there are those of you who are feeling God speaking to you, but who feel uneasy about coming forward, remember the Apostle Peter when, at the Last Supper, Christ told him that he would deny him three times before the cock crowed. Don't be a Peter and deny God. Act now, while He's inviting you. Tomorrow may be too late!"

More people hesitantly rose from their pews and joined the large throng standing hand in hand in front of Pastor Aaron MacAffie, who, by now, was holding his hands over their heads, giving them a blessing while the stage revolved.

When he was through with his blessing, he asked those standing to file to his left, where dozens of church officers were waiting with pre-printed forms ready to document their names, addresses and telephone numbers. There was a large space left at the bottom of the form, just above the signature line, for them to fill in, indicating those items that they wished to give to God. Their age was one of the items that MacAffie had specifically requested on the form.

It had been a good service, but Pastor Aaron MacAffie wasn't through yet. He still had his television audience. Looking straight into the camera while the choir hummed *The Old Rugged Cross*, using his most conciliatory voice, he pleaded with his television audience—the shut-ins, the elderly, those unable to come to God's temple—to contact his office at their earliest convenience by dialing the phone number imprinted on their television screens and make their wishes known to God. They, too, were eligible for the eternal light in the Living Christ Church. "There are operators waiting by the phone, so call now." The camera zoomed in on the church window with Eric and Dawn Nesbit's name inscribed. "Hurry, space is limited."

He let his viewers know that they had special lawyers on staff who could accommodate them in making their last wish, to give to God that which He had given to them during life. Then, when their life was over and they had gone to rejoin their Master, there would be no further need for their earthly treasures.

* * * *

It had been a good service. He was very pleased with himself. It was a great topic and the effect of the stained glass had been a stroke of genius. There were fifty small, slit-like stained glass windows that surrounded the congregation. He would gladly add names to each panel. The first panel, Nesbit's panel, had brought over a million dollars to the church. If he could duplicate that with each window, that would mean fifty million dollars, more than enough to start his next project: the Aaron MacAffie Institute of Higher Learning.

* * * *

Earnest Fitzgerald was flipping through the channels, looking for a golf game, or maybe some football that might be on early Sunday morning, when he passed through the religion channel. He knew that Aaron MacAffie was the Pastor of the Living Christ church, but had never attended one of his services, nor seen him on television.

He sat transfixed as the choir stirred up the emotion of his audience and MacAffie paraded around the stage, his hands raised to the ceiling, pleading for his congregation to make donations to the church through their wills. *Make them feel guilty.* "Giving back to God that which he gave to you," *is a nice touch,* he thought, as he sipped coffee from his cup.

The television screen flashed to the stained-glass window where the names of Eric and Dawn Nesbit had been inscribed on the lower panel. The light showed through from the other side, illuminating it, seemingly giving the glass a life of its own.

The picture of MacAffie standing in the crowd at the Nesbit fire flashed into his mind and began toying with his imagination. There was something about this man that rubbed him the wrong way. One thing he knew for sure, he didn't like him.

* * * *

At that same instant, Jerry Davis was in his bathrobe, sitting in front of his television, watching "The MacAffie Show", as he called it.

"I hope you're not thinking of pledging anything we own," his wife said over his shoulder with a sarcastic voice as she passed by in her bathrobe, towing their youngest behind her. "We're having enough trouble making ends meet as it is. Maybe you ought to think up a scheme to rake in dough, like the reverend there."

"I'm way ahead of you, my dear." He smiled to himself. "Way ahead."

* * * *

As Nevenka stood at the church doors with her husband, holding young Vladimer's hand, greeting those attending the service, she thought that this would be a good day to bring up the topic of bringing her family from Lithuania to America. The church was doing well and, although her husband was much busier now that he was successful, surely he wouldn't mind taking time to sponsor them.

Everyone praised him for being such a good man, a man of God. What son could ask for a better man as his father? Who could ask for a better husband? How could he refuse?

* * * *

Matty McGown smiled to himself as he sat in his rental car making notes to himself after the service. King Arthur wasn't going to believe this!

Chapter 39

"Mr. Horwitz. There's a Miss Lee on the telephone for you. She says it's regarding a deed from a Andrew Mullin you had asked her about several months ago."

"Miss Lee? Oh, yes. Andrew's secretary. Put her through."

"Miss Lee? Adam Horwitz here. It's been a long time. How have you been?"

"Fine, thank you."

"What can I do for you?"

"You remember several months ago you asked me about a deed that I notarized for Mr. Mullin for Pastor MacAffie?"

"Yes, I remember. I was representing Connie Mullin, Andrew's ex-wife. There was some controversy over Andrew's house. Why do you ask?"

"Well, now that he's gone and the office is closed, I'm in the process of storing all of his records, just in case they're needed for lawsuits, depositions or taxes, you know."

"Yes. I've heard. It's a shame when someone of the stature of Andrew Mullin passes away. The wolves seem to crawl out from every rock. Have there been many suits filed?"

"About a dozen."

"I'm sorry to hear that."

"A dozen for every project," she added. "So, I've been locked in the office here for the past month, organizing, sorting, categorizing and labeling every facet of every project he had worked on for the past ten years."

"That's got to be a job!"

"You have no idea! I've got boxes and files covering every square foot of the floor of this office."

"So, how does that bring you to calling me?"

"Well, I was in the middle of the Lake Shasta project when I came across a copy of the Quit Claim Deed on the lot that Mr. Mullin deeded to Pastor MacAffie."

"Lot? Lake Shasta?" Adam Horwitz was confused. He didn't recall asking anything about any Lake Shasta file. "You'll have to refresh my memory."

"You had asked if I had notarized a Quit Claim Deed for Mr. MacAffie."

"Yes, but…"

"At the time, I couldn't remember, but in going through and labeling and filing all the documents, I came across a copy of the deed. It was a Quit Claim Deed for lot 106, dated October 21, 1995."

He nodded, a habit that he had acquired years ago, when talking on the phone, even if the person on the other end couldn't see his acknowledgement. "I appreciate your calling, Myrna, but that wasn't the deed I was looking for. The deed I was inquiring about was the one for his residence. It's been a few months now, and the exact date escapes me."

"I've gone through all his personal documents, and I haven't come across a copy of that document as of yet," she said, apologetically. "If and when I find it, do you still want a copy?"

He thought for moment. "Sure. Why not?"

"How about this deed? Do you want a copy of it?" she offered. "The Shasta lot?"

"I appreciate your asking, but I don't think it's relevant. Thanks anyway."

"Okay."

Attorneys always like to cross reference matters with which they are dealing and, although the issue seemed irrelevant, something in the back of Horwitz' mind made him jot down the date of the Shasta lot anyway. Maybe it was because it had something to do with that shady character, MacAffie, whom he had come to not only distrust, but genuinely dislike. "What did you say was the date on that deed?"

✱　　✱　　✱　　✱

"Detective Terryman, Please."

"Terryman!"

"Pierce. This is Donald Chin, over at forensics. If you've got a minute, I'd like a word with you. Got something interesting to report on the Nesbit case."

"Is it something you can tell me over the phone?"

"I'd prefer to have you here personally. It *is* important."

Terryman sighed. He knew Chin liked baiting him. It came with the territory. "Be right over," he said with resignation.

Pierce Terryman was at the forensics lab twenty minutes later, walking through the double stainless-steel doors. Donald Chin was sitting at a lab table peering through a microscope. "What's up, Don?"

"Thought you might be interested in the results from the victims of the Nesbit fire." He arose to pick up a file on the table next to where he was working. "Sorry it took so long, but we've been busy here. And their stupid dentist didn't want to turn loose his records. Something about patient confidentiality."

"A dentist? Confidentiality? What won't they think up next?"

"Legal had to get a court order to get the filed released." He shook his head. "Some people take their jobs too seriously." Chin handed him the file.

"Mr. and Mrs. Nesbit?" he asked, taking the file from Chin's hand, looking him in the eye. He never did like reading forensic reports. Too much technical verbiage. He'd rather get it straight from the horse's mouth, in English.

"There was no Mrs.." Chin was the type of man who liked melodrama. That was one of the reasons he had gotten into this field. He enjoyed solving mysteries, then doling out information in pieces, making the recipient work for it. For some reason that gave him great pleasure, knowing that he had something you needed, yet secure in the fact that you had to come to him and ask him for it.

Terryman, on the other hand, had no time for game playing and Chin was aware of that fact, too. "What do you mean, 'No Mrs.?'"

Chin smiled that, "Gottcha" smile that he was famous for—the one Terryman hated. "Those bones that were brought in from the Nesbit fire belonged to two males." He paused for effect. "There was no female."

"You mean Nesbit had someone else with him? Not his wife?"

The look on his face made Chin smile even more broad. *Gottcha again.* "Neither of the victims were the Nesbits," he said simply. "Two unidentified John Does, so far."

"Well, if they weren't the Nesbits, then who..." Chin had already answered that question. Unidentified John Does. "So where the hell are the Nesbits?"

Chin shook his shoulders. He loved a mystery. "Did you check the registration of the cars in the garage?" He offered. "Maybe there's a clue there." There was that smile again.

Terryman gritted his teeth, but he knew that Chin was right. It hadn't even occurred to him to check the registration of the automobiles. He had automatically assumed that the two bodies in the house were those of Mr. and Mrs. Nesbit. It would therefore follow that the two cars in the garage were their's too.

Without comment, Terryman handed the file back to Chin and turned to go. Frankly, he was embarrassed. As soon as he was out of Chin's earshot, he dialed Fitzgerald on his cell phone. "You got a few minutes, Ernie? Something has come up on the Nesbit fire. Meet me at the site in twenty minutes, okay?"

Earnest Fitzgerald's yellow Jeep Cherokee was already parked at the fire site when Terryman pulled up in his Bronco. "What's up?" Fitzgerald inquired as he extended his hand to Terryman.

"The remains that we pulled out of the fire?"

"Yeah? The Nesbits?"

He nodded. "They're not the Nesbits. Chin called me down to the lab and, after his little cat and mouse game…"

"Don't you just hate that?"

"You can't imagine. Anyway, after matching dental plates and looking at the bones, it seems the remains you brought in are of two males, neither of which is Eric Nesbit."

"Then who?"

"That's why we're here." He shuffled some ashes with his feet. I hate to be the one to admit this, but neither of us thought to check out the automobiles registration." He looked towards the burned remains of the two vehicles where the garage once stood.

"I thought…"

Terryman shrugged his shoulders. "I know. Me, too."

"Well, that can't be too hard," Fitzgerald said. "I can see the license plates from here. We'll just scrape the ashes off the plate and run it through DMV. That should tell us who they belong to."

"Unless one of the vehicles have been stolen or the plates have been changed," Terryman said, looking at his friend.

*   *   *   *

"I was right," he said over the phone to Fitzgerald. "The plates on one of the burned vehicles were stolen from a used car lot in San Jose. They were probably switched just as a precaution, in case someone saw them pulling into the garage."

"So, let me get this straight. Someone knew that the Nesbits were on vacation and got access to the garage?"

"They obviously had robbery on their mind. And what better opportunity? Pull into the garage of a family on vacation, take their time filtering through everything, then leave under the cover of night."

"Except, when they turned on the lights or lit a match, they got the surprise of their life," Fitzgerald chucked. "Poetic justice. So who were these bumbling fools? Curley and Moe?"

"We checked the VIN number. The vehicle was registered to a Gordon Rothchild. He's got a rap sheet going back ten years…petty larceny, robbery, breaking and entering—a small time hood."

"And his buddy?"

"Who knows? We're looking into past associations, but, it's my guess we'll never know who he was, not that it matters."

"Well, it could matter. It could be a clue as to how they got access to the house or knew no one was home."

"Maybe they just got lucky."

"My bet says luck has nothing to do with it."

"You think it was a set-up all along?"

"An inside job?"

"Come on, Ernie. If it was an inside job, why was the gas left on?"

"To rub them out, of course. It's perfect, don't you see? Curley and Moe bumble a job and get blown up and burned beyond recognition at the same time. Who's to know it wasn't an accident?"

Terryman laughed. "I think you've been watching too much late-night cops-and-robbers television."

* * * *

Adam Horwitz's secretary said, "Here's the Connie Mullin file you requested," handing him a thick, brown file labeled *Connie Mullin—Andrew Mullin Estate.*

"Thanks, Millie."

He quickly thumbed through the file, stopping at the copy of the Quit Claim Deed to Andrew Mullin's estate that had been conveyed to Aaron MacAffie. He glanced at the date: Dated October 21, 1994, recorded February 6, 1995.

He then flipped back to the page in his appointment book where he had noted the date that Myrna Lee had told him the Shasta deed had been executed. They were identical dates!

"Millie. Get me Myrna Lee on the phone, will you?"

A few minutes later she said, "She's on line two."

"Thanks, Millie."

"Myrna! Adam Horwitz here."

"Mr Horwitz. I was just thinking about you."

"Really" How's that?"

"Well, I just finished all of Mr. Mullin's records, and I didn't come across that Quit Claim Deed on his residence that you were asking for. I was just about to call you."

"Great minds run on the same track!" He laughed. "That's why I'm calling you. Do you recall our last conversation?"

"When I asked you if you wanted a copy of the Quit Claim Deed to lot 106 of the Lake Shasta subdivision?"

"Good memory. How much trouble would it be to lay your hands on a copy of that deed again?"

"None what so ever. I've got everything filed and boxed by project. It'll just take me a minute. Why?"

"I'd like to take you up on your offer to get a copy of that deed. If it's not too much trouble," he added, appreciating her attention to detail.

"Do you want me to mail it to you?"

"If you don't mind. I've got a desk full of legal correspondence that'll keep me desk-bound for the next few days, so I couldn't get to it until the first of the week, anyway." He could feel the excitement of the hunt running through his veins. Just like the old days when he first started law. When every case had been an adventure, not a chore.

"Consider it done."

Chapter 40

The next day Pierce Terryman got a call from Fire Chief Earnest Fitzgerald. "Got some news for you."

"You found out that Curley and Moe were set up by Colombian hit men."

"Very funny. With an attitude like that, I just might pull a Donald Chin on you and make you wait."

Terryman laughed. "Anything but that! All right, I'll bite. What's the news?"

"Guess who just walked in, wondering what happened to their house?"

Terryman had been sitting at his desk with his feet propped up on the top. "No!" he said, suddenly sitting erect.

"Yep. None other than Eric and Dawn Nesbit. Said they were at the Grand Canyon when that big storm hit. They've been snowed in ever since. Their cabin had lost power and all communication with the outside."

"How did they keep from freezing to death?"

"They found a gas camping stove in the storage closet. Apparently, they shut themselves in the smallest room of the house to retain as much heat as possible."

"Obviously the telephone line was out."

"That's right. Apparently, they were far enough off the beaten path that they were some of the last ones to be dug out. Good thing, too." He laughed, "Nesbit said that they had run out of food the previous day and were near panicked. Once the roads were cleared, they headed straight home. Apparently, they just hit town. When they saw what remained of their house, they drove directly to my office."

"Fate has an astounding way of jerking people about," he said, thoughtfully. "I can think of three kids who are going to be ecstatic about this news…and one very pissed minister!"

"How's that?"

"You didn't hear?"

"Apparently not."

"Rumor has it that the Nesbits will contained a recent codicil that, in the event of both of their deaths, their house went to MacAffie and his Living Christ Church."

"Aaron MacAffie?"

"The same."

"Well, that does put an interesting spin on things."

"I thought you'd say that."

Fitzgerald was silent for a moment. "You thinkin' what I'm thinkin'?"

"Exactly! Why don't you call the Nesbits in for a little chat about their fire and other related matters. They're liable to be less threatened speaking to you, rather than being invited down to the police station!"

"I assume you'll be here, too?"

"I wouldn't miss it for all the racquet balls at K-Mart."

*   *   *   *

"Your mail, Mr. Horwitz." Adam Horwitz's secretary handed him the neatly stacked pile of opened mail, as she did every day. It was sorted with legal matters on top: copies of lawsuits filed by opposing attorneys needing immediate attention, followed by client billing which needed his initial before being sent out, just in case there had been overbilling or double-billing, which rarely ever occurred. That was followed by non-legal correspondence. Next came the magazines. *The Legal Post* was on the bottom of the pile. All junk mail and advertisements had been previously removed and disposed of by his secretary, Barbara. Bills, such as telephone and PG and E were directed to the bookkeeper. A copy of the Quit Claim Deed from Myrna Lee was in the middle of the pile.

Horwitz quickly thumbed through the mail as he always did, cherry-picking those items he wanted to look at first, leaving the rest as priority dictated: lawsuits and most correspondence that could wait a day or two. Most of the magazines went into his briefcase for bedtime reading and *The Legal Post* automatically went into the round file. He had used to let the *Post* pile up on the corner of his desk, but they never got read. *I don't know why we even take this thing,* he had thought many times as he had chucked them into the waste basket. *No one reads it, and when we use it for legal advertisement, Millie cuts the ad out and saves it in our client's files.*

His eyes focused on the copy of the Quit Claim Deed. A smile came across his face as he compared the deed to the Shasta lot to the deed to Andrew Mullin's house. "I've got you now, you little bastard."

He dialed the telephone number printed on the free give-away note pad from the title company that was on his desk.

"First American Title Company."

"Customer Service, please."

"Customer Service, Jan Akers. How can I be of service?"

"Yes, Jan, this is Adam Horwitz, from the law firm upstairs."

"Yes, Mr Horwitz, What can I do for you?"

"Do you have a branch of your company in Shasta County?"

"No, but we have an affiliate that we reciprocate with."

"I was wondering, could you check on a recorded Quit Claim Deed for me in Shasta County if I faxed you the legal description?"

"Of course. When do you need it?"

"It's not an emergency, but I would like to have it as soon as possible."

"If you'll fax me the legal, I'll send it on to them. We should have an answer back first thing next week.

"That would be great. Thanks. Just make the fax to your attention?"

"That would be fine."

※　　※　　※　　※

Eric and Dawn were at Dawn's sister's house and had left a number where they could be reached. When they got the invitation to meet at Fire Chief Earnest Fitzgerald's office, they were there at two o'clock that same day, along with Laura, their eldest daughter. She stood silently between them, hanging onto her parents hands as if they were about to flee at any moment.

After greeting the Nesbits, Fitzgerald introduced Watch Commander Terryman. "This is Watch Commander Pierce Terryman. I've invited him to sit in on our little chat, if you don't mind."

"Not at all," Eric Nesbit said, offering to shake his hand. "This is my wife Dawn and our daughter Laura."

"Tell me, Mr. Nesbit…"

"Eric."

Fitzgerald nodded. "Eric. In our investigation of the fire of your house, we noted that the gas burner of the stove had been left on. Any clue how that happened before you left for your trip to the Grand Canyon?"

Eric and Dawn both looked at each other, bewildered. "That's impossible. We always check and double-check the burners before we leave the house," Eric said, with a shocked tone.

"Even if it's just to go to the store," Dawn added.

"Actually, when we left, I specifically recall checking the stove, for that very reason, just before I locked up," Eric said.

"And the burners were off?"

"Without a doubt. I vividly recall turning each knob, just to be sure. They were off!" he said emphatically.

"That's odd," Fitzgerald said, first looking at the Nesbits, then at Terryman, "because, when our inspectors investigated the house after the fire, they indicated that one of the burners had been left on."

"That's impossible!" Eric reiterated.

"Did anyone else have a key to your house?" Terryman asked, speaking for the first time.

Eric looked at his daughter. "Laura has a key. We always leave a key with one of the kids, just in case we lose ours or if they have to get into the house for an emergency."

"I'm sorry to have to ask you this Miss Nesbit," Fitzgerald inquired, looking at Laura, "but did you go back into the house after your parents had left and had locked up?" He paused for a moment before continuing. "It's very important."

Without hesitation, she said, "No."

"Did you lend your key to anyone or could anyone have had access to your keys without your knowledge?' Terryman inquired. "Maybe while you were out or at night when you were sleeping?"

"No. My parents keys are on the same key chain as the rest of my keys…my apartment and car key. I keep them with me at all times. And no one sleeps over!" she stated emphatically, as if insulted by the insinuation.

"Why, what's this all about?" Eric asked, suspecting that there was more to this than just a burner left on.

"Well, if you didn't give your keys to anyone and no one else had access to your home, we suspect that your house was in the process of being burglarized when it exploded and burned to the ground."

"How do you…?"

"Does the name Gordon Rothchild mean anything to any of you?" Terryman inquired, ignoring Eric Nesbit's inquiry.

The Nesbits looked at each other blankly and shrugged their shoulders. "Nothing," Eric replied. "Why?"

"Because, Gordon Rothchild was one of two people who have been identified that perished in the fire."

"And the other?" Dawn asked, almost afraid to ask, remembering that Tom Mathews had said if he couldn't have her, no one could. Perhaps he had been in the process of some mindless act and got his fingers burnt, along with everything else.

Terryman shrugged his shoulders. "We don't know. He had no ID that survived the fire and their remains were…well, there was nothing left to identify."

Dawn Nesbit breathed a sigh of relief.

"Well, maybe the burglars decided to make themselves at home and cook dinner or something," Laura said, looking at Terryman. "And they left the stove on by accident, and that's why the house burned down."

The Nesbits looked at Fitzgerald and Terryman. "Maybe," Fitzgerald said, obviously not convinced. "But that wouldn't explain the explosion, now would it?"

Fitzgerald rose from his desk and extended his hand to Eric Nesbit. "Well, we'll get back to you if we have anymore questions. Thanks for coming in."

The Nesbits rose and shook Fitzgerald's hand.

"There is just one more question, If you don't mind," Terryman said, in an off-handed tone. "Yes," Eric said.

"This is in the vein of a personal inquiry, so don't be offended, but I understand you recently added a codicil to your will, naming Pastor Aaron MacAffie and the Living Christ Church as beneficiaries to your house."

Eric nodded, looking at his wife. "That's true."

"Surely, you don't suspect…" Dawn started to protest.

Terryman held up his hand, as it was obvious that she was getting upset at the very thought that Pastor MacAffie's name could be used in the same sentence with the fire or that he could be suspected of tampering with their house. "It was just an inquiry," he apologized. "Our job requires that we look into every aspect of the fire when a crime is involved. And it would appear that there's been a crime committed here," he added quickly. "We just need to know all the facts."

"Speaking of the good reverend", Laura said, sarcastically emphasizing the words, *"good reverend"*. "What about my parent's house? Now that it's obvious that they're still alive, does Pastor MacAffie have to turn over…"

"Laura. Let's not worry about that now," her mother interjected, smiling at the Fire Chief, as if apologizing for her daughters outburst.

"You'll have to consult your attorney on those matters," Fitzgerald said. "Andrea Houseman is a very competent man. Now that it's obvious that your parents are alive and well, I'm sure they'll retain ownership of the lot and the insurance money will go to rebuild their house." He smiled at both the daughter and her mother, not wanting to discuss the matter any further for fear of letting his personal opinion relative to the good reverend be aired.

After the Nesbits left, Terryman looked at Fitzgerald. "I guess that still leaves a few vital unanswered questions," he said.

"Like who turned on the burners?"

"You don't think Rothchild..."

"Not for a minute. I think someone wanted the Nesbits dead. Rothchild and company just happened to come along and saved their bacon."

"Any ideas?"

Pierce Terryman shrugged his shoulders. "One in particular."

"Our revered Pastor MacAffie?"

He smiled. "Our own home-grown Culey and Moe. Who else would profit from the fire and Nesbit's death? That codicil to their will was just a little too convenient." He smiled, then left without shutting the door.

*   *   *   *

"Mr. Horwitz. There's a Janice Akers, from Customer Service with First American Title Company in Redding, California, on the phone. She said it's regarding some deed you asked her to research.

"Jan. Thanks for getting back to me so quick. Have you got something you can fax to me?"

"No."

"No? What do you mean?"

"I mean I don't have anything to fax to you. I researched the legal description you gave me on that lot in Shasta, and there's nothing recorded indicating any title change. The only recordation was to an Andrew Mullin of Shastina Subdivision, Inc., dated back in Eighty-nine. And that was for a hundred-twenty acres, which goes back before the acreage was subdivided by Andrew Mullin."

"So, you're telling me there's been no recorded change of that parcel from Andrew Mullin to one Aaron MacAffie?"

"Nor anyone else, for that matter."

"Thanks. I really appreciate your efforts." *One more nail for your coffin, squirt!* he thought to himself, smiling as he hung up the phone.

* * * *

"Chief. There's a call on line one from attorney Adam Horwitz."

"Adam! What's up now?"

"I've got a couple of Quit Claim Deeds I think you should take a look at. I may have uncovered a giant case of fraud."

Amateur detectives. He smiled, even though he was sure Horwitz meant well. "I think maybe you should be talking to the D.A. They get paid to handle these matters," he joked.

"Haven't you got anything better to do with your time than hassle hard-working civil servants like myself?"

Horwitz ignored his caustic sense of humor. "I have a feeling you might have a personal interest in this one."

Everyone's a junior detective. "All right. Tell me what you've got or stop wasting my time!"

"Remember our favorite citizen, MacAffie? Pastor Aaron MacAffie?" Terryman's eyes suddenly focused on the conversation, as if Horwitz were standing in front of him.

"Yeah. How could I forget?"

"If you recall, one of my clients was Connie Mullin, Andrew Mullin's ex."

"Still trying to get in her pants?"

He ignored Terryman's attempt at humor. "To refresh your memory, when Andrew passed away…"

"Nasty business, that."

"Yes. Well, as I was saying, when he passed away, Connie thought that the kids would get the house, but…"

"But Aaron MacAffie ended up with it instead."

There was a pause. "That's right. It's not necessarily the fact that he ended up with it, but *how* he ended up with it."

"I'm not following."

"You know Andrew Mullin loved that place. The last years of his life, when he started getting in over his head financially, he went through great pains to protect and preserve his house."

"How do you mean?"

"Without going into great detail, let's just say that he formed an offshore corporation, the sole asset being his house."

Terryman nodded. "I get the picture."

"Then, when I read his will, he specified that the house was to be left to his children. But, when I ran a preliminary title report on the property, it turned out that Andrew had recently deeded it to this character, Aaron MacAffie."

"I understand your frustration, but what does this have to do with the price of tea?"

"During the normal course of business, I got a copy of the deed transferring the property from Mullin to MacAffie, from the title company. Upon preliminary examination, for all intents and purposes, it seemed to be in order," Horwitz explained, "even though, to me and my client, it made no sense why Mullin would deed his prize possession to a church and not his kids."

"Did you have an occasion to ask his holiness about the circumstances under which he came to be in possession of the deed?"

"Of course!" Horwitz was incensed. "Any third-year law student would have thought about that!" He was insulted that Terryman had even asked the question. Little did he know Terryman was just giving him a bad time. "He made some lame excuse about Mullin wanting to make a contribution to the church when he was gone, as a monument to himself, or some lame excuse. Yeah, sure!"

Terryman hunched his shoulders. This was all very interesting, but he didn't have a clue where it was going. "And?" he asked impatiently.

"So, when Myrna Lee…"

"Andrew's foxy secretary."

"Keep it in your pants, Pierce."

"Well, she is a fine-looking woman. You can't deny that!" He added with a smile. He had desired her more than once himself. "Not everyone has jugs like hers."

"You really are a horny old goat, aren't you?" Horwitz was getting frustrated. "Can't you be serious for a minute!"

"Sorry. Continue."

"Shit! Talking to you is like talking to a fencepost."

"Don't get nasty."

Horwitz sighed. "Are you fucking interested or not?"

"I told you to continue."

"Where the hell was I? Oh, yeah. I had told her that I had been looking for a copy of the deed, and if she came across it, to call me."

"And she did."

"No. She called me to tell me that she found a copy of another deed, one to a lot in Lake Shasta."

"Horwitz!" His temper was getting short and his attention span even shorter. "I'm a busy man, here. Is this going someplace?"

"Hang in there with me for another minute." Horwitz took a deep breath. "When she mailed me the deed, I compared it to the deed to MacAffie from Mullin's residence and, aside from the legal description, for all intents and purposes, they seem to be identical: same date, same signature, everything!"

Terryman focused on a fly buzzing around the desk for a moment before replying. "Maybe he wanted him to have both properties."

Horwitz was getting exasperated, but held his temper. "Thing is, Mullin was a stickler on keeping copies of everything. He had a copy of the Shasta deed; why not a copy of one for his house?"

"Maybe he forgot. Maybe he didn't want anyone to find it. Maybe he made a copy and his secretary misfiled it. Maybe anything. You said he was a secretive man."

Horwitz ignored his caustic remark. "I took the liberty of calling the title company in Redding and requested a copy of the recorded Shasta deed. Guess what?"

"There's no record of MacAffie ever recording the Shasta deed!"

"See how fast you are? No wonder you're Chief of Detectives."

"I'll ignore your smartass remarks of you'll stop wasting my time. With all this valuable information, you must have a conclusion."

"The conclusion is simple. There was only one deed the whole time. Mullin probably gave MacAffie one Quit Claim Deed for the Shasta lot. I think the larcenous little bastard changed the legal description from the Shasta lot to Mullin's house! That's why there was never a recorded deed on the Shasta lot!"

Terryman stood up and stretched. "That's it! That's your evidence. Only one recorded deed?"

"There is one more thing."

"And that is?"

"The copy of the Shasta deed that I got from Myrna Lee has Santa Clara County typed in—not Shasta." He paused for a moment. "Don't you get it?"

Terryman was thinking. "Tell you what. Bring in everything you've got, and I'll get it over to the lab boys. They'll be able to tell us if it's the same document or not."

Horwitz shot his fist in the year with a silent, *Yes!* "You'll have it on your desk this afternoon."

"Horwitz?"

"Yes."

"Why are you pursuing this so vigorously?"

He took a deep breath. "I've always known that that little bastard is up to something. When he started messing with my client, he picked the wrong guy." There was a pause. "Besides, I've never trusted anyone who wears a rug."

Chapter 41

"Mr. Houesman, I have Pastor MacAffie on the phone." As soon as he had been advised that Eric and Dawn were in fact alive, Andrea Houesman had his secretary place a telephone call to Aaron MacAffie. This was one call that he was going to relish making.

"Mr. MacAffie?"

"Yes, this is Pastor MacAffie."

Houesman smiled. *Always the game player,* he thought. "This is Andrea Houseman, Mr. MacAffie." He refused to call MacAffie "Pastor", even if he purported to be one. "I just wanted to reiterate what I am sure you already know, that the Nesbits, Dawn and Eric, are still among the living."

There was a slight pause, then, "Yes. I heard. Praise the Lord." The words sounded great, but the hollow voice that conveyed them carried a tone of anything but enthusiasm.

"I'm sure it's unnecessary to remind you that the terms of the will have been put on hold, indefinitely." He emphasized the last word vehemently. The tone of his voice conveyed the thought that if he had anything to do about it, the codicil itself would be retracted.

"Yes. Of course," came the flat reply.

"Just wanted to be sure we were on the same page here. Good day, then." Andrea Houseman smiled as he hung up the telephone. It was not everyday that a victory was so deliciously savored.

Aaron MacAffie held the receiver to his temple for a moment before slamming it down angrily. He had already made plans for that money! He had intended to acquire a piece of land for the Aaron MacAffie Institute of Higher Learning.

He opened a brown folder containing sketches he had designed for his new college, and then slammed his fist on the desk so hard that the file fell to the floor.

* * * *

"I received another letter from mother," Nevenka said after dinner, laying the letter in the middle of the table.

Aaron's face automatically tightened because he knew what was coming. It had been a very bad day and he was in no mood to deal with whining relatives halfway around the world…even if they were his wife's family. "Things are getting better?" he offered optimistically.

"No. Just the contrary. Food and fuel are still difficult to come by. Ma Ma says both Niki and Viktor are very thin." Her eyes instantly welled up with tears as she thought of her once-strong, manly brothers wilting away from lack of food.

Young Vladimer looked up at his mother. "Don't cry, Mama." He took his mother's hand and held it gently.

MacAffie looked on, but said nothing.

"We've got to do something, Husband. I just can't stand around doing nothing while my family dies in Lithuania, being held prisoners of Russia."

"Are you sure she isn't exaggerating the situation, just a bit?" He pointed to the television. "I've been watching the news, and it doesn't appear things are all that bad in Russia. I mean, sure, the country is undergoing a change and all, but I don't see anyone *starving* to death, as you put it."

"Russia!" she spat. "They have food and fuel in Russia! Did they show you families in Lithuania? Children freezing, without food? Did they show you that?" She was so angry she threw her napkin at MacAffie and ran out of the room.

Vladimer started crying.

"Oh, shut up," MacAffie said. This was the first time he had seen Nevenka react with any degree of violence. "This is all starting to be very tiring," he said, looking at Vladimer as he poured himself another glass of wine. "I'm beginning to think this marriage thing has been one big mistake."

Vladimer looked at his father, not understanding.

"Yes, and that includes you, little *Vladimer*. You were a mistake from the very beginning!" He pushed his half-filled glass over, spilling the wine on the tablecloth.

* * * *

Nevenka threw herself on the bed and angrily pounded the pillow with her fists. "I hate you!" she said, hitting the pillow with all her might. *If I could get away with it, I would kill that man*, she thought to herself as she buried her face in the pillow.

She closed her eyes and thought of the days when she had run bare foot in the sand of Palanga, holding hands with Vladimer. "Vladimer," she whispered. "Where are you? I need you!" She fell asleep with tears in her eyes and the image of Vladimer Ryzhkov holding her in his arms.

CHAPTER 42

Jack and Lillian Lehman had bought their modest three-bedroom, one-bath house in Los Alamos, California almost fifty years ago, when the area had still been only rolling hills, orange trees and walnut groves, with giant oaks growing abundantly about the unoccupied land. Their parcel contained twelve acres, on which they raised a few cows, pigs and chickens and all the vegetables they could consume. Lillian preserved more than they would consume during the winter, and the balance they sold for pin money. Every year they had a small vegetable stand out on the road. Locals had come to look forward to springtime, when they could buy fresh produce from the Lehmans.

Now that their land had been incorporated into what was now known as Los Alamos Hills, their property had become very valuable. Real estate brokers and developers called every month, wanting to list their property or develop their land. It was now worth well over a million dollars, real estate brokers had estimated.

But, Jack and Lillian were simple folk with simple needs. They had no children, not by desire. Something in Lillian's body, her ovaries the doctor had said, wasn't developing eggs adequate enough to produce a normal child. They had thought about adopting, but somehow never got around to it and, as one year ran into one into another, became satisfied with their life alone as they settled into their quiet, secluded, simple life.

Neither of them had spoken of what to do with their property once they passed on. It was an unpleasant topic, and they had come to avoid such unpleasantness in life. Jack wouldn't even let Lillian subscribe to the newspaper. "They report nothing but crime and despair," Jack would often say to Lillian. "Who needs that?"

Avid Christians, they had been enticed by the Living Christ Church when it first started in Los Alamos and had eventually became members. It was conveniently located just across the freeway in town. They attended church every Sunday, usually the nine o'clock service, as they were early risers. That left them the balance of the day to work around the farm…"and not waste the whole day", as Jack would say.

After they had come home from Pastor MacAffie's stained-glass window dedication to the Nesbits that Sunday, both Jack and Lillian had known what was on each other's mind. They hadn't been among those who had risen from their seats and had gone down before Pastor MacAffie that particular Sunday. It wasn't in their nature to make snap decisions that way. But, now they were in their late seventies and each of them, in their own minds, had been preoccupied with passing on into the hereafter.

When I die, what am I going to need a farm for anyway Jack thought as they drove home in their old Oldsmobile. Being a good Christian, he had no fear of dying. He just didn't want to deal with it until the time came, thus they hadn't gone to an attorney to have their will made, either.

"You know, Lily, I've been thinking," he said, as they sat on their back porch rocking in their rocking chairs, staring out at their land.

"About what Pastor MacAffie said?" Lillian asked with a smile. They had this method of communication. One of them would start a thought or a sentence and the other would finish it, as if they were both tuned in to the same frequency. And they were. They each knew how the other was feeling and what the other was thinking without either of them uttering a word.

"We have no kin, none that I want to leave nothin' to, at least," Jack had said. He did have an older brother with whom he hadn't spoken to in the past ten years. He could be dead, for all Jack knew, or cared, for that matter. The last thing he would consider was leaving him his property! And Lillian had been an only child, so that left no viable heirs.

"So, what do you think? Should we make an appointment with Pastor MacAffie?"

Jack shrugged his shoulders. "I don't see why not. I mean, we're both in good health and I don't expect to go for at least another ten to fifteen years, but you never know when some hair-brained idiot might run us over with a truck or somethin'." He laughed and slapped his knee.

Lillian nodded as she extended her hand over to Jack, who reached over to receive it almost before it was offered. They had both been blessed with good genes. Aside from a modest cold once in a while, they had lived a good, healthy life. And the fact that they both "Worked hard all their life, didn't smoke nor drink and were good, clean-livin' Christians", to quote Jack.

*   *   *   *

"With the urging of Adam Horwitz, I've been doing a little thinking on our friend, the good Pastor," Pierce Terryman said to Earnest Fitzgerald over coffee and donuts. "This guy MacAffie has obviously been riding the crest of other people's misfortunes."

"For example?"

"Take the church. You know who used to own that land?"

"Andrew Mullin. Owned it for years. I heard he got into some financial trouble though and the church bought it."

Terryman shook his head. "Mullin had been in trouble ever since I'd known him." He chuckled. "I think his reckless livin' is what caused Connie to leave him. Oh, sure, he was a name-dropper, but you have to admit, he was a financial genius none the less. No, when he died, rumor had it that he had…"

"Let me guess. He willed it to MacAffie."

Terryman pointed his finger at Fitzgerald. "You're catching on. You should have been a cop."

Fitzgerald ignored the barb. "Seems like quite a coincidence. Mullin deeds his house to MacAffie then he dies. Eric and Dawn Nesbit deed their house to MacAffie and, for all intents and purposes, everyone thinks they died in the fire. Coincidence or fate?"

Chapter 43

"Pastor MacAffie? The Lehmans are here to see you," Nevenka said, sticking her head inside his office.

"Jack! Lillian! I'm glad to see you!" He came around from behind his large dark-walnut desk, walking across the plush, newly purchased, pure-white, imported woolen carpet. There were two stained-glass windows on either side of his desk, positioned perfectly, like a frame, with Pastor Aaron MacAffie's desk in the middle.

Jack and Lillian Lehman entered his office hand in hand, walking lightly, as if unsure that they should be walking on the carpet. Nevenka left the door ajar as she left them alone.

"Such a nice lady," Lillian Lehman said. "You're a lucky man, Pastor. "She's beautiful!"

"And smart, too, I'll bet," Jack said. "Thanks for takin' the time to see us, Pastor. I know you're a busy man." He extended his large hand to MacAffie. MacAffie almost recoiled as he grasped the large hand, rough with callouses, cuts and broken fingers from years of working on the farm. It was quite a contrast to MacAffie's hand, which was as soft as a baby's backside.

He wore a clean pair of overalls with a blue denim shirt tucked in and black-polished, dull shoes. He still had a full head of hair which was combed straight back and held in place by hair oil. Vitalis, MacAffie thought as the odor permeated the air.

Lillian stood a few inches behind her husband, a practice she had adopted over the years, as if letting her large man shield and protect her. She wore a simple, cotton, blue-and-white striped dress with white flats. Her hair was combed back simply, held in place with two blue combs. She wore no make-up, nor any fingernail polish. It was clear she had once been a pretty woman, but never beautiful. Even now her face was almost wrinkle-free, as kind, gentle, blue eyes took in the ambiance of her Pastor's office.

"The Lord's business is always afoot around here." Pastor MacAffie smiled as he extended his hand for the Lehmans to sit on the new white-and-peach-colored pillowed couch. "I'm so glad to see you both in such good health. You must be getting around seventy by now." He smiled, trusting Lehman was in for the reason he had hoped.

Jack nodded without comment.

Just then, Nevenka entered the office with a tray of coffee, cream and sugar. "Hope I'm not disturbing you," she said, smiling to the Lehmans.

"No, not a bit. Why don't you sit a spell? Our business is church business. Nothin' to hide," Jack Lehman said.

She looked at her husband, who motioned for her to take a seat in the matching chair next to the Lehmans. "Nevenka's familiar with our procedure," he said, smiling. "Don't know what I'd do without her."

Jack Lehman smiled. "You're a lucky man," he said again.

MacAffie smiled. "Now, then. What can I do for you two?"

Jack Lehman looked at his wife. "We've been talkin' 'bout your sermon last Sunday, the one 'bout leavin' our stuff for the Lord once we're gone."

Jack was a straight-to-the-point, no-nonsense kind of a man. He had no use for fluffy conversation or small talk. If he had something to say, he got right to the point and said it. Everyone always knew where they stood around Jack, like it or not. He made sure of that. That was just his way.

Pastor MacAffie inched his chair a little closer to his guests and leaned forward, resting his elbows on his knees, giving them his full attention. "Yes. The Lord spoke to many of our congregation that day," he said, studying the man. "But, you didn't come forward at that time, as I recall," he said, rubbing his chin. He shot a glance at Nevenka to see the expression on her face. It was apparent that his wife was taking this all in.

"No, sir. Lily and I had to talk 'bout it first, 'for comin' to a decision."

"That's smart. Shows the Lord that you care. Now then, how can I help you? I'm just his instrument, you know. He works in…"

Jack wasn't interested in a sermon. He had for come for a reason and intended on getting on with it. "Well, Lily and I thought we might get one of those 'life wills' you talked about and make it out, givin' our stuff to the church when we pass on." He was holding his wife's hand affectionately with both of his, but was looking intently at MacAffie. "That way, you could use our home to further the work of the church."

"Living trust," MacAffie corrected him.

"Whatever."

"And maybe put our names in one of those pretty glass-stained windows," Lillian added, smiling shyly, looking at Nevenka for affirmation.

"Of course," MacAffie said, trying to mask his enthusiasm. I can see your names now, 'Jack and Lillian Lehman,'" he said, looking at one of the stained windows in his office, making a frame with his hand in front of his eyes, as if seeing it there himself.

"That would be a wonderful tribute," Nevenka said, picking up the tone of the conversation.

"Everyone will see it." Lillian beamed, squeezing her husband's hand. "Yes. That's what we want to do." She squirmed in her chair from excitement.

"That's a very smart move on your part. God will reward you, I can assure you," MacAffie said, with a broad smile. He could see the Aaron MacAffie Institute for Higher Learning project taking shape before his very eyes. "I can have our staff prepare the documents for your signature by," he glanced at his watch, "lets say, two o'clock this afternoon."

Once a parishioner had made a declaration to make such a commitment to the church, it had been MacAffie's experience to strike while their emotion was hot. He had learned that, when it came to matters of the pocketbook people were prone to change their minds, or even worse, had someone else change it for them, such as a family member, friends or their attorney. He unconsciously snarled as he thought of Houesman getting the Nesbits to change their will back to its original status, cutting the church out altogether. To add insult to injury, they had stopped coming to his services, as well.

"We'll be back around two, then," Jack said, nodding an agreement to his wife, as if asking and telling her at the same time.

"It was so nice seeing you," Lillian said, shaking Nevenka's hand. "You and the Pastor will have to come over for dinner one night."

"I'd like that."

"Pastor MacAffie? Your eleven o'clock appointment is here," his secretary's voice came over the intercom.

"Well, if you'll excuse me, my next appointment is here." MacAffie rose to usher the Lehmans out. Nevenka remained in the office while the Pastor ushered the Lehmans to the waiting room.

MacAffie's next appointment, Jerry Davis, was sitting on the couch, waiting. "Mr. Lehman!" Davis said as he rose from the couch and extended his hand to Mr. Lehman as if they were long lost friends. "You're looking particularly fit," he said as he smiled. "And how are you, Mrs. Lehman?"

"Why, were doin' just fine, Mr. Davis. Thank you for askin.'"

"Haven't decided to cut loose of that hunk of dirt you've been farmin', have you?" He smiled as he winked at Mrs. Lehman. "I could fetch you a pretty penny for that property…enough to buy yourself a free-and-clear condo in Hawaii and one in Palm Springs, with a bundle left over, to boot. You'd never have to worry about workin' again."

"We don't worry none now, son," Jack Lehman said, shaking his hand.

Pastor MacAffie quickly positioned himself between Davis and the Lehmans. "Well, ah yes, well, we'll see you this afternoon, then," he interjected quickly as he took Jerry Davis' hand and led him toward the office, leaving the Lehmans to find their own way out.

Once inside, he said, "Mr. Davis, I'd like you to met my wife Nevenka."

"Nevenka! What a charming name. Russian?"

"Lithuanian," she corrected as she extended her hand to Davis.

"I'm teaching my wife the church's business," MacAffie explained as he smiled at her. "Now then, how can I be of assistance to you? Are you a regular at our church? I don't recall seeing you before. But then," he said with a laugh, "We have a congregation of over two thousand people, plus television," he boasted, looking at Nevenka as if he were performing for her benefit. "One can't expect to know everyone, now can they?" His little inappropriate laugh was becoming irritating to Nevenka. It was if he had a joke on everyone and only he knew the punch-line.

Davis had an eye for the ladies, and found it difficult to direct his attention to the Pastor, especially when such a beautiful lady as Nevenka was present. "Actually, I watch you on television all the time!" He smiled.

"Oh, really." MacAffie beamed, straightening his tie and fluffing at his hairpiece with his fingertips. He loved being stroked and was always delighted to hear that television was working as his outreached arm to the masses…his window to fame, if you will.

"You and your wife should come to one of our services. I'm sure you would be even more fulfilled." He beamed at the man. "It's such an emotional experience, being among the rest of the congregation, feeling the Lord's presence. It's an experienced only to be appreciated by being there—in person. Well, enough of that." He smiled. "Now then, tell me, what can I do for you?"

"Actually, it's more what I can do for you, or, better put, what we can do for each other." He turned his chair so Nevenka was out of his direct line of vision. This way he could focus all his attention of the Pastor. "You see, I'm in the investment business, putting together partnerships for the purpose of buying shopping centers, apartments, convalescent hospitals, that sort of thing."

"Yes. And how do I fit in?" Pastor MacAffie inquired, always interested in money-making schemes.

"Well, I was thinking, between my business contacts and your asset here, I think we have a match."

MacAffie made no comment. Investments weren't his strong suit, mostly because he didn't have the capital to invest. No use showing his ignorance at this early stage of the game. *Let's see what this guy has to offer*, he thought.

Davis had to form his words carefully, figuring that MacAffie must be an astute businessman. He hoped that MacAffie'd have a streak of greed flowing through his veins, as well. Little did he know!

"I've been watching the growth of your church and seen the type of members you have in your congregation. I'm sure you get large contributions that are just sitting in the bank, drawing three or four percent interest, if that."

MacAffie shot a glance at Nevenka, who was taking it all in. He nodded. "What you say is true; we do get regular contributions." He laughed nervously. "As for the bank account, I don't think the church's checking account draws any interest, being a business account and all," he explained.

Davis nodded. "What I'm suggesting is turning your asset into money and still keeping control."

MacAffie liked the sound of that.

"What would you estimate the church and grounds are worth? Just a guesstimate."

"Three and a half to four million."

Davis' eyes lit up as he saw the opportunity he was searching for. "What would you say if I told you I could put a million dollars in your hands and all you would have to do is pay interest on the money?"

MacAffie looked at Davis for a moment. "I'm not following you. I don't have the financial statement to borrow a million dollars, and, even if I did, what would I do with the money?" Full-well knowing that he could do one of many things with it, including retire.

"What I have in mind is not a loan, but a sale with a long term lease and a guaranteed buy-back."

MacAffie shook his head. "Now you've really lost me."

"I'm sorry, let me back up a piece. This is going to sound complicated, but bear with me.

When I'm through explaining, it'll be crystal clear."

"I'm listening."

Davis took MacAffie's paperweight and put it in the middle of the desk. "Let's say this is the church and you want to sell it, but you don't want to relinquish the use of it."

"But I don't want to sell it."

"Bear with me." Davis smiled at MacAffie and turned to wink at Nevenka, after which he regretted the act, thinking that maybe she thought he was getting fresh.

MacAffie sat back in his chair, waiting for Davis to continue, although he was losing interest as he looked at his watch.

"Okay. Let's say that I bring in a group of investors to buy your church and they pay you a million dollars for the property, forgetting that the value is over three million," he quickly added, holding up his hand, just in case MacAffie protested.

"Now, my investor group doesn't want the church, that is to say, they aren't what we in the trade call 'users.' They simply want the church as a vehicle to place their money and get a return."

"So, instead of buying the church, why don't they simply loan us the money?"

"Excellent question. The answer is, if they loan you the money, they just get a return on the investment in the form of an interest rate. If they buy the church and lease it back to you, they not only get the money from the investment, but they get to depreciate it, too, and we'll build in a little inflation schedule, so when you buy back the church from them, say ten years from now, they'll get their money back, plus a little appreciation."

"And what's the advantage for me? This sale and leaseback?"

"I can see that you're catching on quickly." Davis smiled, buttering him up. He took a chance and smiled at Nevenka, too, his eyes lingering a moment too long on her chest.

"I try," MacAffie said. He caught Davis' look.

"I figure, you being the astute business man that you are, you could turn a million dollars into three or four million in ten years. Then, when the lease is over, you buy back the church from the investors and you're ahead two to three million bucks."

"And who pays the lease fee?"

"Why, your congregation, of course. That's the beauty of it. It's simply part of the cost of operation."

MacAffie stroked his chin. He was beginning to see several possibilities with Davis' idea. "I like it," he said. "You don't think I'd be getting in trouble? With the church, that is?"

"Whose church is it?"

"Mine."

"Who makes all the administrative decisions?"

"I do."

"Then, there you have it."

"What do you get out of all this? You're not just doing this for the exercise."

"I'll get a real estate fee for putting the transaction together."

"And just how much would that fee be?"

"Six percent of the purchase price," he said meekly, almost inaudible.

"So, if you bought our church for a million dollars, you would make sixty thousand dollars on the deal."

Nevenka was getting more interested in this conversation by the minute. She could see numerous possibilities herself, not the least of which, if MacAffie got his hands on a million dollars, the church could really afford to bring her family over from Lithuania. She inched closer to her husband's desk, putting her elbows on her knees, straining to hear and attempt to understand every word of this strange conversation. In doing so, the top of her blouse dipped, exposing her breasts. Davis was talking a language that she had never heard before, one that she wanted to learn.

Davis couldn't help but be distracted by Nevenka's breasts. Without being too obvious, he had to look. It was too easy to get distracted here, he thought. He knew where MacAffie was going with his line of questioning, and had to pay attention, breasts or not. He refocused on MacAffie. He'd been here before: In almost every large transaction he had ever been in, someone was always standing with his hand out. If it wasn't the buyer wanting a piece of the action by virtue of asking him to cut his commission, it was the seller telling him to take less so he could get a better price.

Then there were referral fees. If someone had just happened to mention a deal to him somewhere in the past, and later Davis was able to put a transaction together, there was another hand out. "If I hadn't told you about that deal, you would never have done the transaction," was the standard response.

MacAffie didn't hesitate. He came straight in for the kill. "If I'm going to be the catalyst for this purchase and leaseback, what do I get out of it?"

Davis shrugged his shoulders. "I suppose I could pay you a point," he offered. He wanted to establish a relationship for potential future investments. If doing business meant he had to give away some of his fee, so be it. The old adage, that a percentage of something is better than all of nothing was irrefutable.

"A point. I don't understand," MacAffie said, full well knowing what the term meant from one of the many financial discussions he had had with Andrew Mullin. "What's a point?"

"A point is one percent of the transaction. For example, if the purchase price is a million dollars, a point is one percent of that amount, or ten thousand dollars."

"Out of your sixty thousand?"

Davis hesitated. MacAffie was digging deeper and he knew it. "That's correct."

MacAffie leaned back in his chair, looked up at the ceiling as if consulting divine wisdom. He brushed his hand against the back of his toupee and said, "I think half would be appropriate."

Nevenka was so excited, hearing these large dollar amounts, that it was all she could do to contain herself. They were talking more money than her entire family earned in a lifetime! This was what she had come to America for.

"Half?" Davis was astounded. He had been asked for a quarter of his commission by a buyer once, but half? Out of the question! He was doing all the work. Plus, it was his idea!

MacAffie looked at his watch, giving the impression that the interview was about over. "What do you say, Mr. Davis?"

He had just lost fifty percent of his commission, and was doing all the work! *What the hell,* he thought. *That's more than I had when I came through the door. And once I get in bed with this turkey, I'll have him over the barrel. He's dealing under the table, and I'll have him by the balls. He'll have to deal exclusively with me!*

They shook hands on it, and Davis went out to start putting the investment together.

As soon as Jerry Davis had left, Nevenka had a hundred questions. She just didn't know how to ask them. The conversation he had had with Davis was obviously way over her head. She turned her attention to Lehman's will.

MacAffie explained, when people like the Lehmans died and had a living will, leaving their worldly goods to the church, that meant the church would own everything they had willed to the church. "In the case of Mr. and Mrs. Lehman, that would mean their twelve acres would revert to the church."

He smiled and his hand automatically reached for the rendering of the Aaron MacAffie Institute of Higher Learning. He said nothing, but Nevenka nodded as she looked at the sparkle in her husband's eyes. Seeing the rendering in the context of his last comment about Lehman's will, she finally understood.

* * * *

At two o'clock sharp that same day, Lillian and Jack Lehman returned to Pastor MacAffie's office to execute a living trust, naming Aaron MacAffie and the Living Christ Church as the sole beneficiary. Just as an added precaution, Pastor MacAffie had them execute a Quit Claim Deed to their property in favor of the church.

"Just a precaution," Pastor MacAffie said, "in case there is unexpected adverse litigation. You understand."

Jack and Lillian had full faith in their Pastor and signed the document without question.

Chapter 44

Terryman dialed Adam Horwitz's office. He was holding a typewritten report from the document analyst from the FBI's office in San Francisco. The results were more than a little interesting.

"Adam Horwitz," came the lawyer's professional voice.

"Adam. Pierce Terryman here. I've got the results back from the FBI on those Quit Claim Deeds you asked me to examine."

Horwitz sat erect. "And?"

"According to their analysis, the typewriter that typed the Quit Claim Deed on the Shasta lot, excluding the legal description, which had apparently been Scotched-taped to the document, is the same typewriter used to type the Quit Claim Deed to Andrew Mullin's house. The interesting difference is, the typed-in legal description on Mullin's house was also from the same typewriter."

"Let me see if I've got this straight. You're telling me that the same typewriter, and presumably the same person, typed everything except the legal for the Shasta lot."

"There's no way you can prove it was the same person, but, yes, it was the same typewriter."

Horwitz thought for a moment. "Could they tell if the Shasta document and the Mullin residence document were one and the same?"

Terryman smiled to himself. "The FBI's analysis indicates that the chances are a million to one that they're different documents."

"In other words, they're the same document?"

"It's not foolproof, mind you, but when they overlaid the Shasta deed over the Mullin deed, except for the legal description, it was an exact fit, letter for letter, period for period. The clincher was Andrew Mullin's signature."

"Yes!" Horwitz shot his fist into the air.

"Add that to the fact that apparently no one can come up with the recorded deed on the Shasta lot, it lends credibility to your theory that they are one and the same."

"We got him!" Horwitz took a moment to savor the thought, then asked, "So, what's our next move? Are you going to arrest the little bastard?"

"For forgery?"

Horwitz considered the thought. "For grand larceny, if nothing else. He stole Mullin's property, the same as if he had been given a check for a dollar and changed the amount to read a million dollars, by simply adding a few zeroes!"

"I feel confident that we could make a case stick if we charged him for forgery of the Mullin document, and probably grand theft, but what would he get, being a minister and all? Maybe five to seven years?"

"He'd serve eighteen months soft time and be out," Horwitz said.

"Or, worse yet, the court would instruct him to return the property and give him probation because he's a man of the cloth. That is, if we could prove that he made the switch to begin with. He's smart enough to say Mullin made the switch himself on the same deed. Who's going to ask Mullin if he's telling the truth?"

"I see there's more to this iceberg than what's on the surface. What do we do now?" Horwitz inquired.

"I've known Andrew Mullin most of his life, ever since we were in high school together. And I always knew him to be a pretty careful, meticulous guy. I'd be willing to bet dollars to donut holes that he wasn't a party to altering the Quit Claim Deed. It just isn't done."

"My knowledge of Mullin dictates that wasn't one to would deed his property to the church, when he had children to give it to, either. And I knew him fairly well."

"Not necessarily just that, although that facet of the case certainly has a bearing. I'm coming more from the angle that it's a little too coincidental that his plane crashed months after he supposedly deeded his property to MacAffie and his little group of flying angels. The missing Shasta deed is just icing on the cake."

"Go on. I'm with you." Horwitz moved his chair closer to his desk, as if getting closer to Terryman. He was more than interested in his input.

"I reread the FAA file on their investigation. They concluded that the cause of Mullin's losing control of the plane was due to the cable coming loose from the struts. Apparently, they have no case history where this has ever happened before, so they're skeptical as to the crash being accidental. Apparently those cables are locked in. To come loose, someone would have had to deliberately done the deed!"

"So, I'm no pilot, but I assume with one of the struts disabled when he came in for a landing at Shasta, he probably couldn't turn."

"And slammed into the mountain," Terryman concluded. "Now, I'm going to devote some time next week talking to pilots and mechanics at the San Carlos Airport, where Mullin had his plane tied, to see what kind of flying habits he had."

"So, maybe we're looking at a little premeditated murder here."

"We'll let our minister keep preaching a while longer. No sense settling for barbecued leg when we can fry the whole pig!"

Horwitz laughed. "I like your analogy, Inspector. What can I do from my end?"

"You've already got me going with the identical duel Quit Claim Deed switch. Just sit tight and let me do some snooping from this end."

"I do have one additional thought," Horwitz offered. "I know you're going to say that I've been watching too many cop shows, but..."

"Don't kid yourself. You'd be surprised how many cops watch those shows themselves. Sometimes we learn things from them, too."

"It's just a thought, and I'm sure a shot in the dark, but is there any way that you could punch MacAffie's name and ID, that kind of stuff, on your computer to see if anything shows up on the day of Mullin's death?"

"You mean like a parking ticket at the San Carlos Airport?"

Horwitz shrugged his shoulders. "I guess it does sound ridiculous."

"Hey, stranger things have happened. We tripped a guy up once that had killed his lover while he was home taking a shower. After he killed him, he took him and a change of clothes and dumped him in the lake to make it look like he had drowned."

"I don't get it."

"When we fished him out, he was nude. All his clothes were in a neat pile on the beach, as if he had taken them off, stacked them there, then went swimming and drowned."

"And?"

"It took a novice like yourself to find the missing clue that was too obvious for everyone else to see. One of the rookies on the case said, 'Hey, let's dress the guy to make sure the clothes really belong to the man.'"

"So, they did?"

"Oh, the kid got a lot of flak from the senior officers, but in the end, that's what they did."

"And they weren't his clothes?"

"Oh, they were his clothes all right, but the shoes were two sizes too small."

"They weren't his shoes?"

"Right!" Our investigation proved that the shoes belonged to his gay lover, who lived with the guy. Apparently, this guy found out that his lover was seeing a woman on the side and became so infuriated that he whacked him while he was taking a shower. Then he grabbed some of his cloths and took his nude body to the lake, where he dumped him.

"When we realized that they weren't his shoes, we knew he had probably died somewhere else and someone had moved the body to the lake. The subsequent autopsy report confirmed that he didn't drown, because he didn't have any water in his lungs.

"The rest was easy. We traced the smaller-sized shoes to his gay lover. Once we did that, with a little pressure sprinkled with guilt, the guy confessed and the case was solved! So see, don't feel bad about asking the obvious. Maybe he did get a parking ticket!"

Chapter 45

The opportunity for MacAffie to initiate his acquisition of Lehman's land for the Aaron MacAffie Institute of Higher Learning came the day when they invited him and Nevenka over for a spaghetti feed. He hadn't been prepared to move ahead with his acquisition plan quite yet, but couldn't turn down the opportunity. Besides, if Davis was going to come up with the million dollars for purchasing the church, the timing could be perfect. He interpreted Lehman's invitation as a sure sign from God.

This particular Sunday, the Lehmans hung back and were the last of the parishioners to shake MacAffie and Nevenka's hand after the Sunday service. "Why don't you and the missus come over for a spaghetti feed this afternoon?" they had said. "And bring the little one, of course." Lillian patted little Vladimer on his head.

Vladimer, tired of everyone mussing with his head, pulled away and clung to his mother's dress.

"That's very kind," Nevenka said, smiling. "I'd love it."

"Tell you what," MacAffie said, with his arm around Nevenka. "You cook the spaghetti, and we'll bring the spirits."

"You drive a hard bargain, Reverend," Jack Lehman said, patting him on the back. "Why don't you drift on over around four? That way, Lilly can finish making her sauce and she and your wife can jaw in the kitchen while you and I sit out on the porch and spend a little time together. The youngen' there can play with the chickens and ducks." He laughed.

"Duckies!" Nevenka said, tugging at little Vladimer's hair. "Wouldn't that be fun?"

Vladimer looked up at her, then at Mr. Lehman. He wasn't sure if the pleasure of seeing some ducks up close and personal outweighed the dislike to have to put up with having someone messing with his hair all day long.

"You're goin' ta love Lilly's spaghetti sauce. She makes it from scratch, you know. None of that store-bought stuff. She uses basil, fresh mushrooms, garden-grown crushed tomatoes, garlic and parsley. Mighty tasty, if'n I do say so myself."

MacAffie patted jack on the shoulder. "I'm looking forward to it." *More than you think, old man,* he thought, as he held Nevenka's hand so tightly that it hurt as they watched them walk to Lehman's old blue '56 Ford pick-up.

That afternoon, before he went to the Lehmans, he asked his wife to sit down. "You aren't going to understand this right now, but it's important that I go to the Lehmans alone this afternoon. I can't explain, but later you'll understand."

"I think I understand now," she said, holding onto his hand. "It's about their trust and their land, isn't it?"

MacAffie was shocked when she uttered those words. *Could it be that she not only understands, but condones it?* he wondered as he studied her face for any signs of contempt or betrayal. There were none. He smiled and patted her hand. "In due time," he said. "In due time."

∗   ∗   ∗   ∗

Prior to going to the Lehman's, MacAffie drove to a park where there had been a lake that winter. It was mostly dried up now, but the ground was still fairly damp with moisture that had been trapped between the topsoil and the rock-hard adobe soil below. He wore a pair of acid-washed blue jeans, white tennis shoes and a sports jacket with a light v-neck sweater, with nothing underneath, that so a shock of curly black chest hair showed over the top of his sweater. Even if he was a minister, he still liked to look sexy.

He had parked his new black Jaguar with spoked wheels with a cat on the hood in the gravel parking lot. A few moments later, a grey Nissan rental car pulled into the parking lot, and stopped under the shade of a large oak tree. The driver stayed in his car as he took out a pair of binoculars and tracked MacAffie as he walked.

There had been a few cars in the parking lot, but that didn't concern MacAffie as he walked onto the grounds, strolling down where the lake had once stood. He could smell the musty earth as he approached the spot he was looking for. Something in the air made him sneeze several times, stuffing up his nose.

A couple was sitting on a blanket several yards from him, apparently enjoying the afternoon sun, oblivious to his presence. When he had reached his destination, he snapped open a small paper bag and took out a pocketknife.

On the ground, in a shady, damp spot, was the object of his desire, some very desirable-looking mushrooms. Poisonous mushrooms! He knelt to pick them, selecting only the smaller, less-gross-looking ones, cutting them just above the earth. *Once they're cut into pieces, they'll look as normal as can be,* he thought, humming *Just a Closer Walk With Thee,* as he selected another specimen.

Suddenly, he sneezed several times again, without stopping. He pulled out his handkerchief and blew his nose. "Damn sinuses. Must be the damp ground or the mushrooms," he said, looking into his bag. He had to breathe out of his mouth because, by now, his nasal passages had swelled shut due to irritation and congestion.

✳ ✳ ✳ ✳

"Laura! Look over there. That guy's picking mushrooms." The boy pointed to Aaron MacAffie, who was stooped over, cutting the mushrooms, putting them into his bag. "Doesn't he know they're poisonous?"

The girl on the blanket squinted. "That's Pastor MacAffie."

"The minister of your church?"

"Not my church! I wouldn't have anything to do with that guy if he were the last minister on earth. He's the one that nearly stole my parent's house when everyone thought they had been killed in the fire." She sneered. "Let him eat 'em! Maybe he'll croke on 'em."

"Laura! That's a terrible thing to say!"

"It might be terrible, but that's how I feel. I wouldn't stoop to give him water if he were in the middle of the desert, dying of thirst." She got up and folded the blanket with a disgusted look. "Come on! Let's get out of here!"

✳ ✳ ✳ ✳

When MacAffie had returned to his car, he opened his trunk, where he had previously placed a small acrylic cutting board. Under the cover of his trunk lid, he chopped the mushrooms into little pieces, then scraped them into a plastic Zip-lock bag, which he placed in the inside pocket of his sports jacket. He looked around nervously, then drove away.

* * * *

The man in the rental car put his binoculars back in their case and took out a small pad and made himself a note. He slid down in the seat and pulled out a week-old newspaper to hold in front of his face when the young couple came up from the park. He recognized the young woman as the offspring of the parents house that the minister had tried to blow up.

The young couple drove away just as MacAffie finished doing whatever it was that he had been doing. The man waited until MacAffie drove away, then walked down to the dry lake bed. He could see the minister's footprints clearly indented in the cracked adobe soil. "Hmm. Cuttin' poison mushrooms," he said, picking up a mushroom next to the stem of one that had just been cut and holding it under his nose to smell. "What are ya up to, laddie?"

* * * *

Lillian had bragged about how much Jack ate whenever she cooked spaghetti for him. She usually made enough for several helpings, she had said, so it was no imposition for the Pastor and his wife to come to dinner. The fact that Jack Lehman ate a lot was part of MacAffie's plan. He was depending on it.

When MacAffie arrived, he apologized for the absence of his wife, saying that she had just come down with an infectious virus and, not wanting to infect the Lehmans, had stayed home with little Vladimer.

"What a thoughtful wife," Mrs. Lehman said. "I'll give you some spaghetti to take home to her. I'm sure that it will help her recovery."

MacAffie and Jack sat out on the porch, passing the time of day, as promised. It was boring, but MacAffie occupied his time studying Lehman's land, laying out the college in his mind's eye as Jack rattled on about his chickens, cows and pigs.

When the sauce had been cooked and the spaghetti was ready, Lillian called the men into the house. MacAffie poured Jack Lehman a generous glass of Christian Brothers zinfandel wine, and filled his own glass only partially. Lillian didn't drink wine...something about phosphates bothering her digestive system.

She filled their plates with heaping portions of spaghetti, then poured her special sauce over the top, savoring the aroma with a satisfying smile.

It did smell good. MacAffie had purposely left the wine bottle sitting by the stove, near the simmering kettle of spaghetti sauce.

Halfway through the first plate, MacAffie's glass was empty. So was Jack's. "I see you're out of wine there, Jack. Let me get the bottle and give you another snort." He laughed as he rose to pick up the bottle with one hand, removing the package of chopped mushrooms from the inside pocket of his sports jacket with the other. He emptied the contents into the spaghetti sauce, taking care to shield his actions with his body so Jack and Lillian wouldn't notice.

"Umm. You sure are lucky, Jack, having a woman that can cook like this," he said, sniffing the pot as he gave it a few healthy stirs, mixing in his addition before returning to the table to refill their glasses.

Before the evening was over, both Jack and Lillian had another plateful of spaghetti smothered with Lillian's wonderful sauce, plus, Jack had two more glasses of wine. "Have some more spaghetti," Lillian pleaded to MacAffie.

"Oh, my, I'm stuffed now as it is," he said, rubbing his stomach.

"You make me feel bad. You only ate one helpin'. Like you don't care for my cookin'."

"Oh, no. It's nothing like that. My doctor says that I have to cut down on eating. Something about my cholesterol being too high. You wouldn't want me to die of a heart attack, now, would you?" He laughed.

"Maybe you could get yer name on one of those windows." Jack laughed.

By the time dinner was over, Jack, who had had two more plates of spaghetti, was complaining of a stomachache and had asked to be excused. Lillian told him to go sit on the back porch.

"Why don't you go tend to your husband, Mrs. Lehman?" MacAffie offered. "I'll just stay here for a few minutes and clean up a bit."

"Oh, no. I couldn't do that!"

"Go on, there. You did your part by making dinner. Movin' around a little will help settle my dinner. Please," he said, helping her out of the kitchen, out onto the porch, where Jack Lehman had already passed out.

"See, Jack's sleepin' already," she said. "Probably had too much wine." She smiled as she tugged at his ear affectionately

MacAffie tidied up the kitchen a bit, taking care to remove all traces of his fingerprints on the plates, glasses and then the doorknob, before going out onto the porch to thank Lillian Lehman for the nice dinner. She, too, had already passed out, so he quietly left the house and drove away under the cover of darkness, feeling no guilt for what he had done. Just before he pulled out onto the road, he looked back, envisioning a large, colorful laser crafted sign reading, Aaron MacAffie Institute of Higher Learning—Pastor Aaron MacAffie—President.

* * * *

Matty McGown waited for ten minutes after Aaron MacAffie had driven away. His rented car rolled quietly up Lehman's gravel driveway. The only sound that could be heard was the car's tires as they crunched on the rocks. He left his lights off, so as not to announce his arrival to the Lehmans. Once out of the car, he quietly made his way up the steps. He walked on the outermost edge of the wooden stairs, knowing that, if they were going to creak, that would the one place they would be most likely not to announce his arrival. To lighten his weight, he held onto the wooden railing.

He had already formulated his excuse in the event he were confronted by the occupants. He would say that he was looking for the reverend and that the church had said that he was visiting here, knowing full well that he had already left.

The lights were on in the house, but he saw no movement as he peeked through the windows. When a light rap on the door brought no response, he opened the door a crack and softly called, "Hello. Anyone home?"

Still no response.

Matty McGown walked through the house until he saw the two people slumped over in their rocking chairs on the back deck. "Sorry to bother you, but I was told that I could find Reverend MacAffie here," he announced.

When there was no response and they seemed to be asleep, he felt the sides of their necks. Mr. Lehman had no pulse. Mrs. Lehman's heart was obviously struggling and wouldn't last the hour. Matty nodded his head and smiled. "I've got to hand it to you, reverend. You're slick. I don't know what your game is, but you're about to have a partner."

He picked up Lehman's telephone and dialed the international number of King Arthur in Ireland.

* * * *

The bodies of Jack and Lillian Lehman weren't discovered until two days later, when Mrs. Olson stopped by with a fresh apple pie. When no one responded to her knock, she entered the unlocked house, and sat the pie on the counter top. When she peeked outside, she found the Lehman's bodies still sitting on their chairs, exactly where they had been two days earlier. A grotesque was look painted on Lillian's face…the look of excruciating pain.

She screamed and summoned an ambulance. The police arrived, and a routine examination of the dining area revealed two sets of dishes and one wine glass. There was no hint that Aaron MacAffie had ever been there. On first blush, the authorities assumed that Jack and Lillian Lehman must have died of a heart attack.

The autopsy concluded that in fact they had died of mushroom poisoning, which was consistent with the mushroom sauce found fermenting on their stove. The cause of death was noted as accidental poisoning from wild mushrooms, probably picked somewhere on their twelve acres. No one ever checked.

*   *   *   *

Nevenka heard about the Lehman's death on her small desk radio. She had opened the door of Aaron's office to tell him when she noticed that he was intently engrossed in something that was playing on television. "What are you watching?"

Without looking up, he said, "Some Indian fellow back East. He's a faith healer. Just look at the people, will you? Thousands of them. And there are more outside. He can't get them all in the church!"

"I can see why. If I were ill, I would go, too, if I thought that he could heal me."

"That's just the point. Look. He only picks a few people. There! See that old man? They pushed him in on a wheelchair. Then this guy tells him to stand, and he does! Now he touches him, and he falls back, and the guy tells the old man that he's healed. It's beautiful!"

"Yes. Faith can do wonderful things."

He looked at her blankly. "You don't get it, do you? This guy is a fake. He finds a homeless person, dresses him up and gives him a couple hundred, and tells him to pretend that he's crippled. Then, when he 'heals' him, the guy gets lost and everyone thinks he's a hero."

Nevenka looked at him with disdain. "Are you telling me that he's a fake?"

"A genuine three-dollar bill! I've got to look into this. Man, look at the money this guy must drag in. And this televised performance goes nationwide! What was it that you wanted to tell me, Nevenka?"

When she broke the news of Lehmans death to him, she said with a sarcastic tone, "Dinner must have gone well. Perhaps it was best that I did not attend. Who knows," she said, "someone might be talking about me the way they are talking about the Lehmans."

You never know, my pet, MacAffie thought to himself as he smiled at his wife. *You never know.*

* * * *

Major Pennypacker had just finished listening to the latest telephonic transmission from Matty McGown to King Arthur. "This Matty McGown-Aaron Macafy fiasco is getting out of hand. Do we have a man in the States who can take care of this situation?" he asked after hearing the transmission.

"We have Flaraty, but he's occupied with the Trojan project in New York. That's about ready to bust wide open, so I can't take him off that assignment."

"How about Mulligan? Get him over here for a briefing, ASAP. Notify me the moment he arrives."

"Anything else?"

"Yes. Book passage for Mulligan on the first jet in the morning for San Francisco. Have an assault package prepared and ready for pick-up when he arrives at SFO. I'll get photo IDs prepared for him through MI 5."

"Anything to be done in America before he arrives?"

"Yes. Have one of our American operatives get down to this Los Alamos place and locate Matty McGown. I'll want a location and photos of him for when our man arrives."

"Consider it done!"

"Oh, and one more thing: I'll want a complete profile on this Macafy character…photo, living quarters, family, the whole bit. We're going to kill two birds with one stone."

* * * *

Laura Nesbit was having her morning bagel and orange juice, reading the *San Jose Mercury News,* when her eye caught the article relating the deaths of Lillian and Jack Lehman. The deaths were from eating poisonous mushrooms, the article read. Apparently they had picked them and cooked them in their spaghetti sauce, which was attributed to be the cause of death.

Her mind instantly pictured Pastor Aaron MacAffie, carefully picking poisonous mushrooms in the field the day she and her date had ben there studying for a test.

* * * *

The captain at GMPC, the Greater Military Power Group, handed the General a copy of the communiqué' from Major Pennypacker, directing MI 5 to prepare false passport papers for Sean Mulligan. The same communiqué' directed them to compile a complete current file on one Pastor Aaron MacAffie, who was residing in a small western-Californian town in the United States.

"Hmm. I take it our Major Pennypacker is planning on intervening on the MacAffie item."

"Does that mean that he's going to intervene against the Irish, or take steps against MacAffie himself?"

"Good question. My first thought would be that he's going to instruct his operative to eliminate the Irish lad if he's instructed to kill MacAffie."

"If the Sons of Ireland are going to use MacAffie; why kill him?"

"They won't kill him unless he becomes a problem."

"In which case that could become a problem for us?"

"Not necessarily so. If MacAffie has a relapse of conscience, which, from reading his file, I doubt he'll have, and turns the Sons of Ireland down flat, they'll kill him just to protect their own interests."

"Do we care?"

"We've got enough on MacAffie to make good use of his resources ourselves in other areas."

"Like the Kadafy or Saddam Hussein?"

They're a little far afield for our interests. I'd rather keep it close to home, somewhere in Northern Ireland, preferably. I'm sure we could involve the IRA or the Sons of Katy Elder or any of those factions. They're always hard up for money and ready to buy information, munitions and such."

The Captain looked up at the General, the lights from the monitors playing on his chiseled features. "Does it ever concern you that MI 5 might uncover your operation, sir? The Gempac?"

The General smiled. "You mean Major Pennypacker?"

The Captain nodded.

"See these stars," he asked, pointing to the three stars on his shoulder boards. "This is the reason *Major* Pennypacker won't become a problem."

"And if he does?" the Captain persisted.

"We can't risk an MI 5 investigation, so I guess we'll have to make that decision when the time comes."

"You wouldn't have him killed, would you, sir?"
The general simply looked at the Captain and walked away.

CHAPTER 46

▼

Pastor Aaron MacAffie was sitting in his study looking at the rendering for the Aaron MacAffie Institute of Higher Learning for the hundredth time. He had already begun to lay out the buildings on a large piece of drafting paper configured to Lehman's land as he envisioned them to be constructed. The administration building would be the first structure anyone would see as he drove onto the campus. It would be designed as a two-story English Tudor, constructed with used brick. Two coned towers would be constructed at each end of the administration building. One would be his office—the President's office, the other would be the Chief Administrator's office. From his lofty perch, he would have a three-hundred-sixty-degree view of the campus, and everyone would have a view of his office.

Beyond the administration building, the classrooms would be constructed. Although he would love to have all of the buildings constructed of used brick, preliminary construction costs clearly prohibited such extravagance. Instead, the remaining buildings would be constructed of tilt-up exposed exterior concrete walls and metal-framed interior rooms. Although he wanted to have a gymnasium for sporting events, the cost of that facility would be prohibitive, unless he was able to land some independent seed money prior to construction.

If Mullin were alive, I could approach him for a generous contribution, he thought. MacAffie would have even been willing to call it Mullin's Gymnasium. He shrugged his shoulders. At any rate, he reserved some of the land at the back of the campus for a proposed site for a future gymnasium, if and when he located the funds.

He was snapped out of the trance he had put himself in when Nevenka inquired, "Have you given any more thought as to what we talked about earlier?" She was standing at the doorway of his office, almost afraid to come in. "About my mother and brother coming to America?" She was nervously wringing her hands, in which she held a piece of paper. Her head hung low as she looked up attentively to her husband.

She ran her fingers over the paper she held as she talked. It was as if the paper had a life of its own, and needed consultation. "I received a letter from them today. They are starving in Lithuania, Aaron. They need my help. Our help." She fought to keep the tears from running down her face.

For the past hour, she had been watching her husband from the doorway to his office, unobserved, as he savored his new project. He had an obvious look of satisfaction painted upon his face. It was a look that she had not seen for some time. She thought that this might be a good time to once again bring up the subject of sponsoring her family.

Although the final disposition of the Lehmans property had not been finalized, she knew he was feeling particularly proud of himself. She also knew where he would get the land for his college, and how he got it, but didn't dare bring it up. That knowledge would be her bargaining chip, she thought, if it became necessary. She also knew that, once he got engrossed in building the college, there would be precious little time for anything else, especially matters concerning her family in Lithuania.

The look of contentment instantly vanished from his face as he looked at her. He took a measured breath before responding. "I don't know, Nevenka." He tapped the eraser of the pencil that he was holding on his desk, making irritating thumping noises. Nevenka interpreted this thumping as a sign of authority, dominance. She could recall that her father used to rap his fingers on the kitchen table like that when he was upset. It was a sign that he didn't want his judgement challenged. If anyone dared question his authority, punishment usually followed, and it was swift and harsh, and everyone knew it—even his wife. It usually came in the form of a backhand across the face.

He stopped thumping the pencil and looked at her. His lips were firmly fixed in a quasi-snarl. He folded his hands and leaned back in his chair, crossing his legs on his desk. For all outward purposes, his body language had shut off all conversation on the topic. "I have to be honest with you, Nevenka. I don't feel comfortable having your mother and brother here, living here with us. It's bad enough that I have to raise your bastard child!"

Nearly three years of repressed anger suddenly erupted without his even knowing it. Nevenka starred at him with open mouth, too stunned to speak.

"I...I'm sorry. I didn't mean that." He stammered in vain effort to retract his statement.

The look on Nevenka's face changed, from one of subservience to detestable anger. "Oh, I think you meant, it all right. I know you don't love Vladimer as your own son. I can understand that. But this!" She snarled. "I never thought you were capable..." She turned and stormed out of the room without finishing her sentence, too angry to speak and too hurt to care.

That evening, at dinner, Nevenka had had time to cool down and re-evaluate her situation. She knew if her husband kicked her out the house, she would have nowhere to go. She and little Vladimer certainly couldn't go back to Lithuania, although there would be nothing she would like better. At least in Lithuania she had a family that loved her. And then there was Vladimer, if he was still alive—and if he still cared.

"I'm sorry," MacAffie said as they sat down to the dinner table that night. "I just don't see how I can do anything for your family right now. Here." He waved her over. "I've written a check for them, a thousand dollars. If they're as resourceful as you say, they should be able to survive on this. Maybe things will change and they'll find employment in the near future." Giving her money for her family was his way of making everything all right.

Nevenka begrudgingly took the check, bowing subserviently without comment. She would remain silent on the issue of her family's economic state for the moment. Any amount of money was acceptable. Life had taught her not to be proud. A thousand dollars American *would* go a long way in Lithuania.

She looked at the check, suddenly feeling ashamed, like a prostitute who had just sold her soul. Without thinking, she struck back. "When I came to this country, I promised I would bring my family to America," she said, with a firm resolve.

MacAffie stopped eating and looked at her. He made no attempt to mask the anger that suddenly crept across his face. For the first time in their short married life, he felt used. "What do you mean, 'you promised?'" he snarled. He leaned forward in his chair, glaring at her. "Are you telling me that the only reason you came to this country—to marry me—was to bring your family here? And to have...that," he said, pointing to little Vladimer.

The tone of his voice shocked Nevenka, but she held her ground. Nothing was more important than her family and her son. "I resent the fact that you think I married you just to have my child. And, no, I did not marry you just to have my family come to America, but it was the agreement I made when they let me come. It was understood that I would sponsor them when I was settled. I gave my promise!" Her voice had escalated to a shout, which was sprinkled with tears.

The harsh voices startled little Vladimer, and he started crying. She reached over to pick him up, then looked her husband in the eye defiantly. "It is important I keep my promise. Lithuanians do not break their word."

They continued looking at one another with stern eyes, then, without warning, MacAffie's face softened and he broke out laughing.

Nevenka saw nothing funny and was concerned at this inappropriate laughter. "Why you laugh?" she demanded, thinking he was laughing at her.

He stopped laughing, but couldn't help smiling. He went over to her and gave her and Vladimer a hug. Holding her at arm's length, he said, "I think I've met my match!" His eyes twinkled.

She looked confused. "I don't understand."

"I think you do."

She searched his eyes for a moment, then a smile began to creep across her face.

"See, I told you, you understood."

"You can't compare the desire I have, of wanting to take care of…"

"It's not a comparison," he said, interrupting her as he anticipated her words. "You're doing what is necessary to take care of your child and meet your commitment to your family. Don't get me wrong," he said, holding up his hand. "I appreciate that," he added quickly. "By the same token, my commitment is to myself and my church. I'll do whatever is in my power to further that cause, as well." The smile was replaced by a intense look that made his intentions clear.

Nevenka studied the face of the man she had married, before venturing into uncharted, dangerous territory. When she spoke, she chose her words carefully. "Does your faith allow you to commit atrocities on your fellow man to get your way?" she challenged. Since the Lehman's had met their demise she had come to understand the length that her husband would go to get what he wanted. In some respects, she even feared for her own and little Vladimer's safety.

"The Lord works in mysterious ways," was his only response.

"And my family in Lithuania?" she asked, bringing him back to the point.

He nodded. "Let me give it further thought. In the meantime, send them the money."

She had finally come to have an understanding of her husband's ways. When he uttered these last words, she knew that, unless she did something desperate, her family was destined to remain in Lithuania until they died. She vowed on her Sons life that this would never happen. She would find a way.

Chapter 47

"Horwitz! Glad you could drop by! I want you know, for an attorney, you're pretty smart!"

"I'll take that as a compliment."

"It is. You recall, you asked about checking the computer for any entries regarding MacAffie the day of Mullin's death?"

"Yeah. Parking tickets or something like that."

"You lose on both counts, for parking tickets or anything the day of his death," he said with some satisfaction.

Horwitz wrinkled his brow. "I thought you said I was onto something."

Terryman rose to close the door of his office, waving his hand towards a leather captain's chair in front of his desk. "It was your needling me that put me in touch with the computer.

Credit given where credit is due. The day *before* the plane crash, it turns out our friend, Pastor Aaron MacAffie, rented a car from Hertz at the San Jose Airport. He had the rental from the hours of 6:15 PM the day before Mullin's death to 12:20 the following morning."

"Rented a car? What a strange hour to rent, then return, a car! Especially being a local resident! One would have thought that he could have arranged for transportation with one of his church members."

"That's what I thought."

"Any idea where he went?"

"I know that he went to San Jose Blueprint in San Jose."

Horwitz frowned. "What's that got to do with anything?"

"Don't have a clue, but he was apparently in such a hurry that he left some plans or drawings in the back seat of the rental. Hertz found them the following day and had a delivery service return them to MacAffie's office."

"Does that help us any?"

"Only that it confirms that he rented a car that day. In addition to that piece of information, I know that he was in the vicinity of the San Carlos Airport, because he got a fix-it ticket for a broken taillight. The ticket was given by one Harvey Thompson, a California Highway Patrolman, badge number 58943, and it was signed by one Aaron MacAffie."

"Then we got him!"

"Let's not throw the rope around the tree just yet," Terryman said, holding up his hand. "I asked the car rental agency if they checked over their cars for body damage or broken glass before sending them out."

"And they obviously said yes!"

"Correct! It's standard procedure for their attendants to make sure that the car is clean and that there is no body damage nor broken glass before they release the vehicle to the next customer."

"And they have a record of the broken taillight when he returned it?"

"Affirmative."

"So," Horwitz hypothesized, "for the sake of discussion, let's assume the car left Hertz intact, and somewhere along the line, he got into a fender bender, or more correctly put, had some sort of altercation that resulted in a broken light."

Terryman nodded, making no comment, letting Horwitz continue with his hypothetical analysis, then asked, "Wouldn't there have been an accident report filed?"

"There were no written forms filed pertaining to any accident that night. I checked. Having found nothing, I did the next obvious thing. I sent a man out to the airport to poke around, in the hopes that he might find something."

Horwitz was very interested in the story, but it was unfolding too slowly for his razor-sharp mind. Impatiently, he extended his hand. "On with it, man. Then what!"

"Patience, Horwitz. Good police work takes time." He smiled as the image of Donald Chin at Forensics flashed through his mind. He had fallen into Chin's mold, without realizing it. He had to admit, it was enjoyable, enticing the man.

"My man did find some broken glass, similar to that of a broken taillight, on the parking lot adjacent to the tarmac, but," he quickly added, "there is no way to positively match that specific glass to the car that MacAffie was driving. The taillight of the rented car had already been replaced and the broken pieces discarded."

Horwitz wrinkled his brow.

"But we did ascertain that the broken lens was from a '95 Nissan, the same make and model that MacAffie rented."

"That's great! So, we're closing in on a very strong circumstantial case here, don't you think?"

"It's not what you or I think that's important. It's what the DA thinks. I ran it by him before you arrived. He doesn't think we have enough evidence to convict yet."

Horwitz sighed. "I thought we had him for sure."

"Oh, we got him, all right. Now, it's just a matter of technique."

"How's that?"

"We either keep chasing evidence, or confront him with what we have and try bluffing him into thinking that we have more than we do."

"And if he calls your bluff?"

He shrugged his shoulders. "Then, we lose."

"I don't like the sound of that!"

"Didn't think you would. If he calls our bluff, it's not necessarily the ball game, you understand. It just makes our next step all the more precarious."

"Because then he'll know we're onto him?"

"Exactly."

Horwitz thought for a moment. "So, what's the game plan?"

"I'm vacillating between bringing him in to see if I can sweat it out of him, or…" He paused to look at his friend.

"Or fucking what? You shoot him?"

Terryman laughed. "Or I bring both him *and* his old lady in."

"His old lady? The Russian chick?"

"Yeah. I'll put him in one room and work on him for a while, giving him just enough information to make him sweat, then leave him to think about it while I go to work on the Russian. She hasn't been in this country long enough to be streetwise enough to snow us. She's got a kid, and I figure I can fake it enough and scare her into thinking that, if she doesn't cooperate, we'll send 'em back to Russia."

"Anyone ever tell you, you were a bastard?"

Terryman ignored his sarcasm. "And, even if she doesn't know anything, I'll go back to work on the preacher again, making him think that she spilled the beans on him."

"And if all this dancing about doesn't prove fruitful?"

"I can always resort to my ace in the hole."

"You'll shoot the bastard!" He said with a poker face.

Terryman laughed. He pointed his forefinger at Horwitz and said, "Right!" He poured himself a cup of the ugliest black coffee that Horwitz had ever seen, making the styrofoam cup turn black. He took a sip, making a face. "Man, that's nasty!"

"I don't know how you can drink that mud. I'd like to see what your insides look like. Probably a mass of black mush!"

"Beats smoking," he said, then took another sip, making the same disgusting face. Terryman threw the cup and it's contents into the trash. He wiped his mouth with his sleeve. "It's been my experience that the criminal mind invariably makes a mistake when they know someone's watching their every move. Especially, when the person is a novice."

"Like the preacher."

He nodded his head. "Eventually, he'll either get paranoid and do something stupid that'll give him away or say something to someone or, my favorite," he paused to smile to himself, as if enjoying a riddle to which only he knew the answer, "he'll think he's outfoxed us and will continue doing what he was doing all the time."

"No one's that stupid!"

"You'd be surprised."

Chapter 48

It was Friday and, as he did every Friday, Pastor MacAffie locked himself in his study to prepare for Sunday's sermon. The mailman had left his usual three-inch pile of mail, magazines and advertisements on the front desk. Nevenka thumbed through the pile, putting letters in one pile, the magazines in another, setting the advertisements aside to sift through later, when things were slow. Even though she was getting used to the abundance of food, clothing and every other kind of material possession available to Americans, she still loved looking at the pictures in the catalogs, even choosing a blouse or skirt to purchase every now and again.

A cold shiver ran down her spine when she picked up the letter postmarked Moscow, Russia. *Vladimer,* she thought. *He's dead!*

Her fingers trembled as she tore open the envelope. It was a two-page handwritten letter in Russian, with clear, even-handed writing. The first two words fairly jumped off the page.

Dearest Nevenka!

She shut and locked the door to her office so she wouldn't be disturbed.

It seems an eternity since you left Russia. I see you in my dreams every night, but it's not the same as holding you in my arms. I miss you so much! My thoughts and prayers go out to you every night. I dare not even think of our love child, wondering how he is and what he looks like. I hope this doesn't come at a bad time, but it seems that my role is finished here in Russia. Gorbachev has loosened his hold on Lithuania and is on his way out of power. As a result, I am no longer a hunted man. Believe it or not, I have been embraced as a hero and have actually been decorated. They offered me a promotion, but I feel that my job here is done. There are more important things in my life, like you and our child! I have seen your mother, which is where I got your address. She seems to be holding up remarkably well, considering her age and the condition of the country. I do think that you should find a way to either get her to America or for you to visit her, as she is getting on with age.

The Lithuanian Ship Building Company has reopened and your two brothers are back to work. They are fine, strong, young men. I think they'll be all right.

I hope this doesn't come as a shock to you, but I've arranged to fly to America. I know that you're married to an American, but I must see you, if only to hold you in my arms one last time. If I have a child, I will not rest until I have held him in my arms and have kissed the mouth that binds us together.

I'll be in contact with you once I arrive in America.
My deepest undying love,
Colonel Vladimer Ryzhkov

Nevenka held the letter to her chest with her eyes closed, as tears of love for Vladimer flowed down her cheeks. She had almost forgotten what it felt like to feel the warmth of love that she felt towards him.

She folded the letter and tucked in inside her blouse, next to her heart, to be read to little Vladimer later that night. Even if he wouldn't understand, she felt it important that her son hear the words of his father.

It was too good to be true! Vladimer was not only alive, but he still loved her. And he was coming to get them!

Chapter 49

Aaron MacAffie was attending an evangelistic conference in Florida when Nevenka dialed Helena Markarov's office in San Francisco. Since Helena had been instrumental in placing her with Pastor Aaron MacAffie and had extended the invitation that if she ever needed help, to feel free to call upon her, she felt that time had arrived.

Fortunately, Helena had a cancellation the following morning and was more than happy to insert Nevenka into that time slot. After the usual pleasantries spoken in Russian, Nevenka got down to the purpose of her visit. She felt she had to camouflage the truth in order to extract the information she needed. "First of all, I want to thank you for providing me with such a kind and thoughtful husband," she said. "I feel very lucky to have such a devoted mate."

"It pleases me when I hear that my girls are happy. It makes all the hard work worthwhile."

"You must miss your home in Russia."

She nodded. There was a wistful look in her eyes. "Yes, I miss my home and my friends, but I have to say that I don't miss Russia. It was only a matter of time until the foundation crumbled. Look what has happened to Lithuania."

"Yes. That concerns me every time I get a letter from home."

"Tell me about your husband. I understand that he's doing very well. Every once in a while, I catch him on television," she said with an approving smile. "You are very fortunate to have such a man."

"Yes, I am." She smiled for a moment, then transferred that look to a grim impression before continuing.

"Nevenka. I have often wondered about your child. Did he? Was he?"

She smiled and nodded. "Yes. He's a strong, handsome young man. Just like his father. Blond, intelligent and personable. His father will…would have been proud of him."

"I'm so glad for you. Not many people have the opportunity to have a child from one they've lost." She clasped her hands on her desk in a businesslike fashion. "Now then, what brings you to San Francisco?"

Nevenka rubbed her hands, then said, "It is not common knowledge, but…well, you asked about my husband. I'm afraid that he is not well."

"Oh? I'm sorry to hear that."

"He would not be pleased if I told you." She looked at Helena.

"Oh, you can be assured our conversation is confidential. Nothing goes beyond these four walls. Unlike in Russia," she added quickly with a smile.

"Thank you. I appreciate that. You are right, of course. In Soviet Union, such privacy does not exist."

Helena nodded with understanding.

"My husband, he has, what they call asthma?"

"A lung affliction, I believe."

"Yes. That is it. Sometimes he can hardly breathe, and I get very worried for him." The look upon Nevenka's face was clearly one of concern. "He must take medication every night so he can sleep. Sometimes, it is so bad that I have to give him two pills." She held up two fingers. "Otherwise, his nose and throat get so stopped up that he cannot breathe." She paused to let the comment sink in as she studied Helena's face to see if there was any reaction.

"He has seen a doctor, of course?"

Nevenka smiled to herself. She had made the proper impression. "Yes. Of course. He says that asthma is just something that half of the people in California suffer from in the springtime."

Helena nodded. "That's true."

"It is, what did he say, poolen?"

"Pollen."

"Yes, that is it. Pollen in the air. But…" She seemed to hesitate to talk about the issue any further.

Helena nodded. "Please. Go on."

"Well, as you know, I have family back in Lithuania: two brothers, and my mother, who are not well. After Red Army killed Yuri, my other two brothers, Niki and Viktor, have been caring for my mother. My father recently died, of course." She brought out a hankie to dab at her eyes.

"I'm so sorry to hear that. About your father's death, that is."

"Thank you. It is about that issue that I wish to speak." Again she hesitated for a moment, projecting the impression that she was unsure if this would be an appropriate topic to discuss.

"Please. Continue," Helena urged.

Nevenka hesitated for a moment, folding her hankie carefully, as if thinking about how to formulate her next words. "There are two problems that concern me. The first is the fact that Russia has cut off all supplies to Lithuania, as you know."

"Yes. I'm sorry."

Nevenka nodded. "The Lithuanian Shipping Company has been shut down, which means that my family has no money to live on. The winters are very cold in Lithuania and the house is without fuel." She was wringing her white hankie. "And now that all supplies have been cut off by Russia, there is little food." She stopped to catch her breath, and to let that fact sink into Helena's mind.

"Please, go on. You said there were two problems?"

Nevenka nodded, wiping her eyes. She was pleased with Helena's interest in her family's welfare. She took a deep breath and continued. "It is my mother that I worry most about, you see. With no food and little heat, she knows she will soon die, and does not want to be buried in Lithuania." Nevenka looked deep into Helena's eyes for the understanding she needed. "She knows I am here, in America, and that I am trying to bring them here. It is very important to her that she be buried in a free country, along with her children."

Helena nodded. "I understand."

"I want my husband to have the church sponsor them to come over to America, and when I ask him, he says yes, that he will sponsor them."

"That must make you very happy!"

"Yes. Except, you see, he is a very busy man, and now it appears he will be starting to build his university and, well, if I may be frank…"

Helena nodded and inched closer to her guest, so as not to miss anything.

"I'm afraid that he will work so hard that, well, with his asthma and the stress his congregation puts on him operating the church…I'm afraid he may kill himself." She started to cry again.

Helena handed her a box of tissues.

"Thank you. You are kind." She blew her nose and wiped her eyes, then continued. "If something should happen to him, I would be penniless and would be sent back to Lithuania. And if my family can't come to America, I will be responsible. As you see, I'm in a dilemma, Helena. I'm scared. What should I do?" She nervously wrung her hankie.

Helena patted her on the hand. "I understand your concerns. First of all, your husband is an American citizen. When you married him, that automatically made you legal in this country.

No one can take that away from you. Should something happen to him, they would not deport you. You would be treated the same as if you were born in America. The only thing you can't do is vote. You must be an American citizen to vote."

"And the church? What would happen to the church?"

"You would have to look into the by laws of the church to answer that question. If you really want to protect yourself, you should have your husband make a living trust, naming you as his beneficiary. A living trust is…"

"Yes. I am familiar. Husband uses them in his church."

"He does?"

Nevenka bit her lip. She knew instantly that she had said too much.

Helena simply shook her shoulders. "Well then, you know the value of a living trust in the event of spousal death. Are you a signatory the family checking account?"

Nevenka looked blank.

"I didn't think so. In America, most wives are signatories the family checking accounts That means you can write checks," she explained. "In case you need groceries, or in the event you need money in an emergency. I know you're new here and all, but, even so, you *are* his wife. He shouldn't object to that, now should he?"

Nevenka shrugged her shoulders. "Anything else?"

"I hate to sound devious, but you really should try to learn everything about his business that you can. Just to be safe, you understand. You may have to take over someday, if he's as ill as you say he is."

Nevenka thanked Helena for her advice and went home armed with new tools she hoped would result in getting her family out of Lithuania and into America. It would take dramatic sacrifices, of that she was sure, but then, she was used to making sacrifices.

✳   ✳   ✳   ✳

Helena Makarov sat at her desk thumping the eraser end on her forehead, thinking. It had been several minutes now since Nevenka had left and she was certain that she wouldn't return. Reluctantly, she picked up the telephone and dialed a series of numbers.

"Gempac!" The line had a slight echo to it, as it did whenever she dialed overseas to London.

"White Russian calling Bloody Mary."

There was a moment of silence, then another voce came on the line, one of authority. "Helena Makarov! What news do you have to report?" There were no pleasantries. This was strictly business and both parties knew it.

"My Russian pupil just left this office and, in my considered opinion, I feel that she intends to extract the implant."

"Hmm. That would be unfortunate. Seems she and a faction of the Sons of Ireland are bent on the same course. Shooting themselves in the foot! Was this an imminent action?"

"Not imminent, but, in my view, inevitable."

"So, we have some time, then?"

"That is my opinion." There was a pause. "Anything to be done from my end?"

"Not at this time. Let me consult the staff. It would be a pity to have all our planning go without bearing fruit, after all this time."

"I know from past experience that your organization has been waiting for this opportunity for a long time. It would be a shame to lose him now."

The General looked at the large computer board with blinking lights and nodded.

"He's not the only red herring in the sea," the voice said, "but you're right, it would be a shame to waste such an opportunity. We'll be in touch."

Chapter 50

Just as Pierce Terryman pulled into the parking lot of Herb's Deli, he dialed Fitzgerald on his cell phone. "Buy you a donut?" he asked when Fitzgerald answered the phone.

"Beg your pardon!"

"I said, buy you a donut? I just pulled into Herb's, and I thought maybe you could use a bear claw or a twinkie or somethin'."

"Have you been drinking?"

"No, but I might have one after you and I meet and I tell you the latest on our friend the preacher."

"Pick me out one of those fresh apple-filled jobs…and a cup of hot chocolate. I'll be right over."

Terryman had Fitzgerald's hot chocolate and an apple-filled donut were waiting for him when he walked through the door. "What have you uncovered?" he asked before his ass hit the seat. "I can hardly wait!" There was a wide, boyish grin spread across his face.

"Hey! Was your mother a grizzly bear?"

"What?"

"Manners, boy! Where's your manners? Us civilized boys usually say, 'Hi, how you doin'?' 'I'm fine, thank you. Thanks for askin,' before we launch into verbal demands. The very least you can do is take a sip of that fine, brown, hot water I paid a buck for and take a bite out of your cholesterol bar."

Fitzgerald grunted. He was in no mood for Terryman's humor this morning. He had had a spat with his wife about how much money they should give their kids for walking around, pocket money while they were in college, and he had still been agitated over the results of their discussion when he walked into Herb's.

Terryman shrugged his shoulder when he saw that Fitzgerald wasn't buying into his line of humor. "You knew that old Jack and Lillian Lehman kicked the bucket here a while back?"

Fitzgerald nodded as he took a bit out of his apply-filled bar, allowing some of the sticky brown substance to flow down the palm of his hand and onto his coat sleeve. "Shit!" he said as he wiped it on his pants. "Somethin' about mushroom poisonin', the paper had said."

"You read, too."

"You're pushin' it," Terryman said, as he wiped his mouth with the sleeve of his shirt. "Is that why you called me down here, to insult my intelligence?"

"You know I never insult an unarmed man." He laughed as he pushed the napkin holder towards Fitzgerald, looking at the apple sauce on his sleeve. "No, the reason I called you down here was to feed you sticky apple-filled donuts and point out the location of the new Aaron MacAffie Institute of Higher Learning."

Fitzgerald eyes went blank.

"Got a call from Tripper Downs this morning. He's been awarded the job of drawing the layout for the good Pastor. Seems that Jack and Lillian Lehman deeded their property to the good reverend..."

"Then conveniently poisoned themselves with wild mushrooms."

"That was certainly accommodating of them, wasn't it?"

"Sounds an awful lot like the Nesbit fiasco to me. Someone blows up the house when the Nesbits are supposedly home, preacher gets the insurance dough and the heirs get the shaft."

"Only it wasn't the Nesbits who got scorched."

"Details."

"That rug-headed little shit has gone too far this time," Fitzgerald said, angrily. "When are you going to arrest him?"

"As soon as I get some hard evidence. They require that in this county, you know, before we drop the guillotine."

Fitzgerald slammed his big fist on the table so hard that a good portion of his hot chocolate jumped out of the styrofoam cup, onto his lap.

Terryman threw him a handful of paper napkins from the chrome dispenser. "I know how you feel. I want to nail the little shit as much as you do, but so far all we've got is circumstantial evidence. He's been much too clever so far."

"He's not so clever!" he said, wiping the hot chocolate from his pants. "Shit! I just got these out of the cleaners last week!"

"You mean that you've only worn them for a week? Why, shit, man, what's your wife goin' to say? You're goin' to work her fingers to the bone, keeping you in clean clothes, if you keep up this pace."

"Don't push your luck, Terryman, or I'll have someone set fire to your pants." He threw the soiled paper napkins on the corner of the table. "As far as that little fuck is concerned, I still say that he's as dumb as a post. Up to this point he's just been lucky."

"Whatever you wish to call him, he's skated free thus far."

"Well, he doesn't know it yet, but the ice is melting around his fat ass, and I, for one, intend to tie an anchor to his leg when he breaks through!"

"We don't drown 'em in California. Cruel and unusual punishment."

Fitzgerald grunted. "I know. We feed, house and clothe the bastard for the rest of his life, then, when he's run the legal gauntlet, we put him to sleep like a lap dog."

"My job is to get him off the street. What they do with him once he's locked up is the DA's bailiwick."

"So, what's the plan?"

*　　*　　*　　*

Transamerica Airlines, flight 152, landed at precisely 2:53 PM at San Francisco, California, from London. Among the passengers was a slightly built man, with delicate features, his black hair balding slightly at the temples. He wore an open white shirt under a light-brown-plaid sports jacket. The only luggage he carried was a leather carry-on bag containing a make-up kit, two shirts and a pair of pants, extra shorts and socks.

After the Custom's check, he walked straight through the airport, stopping only at the concession stand to purchase a carton of American cigarettes, then proceeded outside to the sidewalk. Within a few moments, a black Mercedes 300 pulled up. The driver rolled down the window and motioned to him. "Mulligan! Over here."

Without comment, Sean Mulligan picked up his satchel and got into the passenger side. "Never could get used to the Americans driving on the wrong side of the road," he said, as he got in. "How you doing, Mark?" He looked straight ahead, without offering the driver his hand.

"Enjoying the California weather. Once ya live here, you'll never go back to England, or Ireland, for that matter."

"You got a package for me?"

"On the back seat."

Mulligan looked in the back seat, where a dark-red, eel-skin briefcase lay. He reached back to snap open the case. "PK Walther with a silencer. Plastic explosives. Fake ID. Gloves. Looks like you got about everything covered. Got some photos for me?"

"In the side compartment. There's a map, too, just in case ya get lost."

He looked at the picture of Matty McGown. "So, this is the bloke I'm to ice." He picked up MacAffie's picture. "And this other chap? The one with the rug. This our preacher?"

"Pastor Aaron MacAffie."

"So, he's the one that we sent over. A man of the cloth, is he?"

"Don't let that fool ya. He's a cold-blooded killer, that one. He looks out for number one, first and foremost."

He drove on for a while, then got onto the Bayshore Freeway. "So, why isn't Pennypacker letting this Irish lad, Matty McGown, do the job for us? He's from the other side. Seems like such a waste, your coming all the way over here."

Mulligan smiled and shrugged his shoulders as he slipped on a pair of leather gloves. "Your guess is as good as mine, mate. You know, as well as I, that bloody intelligence has their own way of doin'. And the left hand never tells the right what's goin' on. Now, lets be gettin' there, lad. I've got work to do."

"When you're done, will ya be stayin' on for a while? I'll show ya the sites and introduce ya to some fine California women."

"Maybe I'll take you up on that. Now then, what will you be havin' for transportation?"

Chapter 51

"Detective Terryman. There's a Laura Nesbit here to see you."

"Send her in."

"Do you remember me?" she asked as she came into his office.

"Certainly. You're Eric and Dawn's daughter. We met under less-than-pleasant circumstances, if I recall."

"You remember the fire at my parent's home then."

"Vividly."

"Does the name Pastor Aaron MacAffie ring a bell?"

Without betraying his interest, he answered in the affirmative with his usual detective poker face. "Why do you ask?"

She slid the current edition of the *San Jose Mercury News* across his desk. A bright red circle outlined the article entitled, "Local Farmer Wills Land to Church."

"Yes. I've read the article."

"So you know that the Lehmans died of mushroom poisoning and, prior to their demise, they deeded the property to MacAffie in anticipation of their future demise."

"I take it you find a correlation here?"

"Don't you?"

"Well…"

"The pattern of their deaths coincides to the millimeter with my parent's situation."

"You think that Pastor MacAffie orchestrated your parent's fire, thinking that they were in the house?"

"Yes! I don't know how he did it, but I'll give my eyeteeth in Hell if I'm not right."

"How does that correlate with the Lehmans situation? Their death was ruled accidental poisoning."

"Give me a fucking break!"

"I beg your pardon?"

"Look. Old man Lehman was a farmer in this valley before Los Alamos Hills even became incorporated. Do you think for one minute he didn't know the difference between a poison mushroom and one from Safeway? Even I know that!"

"Logic would tell you that…"

"Forget logic. Listen. The day before the Lehmans were killed—and I used the word advisedly—my boyfriend and I *saw* that lecherous, rug-headed fart harvesting poisonous mushrooms down at Mulberry Pond. He was picking them and putting them into some small brown bag."

"If you knew they were poisonous mushrooms, why didn't you stop him?"

"'Cause I was hopin' the bastard would take 'em home and eat 'em!"

Terryman tried to refrain from smiling, but didn't succeed.

"You think this is fucking funny? This old bastard tried to kill my parents, then did the Lehmans in, and you can bet your bottom dollar he didn't pay for Mullin's property, either. Who knows who else he's done in or is planning on doing, and all you can do is sit there with a shit-eatin' grin on your face."

He held up his hand. He accepted her analogy, and even a little harsh rhetoric, but downright insults wouldn't be tolerated. "I'd cool down if I were you." He held his thumb and forefinger an inch apart. "You're this far from taking a short vacation in the slammer."

"Sorry. I'm just so damn mad, I could shit."

He rose from his desk and put his arm around her shoulder. In a fatherly fashion, he said, "Why don't you go home and let me do some investigating on my end? We're following several leads that I can't comment on at this time, but, just between you and me, I feel confident we'll have this case closed before you can say Jack Robinson."

"Jack Robinson."

* * * *

"Nevenka! What are these two signature cards from the bank doing in my stack of mail? There's one for the church account and one for our personal account."

"They came in today. The bank's updating all their records. Something about converting everything to computers."

"Well, I'm not signing any signature card until I know what it's all about!"

"Suit yourself. The letter said the bank wouldn't honor any checks from the fifteenth on that didn't have new signature cards. Throw them in the garbage if you like."

"Damn bureaucrats. No wonder Andy Mullin hated them so much." He scribbled his name on the spot marked with a large red X. "Here!" he said, tossing them on her desk. I'm going out. Be back around three."

Nevenka smiled to herself as she signed on the signature line below her husbands name, then slipped them into the envelope that the lady at the bank had given to her when she had requested new signature cards. *Now I can sign checks, too*, she thought, patting the envelope with her forefinger.

*   *   *   *

Terryman had a two o'clock appointment with Rafael Herrera, the County Assistant District Attorney in San Jose. With the Quit Claim Deed from Mullin's Shasta lot, which had apparently been switched to his residential property, followed by his subsequent death, the late-night Hertz car rental, the traffic ticket and the broken tail light, which all tied into the time frame of Mullin's death; the unusual coincidence of the Nesbit fire and subsequent deaths of the intruders, ending with MacAffie being the apparent recipient of the insurance money; the more than coincidental Nesbit fire, with MacAffie as the heir apparent and now the testimony of Laura Nesbit and her boyfriend, Mark O'Brian, seeing Aaron MacAffie purposefully picking poisonous mushrooms the day before the Lehmans death, which resulted in his getting their land, Terryman felt that he had an airtight case against MacAffie, even if it was circumstantial.

"If even half of what you've got here is true, your boy MacAffie has been one busy fella," Herrera said.

"I don't know what else I can do, short of catching him with a smoking gun," Terryman said. "We've really done our homework here. The only surface we haven't scratched is his Russian wife. Personally, I think there's a weak link there, but I haven't been willing to play that card unless it was absolutely necessary."

"If you did interview her, and it didn't pan out, you'd obviously alert MacAffie, and that could possibly endanger your case."

Terryman nodded. "I know. That's why we've kept our hands off."

Herrera slowly nodded. "Good work, Terryman. Let me digest what you've got here. Once I've made a determination, I'll talk to the boss. If he says go, I'll prepare the documents and you can put the collar on him."

"Nothing would give me greater pleasure. You seem somewhat hesitant," he said, sensing some resistance from Herrera.

"It's not that. I just feel sorry for all the poor schmucks that believed in him and have given him their trust and money. They're the real victims here…not discounting Andrew Mullin and the Lehmans, of course."

* * * *

Aaron MacAffie was in the process of drafting a script for the several homeless people that he intended to recruit for his first televised "healing" session when his secretary announced, "Mr. Mathews in on line one, Pastor."

"Tom! I was just thinking about you. How's your investment group coming?"

"That's the purpose of this call. They're ready to close! I was wondering if I could come by with the closing papers and go over them with you? There is one slight problem that needs clarification. Are you free this afternoon?"

"How about lunch? We could go over the documents, then grab a sandwich."

"You got a deal. I'm buying, but only if you bring that lovely wife of yours."

"She'll be glad to come, I'm sure."

"Noon it is!"

At twelve sharp Jerry Davis entered the Pastors offic'e, armed with three copies of each document: one for himself, the original for Pastor MacAffie to sign and a copy for his wife.

"You mentioned a problem," MacAffie said, before looking at the packet of documents. "Maybe we should clear that off the boards before launching into specifics."

Davis straightened his tie. "It has to do with the purchase of the church. I didn't realize that you had a two-million-dollar loan against the facility."

"How do you think I built it? With pocket money?" He laughed as he looked at Nevenka, who simply smiled.

"Yes. Well, since you have a two-million-dollar loan against a property that's probably worth three and a half to four million, give or take a ruble, the investors obviously aren't going to buy one hundred percent of your equity. They wouldn't have any security for the lease—not that you'd walk from the investment," he added quickly, not wanting to insult his client.

"So, what kind of numbers are we talking here?"

"Half a million. That way, assuming you have a million or more in equity, you'll pledge that as security for performance of the lease. Plus, they want a personal guarantee," he added nervously. He hadn't mentioned a personal guarantee in any of their previous conversations.

Davis could see the Pastor's eyes glossing over as if he didn't understand, so he proceeded to explain. "If the investors are going to give you five hundred thousand dollars, they need some security, collateral. The equity in the church is their collateral. If you default on the lease, they take over the church. What they would do with it, I have no idea," he said, smiling. "But, that's their security. As an inducement for you not to just take their money and go on a permanent vacation, they require the personal guarantee. That way, they have access to any additional collateral you might have, in the unlikely event that you default." Having said that, he took a deep breath.

"I understand," was MacAffie's only response.

Davis looked at Nevenka, as if asking if she had any questions. She didn't have a clue what they were talking about, so she simply smiled and diverted her eyes back to the documents stacked in front of her.

"So, is that acceptable to you?"

MacAffie didn't answer. He thumbed through the pile of documents, as if thinking.

"I have the five hundred raised, and a cashier's check ready to hand over to you," Davis said, patting his jacket pocket, as if to say that he had it on his person. "Pending executing the documents, of course. That is, if you're ready to proceed with the deal."

MacAffie would have signed the deal if they had offered only half of that amount. It was found money, as far as he was concerned. He nodded. "I guess I can live with that," he said, forcing himself not to smile.

A broad smile came across Davis' face. "Excellent!"

"So, what's next?"

Davis handed MacAffie and Nevenka the copies of lease, explaining the terms and conditions of that document. "You understand, of course, that you run the church and its business as usual. It's your responsibility to pay the taxes, insurance and existing loan payments, as well as the lease payments as set forth in item two of the lease. Any questions?"

MacAffie shook his head as if he understood everything perfectly, when in fact the only thing he understood was that he was getting a half-million dollars.

"I've got a question," Nevenka said, raising her hand.

"Yes?"

"The money."

"The five hundred thou?" Davis asked.

"Yes. Are there instructions as to its use? What should be done with it?"

Mathews laughed lightly, looking at MacAffie, who smiled as if understood. "The money is yours to use as you wish. You can invest it, take a vacation, build onto the church. Anything you wish."

"Thank you," she said, her mind reeling with the possibilities of five-hundred-thousand dollars. "Does this go into the church account?" she asked MacAffie.

He quickly waved his hand, dismissing the question. "We'll worry about that later." The tone of his voice told her not to ask questions.

"This is the security agreement," Davis said, passing the document to each of them, explaining what a security agreement was and its purpose. One by one he gave the MacAffies the documents, until the pile had been exhausted. "That's it!" he said. "Any questions?"

"I guess I'd like to look them over once more tonight, by myself, before I sign," MacAffie explained. "Just to be sure I fully understand everything. You understand."

He nodded, although he had hoped to obtain their signatures that day. "That's understandable. I'll leave you a copy of the docs for you to read and mark up, just in case you have any questions. I'll keep the other copy and the original until we execute them. We'll need a notary."

"That's no problem. Mary is a notary. She notarizes all of our living wills."

"I'll see you tomorrow, then," Davis said, shaking both Aaron's and Nevenka's hands.

✻   ✻   ✻   ✻

That night, after supper, the phone rang. Aaron answered. "It's for you," he announced. "A Helena Makarov, or something like that. Says she's an old friend from Russia."

A shiver went down Nevenka's spine. *What now?* she thought. *Has something happened to my mother?* "Hello. This is Nevenka."

"Nevenka. This is Helena," she said in Russian. "Don't say anything. Just listen."

"Is it Mother?" she asked, speaking in Russian.

"Can you get away?"

She hesitated for a moment. "I guess so. Why?"

"I'm in town and need to see you. It's urgent. It's imperative that you come alone."

"Where are you?"

"Do you know where Lincoln Park is? It's on First Street and Main."

"Yes. I think so. I'm very close to there now."

"Good! Come as soon as you can. And Nevenka?"

"Yes?"

"Come alone!"

She hung up the phone and looked at MacAffie, wondering what she should say to him.

"Doesn't your friend speak English?" He demanded. "It's rude to speak Russian so no one can understand. What did she want?"

"She…she's in trouble and asked if I could help her."

"Help her? What kind of trouble?"

"She didn't say."

"Probably an illegal alien, and the Federales are after her."

"Huh?"

"Never mind."

"I must go!" she said, putting on her coat.

"Do you need a ride?"

"No. She'll pick me up."

He looked at her suspiciously, but made no objection. "Don't stay out late," were his only words as she left the house.

✳   ✳   ✳   ✳

Nevenka walked briskly down Main Street until she reached the park. From the time she left the house until she reached the park couldn't have been more than fifteen or twenty minutes, at the most. She continually stopped to look behind her, half-expecting Aaron to follow her. *He wouldn't leave little Vladimer alone*, she thought. Nonetheless, she kept a keen eye to her rear, just to be safe. Helena had stressed the fact that she was to come alone.

She was in too much of a hurry to notice the figure of a man that followed her at a distance, slipping from tree to tree like a silent shadow, as she walked towards her destination.

Once she had reached the park, she slowed down, looking around. Helena hadn't said where to meet her. There was no sign of life, so she sat on the bench under a light.

"Nevenka!" a soft, feminine voice came from behind a large pine tree.

"Helena? Is that you?"

"Over here!"

Nevenka slowly walked towards the tree, where she saw Helena leaning against the trunk. "Helena! What are you doing here? Is my family all right? What has happened?" She expected the worst.

"There's someone here to see you," she said.

Just then, a cool pair of hands went over her eyes. It didn't take her but a moment to know that touch. "Vladimer!" she squealed. She spun around, to see the tall form of a man wearing a ponytail. "Is that really you?" she asked in Russian.

"It is, little flower."

She flung herself into his arms and buried her head in his chest. They stood there, clinging to one another for what seemed an eternity. Helena discretely faded into the shadows.

When their eyes met, each saw the other through tears. There was no need for words as their lips met. "Oh, Vladimer. How I have missed you. I am so glad you are safe."

"I can't tell you how often I have thought of you. Not a day went by without you being in my thoughts. Not an hour passed when I didn't feel your touch. It was that feeling that kept me alive all these months."

"Years," she corrected.

"Has it been that long?"

"It's been an eternity, Vladimer. Oh, I have so much to tell you. I am so glad that you are here."

They hugged again, pressing their bodies against one another, feeling every molecule. Nevenka heard a soft groan come from Vladimer's lips. She stepped back, a shocked look on her face. "You're injured!"

"It's nothing. A slight wound. It will heal in time."

"You've been shot! When? Where?"

"It is an old wound. It is not important. What is important is that you are well…that we are here together, if only for this moment. To have you for this moment is to have you for eternity."

Nevenka looked into his eyes. "You have a fine son, Vladimer."

"A son! He is healthy?"

"He is the spitting image of his father. And what a spirit! His hair is flaxen, like the setting sun. He has the skin of a god."

"What do you call him?"

"Vladimer Ryzhkov," she said softly.

Vladimer seemed stunned. "Your husband let you call him that?"

She smiled. "He does not know. I told him I was raped by the Red Army before I came to America. He does not know that I know who the father is."

"Vladimer! What an honor," he said.

"You must see him. Little Vladimer must know his father."

"That cannot be, Nevenka. No one can know that I am even alive, let alone that I fathered your child."

"And why is that?"

"Because it would endanger your position. I could not allow that."

"Vladimer. There is something you must know." She hesitated for a moment, then laid her head on his chest. "My husband is not long for this world."

He held her at arm's length, looking into her eyes. "What do you mean?"

"He has an illness. I feel he will not last the year, maybe not even the month."

Vladimer Ryzhkov could not see the smile that had crept up on her face. "When he dies, we can be together once again."

"But, the people. They will talk!"

"Do I care? What is important is that little Vladimer has his father and I have my husband."

"You have a husband!"

"Yes. I know…you. You have always been and will always be my husband. There is no one else, Vladimer, and there never will be. We can run away. I can get money!"

"I don't know, Nevenka. It all sounds too good to be true."

She kissed him and hugged him one more time. "I must go. I can reach you through Helena?"

"Yes."

"I love you, Vladimer Ryzhkov. Soon it will be as God meant for it to be. Then we will be together as a family. I will call! Soon!"

He watched as she faded into the night.

The figure that had followed her had made his way to a large redwood tree next to where the car had been parked. He swore under his breath, as there was no way for him to follow Nevenka back home. There was no real need for concern, however, now that he knew where she would be going. He knew she wouldn't be departing until Vladimer and Helena left. He had heard enough of their conversation to know that the pastor's wife could soon be leaving him. What was uncertain in his mind, was what to do with the information.

* * * *

"She's beautiful," Helena said to Vladimer after Nevenka had left. "You really love her, don't you!"

"I came halfway around the world just to see her face," he said, sadly. "Come. Let us go."

* * * *

That night, while Aaron MacAffie was sleeping, Nevenka slipped out of bed and went to the drawer that held her underthings. She withdrew a small sealed plastic pouch containing crushed ragweed. Taking care not to wake her husband, she sprinkled a little on his pillow, just beneath his nose.

Within moments he started sneezing. When he was done, his nasal passages were so swollen he had to breathe through his mouth. "What brought that on?" he said, looking at Nevenka, who pretended to be asleep.

There was an evil smile on her face as she drifted off to sleep, dreaming of the beach at Palanga and the tall man with the mane of a lion walking beside her. Only this time the dream was different. A child walked between them, holding their hands.

* * * *

Helena Makarov quietly made her way to a telephone after she was certain that Vladimer Ryzhkov was asleep. The telephone line echoed the hollow sound that it frequently made whenever she made a call to London.

"Gempac!" came the single response.

"Helena Makarov here! Let me speak to the general please," she demanded.

"He is indisposed at the moment. Do you care to leave a message?"

"Yes. Please tell him that the ruby is about to leave the ring, leaving the solitary diamond by himself. If he has any questions, he knows where to reach me, but I have company, so if I can't talk when he calls, he'll understand."

"I'll be sure he gets the message."

When Helena had hung up, the Captain turned to the General standing next to him. "Does this compromise our situation, General?"

He stroked his chin for a moment. "It may actually help us, Captain. You see, stress is a peculiar trait in mankind. Some thrive on it, and others—it destroys. I think this will weaken our man Macafy…make him more susceptible to pressure. We'll let it ride for the moment."

Chapter 52

Jerry Davis had made an appointment to be in Aaron MacAffie's office at ten o'clock the following morning to execute the documents on the sale and leaseback of the church facility. "Did you bring the check?" was the first question out of MacAffie's mouth the moment Davis walked through the door.

He held up the file. "Right here. A cashier's check in the amount of five hundred thousand dollars. Signed, sealed and soon to be delivered. Are you ready to execute the documents?"

"Ready as I'll ever be."

He laid them out on the table, one after the other. Fifteen minutes later, they were all signed and notarized.

Nevenka sat at the end of the table, watching, making no comments, but her mind was racing ahead. Her thoughts were on the previous night.

"Your check, sir," Davis said, handing him a cashier's check.

After Davis had left, MacAffie handed Nevenka the check to hold. "Five hundred smackaroos! Who said religion doesn't pay?"

She smiled and handed it back. She had never seen such a large amount of money before and, to tell the truth, didn't have any conception of how much money it represented.

"I'm going to get this in the bank right away," he said. "Can you take care of the office until I get back, Mary? Care to join me, Nevenka? I'll buy lunch." His smile was wickedly self-satisfying.

"Pastor. There's a Mr. McGown here to see you."

He looked at his appointment book. "I don't show any appointments for this hour, Molley. What's it about?" He was anxious to get that check in the bank.

"He didn't say. Said you would know him from the old country, whatever that means."

MacAffie sighed. "All right. Send him in." He slipped the check into the breast pocket of his jacket, then rose to stand by his desk. This was his way of letting a visitor know that he was in a hurry and didn't have much time for idle chitchat.

There was something distantly familiar about this Matty McGown fellow as he walked into his office. He didn't know if it was the way he lumbered in, the way he carried himself or the ruddy look on his face—signs of a man who had worked outdoors in the cold most of his life. MacAffie extended his hand. "What can I do for you, Mr. McGown?"

McGown's grip was firm and his hands calloused. Somehow he reminded MacAffie of his father.

Matty looked back to be sure that the door was shut, then took a seat, sitting on the edge of the chair with the palms of his hands on MacAffie's desk. He looked MacAffie straight in the eye. "I'm here to talk business, Aaron Macafy."

"It's MacAffie." He hadn't heard anyone pronounce his name Macafy since his mother had trained him and his older brother to learn their new name when they had been children. "The old name will bring nothing but trouble," she had said. "Forget you ever heard it. From this moment on, your name is Aaron MacAffie." She had put the emphasis on "Affie".

The man smiled. "Whatever." He looked around the office and at the stained glass-windows behind his desk. "Nice operation ya got here. A man of the cloth, no less. Very impressive." He took out a cigarette and started to light it.

"Please don't light that. We don't allow smoking in the office."

The little man tilted his head, then inserted the unlit cigarette back into its container.

"Thank you. Now, Mr. McGown, I'm a busy man. What is it I can do for you?" He remained standing as he looked at his watch. He had plenty time to get to the bank. He sighed as he sat down.

"Yeah, ya've been busy, all right. Real busy."

"What does *that* mean?" He had been in his office less than five minutes and already he was starting to dislike this fellow.

McGown leaned forward with his elbows on his desk, looking MacAffie in the eye. "Ya don't remember me, do ya?"

"You look vaguely familiar. Have we met before?"

The man nodded. "Aye. 'Twas a wee bit ago, in Washington State, it was. You were but, how do they say, a minister's trainee? Workin' fer that man of the cloth that got himself blown up by drivin' the wrong car." There was a sinister smile on his face.

MacAffie's face suddenly became ashen. He abruptly stood up and pointed his finger at the man. "Now, I remember you! You were at the church the day that Pastor Magnason got himself killed."

"Aye. And lucky fer you the old man took yer transportation. Otherwise we'd not be havin' this talk."

"Wha...what do you want?"

"Why don't ya be havin' a seat there like a good lad and we'll be having a little chat about the old country."

"What about the old country?"

"Let me give ya a little background before I get ta the point of my being here. As ya might'a guessed, our organization knew yer da back in the old country."

"Your organization. Old country. Ireland?"

"Yeah. Northern Ireland, to be exact. We sort of ran in the same circle, ya might say." He looked at his fingernails and rubbed them on his lapel. "Ya might say that we had the same political aspirations."

"You're with the Sons of Ireland," MacAffie said, pointing to the man, a tingling sensation suddenly running down his spine. It had been a long time since his father had been killed. He had been just a lad at the time, but remembered his mother telling them that their father had been killed trying to bring peace to Ireland.

"My father had nothing to do with your 'organization', as you put it!"

"Aw, lad, but he did. 'Twas working for us that brought him to his demise. He was fighten' the British, ya know. They's the ones that killed his da—yer grandda. Yeah. We were his family. You were but a lad then. What would ya be knowin'?" There was a sort of sneer on the man's face.

"I think you better leave!" MacAffie was getting angry now, and frightened. He stood up. He could feel the heat crawling up his face, which he knew was clearly getting red. It had been a long time since he had thought of the old country and their crude ways of living...and dying. Yeah, he had heard that his grandfather had been killed by the British, but he also knew that his father had wanted nothing to do with the killin', nor those who walked that path...from either side!

Matty McGown didn't move from his seat. "Sit down, old son. We've got a lot of ground to cover, you and I." He smiled and polished his fingernails again. "I know all about yer business, ya see. And yer business is gonna be our business."

"I want you out of my office, right now!" He picked up the telephone and dialed nine. "Molly, would you please call the police and have them get down here right away! We've got an unwanted intruder in our office!"

"That was not a smart move, Mr. Macafy or whatever ya call yourself these days." He grabbed the lapel of Aaron MacAffie's jacket and drew him close. The odor of stale cigarettes made MacAffie wince.

"Ya see, we've been watching ya, real close, old sod. I've seen how ya work. Real smooth, yer are." He let go of his coat. "First it was the airplane wreck, a right smart bit of work, that. Ya must have been plannin' that fer some time." He took out a cigarette and lit it.

"I already told you, I don't allow smoking in here!"

McGown ignored him. "Then blowing up that fancy house where those nice people lived. Now, no Christian man should be doin' that to members of his flock." He smiled for a moment. "I can see that ya did learn somethin' from yer da, at that, lad."

MacAffie was beyond words by this point.

"And those poison mushrooms. That was a nice touch! Only ya left a mite too early that night. When ya left after dinner, the old woman was still alive, laddie. If it hadn't been for me, she might have recovered. I felt obliged ta put me sleeve over her mouth until she passed. Ya can thank me later." He smiled again.

MacAffie wished at that moment that he had a gun in his office drawer. He would surely have shot the man dead and suffered the consequences later. "Wha, what do you mean?"

"I mean she was still breathing when I got there, after ya cleaned up and left." He smiled, then held up his hands. "Don't worry, lad. I covered fer ya. It was a simple task ta cover her mouth and nose with me jacket fer a moment or two, until she crossed over." He got up to take a closer look at the stained-glass window. "Let's just say that it was a favor—in the interest of the partnership."

"What partnership?"

"Ours, laddie. Yours and the organization."

"The only partnership you're going to have is a trip to jail for threatening me! Now, get out of here!"

McGowan walked back to the front of MacAffie's desk. "I'll be on me way, but not 'cause the likes of you says. And, don't be gettin' any ideas 'bout tellin' John Law 'bout the Washington incident, either. Not only do I have an alibi, but you would be gettin' yerself in mighty deep when I got through spillin' me guts, if ya get me meanin', laddie."

Just then, there was a knock at the door and a uniformed policemen walked in. "Trouble, sir?" he asked, looking at Matty McGown.

Matty smiled at MacAffie. "I was just leavin'. Ain't that right, *Reverend MacAffie?*" He tipped his hat to Nevenka and winked at her as he walked by.

*   *   *   *

While Matty McGown was in with Aaron MacAffie, Helena had placed a call to Nevenka. "You shouldn't be calling me here at the church office," Nevenka told her in Russian. "It's too dangerous. Husband might get suspicious."

"Danger is the reason I'm calling."

"I don't understand."

"We're back in town. After meeting you last night, Vladimer wanted to return to see his son."

Nevenka was stunned for a moment. "When?" She was excited about not only seeing Vladimer again, but showing him their son.

"As soon as possible. Can you get away? Where is your son?"

"We have a baby sitter taking care of him at the house."

"Can you get away?"

Nevenka thought for a moment. "I think so," she whispered, although they were speaking in Russian. "I'll meet you in the park in one hour."

Her heart was beating furiously as she tried to act casual. "I'm not feeling well, Husband. Do you have any objection if I go home?"

She was too preoccupied with her own thoughts to notice that Aaron MacAffie had a wild look on his face. "No. Of course not. Do you want to go now?"

She nodded, taking care that her mannerisms didn't betray the anxiety she felt.

"I'll just make out a deposit slip and we'll be on our way. I want to get this check in the bank. Hand me one from our personal account, will you?"

"Shouldn't that go into the church account?"

He glared at her. "You leave the business of making money to me!" he said sternly.

Fifteen minutes later, he dropped Nevenka off at their house. "See you around six," he said as she closed the car door.

"Marie, I'm home," she said, entering the house. "I'm going to stay home for the rest of the day. You can go home now."

She waited for twenty minutes, to be sure that Aaron didn't return and that no one called. Before leaving, she took the telephone off the hook. If anyone called, they would simply think she was talking on the telephone.

As they walked, Vladimer took small steps and had a propensity for picking up every rock and kicking every leaf on the sidewalk. Consequently, it took a little longer to get to the park than she had expected. Just before she got there, a large white limousine pulled up the curb and the door opened. "Get in," Helena said, beckoning from the back seat.

She picked up little Vladimer and carried him into the limousine, but not before she looked around to see if anyone was watching.

Vladimer was sitting on the opposite seat when they got in. Nevenka hesitated for a moment, looking at Helena. "Go on," she said with a smile as she took little Vladimer's hand and gave him a toy to distract his attention. "I'm going to walk around the park for a few moments," Helena said. "When you're ready to leave, just give me a short beep on the horn."

As soon as Helena had closed the door, Nevenka fairly jumped into Vladimer's arms, smothering him with kisses. "It was all I could do to pay attention to business today," she said. "All I could think of was you!"

"So, this is our son," he said, admiring the boy who was playing across the seat.

Seeing the two of them in the car together, it was obvious that he was the father. Little Vladimer had his father's eyes, his hair, his strong jaw and his large hands. "He's going to be a big boy!"

"Just like his father." She beamed. It was a pleasure just seeing them together.

Vladimer wanted to hold his son, but knew that the boy might be frightened by having a stranger pick him up and hug him, so he savored him from where he sat.

"Let's run away, Nevenka. We can get lost in America. No one will ever find us."

"What would we do for money?"

"I could find work."

She smiled at him. "I have a better plan. We have waited three years. Wait a few more days, and everything will be all right. We won't have to run. I'll be free and we'll be rich!"

"What do you have planned, Nevenka?" he asked, a twinkle in his eye. He knew that she was up to something.

She tugged at his hand. "You'll just have to be patient."

"I have no patience." He smiled. "I want you right now!" His hands were exploring the body that he had not touched for three years.

Nevenka was receptive. "What about the driver?" she asked between deep breaths.

"The window is closed. He cannot see."

"And little Vladimer?"

He smiled. "It's about time he saw his parents together," he said as he slipped her undergarments off.

They made love until they were both spent. Little Vladimer watched, not comprehending what was going on, but made no protest. "We are going to be a family once again," Nevenka whispered in Vladimer's ear as she nibbled on it.

"I will give you one week!" Vladimer said. "Then, I will come down like an eagle and swoop you both up like a mouse and take you to my nest, where no one will ever find us."

"One week," she said.

They slipped back onto the seat again as little Vladimer played with the toy that Helena had brought him.

∗   ∗   ∗   ∗

Matty McGown placed a call to King Arthur. "There's been an interestin' development with the parsons missus. Seems she's got a lover. From what I can gather, she's thinkin' of dumpin' the parson.

There was a short pause. "That's interesting, but at the moment, I don't know that it makes any difference to us. Our interest lies in his pocketbook, not what's in his pants or who's sleeping next to him."

"Well, let me tell ya, he's an arrogant little bastard, that one. Just like his da. Threw me out of the office, he did. Even called the law."

"Do you think he'll cooperate?"

"Not without a little pressure, if you get my drift."

"Do what you have to do! I want results, McGown. You've been at this far too long. This is not a vacation you're on there. One more slip-up, and you'll become a permanent resident. And I don't mean aboveground!"

∗   ∗   ∗   ∗

A man with a slight build checked into the Green Parrot, a small motel on the El Camino Real in Los Alamos. His only luggage was a leather satchel and a eel-skin briefcase. "Will you be staying long, Mr. Miller?" the receptionist asked, looking him over as if he were lunch.

Sean Mulligan signed his name and gave the women a week's advance payment.

"I guess that means you'll be here a week," she said.

"I've got a bit of business to attend to. Where might I find the Living Christ Church I've heard so much about?" he inquired.

She nodded with her head. "Just up San Antonio road about two miles. You'll find the building just off Main Street, on the right-hand side of the road as you enter town. Can't miss it. It looks like a giant spaceship waiting to take off." She smiled at her guest. "Anything else I can do for you, Mr. Miller?"

He looked at her left hand and noticed that it was devoid of any rings. "You live here, on the premises?" he asked, looking seductively into her eyes.

"My living quarters are in the back." She nodded toward the back of the office. The door was open and he could see into a nicely furnished living room.

"Maybe you could show a stranger where he could get a good meal this evening? That is, if you're free."

"I'm not only free, but damn good!" She laughed at her own joke and had a twinkle in her eye that transmitted her message clearly.

"Around seven, then?"

"I'll arrange to have the desk covered. Here's your key. Number thirty-one. Around back, where it's nice and quiet."

"Perfect!"

Chapter 53

Pastor Aaron MacAffie had just pulled into the Lehman place, armed with his plot plan. He had visualized how the buildings for the Aaron MacAffie Institute for Higher Learning would be built and wanted to compare them to his plot plan. The yellow tape that had been placed across the property entrance by the police had since been removed. Only a small piece, which had been left tacked to the mailbox, fluttered in the breeze.

He got out of his newly leased white Jaguar and walked around to the back of the house. He had been standing there for several moments, visualizing the location of the administration building and the classrooms, when he was visibly shaken by the sound of a familiar voice.

"It was worth it, eh, mate? Killin' those poor old people just ta get their land? Any Irishman worth his salt would have been ashamed of himself, killin' two old people, but then, if it were fer the cause, I can see where ya can be fergivin'."

MacAffie turned to face Matty McGown. He was wearing a black leather jacket, dark olive pants and a dark-green beret, the same clothes he had worn in Washington when he had killed Pastor Magnason.

"What are you doing here!" MacAffie demanded, as he took a step back, putting some distance between himself and McGown.

"I've got ta be gettin' back ta Ireland, old sod, but before I go, I've got ta be sure we're on the same ground here, you and I. The boys from the organization back home are gettin' a wee bit nervous, what with ya not cooperatin' and all. I'm here to see that the job gets done…if ya get my meanin'."

"And if I don't?"

"Well then, I'll still be going' home and ye'll be stayin'. Only difference is, I'll be above-ground and you'll be below, if ya get my meanin'."

MacAffie glanced around for a weapon, like a board or stick he could use to defend himself. Finding none, he looked for the shortest route to his car. Matty McGown stood clearly in the way. "I don't know what you're talking about! All this talk about killin'. It's got me all nervous. Now, why don't you be on your way, before I call the police again."

Matty laughed as he approached MacAffie. He reached out and pushed him hard, against the porch.

MacAffie's arms went back to break his fall, his hands falling on the two-by-two posts that held up the porch railing.

"Ya've got a mighty nice set-up here, old sod. Ya take in more money in a day than most Irishmen see in a year. There's no need ta be greedy, now is there? All we're askin' is our fair share. That's better'n bein' six feet under, now isn't it?"

"Are you threatening me?" His hand fumbled with the two-by-two post, turning it. The wood was weak from years of neglect when old man Lehman had never treated it with paint or linseed oil.

"Threaten' ya? Why would ya say a thing like that?" Matty punched him hard in the stomach. "That's only a taste of what ya got comin', preacher, if ya don't see our way clear." He straightened MacAffie up and hit him in the stomach again. "That's just in case yer thinkin' of goin' ta the law. And this," he said as he pulled out an old thirty-eight, "is what ya'll get if ya don't cooperate. Ya get my meanin', laddie?"

He shoved the gun under MacAffie's chin, pushing it hard against his soft flesh so it hurt.

"I get your point," he gasped.

"There's a good lad." He eased up on his grip and slipped the gun back into his belt.

Just then, MacAffie, summing up all the strength he had in his right hand, tore the two-by-two bracing off the porch. The nails yielded under the pressure as the wood came loose in his hand.

Aaron MacAffie was now welding a two-inch by two-inch, three-foot piece of lumber that all but resembled a baseball bat. Before Matty McGown could react, he swung it with all his might, catching McGown on the side of his head, sending him flying back into the dust.

MacAffie stood there for a moment, still holding the lumber, looking down at his attacker. A slow trickle of blood made its way down the side of McGown's head.

MacAffie wiped the side of his mouth with his sleeve, dropped the lumber and ran to his car without looking back. He paid no attention to the dark blue Mustang that sat by the side of the road as his tires squealed out onto the paved road, and disappeared from sight within moments.

Sean Mulligan pulled the Mustang up next to Matty McGown's rental Nissan and listened for any sound before quietly leaving his car, taking care not to shut his door, lest he alert McGown to his presence.

In the back of the house, Matty McGown had come to and was groaning, trying to find his feet. Mulligan kneeled down next to him as he screwed on the silencer of his PK Walther. "Feelin' a bit under the weather there, McGown? Must be the climate. They say it takes at least a month for your system to get used to the difference in the California air when you first come from Ireland. Would ya like to be returnin' now, mate?"

Matty McGown held his hands over his eyes to shield them from the sun. "Who the hell are you?"

"It's Sean Mulligan from MI 5. I've come all the way from London to find ya, Matty McGown. Aren't ya flattered now, old sod?"

"You son of a bitch. I'll show ya!"

Matty McGown went for his gun, but his fingers only touched the cold metal as Mulligan's Walther coughed, sending a missile into McGown's brain. He fired one more shot into his heart, just for good measure. "Never can be too careful, can we, old sod? When you get to Hell, you give my regards to all the boys from the IRA, The Sons of Katy Elder and, of course, the "organization", as you like to call it."

He tipped his hat to the body and left.

*   *   *   *

Late Friday afternoon, Assistant District Attorney Herrera placed a call to Pierce Terryman. "Good news! I've been authorized to issue a warrant for Aaron MacAffie's arrest. We're going for an indictment for the murders of Andrew Mullin and Lillian and Jack Lehman, forgery of the Quit Claim Deed to the Andrew Mullin estate, the attempted murder of Eric and Dawn Nesbit and arson."

"Fantastic! When can I pick him up?"

"The paperwork is in the mill. We're preparing a search warrant for the judge to sign, to gain access to his residence and all the church files. We're going to sew him up so tight, he'll have to burp to fart!"

Terryman was impatient. "I repeat, when can I pick him up?"

"Judge Hofmann is out of chambers until Monday morning and the DA doesn't want to ruffle his feathers by bothering him at home. MacAffie's not going anywhere so long as he has no knowledge that we're onto him. Let him enjoy his last weekend of freedom. He'll have the rest of his life to regret that he messed with us."

You mean he'll regret that he ever messed with me! Terryman thought. "I want to arrest the bastard now and let him cool his heels until Monday!" he demanded.

"And have some slick attorney get him out on bail? I can hear it now. 'Your Honor, this man is a pillar of the community…a pastor that has over two thousand people flocking to his church every Sunday, not to mention the millions that see him on television. It would be a sin against God to lock him up. Just the fact that he's been arrested is an atrocity. Release him on his own recognizance.'

"Then he skips out of the country and we lose him for good. No thanks. We're going to do this one by the numbers. I can wait three days. Why don't you enjoy the weekend, Pierce? You'll have a busy week starting Monday."

Terryman shrugged his shoulders. "Maybe you're right. I think I'll take my kid fishing up at Fort Bragg. I need to get away from this place before I lose my sanity."

*   *   *   *

Sean Mulligan reached Major Pennypacker at home, waking him from a sound sleep. "I'm sorry to wake you Major. I forgot about the time difference."

Major Pennypacker wiped his eyes with the sleeve of his nightshirt and squinted at the clock. He swung his legs off the bed and rubbed them to get the circulation going. "That's all right. What have you got?"

"Mission completed."

"Any hang-ups? Witnesses?"

"The package was delivered without incident."

"Good. There's one further delivery that needs interruption."

"And that would be?"

"The man of the cloth."

There was a silence as Mulligan thought for a moment. "Thought he was the lamb that needed protection."

"Turns out the lamb has converted himself into a predator. As you know, predators feed on others. Intelligence has determined that he's eaten more than his share. If he continues on this path, it could prove embarrassing. The trail must stop here. Do I make myself clear?"

"I read you loud and clear. And the dependents?"

"They're of no interest to us. Treat them as protected goods. Under no circumstances are the woman and her child to be harmed."

"Message received."

"I take it that you've taken all precautions to protect your anonymity?"

"As always, Major."

Without waiting for a reply, Sean Mulligan hung up the telephone and thought for a moment. He was hungry and had a yearning in his loins ever since he had checked in. MacAffie would wait.

* * * *

Aaron MacAffie came home late, around seven that night. He threw his briefcase on the floor and collapsed on the couch. "What's for dinner?" were his only words.

"I made a nice, hot Russian stew for you, your favorite," she said from the kitchen. "It'll be ready in a moment. Why don't you wash up, dear?"

Little Vladimer walked over to MacAffie and grabbed at his pant leg, asking to be picked up. "Get out of my sight, you little Ruskie," he said, pushing him on the head so hard that he fell on the floor.

Vladimer let out a scream, more from the harsh rejection than being hurt.

Nevenka rushed into the room to pick up her child. "What happened?" she asked Vladimer, looking at her husband.

"The kid fell down," he offered, then walked into the bathroom.

"I'll bet!" Nevenka glared at Aaron as he closed the door. *We'll see who falls down!* she thought to herself.

She served Aaron his dinner at the table with two candles and burning incense. A bottle of his favorite wine was chilling on the table by his plate. "What's the occasion?" he asked. "Aren't you eating?"

"I just wanted to set a nice table for you. You've had such a hard day. Vladimer and I ate earlier. Maybe after you eat, you'd like to take a little nap," she said, pouring him a generous portion of wine.

The stew was delicious. He ate two helpings and had three glasses of wine. Fifteen minutes after he had risen from the table, he was so tired he could barely make it to bed. He was snoring when Nevenka removed his clothes and tucked him in. "Sweet dreams, Husband," she said, patting him on the shoulder.

In the kitchen, she washed the stew pot in scalding hot water, then placed it in the dishwasher to be rewashed for good measure. She did the same with the plate, his silverware and even the wine glass. She didn't want any trance of the four sleeping pills that she had mixed in with the stew to be found, just in case anyone was inclined to look.

Satisfied that everything was in order, she returned to the bedroom, where she had left the light on. She looked down at her husband, then began shaking him, gently at first, then violently, but he was in such a deep sleep from the wine, dinner and four sleeping pills that a bomb wouldn't have stirred him.

She went to his closet removed one of his large black belts, wrapping it around his midsection, restraining both of his arms. Now he couldn't raise his hands above his chest. Next she went to little Vladimer's toy box. He had a colorful, baseball-sized nerf ball that he played with. It was soft and pliable, so it wouldn't hurt himself, nor anyone else, when he threw it. Nevenka propped open MacAffie's mouth and gently stuffed the ball in, forcing him to breathe through his nose. MacAffie kept sleeping, snoring through his nostrils.

She stood back, looking at the man who was her husband. It amazed her, how calm she was. Next, she went to her drawer where she kept her fine lingerie and removed the small plastic sack that contained the crushed ragweed. Sprinkling it generously on his pillow, just under his nose, she stood back and watched for a moment while his body started to convulse as he breathed in the powdery substance.

While he was thrashing around, Nevenka walked out of the room and shut the door behind her. It wasn't until she had watched the ten o'clock news that she shut off the television and calmly walked back into their bedroom. Aaron MacAffie was lying on his back with his eyes wide open. His body was still.

She put her fingers to the side of his neck for a moment, removed the belt from around his waist, then the nerf ball from his mouth. When she was done, she closed his eyes and removed the pillowcase that contained the crushed ragweed, replacing it with a clean one. She tossed the old one into the clothes washer along with a cup of soap and an equal amount of bleach, then washed it twice.

She would sleep on the couch tonight. Tomorrow she would wake up and find that her husband had passed away during the night. She would frantically dial 911, and then wait for the paramedics to attempt to revive him. She would explain that he was violently allergic to many plants and that earlier that day he had said that he was going to look at some land in the country for a site for a new house before he came home. She had noticed that he had been wheezing badly. After he had eaten dinner, he said he was going to bed, but couldn't sleep. The last thing she remembered was his going to the medicine cabinet for sleeping pills. When she woke up in the morning, she found him dead.

She would, of course, be devastated and cry, wondering what would become of her and their son.

CHAPTER 54

▼

The hot shower felt good as the water pelted the top of Sean Mulligan's head. After he had showered, he shaved, splashed on some Old Spice, combed his hair and put on some clothes then walked to the motel office. "You know, I didn't even ask your name," he said when she came out of her living quarters.

"Joyce. My friends call me juicy Joyce," she said with a light laugh.

"I assume that has a special connotation."

"One which we won't go into at this moment." She giggled as she shrugged her shoulders in a little-girl fashion.

She had on a black dress with a "V" that came down to her breasts, exposing a good portion of two well-developed breasts.

"Well! I didn't realize how much of a woman you were, there, Joyce," he said, taking no care to mask his admiration for her shape.

"I have a feeling that this is going to be a night to remember," she said, as she took his arm. "Hungry?" There was that seductive look again.

"You bet!"

"What's your pleasure?"

"Why don't we start with a nice juicy steak?" he smiled. "Then, we'll come back here for dessert." Their eye contact left no doubt as to his meaning.

They had dinner and a bottle of wine at the Brave Bull, after which they retired to the lounge for cocktails. Joyce had two Long Island Ice Teas and was feeling no pain. The alcohol was making her feel very amorous and she was all over Mulligan, to the point that the other patrons were making snide comments and continuous stares in their direction.

"I think it's time we retire to your place," he said, putting his arm around her waist, lifting her up out of her seat, then guiding her out of the lounge.

By the time they had arrived back at the motel, Joyce was in that thin margin between passing out and semiconsciousness. She was just alert enough to not want the evening to end. "Let's go to my place," she said slowly, her words barely making it out of her mouth. "I'll put the 'No Vacancy' sign out and shut off the phones. We'll put on a little music and let nature takes its course." She smiled a self satisfied look that said, "Take me."

Sean Mulligan was only too obliging. Within ten minutes from the time they had entered Joyce's apartment, they were in bed making love. Joyce was limp as a rubber hose and passively receptive to anything. "I love you foreigners," she said with her eyes closed. "You have such abandoned passion. And to think, you'll be here for a whole week! Grrr!"

"There's been a change of plans, love. I've got a job to finish tonight, then it's off to good old London."

"Oh. I'll miss you," she said looking up at him through sleepy eyes.

"And I, you," he said. "Now, it's time to say good-bye and good night."

The look on Joyce's face was one of horror as he forced the pillow over her head. "Sorry, love. But, you see, I can't be havin' someone identify me once I'm gone."

In her inebriated state, she struggled only for a few moments. The liquor had made her weak and she succumbed quickly.

Sean Mulligan left her there in that position, with the pillow over her head. He showered and dressed. After making sure that he had wiped all the fingerprints from the places he thought he might have touched, he departed back to his room. Chances were, no one in the States had his prints on file. No use starting their collection at this point in time. He packed his leather satchel, picked up the eelskin briefcase, made a quick visual scan of the room, then left. As he retrieved his weapon from the briefcase, he said, "Aaron MacAffie, prepare to meet your Maker."

* * * *

It was well after two in the morning when Sean Mulligan pulled up in front of Aaron MacAffie's home. He looked at the paper that he had been given that noted his address, then double-checked the number on the door of the house. They were identical.

The house had no lights on, so he assumed everyone must be asleep, as expected. The kitchen and living room appeared to be situated at the front of the house, with sleeping rooms at the rear.

Sean Mulligan was no stranger to illegal entry. Within ten seconds, he was standing in the interior hallway. He listened intently. The house was quiet…almost too quiet.

The first door proved to be the child's room. The next bedroom had a single figure lying in bed. The question was, who? The third bedroom turned out to be an office. *Was there only one adult? What happened to the other person? If the child was there, then the figure in the bed must be the mother,* he thought.

He backtracked to the living room, then froze in his tracks. There was a slight breathing sound coming from the couch. Mulligan softly walked over to the couch, peering over the edge, holding his Walther with the silencer extended out in front of him. The person sleeping there had long blond hair. *His wife.*

That left the figure in the bedroom to be Aaron MacAffie. Mulligan quietly, but quickly, walked to the room, stood a few feet from the figure and pumped six rounds into his body. There had been no movement. *Must have killed him with the first round*, he thought.

Moments later, he was in his car and on way to San Francisco, where he would turn in his rental car, then catch the shuttle back to the airport. There, he would rent a storage locker, put the eel-skin briefcase in it and send the key in a pre-addressed envelope. Now there was nothing to do but wait until morning, when he would catch the first TWA flight to London.

Chapter 55

It had been a long time since Pierce Terryman had spent a weekend with his son. The fishing trip had been a welcome change. "This is something that we've got to more often," he had told his son. "We don't spend enough time together."

Even while they were out on the boat, fishing for salmon, his mind was still preoccupied with the arrest of Aaron MacAffie. Any time a criminal could make a fool of him, it was not only embarrassing, but a blow to his ego, as well. And this little worm had all but flaunted his crimes in their faces. Just the thought of it made his blood boil!

* * * *

Monday morning, Terryman went straight to the District Attorney's office to pick up the search order, which, by now, would have been signed by the judge. This was one arrest that he was going to enjoy!

"Well, where's my paperwork?" he asked Herrera the minute he walked into the District Attorney's office.

"Paperwork?"

"Yeah. Don't play games with me." There was a scowl on his face. "All I could think of this weekend was seeing MacAffie's face when I arrest him!"

"I guess you haven't heard."

"Heard? Heard what!" The blood visibly drained from his face. "Don't tell me! He skipped!"

"No. He's not going anywhere."

"What do you mean? What's up? What's happened!"

"It's MacAffie. He's dead."

"What! Dead?"

Herrera nodded. "Friday night. Apparently there was a burglary. According to his wife, the previous night he had came home after walking around some hills looking for a place to build them a new house, he ate dinner, then went to bed. She said that he was so exhausted and had been snoring so loudly that she went to sleep on the couch. Good thing for her, too." He nodded with emphasis.

Terryman shook his head in frustration. "I'm not getting all this. Tell me what the hell happened!"

"That's what I'm trying to do. Chill out for a minute." He took a deep breath and continued in a quieter tone. "No one knows for sure what happened, but MacAffie must have heard something and surprised the burglar, because whoever it was, they pumped six rounds into his body."

"Six rounds! That doesn't sound like a burglary. That sounds like a hit!"

"That's what we thought, too, but who would want to hit a minister?"

"And the wife? What did she do when she heard the shots?"

"That's the funny part. She claims that she didn't hear a thing. Apparently, even the baby didn't wake up."

"So, he was using a silencer. I've never heard of a burglar using a silencer on a job. In the first place, they don't plan on using their weapon, and in the second place, a silencer always adds length and bulk to a weapon, which is the very thing a burglar doesn't want!"

Herrera shrugged his shoulders. "They've scheduled an autopsy on him for later today. At least we'll know the type of weapon that killed him."

"Shit! Terryman slammed his big fist down hard on the table. "I was so looking forward to collaring that guy, and now he goes and gets himself blown away."

Herrera shrugged his shoulders. "Sorry. I thought you knew. It was in all the papers and made the six o'clock news."

"I got in late last night from Fort Bragg. Put the kid to bed and took a shower and hit the hay myself. I didn't read a paper or talk to anyone until I saw you this morning."

"Catch any fish?"

He nodded. "A couple salmon." The enthusiasm seemed to have left him as he turned to go. "I think I'll take the day off."

Herrera walked him to the door. He put his big hand on Terryman's shoulder. "Look at the good side of it all."

"Yeah. And what's that?"

"Look at the money we save not prosecuting the bastard."

Terryman walked away without comment. *I think I'll get drunk!*

* * * *

Jerry Davis was beside himself when he read in the paper that Pastor Aaron MacAffie had been killed. "I raised a half-million dollars for that man, and now he's dead!" he complained to his wife.

"Can't you get the money back?" was her simplistic response.

"I don't think so." Then he thought of Nevenka. Maybe he could trick her into returning the money and cancelling the deal. After all, if MacAffie was dead and gone, who would run the church and pay the lease? And, obviously his personal guarantee was no good.

The investment money he had raised was from some heavy-duty-type investors from San Francisco. They looked dimly upon losing money. He had heard stories of people who had either welshed on deals, or didn't pay off on time. He didn't like what he had heard.

"Maybe he didn't cash the check," his wife offered.

"God, I hope you're right!"

* * * *

Obviously, no one expected Nevenka to go to the parish office. In fact, the office was closed. When Jerry Davis couldn't reach her, he tried calling her home, but she wasn't answering the telephone, either. Reporters and well-wishers had been calling ever since the news of MacAffie's death had been reported. For all intents and purposes, Nevenka had shut herself and their child away from the world. And who could blame her? Her husband had been murdered. It was a miracle that she was still alive.

Davis finally resorted to going to her house. Nevenka recognized him through the peephole and at first declined to answer the door, then thought better of it. *Better to cut him off right here,* she thought, *than have him making waves about the money at the church.*

"Mr. Davis, won't you come in?" Her eyes were red from crying.

"I'm really sorry about your husband," he said, "but, as you know, just last Friday I gave him five hundred thousand dollars. Now that he's gone, he can't perform on the lease. I need to cancel the deal and get our money back. Tell me you didn't cash the check. Tell me that you still have it."

"I'm sorry. My husband took it to the bank the day you gave it to him."

"I've got to get the money back! Can you take care of that for me? I'll make it worth your while." The look of desperation on his face almost made Nevenka feel sorry for him.

She shook her head. "I"m sorry. Only Mr. MacAffie can sign on the checking account. Besides, I thought you took the documents down to the Recorder's Office last Friday. At least, that is what you said you were going to do."

He looked down in despair. "Well, yes. But, who was to foresee what has happened?"

"Don't things ever go wrong in these types of transactions?" she inquired innocently.

"Not often, but, yes, sometimes."

"And what do you do then?"

"If the party can't perform, we usually have to foreclose. But my investors don't want a church," he added quickly.

"Maybe, in this case, they will have no choice. If you need to protect yourself with the recorded documents, then I can only assume the law would take its normal course."

Davis looked at her, not knowing whether she was deceptively intelligent or incredibly stupid. Either way, he was wasting his time.

✳   ✳   ✳   ✳

Tuesday morning, Terryman walked into his office with an oversized headache. "The autopsy on MacAffie came in this morning," his secretary said as he hung up his coat.

"Who cares! Dead is dead. Why do I care how he got that way? The son of a bitch cheated me out of an indictment."

"Just thought you would like to know," she said. "It was your case."

"File it. I really don't give a rat's ass if he died of bullet poisoning, a cat bite or was hit by a truck."

"I'll just put the file on your desk," she said.

"Fine." He walked into his office. "And, Dora?"

"Yes, sir?"

"Bring me a handful of aspirin and a cup of that black sludge you call coffee."

"You're in a great mood," she said to herself.

* * * *

The day the coroner released Aaron MacAffie's body, Nevenka arranged to have his remains cremated. Instead of having a funeral, she decided to just have a memorial service at the church. Anyone who wanted to attend the services, could. Anyone wanting to get up and speak about their Pastor could do that, too. She had no desire to take an active participation in the proceedings.

She and little Vladimer simply sat in the front pew and listened. She was appropriately dressed in black, wearing a black veil over her face, and Vladimer wore his Sunday suit with a little blue tie.

Everyone present came up to her and offered their condolences. "I can't understand how anyone could have murdered such a nice man." "Whoever it was that did this, obviously made a terrible mistake."

"At least he's in Heaven now."

The comments were sincere. *If they only knew the kind of man he really was, she thought. No one would have shown up at the services.* When it was over, she went home. She had already packed her personal belongings in a single suitcase. She had arrived with one suitcase and she would leave the same way. This would be the last day she would spend in this house. Or in California, for that matter.

* * * *

Nevenka called a Yellow cab to pick her up, instructing the driver to take her to the Bank of America. The lady at the bank stared at the withdrawal slip for a moment and requested the bank identification card with her picture that had been issued to her when she had deposited the new signature card.

"Please wait here while I get approval from the manager," the young cashier said, locking her cash drawer. "I'll be right back."

She and little Vladimer waited until the teller had returned and asked how Nevenka wanted the money. "Obviously, we don't have this much cash on hand." She chuckled, as if Nevenka wanted it all in cash, which she did.

"How much could I get in cash?"

"Probably no more than twenty thousand dollars. But that's a lot of money to carry around," she advised.

"I'll take as much cash as you can give me and the rest in a cashier's check, please."

Again the manager was consulted, and fifteen minutes later, the manager counted out twenty-five-thousand-dollars in one-hundred-dollar-bills, then issued a cashier's check in the amount of four-hundred-seventy-five thousand dollars.

"May I have an envelope to carry this in?" she asked, after the cash had been piled in front of her.

"Certainly."

Nevenka briskly walked out the bank, holding the money in one hand and little Vladimer's hand in the other.

"Where to, lady?" the cab driver asked.

"How much to San Francisco?"

He looked at her as if she were joking. When he saw that she wasn't he replied, "I'd have to call the office for special permission."

"Please do."

*   *   *   *

They arrived at San Francisco an hour later. "Where to, lady?"

"Where's a famous spot that anyone can find in this city?"

He thought for a moment, then said, "Fisherman's Wharf."

"Then take me there, please."

The cabbie shrugged his shoulders and drove towards the Bay. "This is it! Fisherman's Wharf."

He had stopped in front of Pier Thirty-Nine. Even though it was a weekday, there were a lot of people milling around the stores. "How much do I owe you?"

"Sixty-eight dollars and seventy-eight cents."

She handed him a hundred-dollar bill and told him to keep the change. There was a telephone at the entrance of the shops, and she dialed Helena Markarov's number.

"Where are you?" she said. "We've been trying to call you, but there's no answer. We heard about your husband's death. I'm so sorry. You must be devastated."

"Is Vladimer with you?" she asked, without responding to Helena's concerns.

She hesitated for a moment. "Yes. He's been worried about you ever since we heard the news."

"How far are you from Fisherman's Wharf?"

"Maybe ten minutes by cab. Why?"

"Because that's where little Vladimer and I are."

"You're here? In San Francisco?"

She nodded, forgetting that Helena couldn't see her.

"How did you get here?"

"I took a taxi."

"From Los Alamos?"

"Yep. Cost sixty-eight dollars."

There was a silence for a moment. Nevenka heard her talking to Vladimer, but apparently she had her hand over the receiver so Nevenka couldn't hear what she was saying. "Tell me exactly where you are and I'll come to pick you up," she said, when she came back on the line.

"No. I'd rather have Vladimer come, if you don't mind."

Again, a conversation with her hand over the receiver. A moment of silence, then Helena said, "He'll be right there as soon as he can get a cab. Where are you?"

"Pier Thirty-Nine. Do you know where it is?"

"Of course. Wait at the entrance. Vladimer will be there in a fifteen minutes."

* * * *

As soon as Vladimer Ryzhkov had left Helena Makarov's apartment, she dialed the telephone number in London.

"Gempac!"

"Get me the General, quick. This is an emergency!"

"May I ask who is calling?" Although this was a highly secretive operation, known only to the highest of military officials, there had been wrong numbers dialed on this number from time to time. Not even the Queen herself, nor MI 5 nor MI 6, was aware of their existence. The only reason Helena Makarov had any knowledge of them was because they had formulated, founded and capitalized the Lifetime Partners organization for her when she had been in Russia.

"Henela Makarov!" she responded impatiently.

There was a moment of silence, then a strong, assertive male voice came on the line. "General Macintosh!"

"General. This is Helena Makarov. I wanted to let you know that Aaron MacAffie has been killed...apparently assassinated, although the news media says that it was a burglary."

There was a loud sound on the other end of the line, as if something had been thrown or smashed. She heard the General curse, then order someone to do something which she didn't understand, as he had apparently held his hand over the receiver.

"The woman and child?"

"They're here, in San Francisco with her lover, Vladimer Ryzhkov, a Lithuanian general retired from the civil war with Russia."

"I'm aware of the relationship between one Nevenka Adamovich-MacAffie and the good General. What are their plans?"

"I'm not sure, but if I were to make an educated guess, it would be that they're planning on getting out of the area."

"So, she's abandoning the church?"

"That would be my guess."

"Then she would be of no further use to us. Our interest was in the institution that MacAffie had formulated."

"What do you want me to do?"

She heard a sigh from the General. "I guess nothing, for the moment. We'll regroup at this end, but it would appear that we've come to a dead end on this one."

"Sorry."

"It's not your fault. You did everything that was required of you. Once we had access to MacAffie, we had to rely on the Irishmen to follow through. Apparently, they either saw no further merit in MacAffie, or, worse yet, our own people intervened."

"Your people?"

The General nodded out of habit, forgetting that Helena Makarov couldn't see him. "We have it on reliable information that British military intelligence has been intercepting messages from their agent in the States to King Arthur...the Irish," he explained.

Helena shook her head. "I'm afraid you've lost me."

"That's okay. It's tricky business. Thanks for your assistance, anyway. If I'm ever in the States, I'll look you up."

"I'd like that. All I've ever gotten all these years is just a voice in the dark. It would be nice to see the face that goes along with it."

*   *   *   *

The coroners file on the report of the results from Aaron MacAffie's autopsy sat on Pierce Terryman's desk, unopened. Begrudgingly, he flipped open the file and began to digest it. Within moments, he was sitting erect, his mind consuming every word.

"My God!" he said aloud. He picked up the telephone and called the parish office at the Living Christ Church. "May I speak to Mrs. MacAffie please!" His voice had a tone of immediate urgency.

"I'm sorry, but since Pastor MacAffie's passing, we haven't heard from her. She's probably home."

"Thank you."

He rushed out to his automobile and drove to MacAffie's residence, not sure what he was going to do when he got there. He pulled into the driveway and sighed a breath of relief as he saw MacAffie's white Jaguar in the driveway. When no one answered the door, he was tempted to pick the lock, but thought better of it. *Breaking and entering would only exacerbate the situation if I need to make a case for search and seizure of evidence,* he thought. *Better get a search warrant from Judge Hofmann.*

* * * *

The first thing Vladimer said as he jumped out of the taxi, when he saw Nevenka and little Vladimer, was, "When I heard about your husband being murdered, I wanted to call you, but no one answered the phone. It's been on all the television stations and in the papers." His face took on a sly look. "Forgive me, but to be perfectly honest, my sorrow doesn't run that deep."

"Husband?" she said with a smile. "I have no husband, Vladimer. Aaron MacAffie was a momentary detour in our lives. May his soul rest in peace. As of now, Nevenka MacAffie no longer exists. I am Nevenka Adamovich of Lithuania, and this is my son, Vladimer Adamovich. We are here in San Francisco in search of a place to live. It is my understanding that Hawaii is beautiful…the crown jewel of the Pacific Ocean, I hear, where the water is clear and warm. Would you care to join little Vladimer and myself there?" The look on her face conveyed her meaning as well as her words. "And leave California?" he asked.

"California is no longer a place that is appropriate to raise little Vladimer. He needs a father. I must be about the business of filling that role. Don't you agree?"

The twinkle in her eye made Vladimer laugh. "I think that it is a very admirable goal."

"Do you have anything that must be picked up at Helena's? Clothes, personal items?" Her question had a duel meaning, and Vladimer knew it.

"Just a few pieces of old, worn clothing. Nothing I can't do without."

"Then let us take a taxi to the airport."

Vladimer shook his head and smiled. "To go to Hawaii will take money, Nevenka…a lot of money."

"More than this?" She handed him the envelope containing the twenty-five thousand dollars. "Or this? She showed him the cashier's check for four hundred, seventy-five thousand dollars.

He whistled as he thumbed through the money and looked at the check. "I'm not even going to ask where you got this money."

"No need. It came from a business transaction that Mr. MacAffie concluded last week. Now that he's gone, he won't be needing the money, so I figured that Little Vladimer and myself might as well make use of it."

He really didn't want to ask this question, but knew that he had to. "You didn't have anything to do with the death of your husband?"

"Vladimer. You, of all people, must know that I could never shoot anyone."

"I knew that. Forgive me for asking."

She simply smiled and took little Vladimer's hand. "Shall we go?"

On the way to the airport, she asked Vladimer, "I have just one question?"

"Yes?"

"How do you feel about Mother, Viktor and Niki coming to Hawaii? Not to live with us, you understand, but to leave Lithuania and be nearby?"

He put his arm around her, drawing her close. "How do you feel about me making you an honest woman? After all, our son needs a father. And we can always use a grandmother to baby sit, especially if we're going to honeymoon in Hawaii."

Chapter 56

Major Pennypacker sat at his desk studying the report the Captain just handed him. It was a report from one Sean McTavish, their communications expert that had discovered the tie-into telephone line in the industrial building in Ireland...King Arthur's telephone connection.

"Sergeant! Get McTavish in here, ASAP!"

Twenty minutes later, Sean McTavish was seated across from Major Pennypacker. "McTavish. I've been in the Queen's service for nigh on twenty years now." He studied the report that McTavish had prepared for him. "Do you know what this report could mean to my career?"

"Sir?"

He slapped the report with the back of his hand. "This report! This could well spell the end of my career and any pension that I might derive therefrom. Do you have any conception of the implication here?"

The man studied his hands for a moment before speaking. "Yes, sir. I have full knowledge of the contents. I prepared it."

Pennypacker sighed. "Has anyone else seen this?"

He shook his head. "No, sir."

"You're certain there's no mistake in your discovery?"

"None."

"Very well. That will be all."

Sean McTavish rose to leave Major Pennypacker's office. "Oh, McTavish?"

"Yes, sir?"

"Good work."

"Thank you, sir."

Pennypacker held up his hand. "There is just one more thing. Do you have a tracking device in your arsenal of electronic equipment?"

"Tracking device, sir?"

"Yes. Something small, easily hidden on a person, but with a wide field."

"Yes. I think I can devise such an instrument ."

"How soon can you make it available to me?"

"It will take a couple of hours to pull all the necessary equipment together, but I'd say, four to six hours."

"Good. Meet me back here as soon a you can arrange the merchandise. I'll have some additional special instructions for you at that time." He handed him a file. "This is a sealed file that I wish you to keep in your possession, to be opened only in the event of my demise. There are instructions inside."

McTavish looked at Pennypacker with questioning eyes, but made no further inquiry. "As you wish, major."

* * * *

The next day

"General Macintosh! There's a Major Pennypacker on the line. Says he's with the Queen's security."

The General held the telephone for a moment before putting it to his ear. He knew this was a call that he had long been dreading, hoping that it would never be made. Yet, here it was. "Major Pennypacker?"

"General, I don't know if you even know who I am, but…"

"Yes. I know of your position," he said quietly. "You're with the military intelligence."

"Yes, sir."

'What can I do for you, Major?"

"I realize that this is highly irregular, but I've got to speak to you at once, sir."

"How did you get this number, Major? This is a highly classified line." He knew the answer without asking the question, but rank and order dictated such an inquiry. He hoped against hope that he could intimidate the Major, but in reality, knew better.

Pennypacker ignored the question. "Sir. We need a meeting at your earliest convenience. I can't stress the urgency of this matter enough. I'm in possession of highly sensitive material that cannot be discussed on the telephone…material that can affect you and your operation significantly." He emphasized the word "operation" as if it were distasteful, and it was.

Macintosh tried to defuse the issue, knowing that it would be in vain. Pennypacker wasn't Chief of Military Intelligence because he was easily put off or intimidated. "I'm a very busy man, Major. Isn't this something that can be cleared up at a later date?"

"The matter is too sensitive, General. I think you know that. I don't want to sound pushy, but if I can't satisfy myself as to the disposition of this matter within the next twelve hours, I'll have no choice but to turn my findings over to the General Security Council."

The General held the receiver to his forehead for a moment without responding, feeling the coolness of the black plastic against his warm skin. "All right, Major. Considering the fact that you've located this telephone number, can I assume that you know where we are situated?"

Without hesitation, Pennypacker responded in the affirmative.

"Very well. Be here at seventeen-hundred hours today. And, Major?"

"Yes, sir."

"Come alone."

* * * *

Pennypacker's destination was a large, old abandoned building, located at the back of one of the airfields just off the Thames River at the mouth of the North Sea. Churchill had built this airway specifically for the war effort during the war with Germany. The airfield had since been abandoned and had been fenced off and the entrance gated and locked. Pennypacker wasn't surprised to see that the guardhouse was manned with armed military personnel, although, from the entrance, for all intents and purposes, the facility appeared to be abandoned.

He leaned out of his car window to talk to the guard. "Major Pennypacker, to see General Macintosh." He showed the guard his military identification without being asked, knowing that that was protocol.

"Straight through to the large building on your left, Major."

The airstrip had cracks in it due to lack of maintenance over the years and was covered with dust and dirt. Tufts of wild grass and weeds had forced themselves through the pavement. The conning tower stood silent, like a frozen centurion, its windows dusty grey with years of dirt and dust. All the buildings were in like condition. For all outward purposes, this was an air base that had not seen a human hand for twenty years or more.

Pennypacker had come alone, as requested, although he had left a detailed memo along with his complete notes and of the "King Arthur" file with Sean McTavish, with instructions that they were to be delivered to the General Security Council in the event of his turning up missing or dead. It shamed him to think that he couldn't trust his own superiors, but it equally angered him to think of what they had done to their country. His country! The country that he and so many of his contemporaries had fought to preserve, not to mention those who had given their very lives in the interest of peace and freedom.

He parked his car and entered the building. He was immediately met by two burly armed guards who apologized before searching him for weapons, but did so without permission.

Having found none, they ushered him through the large vacant building to a freight elevator. The elevator came to life as one of the guards punched a code into the electronic elevator panel. The elevator slowly sunk to what Pennypacker judged to be thirty feet below the surface, then opened into what appeared to be a large, dark war room with brightly colored, twenty-foot, television-like screens. One screen outlined the form of Britain and contained various green and amber flashing lights. Another screen displayed the outline of the world with bright-red pinpointed blinking lights. An adjoining screen had a blow-up of Ireland with corresponding red and orange blinking lights. It took his eyes several minutes to adjust themselves to the darkness before he could see the detail of the rest of the room.

"Impressive, isn't it?"

Major Pennypacker turned to face a tall man dressed in military uniform bearing a chest full of ribbons depicting various battles, metals of bravery and military actions. On his shoulders stood the markings of a General.

"General Macintosh," the man said, offering his hand.

Pennypacker ignored the General's hand as he continued glancing around the room, which not only contained the large television screens, but several uniformed men manning computers, sending and receiving messages and adding to or deleting code names and numbers on their computer screens. Aside from the occasional clicking of computer keys, the room had an eerie silence.

"Do you know the significance of this magnificent room, Major?"

Pennypacker continued looking at the screens for several moments before replying. "At first glance, it would appear that you've got a display of every known hot spot in the world outlined in those little red dots," he said. "And the amber ones?"

The General smiled. "You're very perceptive. The amber lights indicate potential civil or military hot spots that we're working on. If and when a conflict breaks out, we convert the amber lights to red," he said with a certain air of pride.

"I see. I notice that you've got an amber in London," he said, tapping the light. "The Queen's castle?"

The General's face flushed a little, but in the darkness of the room, Pennypacker could not detect the facial change. He made no comment to the Major's inquiry.

Pennypacker nodded. "And the green lights." He looked at the map. "Let me guess. They're friendly forces working on creating amber lights that will hopefully be converted to red lights."

"Very good, Major."

Pennypacker pointed to the United States, where a green light was blinking in Central California. "I take it this is King Arthur's contact?"

The General had an uncomfortable look on his face. "I see there's no use denying it, Major Pennypacker. Again, you are well informed. I commend you on living up to your reputation. Now, as to the purpose of your visit?"

Looking at the lit panels, he said, "If you'll pardon the inquiry, General, what the bloody hell do you think you're doing? I know you're tied in with the Sons of Ireland in some manner. We've been able to track the telephone lines and intercept messages between Irish operatives to this location. To the degree that you're connected to the other bloody Northern Irish factions, I don't know." His voice was rising and he knew that the anger was betrayed by the blood that he felt flowing to his face. "Additionally, we've been able to identify a Russian source in California reporting to you on the Irish activities."

"Don't condemn that of which you have no knowledge, Major."

"That's precisely why I'm here, General. I've given my life to this country, as have many, living and dead. What you appear to be doing brings my blood to a boil. I wanted to come here and listen to your reasoning before going to the General Security Council with my findings. I don't want to jump to conclusions."

"I appreciate that, Major." He put his arm around the Major's shoulder to turn him away from the lit boards, but Major Pennypacker turned his body so that the General's arm slipped off. He wasn't going to be swayed with a little slick attempt at copinquity. "We're both military men, Major. Fighting wars and protecting the Queen's country is our livelihood." He looked the Major in the eye. "Without conflicts, our profession has no purpose."

Pennypacker looked into the General's eyes and, for the first time, understood. "Let me see if I have this right. You *want* civil and military unrest so *you* can have a job?"

"It's not just a job, Major. It's far more complicated and deeper than that. It's ethnic cleansing, population control, economically stimulating and, above all, it keeps us in military readiness. If certain civilian fat cats who have nothing better to do with their lives than sit around smoking large cigars and sipping brandy while they find ways to confuse our lives with new laws had their way, the military organization as we know it today would be abolished. And, yes, it does give those of us in this profession a purpose. Look at what history has taught us. During *the* war, Hitler tried to cleanse the world by eradicating the Jews. We got drawn into the conflict—not by pure accident, I might add." He smiled.

"Are you trying to tell me…"

"Our economy was sluggish. People were out of work and our country was overpopulated. Getting involved in the war with Germany gave our country a purpose. Men were trained to fight on the land, in the air and on the sea. We were a vibrant power again. Women and men not eligible to fight were employed making ships, aircraft, tanks and munitions for the war effort. Even the children were energized when the were brought in to do their part by raising money for war bonds. Our country was rolling in high gear! Even you, major, rose in rank due to the war. You went from a single-grade officer to Major in no time flat. Now, don't tell me that the war wasn't good for you!"

"And I've been a Major ever since, working at a desk job in intelligence."

"Pending our little conversation here, Major, I've arranged for your retirement promotion." He had a smile on his face, obviously pleased with himself.

Pennypacker ignored the General's effort to buy him off. "You speak of men and women being trained and employed in the war effort. What of the men, women and children who were killed because of the war? And all the bombed-out buildings from the German U-2's launched on us? Was that all part of your plan, too?"

"It was calculated that we would lose a few lives, of course. Every war has its casualties. Look at it as population control. Aside from that, we had inside knowledge of the U-2's progress, but we calculated that the Germans were suffering great monetary losses and had fallen behind on their production schedule. We knew, if we could draw the Americans into the war, the Germans would be defeated. And they were!"

"Wait a minute. Are you telling me that *you're* responsible for the Americans getting involved in the war?"

He shrugged his shoulders and had a sly smile on his face. "After the Japanese attacked Pearl Harbor, the Americans were already gearing up to fight. The next step was easy. We simply captured a German sub, manned it with our men and had it attack a couple American ships. Roosevelt was quick to anger, especially after being attacked by the Japanese, so it was no great feat to lead him in the right direction."

"So you also sacrificed British lives to get the Americans to fight in a war that you got us into."

"It worked, didn't it? I figured we did Roosevelt and the Americans a good turn. Look what happened to their economy. They're the leading country in electronic technology, machinery, space exploration and automotive industry. They wouldn't have been anywhere near where they are today, hadn't it been for Gempac!"

Pennypacker shook his head. "Gempac. Tell me, what exactly does that stand for?"

"Greater Elite Military Power Control." His voice had an obvious tone of pride as he said the words.

Major Pennypacker simply shook his head. "And exactly how large is this organization of yours, General?"

"We are headed by one elite member of each military organization: the Air Force, Army and Navy. Within each group, there is a secret military organization formed that is answerable only to higher command.

"And higher command would be you, of course."

"And my fellow officers."

"Funded by the Queens military budget."

"Of course. So, you can see, Major, our organization serves as a very important, how shall I say it, equalizing function."

"And how does this King Arthur Northern Irish faction fit in the scheme of things? For example, this Macafy guy: He was just the child of a widow of an informant who was working for me. We were grooming his father to infiltrate the Sons of Ireland organization, the very organization that you seem bent on helping."

The General smiled. "When we learned of your plot to infiltrate the organization with this Macafy fellow, we had no choice but to stop him. Sorry, but for the betterment of the organization, he couldn't be allowed to succeed, you understand. If you would have succeeded in eradicating the Sons of Ireland, the IRA and the Sons of Katy Elder, who knows what would have been next? Eventually, you would have been successful in negotiating peace between the Irish and our country!"

"That was the whole point."

"So, now you understand why we couldn't let you succeed."

"Let me get this straight. You killed our guy?"

"Someone had to. Where would we be if you were successful in your peace efforts?" The word "peace" seemed to roll off his lips like a distasteful bug.

Pennypacker shook his head. "And Macafy's son in America? What was your interest in him? He was no more than a cold-blooded killer, killing everyone in his church just to better himself. If anyone deserved to die, it was him."

"Aw, but you see, you're missing a piece of the larger picture, Major."

"Tell me about it, then."

"It's complicated."

"I may appear to be dense to you, General, but I found you and your…your Gempac group."

"Touche'." The General took a deep breath. "All right. As a routine of Gempac's normal business, we find it advantageous to fund certain people migrating to prosperous countries from time to time, with the hopes of getting into the pocketbook of some of the more energetic, prosperous individuals."

"Like Macafy?"

"In a left-handed way, yes, like Macafy."

"How do you mean, 'in a left-handed way'?"

"In the case of Macafy, we created an organization called Lifetime Partners in Russia, which was designed to take desirable, eligible Russian woman and find them homes with wealthy American men. The idea was that once we had positioned them in the American society, there would be one or more of them that we could induce to, how shall I say, make substantial contributions to certain organizations."

"Like the Sons of Ireland."

"Exactly."

"So…"

"So, they could buy guns and munitions to fight their enemies."

"Like the British."

"Exactly."

"Then, when they fight the British," he pointed to the red flashing light in Ireland and the amber one at the Queen's castle, "that would get the British military involved, thus justifying the goal of your organization."

"You see the picture clearly, Major."

"I don't see the picture of this jerk Macafy clearly. He was simply an Irishman transplanted to America, gone rotten from greed."

"Unbeknownst to us, when the Sons of Ireland killed Sean Macafy, they also decided to eradicate his family, which, in reality, made no difference to us."

"Because they had killed their father."

"And the Sons of Ireland don't like surviving children coming back and hunting them in the shadows of night...even if they move to America."

"I still don't get it. So, the Irish want to kill Sean Macafy's descendants. That I understand. Then, one of the children marries one of your Russian women. Of what significance is that to anyone?"

Again the General smiled. It was a look of "Gotcha". "As you have learned, we monitor all of the calls coming to King Arthur."

"Which I assume they're unaware of."

"Exactly. No use letting the enemy know you're trying to help them. They might end up biting the hand that feeds them."

Pennypacker nodded.

"When we learned that Macafy, or MacAffie, as he now called himself, was weaving himself a golden coat of riches from his flock's fleece, King Arthur apparently decided to give him a reprieve pending their ability to persuade him to funnel funds to their organization..."

"Through whatever efforts, be it by force or blackmail."

The General shrugged his shoulders. "That is of no concern to us. From what we learned of Macafy, or MacAffie, it was determined that we had ourselves a golden calf."

"MacAffie's church affiliations."

The General nodded. "And it was all working according to plan, that is until you chaps interfered." The expression on the General's face momentarily changed perceptibly. "Too bad, too. MacAffie was a master at bleeding his sheep, and I don't use the term metaphorically. If your man hadn't interfered, we could have funneled a ton of money to the cause."

Major Pennypacker smiled, more to himself than anything. "At least I did something worthwhile."

The General turned to look at Pennypacker. "Am I to take that as an indication that you don't approve of our little camp, Major?"

"General. Not only do I not approve of your camp, as you delicately put it, but I think your organization is rotten to the core, sir." He turned to leave. "Now, if you'll forgive me, I've got an appointment with the General Security Council. I don't know how I'm going to explain all this to them, but, by God, even if it means losing my retirement, I'll see that you're closed down, General, sir."

The General made a motion with his head to the two burley armed security guards. "It is unfortunate that you think this way, Major. With your quick mind and clear understanding of our national security system, you could have been a valuable asset to our organization."

"General. You may kill me, as I'm sure I'm no more than a fly on your cap, but be rest assured, I didn't come here unprotected."

The General paused for a moment. Pennypacker wasn't chief of MI 5 because he was incompetent, that he knew for sure. He assumed that he would have anticipated an adverse reaction from Gempac and would have prepared for the worst. "No, Major, I'm sure you didn't." He paused again. "Then again, I don't know that for a fact, do I?"

Chapter 57

9:18 A.M. the following day

The fog hung just above the ground as Sean McTavish followed his electronic locator down the unpaved road approximately sixty miles outside of London, along a cow pasture near the Thames River. The beeping radar sound was coming in shorter intervals now, indicating that they were getting near the source of the signal, hopefully leading to Major Pennypacker.

Ahead, through the fog, he saw Major Pennypacker's car. It was parked just off the bank of the river, where, eventually, the tide would erode around the bank and the car would slip silently into the water.

Sean parked his car twenty yards behind the Major's car and approached the rest of the way on foot, listening carefully for any unusual sounds. The windows had all been rolled down. As he peeked through the rear window, he saw the Major's head lying on the back of the seat, as if he were sleeping.

Sean quickly opened the door and put two fingers to the side of the Major's neck. His pulse was weak and he appeared to be in a coma. In fact, he was near death.

"Major! Major! It's Sean McTavish, sir. Wake up! Snap out of it, sir." Sean slapped him on the side of his face, trying to awaken the Major.

Unable to arouse him, Sean called for an ambulance, telling them that he was driving towards London and would flash his lights when they came into view, indicating that they had met one another. Twenty minutes later, as Sean drove down the highway at the maximum speed his car would safely travel, the flashing lights of the ambulance came into view.

Major Pennypacker was loaded onto a gerny and transferred to the ambulance. The attendants concluded, from his vital signs and the fact that he appeared to be in a coma, that he had suffered a stroke. He was administered oxygen and injected with medication to stabilize his vital signs, then rushed on to London's General Hospital.

* * * *

Sean McTavish had been sitting in a chair next to the Major's bed for six hours when he gained consciousness. "You gave us quite a start there, Major."

The Major looked at Sean, then quickly scanned the room. "What happened? Where am I?" The look on his face was a mixture of confusion and fear.

"I found your car several miles out of town, Major. You were unconscious. The doc said you had a stroke."

"How long have I been here, Sean?"

"You've been out for the past two days. The doc said something about your system needing to recover. That's why you were unconscious. Good thing you had that homing button sewed into the lining of your coat. When you didn't show up for work, I followed the homing beacon like you asked. It took a bit of doing. You really outdid yourself, Major. Any idea what you were doing way out there, parked by the river? I mean, there was absolutely nothing or no one within miles...just an old abandoned farm house."

Major Pennypacker closed his eyes. "You know, Sean, the last thing I remember was being horsed around by these two burley guards of Macintosh's." He licked his dry lips. "Any water there?"

Sean handed him a glass of water with a glass straw and held it for him while he took a sip. "Thanks. Never thought water could taste so good. What's this about a stroke? I'm as healthy as a horse and just about as ugly." He made an attempt at smiling.

"They're running tests on your blood, but, as I said, they thought you had had a stroke and just drove yourself into the river. Probably got lost or confused."

"Or drugged." He looked cautiously around the room, then motioned for Sean to lean close to him. "That file I gave you to hold. You still got it?" he whispered.

Sean nodded towards the door. "In the trunk of my car. Want me to get it?"

Pennypacker's eyes glanced around the room suspiciously, as if he expected to be overheard. He motioned Sean to lean towards him. "Take it over to General Standish," he whispered in his ear. "He's Chairman of the Security Council. Tell him to move on this right away. If he has any questions, he's to see me straightaway."

"Yes, sir."

"Now, off with ya. And, Sean?"
"Yes, boss?"
"Thanks."
"It was a pleasure."

*   *   *   *

General Standish examined the file, then picked up the telephone and dialed the number at Number 10 Downing Street. "The Prime Minister, please. General Standish at this end. Tell him it's urgent."

There were several minutes of silence, then, "General! It's been a long time. How's the family?"

"Just great, sir."

"And Margaret? She's such a lovely lady."

"Yes, sir. Thank you, sir. Sir, there's been a development that's come across my desk. I think it's a matter of the utmost urgency, too delicate to converse over the wire. Could I buzz on over?"

There was a moment of silence, then, "Yes, by all means. Be here at 10:30. We'll have a spot of tea and see what you've got."

General Standish was waiting in the outer room at precisely 10:15, anxious to see the Prime Minister. At 10:48 he was ushered into his office. It was an impressive office. The walls were paneled with dark walnut and held pictures of heads of state, presidents of other countries with their arms around the Prime Minister and, of course, a picture of the Queen and Winston Churchill. The plush carpeting on the floor was a deep blood-maroon. A chandelier, ten feet in diameter, hung in the center of the large room. Leather couches surrounded a thick glass coffee table. On the far end of the office was the Prime Minister's desk, clean of everything, save a glass paperweight containing a spent bullet that invited inquiry, a gold fountain pen and a green writing pad. The General had been here several times before, but each time he seemed humbled by the experience.

"I'll come right to the point, sir. We've had one of our men, a Major Pennypacker from MI 5, report a very disturbing incident regarding several of our top military officers. I've not spoken to anyone about this, sir, as it is a very sensitive issue. It's all here in the file." He shifted his weight nervously, as if he were uncomfortable with the issue. "If what's in this report is true, we've got a serious group of rogue generals taking the course of, not only our country, but certain sections of the world, down dangerous paths. If the United Nations were to get a hold of this information, I don't know…"

He handed the file to the Prime Minister, then paced back and forth in front of the Prime Minister's desk while he read it.

"Do sit down, Standish," he finally said as General Standish shuffled nervously. When he had consumed the file's contents, he looked up at the General. "Very disturbing."

"Yes, sir."

"These are very severe accusations, Standish. The reputation of some of our best military minds are at stake here, not to mention their military careers. What do you make of it?"

"Well, sir. I've given this a lot of thought. If what you read in that file is true, then we have a very serious situation on our hands, indeed. We can't go about creating national and international conflicts simply for the sake of generating internal military interests! I mean, I like a good fight as well as the next man, but this..."

"Indeed, Standish. Indeed."

"If I may be so bold, sir."

The Prime Minister waved his hand. "Yes, proceed, Standish. By all means. Feel free."

"Well, sir. I think we should investigate the matter with the utmost discretion. I would hate to have this information get outside our immediate control, if you know my meaning?"

"Indeed, I do, Standish. Indeed, I do."

"Shall I compile a team to investigate, sir? On the QT of course."

"And if what you find is accurately portrayed in this report?"

"Then, sir, we would be honor-bound to terminate their operation and turn the matter over to the National Security Council."

"Humph. Exactly. Good idea, Standish. You take charge. See to it, and report back to me first thing in the morning."

*   *   *   *

The following morning, General Standish had assembled a company of thirty highly trained commandos armed with automatic weapons. Before dawn, they arrived at the abandoned airport without notice. The gate was locked with a large rusty chain which was held by the largest lock the General had ever seen, which was equally rusty. "Corporal, remove the lock."

With a large bolt cutter, the chain was cut in two, and the gate was forced open. They proceeded to the large, abandoned warehouse, where the entry door was also locked.

"Kick it in!"

The door gave way easily under the force of a boot and fell noisily to the floor. The General dispersed a number of his men around the building, then took the remaining men into the building. Their search revealed nothing.

"There's no sign of a soul, General. The building is empty of man and machine...not even a rodent. We even checked the underground freight elevator, where munitions must have been stored. Nothing there, either."

"No sign of anything or anyone?"

"No sir. Just this one thing. Makes no sense, what it was doing down there."

He handed the object to the General. It was a shiny button from a military dress uniform worn by only by high-ranking officers.

"Assemble the men and prepare to return to base."

* * * *

"General Standish to see you, sir."

The Prime Minister swirled the burnt-orange-colored liquor in his large snifter glass. "Show him in."

"Well, General, what did you find? Pirates and galleons?" He laughed at his own humor. He waved the General in towards his desk. "Care for a brandy, General?"

"No thank you sir." He remained standing at attention while he spoke. "We raided the warehouse and found it empty. The only sign of its ever being occupied was this." He handed the brass button that they had found to the Prime Minister.

He examined it, then tossed it in his hand for a moment. "Just a button?"

"Yes, sir. Just a button."

"No men?"

"No men."

"No radar?"

"None."

"No computers or electronic equipment?"

"None, sir."

He laid the button on his desk. "I guess Major Pennypacker must have suffered a delusion when he had his stroke. Wouldn't that be your assessment of the situation, General?"

"That would seem to be the case, sir."

The Prime Minister emptied his brandy glass with one swallow, then sniffed the glass before setting it down. "I guess that closes the case on the diabolical generals."

"Yes, sir. Sorry for the false alarm, sir."

"Nonsense. If we don't have false alarms once in a while, we wouldn't know how to prepare for the real thing, if and when it ever happens, now, would we?"

"I guess not, sir."

The Prime Minister walked the General to the door, shook his hand and watched as the old warrior made his way down the long marble corridor. "Good man, that."

He went to his desk and picked up the telephone. After he had dialed a series of numbers, a voice came over the phone. "Gempac."

"I understand you're missing a button, General."

General Macintosh fingered the vacant hole in his dress coat.

"I'll bring it with me to dinner tonight. Look forward to seeing your wife Nancy. Lovely woman, general. You're a lucky man."

"Thank you, sir."

"I'll expect you to bring me current on the Prince Charles situation over dessert, General. I think the troops are getting restless. They need a good fight."

"I agree."

"Thought you would. See you tonight, then."

The End

About the Author

Howard A. Losness is the author of over a dozen fictional novels, has written and illustrated seven children's books and is an artist. He has a master's degree in clinical psychology and worked for two years in the Clinical Psychology Department for the U.S. Army. He plays the tuba and has been the president of his own commercial real estate company for the past 40 years.

978-0-595-38206-4
0-595-38206-1

Printed in the United States
41949LVS00003B/97-117